T0158779

"Cloying temptation to turn each page."
—Ripley Thirdy (*History Librarians' Quarterly*)

"Wunderbar!"
—Kinzly Pippin Kelby (*Deutche Stimme Heute*)

"Lincoln's legacy lives!"
—Daxx Stetson (*New York Morning News*)

"Hauntingly, historically hilarious."
—Nyx Wrigley (*New Science Review*)

"Seldom have history and truth and futuristic fiction wedded so harmoniously. An unholy trinity in a non-conventional perspective."
—Amorette Harlowe Duda (*Genomic Abstracts*)

"Kudos to Klein!"
Braulio Finch (*Literature in Review, Studies for Mensa*)

"典型的资本主义宣传。应回到生活带来了毛泽东"
—下巴下巴昌 (每个季度中美)[1]

---

[1] "Typical capitalist propaganda. Should have brought Mao back."
—Chin Chin Chung (*Sino-American Quarterly*)

REDIVIVUS

Redivivus: (adjective) ray-dē'-vē-vous
1. Brought back to life 2. Reborn (Latin)

NIKOLAUS KLEIN

REDIVIVUS
REDIVIVUS: (ADJECTIVE) RAY-DĒ'-VĒ-VOUS
1. BROUGHT BACK TO LIFE 2. REBORN (LATIN)

iUniverse books may be ordered through booksellers or by contacting:

iUniverse
1663 Liberty Drive
Bloomington, IN 47403
www.iuniverse.com
1-800-Authors (1-800-288-4677)

Because of the dynamic nature of the Internet, any web addresses or links contained in this book may have changed since publication and may no longer be valid. The views expressed in this work are solely those of the author and do not necessarily reflect the views of the publisher, and the publisher hereby disclaims any responsibility for them.

Any people depicted in stock imagery provided by Thinkstock are models, and such images are being used for illustrative purposes only.
Certain stock imagery © Thinkstock.

ISBN: 978-1-5320-0732-3 (sc)
ISBN: 978-1-5320-0731-6 (e)

Library of Congress Control Number: 2016916673

Print information available on the last page.

iUniverse rev. date: 10/31/2016

Redivivus (adjective):

ray-dē'-vē-vous

1. Brought back to life
2. Reborn

(Latin)

CHAPTER 1

Me

My name is Anton Bauer. My friends call me Tony. (No one calls me Tony.) I was born on July 5, 1996. More about that later. Today is July 5, 2058. I am now sixty-two years old. This is my story.

Anton, I am told, was my great-grandfather's name. He had been a government official in the Viennese diplomatic core. His son, Wilhelm, was deported shortly after the Anschluss, but not before having fathered my own father, Petr. The rather pedestrian family name surely predates the first Anton, but names are names, and evidently Anton escaped his agricultural destiny. Dank sei Gott![2]

My mother's family origins are less certain. Her own grandmother had no recollection of her parents, since she had been orphaned young. She came to the Midwest on one of the famous orphan trains near the end of the era of disposing of unwanted children in the early years of the twentieth century. She was adopted without papers, on sight, at the Saint Louis train station. The elderly man and woman who selected her from the remnants of the cross-country journey were named Louis and Ethel Lewis. (Louis Lewis—oh boy!) They named their daughter Henrietta. She married a vaudeville performer named Henry Leitner who used to perform as a comedian before the main act came to the stage. They traveled the country from theater to theater and from coast to coast, which is why my mother, their only child, was born in a dressing room. They named her Gracie—not Grace, but Gracie—in admiration of Gracie Allen, the scatterbrained wife of and coperformer with the great George Burns. Her folks idolized that famed duo.

I am quite brilliant. This statement is not a lack of modesty; it is

---

[2] For those who are monolinguists, "Thanks be to God!"

simply the truth. I am actually incapable of modesty or braggadocio. It is part of my DNA. I have an eidetic memory.[3] I remember being born. I remember the nurse who swatted my bottom. Her name was Margaret Tompkins. (I got my revenge for that abuse. More about that later.) My IQ cannot be measured. No psychological tool exists that can adequately encompass my abilities. Some thought I had an unusual form of Asperger's disease. The simple truth is that I am probably the brightest person ever born. Think of me as the spawn of Sheldon Cooper and Temperance ("Bones") Brennan.[4] Then add a dash of Einstein and a soupçon of Hawking. You get the idea.

I finished grammar school in Morristown, New Jersey, by the time I was seven. It took two years for me to finish high school, only because the school district couldn't provide teachers rapidly enough to deal with me. I actually would have preferred a private academy, but the better ones are all residential, and I was too young to be tossed into the mix of adolescent hormones and pranks. I learned early that I could recall anything, associate concepts and facts, and create new things out of the knowledge I accrued. The sheer act of remembering everything wouldn't make me more than a machine. It was the ability to create with that knowledge that was my particular genius.

It was difficult to decide what kind of life path to pursue. I was always being courted for various medical and psychological studies, which, thank God, my parents were bright enough and kind enough not to allow. My brain would have been biopsied into oblivion if they had allowed that.

I enjoyed history, but there wasn't really much challenge to that. I went to Harvard and finished my undergraduate work in eighteen months. It took six more months to earn an MA, and I completed my first PhD in eight more months. That accomplishment took a bit longer than I expected because I decided to write my dissertation on *Cardinal Mazarin and the Fronde* in seventeenth-century French. The French wasn't a problem for me. It was a problem for my examiners,

---

[3] Oh, I am so grateful for my photographic mind!

[4] These are characters from the popular early twenty-first-century television programs *The Big Bang Theory* and *Bones*.

whose French was not up to snuff. It took them time to learn the grammar and specialized vocabulary of that era. I defended the thesis the same day I celebrated my Bar Mitzvah. Yes, I am Jewish—through my mother's side, of course. I also remember the mohel who circumcised me. I remember it all painfully well. His name was Samuel Weinstein. He was a tad tipsy that day and sliced more deeply than he should have. Some might think that inhibited my psychosexual development. Maybe it did, but I didn't care. I always had other things on my mind. More about that later.

I really didn't plan to do much with that background. I was still only thirteen years old. To be sure, I was much sought after by the more impressive schools, including Harvard, Oxford, the Sorbonne—and the CIA. My interests, though, were drifting elsewhere. I was, of course, also a genius at anything scientific (well, actually at anything). A career in computer technology could have enriched me more than it did Bill Gates, but I wasn't interested in money or power. I was interested in knowledge. I could not read fast enough. In the months after the dissertation defense, I picked up Carl Sandburg's *Abraham Lincoln: The Prairie Years*. That began to open the path for my future. More about that later. You, my reader, know that Abraham Lincoln's fame rests upon his presidency during the American Civil War. Cardinal Mazarin's fame, of dissertation memory, rests upon his activities during the Fronde, a type of civil war that predated the French Revolution.

That spring, I enrolled at MIT. I was allowed free tuition, room and board, and a lot of other perks, as long as I conducted one advanced doctoral seminar. I didn't plan to stay there long, but they were kind, so I took two semesters to polish off another master's degree, and one more semester to complete a doctorate in biomedical engineering. Naturally, it didn't take long to surpass the professors, and they began to come to me for assistance. The doctoral defense was fascinating. No one was able to ask a question for which I couldn't offer both an answer and textbook citations, including publishers and dates. But there I was, still young, only fifteen years old. I did take some time out of the day for exercise and sports. I taught myself piano, classical guitar, and, for the fun of it, bagpipes. I played the bagpipes as I entered the hall for my defense. A guy's got to have some fun! I even wore a kilt!

I was also moving ahead along the normal lines of physical development. I would have pleased Adolph Hitler with my very German name, my very German blue eyes, and my very German dirty blond hair. I would not have pleased him with my Jewish background, but by age sixteen I was six feet two inches tall and a robust 180 pounds. I was intimidating physically as well as mentally. I liked to dress the part as well. The right clothes with my very right look always got me second glances from men as well as women.

After MIT, I traveled. I made it my duty to learn the language of any place I planned to visit before I got there. Fortunately, most universities were eager to have me make an appearance and talk about something—about anything—so my way was paid. I spent several months in South America and then went on to Spain, Portugal, France, Germany, Austria, Italy, England, Belgium, Greece, and Israel. I rather enjoyed the whole experience—especially my time in Haifa at the Technion, the Israeli equivalent of MIT.

From there I went to Cairo and South Africa. I skipped the rest of Africa. I spent some time in Mumbai, Sydney, and then China. China was sufficiently different. It took me three months to be completely fluent in Mandarin, but I enjoyed it. I was eighteen years old, and by then, as often happens with the especially unusual aspects of a person like me, some darker manifestations were beginning to seep into my conscience. I didn't know whether to fight them, laugh at them, or be afraid of them. They were there, but I was too young to care a lot and too naive to worry about it.

I really had no friends. No one could hold a conversation with me, so I took to a great deal of talking to myself. I would bounce from language to language and enjoy telling myself stories and trying to translate jokes into various languages with sufficient idiom approximation that paronomasia could make the leap from one tongue to another and still be funny.

It was during my time in China that I decided to pursue my third PhD. I didn't really need it, but it is easy to get into schools that are eager to brag about your presence. I matriculated into the Beijing Academy of Science and began to enhance my biomedical knowledge with the opportunity to use the labs at the school. I found they are much less regulated than US university study centers, and my language prowess made it possible to get whatever I wanted with a minimum of questions being asked. I could also dazzle as well as baffle, not to mention lie. I rather enjoyed lying, once I found out how socially unacceptable it was. Honor was a concept I chose not to understand. Fortunately, I met some fellow students from Scotland; we had a great deal of fun together. More about that later.

I towered over the other students academically. I did not tower above Hun Sang Ho. He was another doctoral student who had made his fame playing basketball in Europe. He was bright enough, and at six feet eleven inches tall and weighing 150 pounds, could be physically intimidating in a skeletal kind of way. I outweighed him and outsmarted him. He kept his distance.

My work this time involved genetic studies, a natural follow-up to biomedical engineering. I wrote the dissertation in Mandarin. The week before the defense, I rewrote it in German just to have some fun.

So there I was: Anton Bauer, PhD three times over (or PhD^3), just turned nineteen years of age. I could vote in the United States. I could write my own ticket. I could make a fortune. None of that appealed to me. Instead I decided to start assimilating some of these experiences and all of this knowledge and do something no one else had ever done before. Why not? And that, my friends, is the stuff of this book.

I mentioned a certain fascination with Abraham Lincoln. I set aside science for a bit and began to do some more reading. There is, of course, that classic work by Carl Sandburg. I added to that list the following: *Lincoln*, by David Herbert Donald; *With Malice Toward None—A Life of Abraham Lincoln*, by Stephen B. Oates; *Team of Rivals: The Political Genius of Abraham Lincoln*, by Doris Kearns Goodwin; *Honor's Voice: The Transformation of Abraham Lincoln*, by Douglas Wilson; *Lincoln's Virtues: An Ethical Biography*, by William Lee Miller; *Prelude to Greatness: Lincoln in the 1850s*, by Don Fehrenbacher; *A New Birth of Freedom: Abraham Lincoln and the Coming of the Civil War*, by Harry V. Jaffa; *Lincoln at Cooper Union: The Speech that Made Abraham Lincoln President*, by Harold Holzer; *Abraham Lincoln: Redeemer President*, by Allen C. Guelzo; *Abraham Lincoln and The Second American Revolution*, by James McPherson; *The Eloquent President: A Portrait of Lincoln Through His Words*, by Ronald

C. White; and, of course, *The Lincoln Murder Conspiracies*, by William Hanchett. Of course, a man's secretary or valet always knows the most about the character, so I gave a careful study to Joshua Zeitz's *Lincoln's Boys: John Hay, John Nicolay, and the War for Lincoln's Image.*[5] I confess it took me a week to read the famous *Lincoln: A History*, by Nicolay and Hay. After all, it is ten volumes!

I even lowered myself to the level of the common person and bought some DVDs of Lincoln movies: *Saving Lincoln* (2013), *Lincoln* (2012, Steven Spielberg), *Abraham Lincoln* (1930, the D. W. Griffith classic), and *The Civil War* (Ken Burns). [6]

---

[5] All of these are actual tomes about the life and legacy of Abraham Lincoln.

[6] The old celluloid and digital versions have been converted to the newest microchip technology.

CHAPTER 2

The Plot Hatches

I needed to go to Washington, DC, after reading those books. I had been there many times before, but I never looked for certain things the way I needed to now. I didn't know how long I would be there, so I arranged to respond to some older invitations from the local universities to lecture on genetics and morality. (I laugh out loud.) That would give me a legitimate excuse to be in DC. The talks would be easy enough to prepare; I would just pull out some old notes. That would leave me plenty of time to sleuth about.

I booked an open-ended ticket on Hoverair—first class, of course. The landing at New Reagan/Obama International was a little rough because of a snowstorm that raged through the city overnight. Evidently these East Coast types don't know how to plow snow. On top of that, the Jetway was frozen and would not come out to the door of the plane, so we had to back up and wait while the ground crew rolled out a portable stairway. It had not been shoveled. Being in first class, I was among the first passengers to maneuver down the slippery, ice-covered, ankle-deep snow on the steps. I was tempted to fall on purpose so that I could possibly sue the airline, but I was more concerned about keeping a relatively low profile while in Washington. I certainly didn't need the money.

I took the metro to the Pentagon Arms, checked in, showered, and took a nap. Tomorrow would be the first of many busy days.

In the morning, I went to the university to see what sort of schedule for lectures had been arranged. I had left it open so that I would appear the picture of cooperation. The schedule was light enough: one lecture on Tuesdays and one on Thursdays for three months. I had free use of the laboratory, a lab assistant, and $5,000 a week for my efforts. If only they knew! Fortunately this little arrangement also set up some precedent that would prove useful later.

There were a lot of places to visit, to study, and to absorb. For the fun of it, I filled out the online volunteer form for Ford's Theatre. The theater needed ushers. I had evenings free for those months, so I went ahead and sent in the form. To my delight, I was accepted. I don't think the overview committee really recognized my name, but the volunteer position would give me access to places the public did not see and would give me a legitimate reason to be in the theater when the public wasn't around. The National Park Service still runs the theater.

But first things first. If you recall, Samuel Weinstein was the mohel who circumcised me so many years ago. Anyone who thought that the ceremonial drop of wine given to us babies was some kind of comfort food was sadly mistaken. It hurt. It really hurt. And no one hurts Anton Bauer without paying a price.

I don't think much of modern things unless they help me get what I want, such as my personal science adventures. Technology has been a great assist to me, but I am not a frequent customer at big-box stores to get the latest again and again—unless it helps me in my intentions. Sometimes I can be a bit of a Rekabite.[7]

I had used various search engines a few times, and I used one today to look up my old buddy Mohel Samuel Weinstein. His address was listed. He is now eighty-four years old and a resident at an assisted living / acute care facility in New Jersey. Not too far, not too close. Perfect!

The facility was named Sinai Sion Home for the Elderly. I phoned the place, pretending to be his nephew, checking on dear Uncle Sam's condition. The receptionist answered on the second ring. Her New Jersey accent was heavy and irritating. She connected me to the floor nurse, who evidently had never heard of HIPAA, because she blabbed freely about dear Uncle's dementia (his being in and out of it) and his foul mouth, foul smell, and habit of sleeping all day and being awake all night. Again, perfect. I was afraid I would find out some financial difficulty existed, but she said nothing.

I let my chin whiskers grow out for a few days into a respectable

---

[7] Look it up!

goatee, purchased a pair of very clunky thick-lensed, black-framed clear-glass spectacles, shaved the pate of my head, colored the remainder gray (as well as my rather handsome goatee), stole a yarmulke from the local synagogue, and bought a round-trip train ticket from Washington, DC, to Middleboro, New Jersey, a stop on the local line. I made sure to be sufficiently obtrusive and interruptive on the train that people would remember me, but not so much that I would cause a disturbance requiring the intervention of security. I might need an alibi later. I wore a Bavarian fedora, complete with feather. My overcoat was from Goodwill, dated but not tattered. My shoes were wonderfully comfortable old black oxfords, sufficiently scuffed to look used but not so much as to look shabby. With a pair of gray slacks, a wrinkled blue shirt, and a thin, yellow striped tie, I was set to go.

The 8:43 a.m. train was twenty minutes late that day, but I had plenty of time. I took some reading material in German with me. With the foreign-language book, odds of anyone trying to strike up a conversation with me were diminished. Off we went.

As I had hoped, the German novel staved off any busybodies. I hate people who try to become my best friend in restaurants, trains, or hoverplanes. I have also found that mumbling to myself tends to keep folks away. So does drooling.

Upon arriving at Middleboro, I walked the two miles to the home. I shuffled into the reception area looking and acting twenty years older than I am. I looked sufficiently old to be harmless, but not so old as to look like an escaped client of the home. I was going to ask which room was dear old Uncle Samuel's. No one was at the reception desk. (How these places get away with unlocked doors 24-7 is beyond me, but it was a great help.) There was a handsome imitation of a Torah scroll fastened to a pillar just to the right of the receptionist's empty desk. There every resident had a photo, a name, and a room number. I sure hoped that nurse had been right when she said the old bastard slept most of the day. I shuffled off to room 147 and gently knocked. No response. *Good.* He was probably asleep.

I entered slowly, quietly, and gently closed the door. There was no window in the door. I shut it just shy of total closure, lest it look suspicious. No other doors were tightly shut. I had seen a number of Do

Not Disturb signs on other doors along the hallway. *Perfect*. I slipped Sammy's onto the outer door handle. Given the wonderful personal information shared by the nurse, the staff would probably be glad not to deal with him.

Approaching his bed, I cleared my throat. There was no response from him. I shook him gently, and he stirred. I shook him just a little harder, and he awakened. I don't know what he thought, but he looked up at me and smiled, revealing yellowed teeth stained from years of tobacco abuse. He made no sound. He had on a pair of bright red flannel pajamas. A light on the bedside table was the only illumination.

I would have preferred to use a mohel's knife on him. The irony would have been superb, and the revenge would have been poetic justice, but I didn't want to risk getting any blood spatter on myself. It would be too hard to explain away should anyone see me. I simply took his phone, the now old-fashioned desk model kind, and hit him four times on his head—twice on top and once on each side. It made the sound of thumping a soft melon, which is not a bad image for that old head. Satisfied, I wiped my fingerprints off the phone, took off my glasses and placed them in my coat pocket, put my gloves back on, and exited quietly through the sliding door, which led to a small patio. The room was on the first floor, so I simply walked around the building to the sidewalk in front. It was the perfect crime—the first of many.

After a quick walk back to the train station and a book to enjoy on the ride, by evening I was back in my place outside Washington. I left all the old clothing in a trash bin at the train station after changing into my regular clothing that I had stored in a twenty-four-hour lockbox in the terminal. Revenge, truly, is a dish better served cold. It was murder, pure and simple. Revenge. As Poe wrote in "The Cask of Amontillado," "Nemo me impune lacessit."[8] Well, I must say, that wasn't as hard as I thought it might be.

---

[8] "No one injures me without revenge." This is the motto of the British Royal Family. The term is used in Poe's story on the lips of Montresor as he bricks up his mortal enemy within the wall.

CHAPTER 3

Tuesdays with Abraham

Ever since star phones replaced the omnipresent early-twenty-first-century cell phones, only the receiver intended could hear the ring. My own ringtone was *The Battle Hymn of the Republic*. It was chiming now.

"Hello."

"Is this Anton—Anton Bauer?" the woman's voice asked. (I knew who it was. Caller ID is still popular.) It was Allyson Gray, the coordinator of volunteers for Ford's Theatre.

"Speaking."

"Oh, Anton," said Allyson. "We are having that special performance tonight at the theater for the Diplomatic Corps. Would you be able to assist us? The museum, which is usually not open in the evenings, will be available to the curious after the performance. Is there any way you can help?"

"Madam," I said, "I would be delighted." (I said this with the same exaggeration of voice that Teddy Roosevelt used when saying "delighted". It was my custom of imitating various presidents that endeared me to Allyson and most of the rest of the staff at the theater. Besides being a reliable worker, I could entertain them in this most boring job.)

Allyson said, "Oh, Anton. Thank you so much. You have saved the evening. Please wear the 1865 uniform and see me at seven in the lobby."

"Dear, I cannot wait to see you again." I disconnected with the customary double blink of my eyes. This was perfect. I'd managed in these first weeks to endear myself to my students, to the university administration, and to the staff of the National Park Service at Ford's Theatre. My interest in Lincoln had become a fetish, and my plans for the dead president were firming up daily. If I did all this correctly,

Allyson and the entire Diplomatic Corps would become unknowing agents of my scheme.

I finished my notes for tomorrow's lecture. I cleaned up, ate a light dinner, and then changed into the 1865 usher's uniform, which, I admit, made me look quite dashing. I was just a bit taller than most people of our time, just as Lincoln was a giant among the people of his time. One withering stare, oft practiced in the classroom, would get any patron to obey. I didn't have much time to work out my plan, but I could not waste this opportunity. I sat down and closed my eyes, and the plot became clear. There were a lot of surds (as we math folk like to say), but it was workable. I took a cab to the theater rather than be seen by too many folks on the metro.

The cab dropped me off in front of the theater at a quarter to seven. Allyson would be busy, so I had fifteen minutes to scout the area.

The crowd was already gathering in the theater, and the usual usher crew was explaining over the telecast chromoreceptors what the situation was like on that fateful evening of April 15, 1865. I knew the speech by heart and could deliver it in several languages. That was part of what made me so popular among my peers here: I gladly took any foreign group and amazed them with my little speech. It was filled with much more than the standard English version that we were supposed to offer tourists. Few knew the truthful but sometimes scandalous additions to the text.

This evening was working out fine. Allyson saw me and waved me over.

"Anton. Anton. The theater is filling up, and the curtain is about to go up. All of that is business as usual. Let me show you what I need your help with."

With that we went to the lower level of the theater—to the museum. Of course, I'd scouted this out many times, and I was well aware of exactly what I wanted. This evening offered the perfect opportunity to follow through on my plan.

My instructions were to open the door to the museum the moment the final curtain fell, at about nine thirty, if all went well. Then I was to escort the first group of the Diplomatic Corps, all South Americans, to the exhibits and give an explanation. I was asked to do this in Spanish.

Allyson either forgot or did not know that South America includes Brazil and the language there is Portuguese. No problem. I would use both and amaze the arrogant corps members as I switched from one to the other.

The play that evening was not *Our American Cousin*, the play that was performed during the infamous assassination. Although everyone wanted to see *that* play in *this* theater, there were other plays as well. This month the attraction was Shakespeare's *Macbeth*. There would be no raucous laughter to cover up the assassin's pistol shot as there had been that famous night. This was not a problem, for there was not going to be an assassination. There was going to be a theft.

"Allyson," I asked, "Would it be helpful for you if I had a second group at the end of the tours?"

Each group would be escorted outside to Tenth Street (as it is known now) for refreshments. The evening air was quiet, and the slight breeze disseminated the effects of the light humidity.

"Yes, of course, Anton," she replied. "The last group, in fact, is the Chinese, and you know how they get if their own language isn't used. You can handle that, can't you?" I smiled at her and said, "当然."[9]

Tuesday was the usual day of my volunteering. I had gotten used to the inane questions of the crowds. One would think none of them ever read anything. If a play were being presented, the ushers' tasks were to be at the theater one hour before curtain. Besides the usual job of helping people find their seats, we also were expected to answer questions about the history of the theater and, of course, the events of that fateful night. It seemed everyone thought he was the first one to quote the line "Other than that, Mrs. Lincoln, how did you like the play?" "Tuesdays with Abraham" became my regular social pattern.

I knew all the history and could repeat it easily. What my supervisor did not know was that each time I was in the theater, I also took advantage of my volunteer position to reconnoiter the museum. While many of the artifacts there were interesting, and all were connected to Lincoln, my special concern was the display of the frock coat he wore on the night of his assassination.

---

[9] Mandarin, not Taiwanese, for "of course."

Each Tuesday, I did my duty. I did it well. And each Tuesday, I got to know the theater a bit better. I had the chance to ingratiate myself to the officials of the National Park Service as well as the other volunteers. Little did they realize what I was really up to! They trusted me, and with that trust came more responsibility. My plan was working well. Only two weeks passed before I was given my own set of keys to every lock on the property.

By the evening of the Diplomatic Corps soirée, I had everything in place. I was the favored guide—not only for my knowledge but also for the humor and minutiae I could bring to the presentation.

I finished with the Spanish-speaking group (with many dashes of Portuguese) and led them out to the street, which had been closed off—as it often was—for refreshments and mingling. Lincoln captures the imagination of many, many people, but this group was not overly moved by the tour. Most of them came from nations where political assassinations were as common as houseflies.

While they were mingling and mixing among themselves, I was able to leave their exalted company. I went to the subbasement and used the access key to enter the control room. For some reason, the same key that opened our break room was a kind of master key. The control room contained all the equipment for the air conditioning system, the heat, the surveillance paraphernalia, and the electrical system. No one was stationed in this room. It had nothing of historic value, so it was easy to access it while the other groups were being led through the museum. I entered to do my deeds. I simply turned off the surveillance system that recorded every movement from every angle. Earlier in the century, one could always tell if there was a spy system. By now the microchip was all but invisible. The room and the system controls had no alarm, since anyone with access to it was considered safe. Turning it off alerted no outside alarm monitors and no security personnel. It took seconds.

Next was the electrical system. I couldn't just shut down the master power; that would be too obvious and would alert the security team. In fact, it would alert everyone. Instead I inserted a remote-controlled timer chip into the mainframe. I could activate it by tapping my cufflink—an essential part of that stuffy, uncomfortable, yet dashing 1865 uniform.

I placed my chip in the spot of the regular automatic timing chip and quickly and silently left the room. The whole operation took only one minute.

Back on duty, the Chinese group was waiting. They were already upset that they were the last to get the special tour. No one trusted them. Everyone knew the group was part of the Beijing spy cabal. To me it made no difference; they served my purpose well.

After the usual round of phony polite introductions and bows—a vestige of imperial kowtowing, if you ask me—we began the tour. I explained the history of the building, that disgraceful night, and the eventual renovation as a working theater and museum. As we approached the glass case that contained the clothing Lincoln wore on the night of his assassination, the group was chattering away in its polite, mumbling way. They were tired and bored and actually didn't care a bit about the history. This was Western history, and they were as interested in it as we were in theirs. It was then when I tapped my right cuff link, signaling the electrical system to fail. With the surveillance system out, the whole power grid was down, and none of the backup lights came on. We were in total darkness.

The soft chatter became the excited and loud chaos I had hoped for. It wasn't the laughter of the audience at the funny line of *Our American Cousin* that gave J. W. Booth his cover, but it was the second time this theater was going to be part of history. Earlier in the century, I would have feared the myriad of portable devices that everyone—especially the Asians—had. Their protoplasmic optical simulators would not function without an active plasma cell unit (now the equivalent of early century Wi-Fi; it had been rendered unworkable by the power outage). I had to act, and quickly.

I opened the back door to the small display case with its key, and sneaking on my night vision goggles, I went to the manikin of Lincoln. I snipped away the small piece of pant that still held the dried bloodstain from that fateful evening. Backing out of the case quickly, I shut the door to the exhibit. I would relock it later. Then I pressed my cufflink again, and the power came back on. As the lights came on, I raised my voice and ordered everyone to follow me quickly.

Urging them to safety, I led them out to the street. Folks there were blissfully unaware that anything had happened inside the building, but the Chinese soon dispelled them of any sense of calm. Capitol police cars began to block the entire neighborhood. Other volunteers rushed to the front office, and a distraught Allyson was frantically trying to speak to the police, the FBI, and the Department of Homeland Security (yes, it's still around); talk on the phone; and deal with the on-the-scene National Park Police.[10]

I dutifully reported to her that all the groups were out of the building and it could be shut down. I volunteered to check the restrooms for any possible stragglers. No one would ever detect the chip in the electrical system. Charlie McKnight, the security man in charge that night, was just emerging from the control room. Out of breath already (too many doughnuts), he gasped out the "news" to me, said he had turned the surveillance system on again, and went on his way. On my own way to dutifully check the restrooms, I walked behind the display case and relocked it. No one noticed the small patch of cloth missing from Abraham Lincoln's pant leg until two days later, when a small boy on tour began laughing at the missing piece. His height was equal to the height of the missing cloth on the pants. It made Lincoln's pants look just like his own torn clothing.

That discovery brought a whole new level of interest to the event and led to the closing of the museum and theater until further notice. That precious piece of cloth, about 1" × 1", was safely stored unobtrusively in my hotel dresser, sandwiched carefully between my socks and my handkerchiefs.[11]

Well, if I said it once—in fact, I did—I'll say it again: "That wasn't so hard!"

---

[10] aka the Keystone Cops

[11] The suit Lincoln wore that night was from Brooks Brothers. Because of his size, it was made to order. In the lining of the coat, there was a hand-stitched eagle and the words "One Country, One Destiny." Lincoln had worn the coat originally at his second inauguration. The night of assassination, the contents in his pockets included a linen handkerchief, some candy, two pairs of glasses, and a wallet.

Ford's Theatre

CHAPTER 4

Meanwhile, Back at the University ...

Meanwhile, back at the university, I had students involved in a number of projects that would assist me. Others were legitimate-looking enough but in reality were exercises in futility. I employed that wonderful Byzantine (some say Vatican) policy of splitting up the information so that one group would not know what the other group was doing. But I knew. I alone knew how the pieces would fit together to move my little scheme along. But the students did not know. Bright as they were, as each one truly was, they would never figure out the scheme. Why, it was Jesuitical!

There were four groups of four students. I mixed them by sex, by nationality, and by intelligence levels, as discerned from their application transcripts. I lectured all the students in the doctoral program on Wednesdays. It was a little bit of a chore because of my late Tuesday evenings at Ford's Theatre. On Thursdays I had a seminar with the sixteen subgeniuses. I made sure to make the general lectures interesting and enticing—so much so that others would someday build on the lead I was creating. I did have to be alert to the brightness of the Gang of Sixteen,[12] but by divvying up the projects as I did, and by making them as complicated as possible, I was satisfactorily assured that they would never catch on. They didn't.

They had two months to labor on their projects. I programmed two of the groups to fail utterly. It was cruel, but it was necessary to keep them busy, as well as to keep some level of competition alive.

It was the two groups programmed to really assist me that I monitored

---

[12] I rejected the basketball metaphor, still around, of the Sweet Sixteen from March Madness.

most carefully. I wanted them to work with active DNA as well as the DNA from deceased animals. The assignment was to create the kind of DNA particle I needed. What did I need, you ask? Well, I just told you. I needed a formula for a resuscitated—no, a resurrected, or redivivus—DNA molecule to move on in my work. The rest of everything I did was cover-up. It was sham. I had no shame in creating the sham.[13]

Two Tuesdays after the mysterious events at Ford's Theatre, I went back for my usual evening volunteer session. Everyone was now electronically scanned as we entered the building. This made no difference to me. I knew better than to carry anything remotely connected to the theft.

That evening I was given a new assignment. I was to be the guide for the Petersen House—the building across the street from Ford's Theatre. It was the house that was borrowed on the night of the assassination for the care of the dying president. Like the museum, it had been restored to the condition of that night of April 1865. It would be about one hour before anyone would be coming for the tour. I knew all the information to be disseminated, but I could not resist one temptation. I had to rest in that famous bed. I tossed my frock coat over the bookshelf where the surveillance chip was located. No one would be watching the monitor yet, because the home wasn't open to the public until later in the evening.

I climbed onto the bed. I lay down on my back. I was just a tad shorter than Lincoln who did not fit on the bed, but my feet still dangled over the edge. I closed my eyes and let my imagination run away with me. (I don't do that often. It's illogical, but it can be fun!)[14]

There I was, in the second most famous bed in the world. Only the Lincoln bedroom is more famous. (More about that later!) I have a bit of a built-in alarm clock, so I wasn't worried about overnapping. I closed my eyes and tried to imagine the chaos and the hush alternating in that small space.

Mary Lincoln was dragged out of the room because of her

---

[13] Read that sentence out loud three times!

[14] I knew that the actual deathbed was in the Chicago History Museum in Illinois, but I wanted to get a *fingerspitzgefühl* for the experience.

constant—dare I say theatrical at times—hysterics. Edwin Stanton, wary of Lincoln but supportive of him as well, remained there. I pictured in my mind's eye his anxiety alternating with his ambition. Twenty minutes later, I opened my eyes, stretched, retrieved my coat, and proceeded to have another Tuesday with Abraham.[15]

After we locked up the house, I took a hovercab back to the university. Time was running out on my stay there. I had only a few more things to accomplish before this part of my plan would be complete.

I reminded the postdoc students that their final reports would be due in one week. Two groups panicked, of course, because they had been set up for failure from the beginning. There was no grade for their work—no prize, no payment—but the embarrassment would follow them forever. Too bad. My greater interest was in the two groups whose work was going to be helpful to my own plans.

That Saturday I finally accomplished the last of my typical tourist adventures. I stood in the long line of people waiting to be admitted to the White House. Ever since the attacks of 9/11 so many decades before, and in the light of the current standoff between the United States and Canada, greater care than ever was assigned to the National Park Rangers, whose responsibility it was to guarantee the safety of this historic place. (The Secret Service was also anointed as guardians, but earlier in the twenty-first century their reputation for reliability floundered.)

I wore my own national park ranger volunteer badge as I made my way to the front of the line. While I still had to undergo the electronic surveillance, I was allowed to skip the infrared and biochemical scans. That put me closer to the front of the tour line. I had no intention of making trouble on this gambit, but the temptation was great.

The security system was considerably more thorough in this famous place, so I behaved. My main goal was to see the famous Lincoln Bedroom. I had done my homework, naturally, and I was rather appalled to learn that Abraham Lincoln himself probably never slept in this bed or the bedroom itself. The bed has a peripatetic history of mild

---

[15] Yes, as I stated, I am well aware that the actual bed is no longer in the Petersen House, but give a guy a break, will you?

interest, wandering about the White House from room to room and from storage to a room and back to storage. Nonetheless, I wanted to see it and to be in that building where Lincoln was so consumed with the task of leading the Union forces to victory—that place where his overly dramatic but typically Victorian wife had her séances and hissy fits. I also wanted to experience the sadness of the place where the Lincolns' young son Willie died.

I was not disappointed. There is a respectful hush that washes over the crowd as the guide reviews the story of the most famous person to occupy this site.

The rest of the tour had its moments of interest, but I had seen what I wanted to see. I purchased a book with photos of the exterior and interior of the White House—one of those coffee table albums. No one but me would ever see it, but if I got discouraged in my work, it would serve to renew my resolve.

At any rate, Lincoln moved from a one-room log cabin, the place of his birth, to the magnificence of the White House, which was still quite new at his inauguration.[16]

I went home satisfied.

The next day was report day for the students. Faces betrayed the frustration—and failure—of the two groups whose projects were sabotaged. The first group of four came forward slowly and awkwardly. An embarrassed silence smothered the room. The spokesman, Daniel Corrigan, began: "Sir, we have not been able to solve the problem. Our test results, no matter who managed them or who performed them, resulted in absolutely nothing." The silence continued.

I said nothing.

Then the representative from the second programmed-for-failure group stepped forward. She was a very plain girl, wearing dark, professorial glasses and a kind of Quaker-length gingham dress. She looked a bit like Granny from the 1960s TV program *The Beverly Hillbillies*.

"Dr. Bauer," she began. "We ran the samples over two hundred times. We studied the results with every tool available, and some we

---

[16] His birthplace was a room about 16' × 18' with a dirt floor in Hogdenville, Kentucky. For images of the Lincoln White House, see www.lincolnwhitehouse.com.

tried to manufacture for our use. There was no way we were able to successfully conclude our project. We are sorry."

She sat down. The silence continued. I said nothing.

Jeremy Cutler, the image of a future professor, stepped forward. He had a rather large grin on his face. I knew he would report limited success. It was thus programmed. He always wore a shirt one size too small in order to emphasize his physique, which was quite attractive to the coeds. His hair was sandy and moppish—foppish, almost. He put on a pair of reading half-glasses and began.

"Dr. Bauer, classmates: group three is proud to present limited success in our endeavor. The center of our study focused on the resolution of highly charged protoplasmatic cells and their ability to regenerate and duplicate the source cell. We did not know what the source cell was, so we were never certain about our actual success. We only know that the continued application of the formula we devised resulted in the same end product. For this reason, we consider ourselves fortunate and moderately successful."

Jeremy sat down. The class said nothing. I said nothing. I called the representative of the last group forward. This group had been given all the material it needed to be successful. On paper, it looked as if each group had been given the same information and lab materials needed, but the truth was that there were just the slightest discrepancies. I counted on them not figuring that out, and despite their being as bright as they were, they did not. The most beautiful girl in the class was their representative.

Clara Elsinger was the brightest girl I have ever taught or ever met. She was also knockdown gorgeous. As she made her way forward, I could read the envy in the eyes of the other girls and the lust in the eyes of the boys. She didn't so much walk as sashay to the front. Her skirt was just the proper length for serious academe, yet it was provocative, and her choice of colors was appropriately muted. She knew who she was and what she could accomplish and the effect her presence had wherever she went. That was the reason I gave her group the possibility of success. More about that later.

Clara began. "Dr. Bauer and classmates: our group isolated the genome that we had hoped to find. At the end of session one ..."

She continued speaking for an hour, detailing all the fine points of the group's research, the contribution that each member had made, and the startling success they had achieved. I wasn't terribly surprised, but I was very happy. The result was just what I had expected and hoped for. It would also save me a great deal of time in the future. The group unwittingly created the formula I needed to regenerate lifeless DNA into living and thriving cells. The group also succeeded in identifying the source of the DNA—a wombat: primitive, yes, but all that I needed.

Each group handed in its reports along with all the computer data that backed up their research. I claim copyright to anything I direct. I excused myself momentarily and placed that information in my study, which was attached to the lab. I shredded the paper copies of the first three reports and then quickly burned the dot recorders with the computer results. Their own hard drives, which they brought into the lab and into class with them at my insistence, were at the same time being clandestinely erased by a supercharged ultrasound wavelength. Their computers were now good for nothing, with the possible exception of use as paperweights, even though computers weigh next to nothing now and paper is harder to get ahold of than a gaggle of dodos. I took the fourth report and likewise shredded it, but I placed the dot recorder into the sluice drive of my office supercomputer, checked that it had all the pertinent material, and then flash-mailed it to my home computer. Another five seconds and I verified it was there. This phase of my plan was almost complete.

I knew that when the final revelation of my work took place, I could take no chances that anyone else might step forward and remember this group, much less claim credit. I almost felt bad for them because they were really very attractive people—the kind any university would delight in recruiting for faculty and research. But that, alas, was not to be.

I came back into the lab. No one spoke. The air was heavy with anticipation. I began: "Groups one and two, you are aware that despite your best efforts, you have failed. Failure is not an option in the scientific community. Group three, you are aware that you, also, have failed. Although you came further along in your work than your peers in groups one and two, you too failed. Partial success is not an option in the scientific community. Group four, you have been happily successful and have every right and reason to celebrate your accomplishment. You have not failed. Quite the opposite, you have succeeded beyond expectation. I am well pleased.

"I want to invite all of you to a celebration of the conclusion of our work and time together. Please meet me this evening at *Barnacle Bill's* for dinner and discussion. It is my treat, and we will discuss our next steps at that time. I have rented a limousine to pick all of you up here, in front the lab, at 7:00 p.m. tonight. Don't be late, or you will miss the ride." (Insistence on punctuality is so German!)

This was unexpected. The reclusive, silent professor was actually going to socialize with underlings. They walked out on air. I walked out with my sluice drive and took a hovertaxi to my apartment.

At seven that evening, the Hover Hermosa Limousine, shining bright blue and yellow—the colors of the university—floated up and then hovered just off the ground in front of the university lab building. The driver was Pakistani—still not unusual in DC. What he did not know was that the limousine had been tampered with. On the way to the restaurant, lethal fumes would slowly fill the passenger area. I had arranged for champagne and beer to be available. Knowing that students who have just completed a major effort would be in a partying mood and would get sufficiently inebriated, I was sure they would not notice the gradual and then increasing doses of the newest chemical/gas death agent, Radocarbon 143.

I waited at the restaurant, having reserved a small banquet room for the soirée. All the food had been ordered. Places were set for the seventeen of us. An open bar was awaiting the thirsty guests, but no guests arrived—well, not alive, anyway. When the hoverlimo pulled up to the restaurant, the valet opened the driver's door. He, in turn, opened the double door on the vehicle only to find that all his riders were sound asleep. Only they weren't sound asleep; they were quite dead.

The autopsies showed that poison gas was the cause of death, but it was attributed to a malfunction of the discoscope HVAC unit in the hoverlimo. It had never happened before, but now all the recent models of Chevford Motors vehicles were being recalled for safety checks.[17]

---

[17] Yes, despite all the modern technology, such things still happen.

The news media, of course, made much of the tragedy. I was interviewed by all the major networks and the various Washington media pimps. I was a good thespian and showed great personal compassion for the families and regret for the loss of these rising academic stars.

I spoke at the university memorial service. I was dressed appropriately for mourning and managed to stumble through my moving obsequies for the deceased. I spoke about how dedicated they had been to science and to me. I spoke about how sixteen brilliant lights for the future of our universe had been extinguished. I awarded each of them an honors grade posthumously, even though there was no real grade for their participation. The crowd was deeply touched. On the other hand, I was greatly amused. I accepted condolences humbly and then returned to my apartment, packed my few things, and took the evening flight from New Reagan/Obama International Airport to Chicago. From Chicago I took a train to Springfield. (Yes, there still are trains, but they are a far cry from the AMTRAK of old.) In Springfield I rented a fine suite of rooms (for the time being) and then sat back and laughed.

My plan was working!

CHAPTER 5

Springfield, Illinois—Home, Sweet Home

I did not want to stay too long in a rented place. I needed privacy and space. I spent a few days driving around Sangamon County, looking for a residence that would not be too far from the Interstate Hover System (I had to get to the university, after all!) yet far enough to keep trespassers at a distance.

The area hasn't changed much since Lincoln's time. It is easy to picture him riding the circuit. The rivers and streams are relatively unpolluted—not a bad reality given the ecological disasters of the twentieth century. Great trees soared in primitive woodlands. Miles of cultivated farm fields had been everywhere in his day, and they still graced the countryside.

In Lincoln's time, the population of Sangamon County was 32,274. By the middle of the twenty-first century, it was almost 200,000. That's not a terribly significant growth factor. The county is in the center of Illinois, slightly west of perfect center. It was named for the river that runs through it. It might be a French name or a Potawatomi name—makes no difference to me. Lincoln was a representative of the county to the Illinois State Legislature. Sangamon County was also part of the territory Lincoln represented when he was in the House of Representatives. Since Springfield was the capital, Lincoln had a vast knowledge of the local politics and the local terrain. Soon I would also.

It was late on a Friday afternoon when I finally found my new domicile. It was about eight miles north of Springfield. It was an old farm—one that hadn't been worked for almost one hundred years. There was a great Victorian farmhouse on the knoll that overlooked the Sangamon River. The closest paved road was two miles away. There was a challenging, twisting dirt road that led to the place. It sat there, sad and empty. The For Sale sign was an old one, but the cybercommunication number was twenty-first century. I decided to poke around a bit on my own to make sure this was what I wanted.

There was an old barn, its main door askew. Perhaps it had once been red, but now it was weatherworn gray. There was a two-seat outhouse, complete with a half moon carved into the door![18] What a far cry from contemporary sanitation science—our instant-suction sanitary inserts. The house itself was two stories, with three dormers and a splendid wraparound porch. There was even a broken swing on the porch. This was getting better and better.

The front door was closed, and a padlock attempted to secure it. With a firm push, the door gave way. A medium-sized foyer lay within. There was an old boot holder, complete with coat hooks and a tarnished mirror. An empty lighting fixture announced that at least at one time there was gas lighting in the home. I don't think it ever knew electricity, much less modern power systems.

The foyer opened up in three ways. To the right was the great parlor. (I suspect that is what it was properly called in Victorian days.)[19] There was no furniture, but there were splendid windows that reached from a few inches below the high ceiling to about one foot from the mahogany floor. A large fieldstone fireplace filled most of the west wall.

To the left, the foyer led to what must have been the ladies' sitting room. It was the same size as the main parlor and had another fireplace—a twin to the one in the parlor. The windows, likewise, mirrored the parlor. It was once magnificent and could be again. Rotted red lace draperies hung from valances.

Off each of these great rooms, on either side of the long entrance hall, were two other rooms of matching dimensions. Off the ladies' parlor was the dining room. A splendid walnut buffet lined an entire wall. It was scratched and worn but could be restored to its original beauty, just like the floors in each room. Its counterpart was the kitchen. An old pump sink and wood-burning stove were still there. They were

---

[18] Two seats—think about that a moment!

[19] "Parlor" comes from the French word for "to speak," you know.

quaint but useless. There was even a dumbwaiter that went from the kitchen to the cellar.

In the back of the house, a stairway led to the upper level and down to the cellar. In the front of the house, parallel to the hallway, was a grand staircase of mahogany. It was easy to picture farm children sliding down the hand railing to the chagrin of their mother.

Upstairs there were five bedrooms. Each lacked a closet—a typical feature of Victorian homes. Houses were taxed according to how many rooms they had, and a closet was considered a room. The armoires that certainly graced the bedrooms were missing. In fact, there was no furniture in any of the rooms. More gas lighting fixtures still jutted out from the peeling wallpaper, which bore hideous floral designs typical of the era.

The grounds were more than adequate. The barn was falling apart, but that could be repaired. There were two hundred acres of woodland around the house. The tilled fields had vanished from neglect long ago, and nature had begun to rebuild its own habitat. In fact, a splendid woods encircled the property.

I called the agent listed on the fading sign, Dexter Cabot of Sangamon County Realtors. I didn't know if the agency would still be in business. The person who answered was astonished that I was inquiring about the place. I think Dexter thought it was a prank call. He sounded like a talking antique. The property had been bank-owned for seventy-five years! Any offer would be accepted, I was told. I offered $250,000 for the whole property. Before the day was over, I owned it. There was no question about anything. Cash can do that. It did take a few days to get the paperwork out of the way, and then the real work began.

Next I had to hire contractors to renovate my find. I had landscapers put paths through the woods, trim the wild growth back one hundred yards around the house, plant perennial flowers and shrubs, and put in a brick path to the river, as well as a pier and dock. I bought a pontoon boat and named it the *MARY TODD*.

The house was structurally sound. I had all the woodwork, stairways, and floors sanded and varnished to a proper sheen. Every wall was stripped of its ancient wallpaper and replastered. I had Solarvec installed to provide power for the house and my various upcoming projects—particularly the project that has become my raison d'etre. Solarvec was the most recent technological innovation for power—microchips that captured wind and solar energy. (These are a far cry from the ugly windmills that dotted the landscape at the beginning of the century.) Once installed, they lasted forever and cost nothing. The purchase price, however, would scare most people away. Many still preferred the fossil fuel route, even though there was only an estimated ten years of supply left and use of such fuels had been outlawed in many places.

Two new wells were dug, and twenty-first century plumbing was installed, complete with an en suite in each of the five sizeable bedrooms. That was the one nod to modernity I could not control. I preferred to use my own splendid well water; it would cost a fortune to connect to the county sewer line, but there was no legal way around it, and I didn't want to create any reasons for investigation down the way.

The perimeter of the whole property was secured with an electric fence with all the appropriate warning signs in English, Spanish, Chinese, Arabic, and Hmong. There were only two entrances: one for the "public" and a secret one only I would know about—just in case. Then I had an underground security fence installed—the kind that people use to keep pets within their boundaries. More about this later.

Furnishing the house would normally have been a fun challenge, but I didn't have the time to do it myself. I was in a hurry. I hired McNabb and McCarthy out of Saint Louis and gave their decorators carte blanche. My only instructions were that the kitchen and great parlor were to be paragons of twenty-first-century decor. The ladies' parlor was to be a great music room, with a harpsichord and grand piano, furnished according to the Lincoln era. The latest sonograph technology would be employed, however. It was now possible to simply state the music one wanted to hear, either genre or specific opus, and it would be telesounded to the system.

Leslie Lappendorf was the design consultant from McNabb and McCarthy. She was a very competent woman, and she understood almost intuitively what I wanted in the house. I was particularly pleased with the Victorian recreation in the ladies' parlor—not that it would ever be used. She managed to find a splendid rosewood carved sofa with deep red covering, a rare walnut Sutherland table and matching sideboard, an inlaid rosewood ladies' writing table, and a loveseat to match the sofa. A huge Oriental rug covered all but a three-foot perimeter of the wood floor. Hummels and Waterford fit into the floor-to-ceiling glass display case. Four gas-lit sconces decorated the walls, and at the center was a splendid gas chandelier that she had found on Royal Street in New Orleans. It, too, was Waterford.

The kitchen and bathrooms were outfitted with the best and most progressive eye-catching designs from the Kohler showroom in Kohler, Wisconsin. No two rooms were identical. Sadly, the kitchen, like the ladies' parlor, would seldom, if ever, be used—at least not by me personally. Perhaps I should hire a cook.

I also ordered the construction of a three-car garage[20] discreetly positioned inside the front gate. I did not want it to be visible from the road. I also did not want to change the splendid old bricked bridle path to the house. I purchased a Lincoln MKZ hovercar for my real transportation and an old Trabant[21] (like there are any new ones!) as a nostalgic vehicle to take me from the garage to the house, should I so desire.

The one order that governed all the contractors was the time line. I had sought bids, only to keep things looking normal. I took the highest bid from each area of expertise. I wanted the best and didn't mind paying for it. Then I promised a 50 percent bonus if all the work from each area was completed in three months' time. Time, you see, was of the essence. You can imagine the flurry of activity that took place. It was costly, but it was worth it.

My main concern was actually the barn. That would be my home laboratory. Given what they all knew about Anton Bauer, my rather eccentric requests for the building went unquestioned. The entire exterior was updated and painted and looked exactly like a red barn ought to look—from the outside.

---

[20] Garages are actually obsolete at this time, but I wanted a storage area for the antique vehicle.

[21] This is the infamous car manufactured in East Germany in the middle of the twentieth century. It was renowned for its inefficiency, pollution, and frequent breakdowns. But it was (East) German.

On the inside, however, things were quite different. I had the entire space gutted. The ceiling was installed for the first level at twenty feet off the ground. The space above that was left open. I didn't need it. The interior walls of the barn were covered with three-foot-thick concrete. Four smaller rooms, each twenty feet by twenty feet, surrounded the large central lab area, which was forty feet by forty feet. There were no windows, but a series of exhaust ducts made the place look like a meth lab from earlier in the century. Oblong tables and shelves lined the walls. One of the rooms was the cool room, with hundreds of vials of my concoctions. Plenty of power outlets were installed along with the best lighting available, worthy of the International Space Administration. The barn, too, was equipped with Solarvec, but I had a huge emergency generator system installed on the property—just in case. And just in case once again, I had a second generator system ready.

I hired a Hispanic couple to assist. I installed them in a nearby home I purchased so that they could get to the estate (Tadwil) in a few minutes. I would have preferred some undocumented aliens, but ever since the Obamagration Laws of 2015, it was too much of a risk to take.

Humberto, the man, was about fifty years old, short, and stocky, with an overgrown gray moustache. I ordered, "¡Nunca entrar en el granero!"[22] and "¡Cortar y recortar el césped!"[23] Also "¡Mantener el coche limpio y gaseados!"[24] My command of Spanish intimidated him sufficiently. He would be no problem.

His wife (or partner—I wasn't sure which and didn't care) was named Isabella. She looked like her husband, sans the moustache. Then again, there was an outline of one above her lip. Her orders were similar to Humberto's: "¡Limpiar la casa tres veces por semana!"[25] and "¡Nunca entrar en el granero!"[26]

I did not think I would have any trouble with them, but little did

---

[22] Never go into the barn!

[23] Cut and trim the lawn!

[24] Keep the car clean and filled with gas! (Remember, it was the old fossil-fuel-driven kind.)

[25] Clean the house three times a week!

[26] See footnote 21.

they know that if there was any violation of my orders, there would soon be a cemetery on the property!

In the end, the work was done on time. I paid out the contractors and checked my figures:[27]

Item	Expense	Above/Below Budget
House	$250,000	No bonus necessary
Power (Solarvec and generators)	$350,000	Plus 50%
Landscaping	$150,000	Plus 50%
Pontoon Boat	$25,000	No bonus necessary
Woodworking	$125,000	Plus 50%
Furnishings and Planning	$400,000	Plus 50%
Security Fences	$75,000	Plus 50%
Misc.	$52,500	No bonus necessary

I moved in on February 12. It was an auspicious beginning!

My Completed Victorian Farmhouse
(photo from Thinkstockphotos.com; Used with permission)

---

[27] Dollar amounts, of course, are in new American dollars (NAD).

CHAPTER 6

"Heigh Ho, Heigh Ho, It's off to Work I Go"

Everything was going splendidly. I really liked the way the property adventure turned out. It was everything I had hoped for. I am neither easily nor often satisfied, but I allowed a grin of self-delight to decorate my visage.

I took to swimming in the river every morning—just a quick three-minute dip to open up my pores and invigorate my mind and body. I noticed on the third day that there was a kind of reflection in the woods on the other side of the river. It was there again at dawn on the fourth day. I asked Humberto to spend the night in the pontoon boat, and when I came for my morning plunge, he was to surreptitiously scout out the reflection. This he did, and he reported to me back at the house, "Señor, es un hombre con binoculares."[28]

Well, now, isn't that interesting! I thought. Undoubtedly someone had learned that the famous Dr. Anton Bauer had bought the old property and renovated it, and he or she was now either eager to view the result or to spy on me. I did two things: I doubled the number of lock mechanisms on the barn. I had equipped it with all the needed and most recent devices. I actually had more money to spend on such things than the university, but I did not tell them my private laboratory was larger and better. Much of that was due to the equipment I had designed and built myself for my work. I was especially proud of the genome transmorgrofier. More about that later.

The other thing I did was purchase property across the river for one mile upstream and downstream from my own property. I then surrounded it with the same kind of electric fence, both above and

---

[28] I believe you can translate this yourself.

below ground, that I had placed on the perimeter of the estate.[29] No more worries about intruders!

It was now mid-April and time to return to work. I did not need the money, but I did need the academic public life to cover my personal research. I bought a chauffeur's uniform for Humberto and had him drive me to the university. It was only about twelve minutes away in the hovercar, but I preferred not to worry about anything except my research thoughts.

We arrived on the campus on a splendid spring day. I went to the science building, which had been named for Louis Pasteur, and sought the head of the Department of Bionomic Sciences. She was expecting me. Her name was Dr. Madison Jeffries. Her rather frumpy secretary led me into her office, which was lined with all the proper volumes and framed certificates of her own considerable accomplishments. Her degree, earned twenty years before, was from Stanford, a credible enough institution. Her publications were respected, especially because they usually quoted mine.

"Dr. Jeffries," I said, "It is a pleasure to meet you!"

"Ah, Dr. Bauer," she said, "The honor is truly mine. I am so pleased that you have chosen our school to continue your work. You are the talk of the campus."

"Please," said I, "call me Anton."

"Oh!" said she. "I don't know if I can bring myself to do that."

"Please do," I insisted.

"Very well, Dr. Bauer ... uh ... Anton. Please, let's discuss the terms of your work here, and then I will show you around your lab and the campus. We are scheduled for a noon meeting and lunch with Chancellor Adamson."

I do not like most people, but Madison Jeffries was going to be hard not to like. She was as beautiful as she was pleasant and intelligent. That meant I would have to be wary of her. She was wearing a white lab coat with her name embroidered on the pocket. A pair of sensible white shoes gave evidence to the hours she must spend in the lab and not just at her desk. She had on a very interesting pair of earrings—copies of

---

[29] By the way, I named the estate Tadwil as a reference to two of Lincoln's sons.

the cartouche of Cleopatra.[30] I commented on them, and she said she had received them as a gift in Egypt from the famous archaeologist Edwin Stanley Fetherston. I was impressed. Evidently she could wield feminine wiles as well as Cleopatra did in antiquity. The rest of her outfit was just as proper. She was wearing a buttercup-yellow dress with short sleeves that betrayed the tan from a recent vacation—spring break no doubt. Intelligent eyes danced with curiosity and charm at the same time. While I would not be working with her in any real sense, she would be a pleasure to have around—or so I hoped.

We walked through the lab section of the building. While it was quite well supplied, it was not the same state-of-the-art laboratory I would have preferred. I was glad I had my own in the barn. This would do, however, for public consumption.

We discussed a teaching/lecture schedule and settled upon five summer lectures, one a week, all to be delivered before the July 4 break. In the meantime, I had free access to the lab—which I didn't really need. But I fawned gratitude nonetheless.

Then I made a request that was totally superfluous to my needs but I knew would make her and the rest of the staff quite happy. I offered to conduct a weekly seminar on the genome projects that were taking place around the globe. We would be connected via interstellar satellite communications. Every scientist of whom I approved could participate in the discussion, should he or she want to. I would coordinate and moderate the sessions. This was child's play to me, but it would endear Madison to the university's funding gurus.

After that discussion, we went on a quick walk around the campus. The spring weather was fickle—sunny a bit, and then chilly and cloudy, but no rain. Most campuses, unless in a completely urban setting, are rather much the same. Their field house was state of the art, which told me where the money came from and where it went. Two Nobel Prize winners had come out of the school—one in literature and one in chemistry. That boded well. Several Pulitzer prizes were also claimed by the English Department, but who cares?

It was twelve thirty now, and we were to meet and dine with the

---

[30] Yes, I also know hieroglyphics, having mastered Gardner's classic textbook.

chancellor. Dr. Wilson Adamson had brought the school from near bankruptcy eight years ago to having one of the finest endowments of any university in the country. I had done my homework on him. His own (singular) doctorate was in chemistry. Had he not been so successful, I would have thought him worthy of a kindergarten classroom. His office, naturally in the centrally located Administration Building, was the caricature I presumed it would be. A large concrete stairway, flanked by copies of the lions from the Chicago Art Institute, led into the five-story Georgian brick building. I admit it was a handsome structure. The lions had been sculpted in 1893 by Edward Kearny and were a gift to the Chicago Art Institute from the Marshall Field family. I would not mind a duplicate set for my own estate, truth be told.

We entered Adamson's office. Walnut bookshelves, trophies, and photos of him hobnobbing with national and world academic and political figures adorned the walls. His desk was discreet; it had only his working papers on it, along with an antique pen and inkstand. A door to the left rear of the office led either to a privy or to his real work office; I didn't care which.

Madison introduced me. "Dr. Adamson, I would like to introduce you to the world-renowned and now special faculty member of the College of Sciences, Dr. Anton Bauer. Actually, sir, it is Dr. Dr. Dr. Bauer."

Dr. Adamson replied, "It is an honor to meet you, sir, and to welcome you to our institution. I trust that Dr. Jeffries has been helpful."

I smiled and replied, "Doctor, Dr. Jeffries has been most cordial."

Then Jeffries interjected, "Dr. Adamson, we have come to an agreement I think you will find most beneficial to our school, our alumni, and our students."

Dr. Adamson said, "Dr. Jeffries, your labors are not unnoticed."

I said nothing. At this point, I was beginning to think that all the sentences beginning with "Doctor" were starting to sound like a scene from a Marx Brothers film.

Finally I added, "It will be my delight. Now, I hate to be rude, but I was informed we would dine together. I do need to keep my schedule, and my chauffeur will be expecting me out front in a little more than one hour."

"Dr. Bauer, of course," stated Dr. Adamson.

This is getting wearisome, I thought.

We left his office and went down the hall to the Regents' Dining Room. There, a choice of truffled salmon or Bavarian pork shank with a dill reduction sauce awaited us. I was true to my Teutonic background and selected the pork shank. If Isabella could duplicate it, I would be happy. It was a good meal, despite Adamson's droning drivel.

At the end of the meal, I demurred on a dessert, forcing them to do the same. I did have a splendid demitasse of espresso. I took it as a good omen that they did not offer cappuccino. No civilized person drinks that beverage after eleven in the morning! It would be a faux pas equivalent to having weißwurst after twelve.

Humberto picked me up promptly in front the Administration Building. We took the hovercar home, and I dismissed him for the day.

The next day, I set about getting a job. Oh, don't be confused. I did have a real (though unnecessary) job at the university. I needed a cover job for my true intentions. I wouldn't have needed a private laboratory if all my plans had been honorable.

I went to a secondhand store and purchased a pair of basically clean but slightly worn-looking work jeans. I complemented this with a red plaid flannel shirt, heavy-duty work shoes, and a baseball cap. Since I didn't know if my interviewer would prefer the White Sox or the Cubs, the Illinois teams nearest to Springfield, I got a hat for the Saint Louis Cardinals. That was close enough to Springfield to be excusable.

More difficult was to disguise my face. My hands I simply worked around some rough wood for a few days to get a worn, tough feel for the deal-sealing handshake. I purchased a toupee of brown with slight tinges of gray and grew my beard out for a few days—not enough to be scruffy, but enough to make me look like a working-class person.

Then I had Humberto take me to downtown Springfield and hired a hovercab to take me to Oak Ridge Cemetery. I knew there was a job opening there for a part-time night watchman / cleaning man. I knew that because two days earlier I had arranged for the former watchman / cleaning man to become deceased.

I entered the cemetery's office looking a bit haggard, but not too much so. I wanted to get this job. I had fixed all the phony credentials

I would need in advance. Technological piracy is still easy. I met with Mr. Jason Wembly, the director of Oak Ridge Cemetery, and also the local administrator for the Illinois State Historical Site Service.

Mr. Wembly invited me to be seated as he reviewed my paperwork, looking over the top of his reading glasses at me the way grade-school teachers still do in places that are not completely cybereducational.

He looked the part of a cemetery director or a funeral director. He was about fifty-five years old and had a shocking crown of snow-white hair. It was immaculately groomed, as were his fingernails, his eyebrows, and his goatee. He was wearing, appropriately, funereal black. I would guess this suit had set him back about $200 NAD.[31] His starched, long-sleeved pale blue shirt was matched with a smart black and deep blue striped necktie. When he moved his hands forward or backward, a splendid set of matched cufflinks caught the light. Hardly anyone wears this kind of shirt anymore, but it made sense on him. The cufflinks, I could see, were made of opals with slight bas-reliefs of the Lincoln tomb on them. How quaint! I would arrange to get them or a similar pair sometime in the future as a little memento of my time here.

Mr. Wembly asked, "How did you find out about this open position?"

I responded carefully: "Sir, the former caretaker/watchman lived in my apartment building. I was there when the coroner took his body out. We would share a beer once in a while in the evening while watching football or baseball. We weren't great friends, but we were friends. When I learned about his death, I knew there would be an opening here. I had been looking for something a little closer to Springfield, where my apartment was. As you can see, I have had a lot of experience in both cemetery maintenance and watchman service."

Wembly said, "Yes, I see that. You are practically a godsend. The hours are not very pleasant, and it can get lonely."

I quipped, "Yes, sir. I am accustomed to that. I don't mind being alone. I think my résumé shows that I am quite responsible. I just need someone to familiarize me with your grounds, where equipment is stored, whatever procedures you prefer to follow in case of a problem, and so on."

---

[31] Not too expensive, not too cheap!

Wembly noted, "We can do that. I can have a member of the day team take an extra shift. You know this is only three nights a week, yes?"

I affirmed my knowledge of this. It was not a limitation for me but good fortune. It would allow me to have enough time to keep up my phony work at the university, as well as still give time for my private research at the estate.

Wembly stood and put out his finely manicured hand. "Well, Mr. Kenally, let's try the customary six-month probation period. If you can be here tonight at ten thirty, I will have Wilson Limon, our day chief, show you the ropes."

I answered, "That would be fine. I will be here. And please, just call me Jim."[32]

Wembly ushered me to the door and said, "That's fine, Jim. In a few weeks we'll have a little review session to see how things are going. Best of luck."

We shook hands, and I left his office, used a worn and untraceable

---

[32] I knew that Jason Wembly might well have been a relatively important person in the trusting community of Springfield, but I hoped that he did not know his history. I took a chance on the name James Kenally. You see, in the mid-1870s, James Kenally was a two-bit Illinois hooligan, an Irish crime boss, and a counterfeiter (somehow Illinois seems to produce a lot of these, though more recent criminals have been Italian mobsters). In 1876 Kenally had a companion who was in prison. Kenally concocted a scheme to get his compatriot out of jail and get a fistful of money besides. He plotted with two acquaintances to steal Lincoln's body (Yes!), bury it in the Indiana sand dunes, and hold it for ransom. His coconspirators (what a strange phrase—doesn't "con" already mean "with"?) hired two other fellows to help. They did not know that these assistants had FBI connections. (The FBI was involved because of Kenally's counterfeiting reputation.) It seems that "in vino veritas" is an apt saying. The same could be said about beer. While they were bragging at a tavern, the plan became known. They easily cut through the cheap padlock that had been installed on an iron grate in front of the sarcophagus (Greek for "flesh-eating thing"). When the would-be grave robbers arrived, they managed to get the top off the great white sarcophagus, but the casket itself, weighing some five thousand pounds, worthy of a president, was extraordinarily heavy and could hardly be budged. It was moved only a few inches before the FBI, who had been waiting in another part of the tomb complex, came and arrested them. I just thought it was exquisite irony to use that name, given my real purpose for being there.

telecom to summon a taxi, and went back to where Humberto was waiting for me and then back home. I was well satisfied, but I would need a nap before the evening's activities.

Lincoln Tomb, Oak Ridge Cemetery, Springfield, Illinois
(photo by the author)

That night I had Humberto take me by hovercar back to Springfield, where I repeated the taxi ride to the cemetery. The front gate had been locked for the night, but the day man, Wilson Limon, was waiting for me.

We went to the worker's station, and he gave me a long-sleeved cotton shirt—light tan with the cemetery logo in deep blue over my heart (of all places!). We chatted a bit and hit it off nicely. He had been worried that he would get weeks of double-shifts until the new guy was hired. I relieved him of that fear, and he was grateful.

We began with a drive around the perimeter of the cemetery and then the various roads that crisscrossed through it. All I had to do in this part of the job was look for anything suspicious. Evidently there were always college students or low-life tourists trying to get something out of this famous place. Every two hundred yards, there was a visi-dome, a kind of microchip processor. As I placed my hand in front of it, it stamped the day and time in the central security office—proof that I, and only I, had sent the "okay" signal.

Limon showed me the site where Lincoln's casket had been placed when it first arrived at the cemetery—the "holding grave." Then he showed me the temporary resting place on the hillside opposite the famous tomb where Lincoln's body rested until the great edifice was finished. I had to choke back laughter as he narrated the tale of the would-be tomb robbers. Fortunately he knew the sketchy elements of the story but not the names of the bungling burglars.

He was quite the tour guide. He showed me the copy of the famous Gutzon Borglum bust of Lincoln.[33] The nose on the bronze bust shines brightly. Tourists, for decades now, have rubbed Lincoln's nose for luck.[34]

It was time for a coffee break. The workers' station was fully supplied with all sorts of snack foods and beverage options. Limon even said that I could order a pizza—or anything else—if I wanted; but it had to be before one in the morning, when the local restaurants stopped delivery, and I also had to meet the delivery person at the front gate. Well, that would not be a need for me.

After our break, we went into the tomb. I had scouted it out many times, of course, and I lied and told Limon I had seen it twice as a tourist. Now, however, I was to get the royal tour and keys to access its hidden parts (which weren't particularly useful to me). We circumnavigated the

[33] Yes, it is the same man who blasted and carved out Mt. Rushmore. He did a Lincoln figure there too, you know. More on that later. This work is a copy of the marble piece in the US Capitol Building.

[34] Not unlike the worn-smooth foot of the statue of Saint Peter in Saint Peter's Basilica, Vatican City State.

structure inside and out. He showed me not only the visi-domes in the structure but also where all the surveillance microchips were located. I had, he said, in my shirt monogram, a special transmitter that would prevent the visi-domes from announcing me as an intruder. This seemed too good to be true!

I was glad that, unlike in the usher role at Ford's Theatre, I would not have to interact with any of the public. The job was brainless, but it gave me access to what I required and what I wanted to know for the next phase of my master plan.

Limon had me make the second round with him; this time it was I who explained locations and procedures to him. I made a few deliberate mistakes, lest he think something about me was peculiar or amiss. Little did he know!

At five in the morning we parted company at the main gate. Again I called a hovertaxi, which took me back to my apartment building in Springfield. Humberto met me there, and he chauffeured me back to the estate.

I took a little snooze. The plan was working fine.

CHAPTER 7

Days with Madison, Nights with Abe
Life in the Cemetery (Ha ha—get it?)

My new schedule was working fine. I could spend as much time at the university as I chose, sleep when I chose, and still get to the cemetery for my night rounds. The cleaning was minimal; the day crew did most of it. I just had to make sure that everything was in order after the cemetery closed at dusk. Restocking bathrooms was the most arduous task I had. Despite all the advances in science, toilet paper remained a necessity in public places.[35]

I spent two weeks dutifully doing my rounds. It was boring but necessary. Fortunately, the mindless work afforded time to let my great mind dart about other things. I needed those two weeks to establish credibility. I made sure that everything was done as expected and then some. I was an exceptional employee. The dark hours of the night fit my personality perfectly. I much preferred this to the busyness of Ford's Theatre and having to deal with the curious, ignorant public.

I took to talking to Abraham Lincoln as I made my rounds—talking to, not talking with! I found it helpful to articulate my plan orally and then use an imaginary Lincoln as a foil for any possible weaknesses. Of course, there were none.

At home, in my lab, I was happy as could be. I knew exactly how

---

[35] Although homes had the advantage of the scientifically advanced personal sanitation devices, public places still relied upon the old-fashioned toilet. By the way, Thomas Crapper (1836–1910) did not invent the flush toilet. It had been around for some time before him. However he did invent the ballcock flushing mechanism and made the toilet rather popular, given the questionable hygiene of his era.

to proceed and began working on the machinery I would need to accomplish the tasks at hand.

In the earlier years of the twenty-first century, the US military employed drones to make attacks on enemy positions. They were primitive but efficient. The technology improved over the decades, but the military, you know, always thinks big. I recall reading that in the early 1950s, it was projected that computers, which were an entirely new phenomenon at that time, would get faster and faster. And they did. But they also predicted that to accomplish that, computers would get larger and larger. The 1950s computers were already the size of a small room. In predicting ever-larger computers, they were wrong. Oh, were they wrong!

This was not unlike an 1890 meeting in New York. As the city was growing, experts predicted that by 1950 the city's population would be about eight million people. And they were right. But they also predicted that because of that increase in population, the city streets would permanently be under three feet of horse manure by 1950. Anyway, I digress.

I worked on my own drone technology for this project. I needed something that would be practically invisible, not show up on any of the omnipresent radar and cybersurveillance tools of the times, and yet be effective. It carried no bomb. I needed no bomb. It would carry an infinitesimally small camera that would use the newest digital electron signal to send the images back to my lab, where they would be safely stored in my own computer.

I needed that job at the cemetery for two reasons. This was the first of them. I needed to get accurate measurements of the whole tomb complex. The infrared technology of the drone would take photos in three dimensions. I wanted to be absolutely sure of the location of the Lincoln casket. I knew the red granite marker in the main room was just that—a marker. The tomb-robbing incident from 1876 had a lasting effect. The casket was hidden while new work was done to improve the safety of the tomb and the sturdiness of the structure (built on less-than-desirable land), and to complete the aesthetics of the tomb for the public.

Accordingly, the actual casket was not directly under the marker.

Articles from the newspapers (imagine—they read newspapers instead of having information forwarded into their implanted microprocessors!) had stated that the casket was actually some thirty inches behind the marker and its top was some ten feet under the floor.

A further complication was the fact that in 1901, the last time the casket was disturbed, that meddlesome Robert Lincoln, the only immediate blood relative not buried with the family,[36] insisted that his father's casket be protected from future vandalism. Evidently he had no idea that time would pass him by and future technologies would undermine his misplaced wishes.

At any rate, the casket was lowered into a large steel cage, and then the cage was covered with concrete, placed below the floor of the tomb those ten feet, and sealed "forever." Well, Robert Lincoln had no idea that one day Anton Bauer, PhD × 3, would one day come along.

The drone was the size of a small fingernail—No longer, no wider, and not even as thick. Embedded in it was a global positioning system that would respond to commands from my lab after a series of passwords had been used to initiate its flight. I had some fun with the passwords, of course. I just used the names, in order, of Lincoln's children. As the drone, which I nicknamed TAD (for Technologically Advanced Detection), made its way from the estate to the cemetery, it had enough self-knowledge to avoid any obstacles while flying only one hundred meters off the ground. Once I directed it to the tomb complex, I activated the cameras. Two hundred photos per second were transmitted to the lab. I had the drone fly around the exterior of the tomb twice. I needed measurements from all sides to determine which would be the best to use for the next part of the project. Then I had to get precise measurements on the location of the concrete block, where the steel bars of the cage were located, where the walls of the casket would be found, and last and most importantly of all, exactly where Lincoln's body was located.

The images were crystal clear. I had what I needed. I then directed the drone to fly into the Sangamon River, where the water would deactivate the drone's power systems and the natural chemicals in the water would dissolve the drone.

---

[36] He is buried in Arlington, Virginia.

"Mission Accomplished," as one hapless US president once said.

I categorized the photos into shots from the outside and the x-ray-like internal shots. I compared the photos from each pass to one another to make sure all the angles and measurements would be accurate and useful. And they would be.

Now that part of the project was finished.

Meanwhile, Back at the University

I wasn't at all tired from my nocturnal escapades. Quite the opposite. The adrenaline rush from pulling off this caper more than made up for any lack of sleep. I never needed that much sleep anyway, if you recall. My duties at the university went on without a hitch. I had gotten the information I needed for my personal project. The students would be working pretty much at the same kind of tasks that I had assigned in Washington. I varied the parameters just enough for each group so that there would be no duplication.

The lectures went fine. The international stellar satellite sessions went smoothly. Madison proved a capable administrator. She had not lost her scientific edge. She was particularly (and unnecessarily) active in the actual discussions. Her point of reference, however, always revolved around the ethics of the project. That always seems to get in the way of true scientific advancement.

I must admit, I did like her. Her mind was sharp. Her physical presence was not hard on the eyes—not that such things mattered to me (thanks, again, Mohel Samuel Weinstein). At any rate, we got along well. We were in the university cafeteria one day sharing a few quiet moments.

Madison stated, "The students seem to have taken to you. They enjoy the challenge, and they will particularly enjoy putting your class on their résumés."

I responded, "Well, yes. Everything seems to be going just fine."

Madison spoke again. "Anton, I mean Dr. Bauer ... no—I mean Anton: the international stellar satellite sessions are making the evening news. Your commitment to the genome project stirs interest as well as controversy. How do you deal with that? You seem so calm."

"My dear," I said, "I am always calm. It does no good to let anything beyond one's control take over a sense of intellectual or physical well-being. The Greeks, you know, were sound believers in self-control. I try to imitate them in that regard."

Madison answered: "However, most of the news broadcasts are negative. The students are bright, and they follow your lead, but the average citizen cannot."

"I know, my dear. I know. It's the price scientists always have to pay. Ask Robert Fulton. His 'folly' paved the way for modern commerce."

"But what about public opinion?"

Her line of questions was beginning to irritate me. I am not used to conversing with others, much less being contradicted or expected to explain myself.

"Madison, this is my philosophy: their opinion of me is none of my business."

"But," she retorted, "the ethics of the program is my concern, and when the public gets involved, I am the one who has to respond. What should I say?"

"Tell them to go and get some education in the field. If they held a doctorate or two, I might converse with them."

Madison frowned. It was a rather pretty frown, actually, but a frown nonetheless.

"Oh, I could never answer that way. Some of their concerns are actually my own."

"Are they now?"

My mind was beginning to move quickly. I wanted to end this little exchange quickly lest I betray myself.

"Yes, they are," said Madison. "We need to speak more about this as the project moves along." Little did she know the project at the university was not going anywhere. Once again I had seen to that.

"Oh, Anton."

"Yes, Madison?"

"I almost forgot to mention to you that there will be a new student in Section 3. Her name is Claudia Elsinger. She said her sister was one of your students in Washington—one of the unfortunate students who died in that strange car episode."

Crap! I thought I had all those ends tied up. "Thank you for letting me know, Madison. I look forward to meeting Claudia. If she is half the student her sister was, she will be a great addition to the project."

All the time, I was actually thinking of ways to deal with this. All would depend upon our first classroom encounter, which was to take place two days in the future.

"Well, time to return to the desk."

"Bye, Madison. See you in two days."

Now to My Personal Lab

I had to put that conversation out of my mind for a bit. I will return to it later, this minor glitch in an otherwise flawless schema. Humberto and Isabella always made sure I had my favorite things to eat waiting for me. They respected my privacy and the lab's sanctity. The photos showed me the information I needed to move on to the next level of this endeavor. While I prefer dealing with chemicals and formulas, the task at hand was the creation of a tool. I felt like *homo habilis redivivus.*[37]

I needed to invent an unobtrusive, boring tool. It had to be unobtrusive so that I could take it with me to the cemetery without arousing any possible suspicions should someone see me. Laser technology, that brainchild of the last century, would serve my needs.

I needed a kind of extendable eyeglass that would be able to penetrate the width of the Lincoln tomb, from the dirt outside on the hill into the casket—indeed, into Lincoln himself! The circular tube would contain a kind of periscoping extension. Most of the work would be quite easy. Using a laser to blast through the earthworks was the easiest part. The rest was more problematic, but I solved it.

Now to the Cemetery

The next night, I determined to begin my assault upon the tomb. I took my little laser invention, which I code-named LAUGH, for "laser Abe underground heist." It could fit in my jacket pocket, a miniature

---

[37] Stone Age toolmakers brought back to life.

of a pirate's eyeglass of old. It needed no external power. I had used a blast of atomically charged electrons to power it. The research formula, abbreviated, is:[38]

Incident Photon E$_2$

$\searrow$

$\searrow$

$\rightrightarrows$ **Trilated Neutron E^4**

$\downarrow$ $= E^2 - E^4 + \Delta^6 =$ **Laser**

$\downarrow$ $\nearrow$

plus Electron $^{\Delta 6}$ $\nearrow$

Penetrating the ground would be the easiest part. I planned to accomplish that in one night. It would take less than five minutes for the concentrated light beam to cut through and vaporize the dirt. Even if rocks or stones got in the way, it would blast them into nothingness. The bored hole would be only one inch in diameter, but it had to go some forty-two feet into the hillside. As I bored the small tunnel, I pushed in a plastic pipeline. This would keep the worked area from collapsing. It was small enough that when I finished, I could just leave it. It would be a long time—if ever—before it was discovered. I knew that two in the morning was the best time for this. I had made it my routine weeks before to patrol this section of the cemetery at that time. Just in case someone should be watching, I would be safe. All I had to do after that first night was plug up the external hole in the hillside. It would be next to invisible, but I wanted to cover all possibilities. I used a small straw just above the borehole to mark the site at shoulder height. As I hoped, I was done with this part of the project in minutes. I placed LAUGH on the ground to cool off a bit, walked around the exterior of the tomb as usual, and then retrieved LAUGH, placing it in my jacket pocket. So far, so good.

After I returned that night, I felt good. I took a dip in the Sangamon, followed by a shower, and then I went to bed. I wanted to sleep as much as possible for the sheer enjoyment of it. The next night, I returned but

---

[38] Short form of laser creation, all the original work of Anton Bauer!

did nothing special. I followed my regular routine, but I did carefully check the bore area. All was exactly as I had left it. *Good. No other grave robbers around.*

Madison, Part 2

That interfering bitch! Her ethical concerns meant nothing to me, and I was tiring of keeping up the charade of cooperation. I decided to let her think I was carefully mulling over her various moral postures, all the time actually plotting how to deal with her a little more severely.

To begin, I began to infer that I thought something was a little wrong with Miss Claudia Elsinger. We sat down at a small table in the faculty lounge, at a distance from any other people. I had my usual cup of chamomile tea, and she had a coffee with some vile syrup poured into it. Both of us munched on buttery croissants—a specialty of this dining room.

"But Anton," said Madison, "her credentials were impeccable. You said so yourself."

"Yes, I still support that reality. It is not her scientific abilities that are the problem. It is her personality. She is always finding excuses to stay a little later than anyone else, to saddle up a little too close to me, brushing against me, trying to hold my hand while speaking—all of this is making me quite uncomfortable. If you recall, Madison, all the sexual harassment difficulties in the workplace earlier this century—it is as though she never was instructed about them." (None of this was true, but I was laying a scenario for future action.)

Madison responded, "Well, I know that the students are trying to impress you. Perhaps she is trying too hard. Do you want me to speak with her?"

"Oh, no. Not yet, anyway. Let me see if some more challenging lab projects might make her too busy—or too embarrassed—to disturb me."

Madison thought that would be a better route than having to have a formal academic grievance issued against her—at least at this point. Thankfully, she did promise to keep her eyes open for the problem. All I had to do was make sure I manipulated myself around Ms. Elsinger to make the complaint appear to have some validity. I really just needed to get her out of the way. I had no idea how much information, professional or personal, her sister might have shared with her.

A great opportunity presented itself that very evening during one of the international sessions. I rearranged the chairs in the lab so that it was less like a classroom and more like a setup for a college exam study evening. I even had beverages for the group and had crystal goblets with each student's name engraved at each station. (Mall shops still specialize in catering to this kind of wedding party gift.)

I placed Claudia's goblet on the station next to mine. Unknown to her, the inside of her goblet had been carefully rubbed with a minor amount of Rohypnol. It was just enough to make her a little drowsy without knocking her out. In that drowsy state, however, she would reach out for support whenever she stood—and I would be right next to her. To the casual observer, it would look like questionable behavior.

The session went as planned. Madison, as always, was there. She, too, had a crystal goblet and commented ahead of time how kind it was of me to provide each student with such a fine token of the experience. She also saw what looked like a besotted Claudia Elsinger trying to touch me at frequent intervals while I was trying to lead the seminar's discussion. Claudia would feel fine in another hour, but on the way out the door, Madison, who always stayed to make sure all was set for the next day, gave me a knowing look.

And Back to the Cemetery

The afternoon went well. I was delighted that Claudia had unwittingly proven a tad emotionally off. But I had work to do. After Humberto dropped me off, I began my regular rounds. There had been several school groups at the tomb that day, and it was easy to see the results of those undisciplined brats. The regular maintenance crew was still cleaning the toilets when I got there. I hadn't seen any of them in weeks. They invited me to share some sandwiches and coffee during their break. Ever the gentleman, I agreed, even to the point of drinking coffee, not tea, from a paper cup. I assisted them in cleaning (it was, after all, in my job description) and got them on their way.

I got to the bore site a little later than I would have preferred. I did not have as much footage to go through this time, but it was a more difficult task this evening. I wanted to make the cut through the concrete that surrounded the coffin. Since the concrete was considerably harder than the dirt, packed as it was, I increased the intensity of the laser. It would be silent, but I had to be very careful to cut only through the concrete and not into the casket itself. I programmed in the measurements that I had obtained from the drone flyover, removed the patch covering the borehole, and slid the telescoping equipment into the hollowed part of the hill. The plastic tubing was holding just fine. Fortunately nothing had collapsed since that first night.

The spectrometer that I wore, which looked like an ordinary old-fashioned analog watch, showed me the progress. This laser cut just as wide as the ground laser did. I needed that one-inch circumference to have enough room for the next part of the project. It took slightly over twelve minutes. The cement quality from 1901 was not spectacular, and it, like the ground, vaporized with the onslaught of the laser beam. At exactly 4 feet $11\frac{1}{2}$ inches, the laser had cut its swath through the concrete cage. I withdrew the device and again placed it on the ground to cool, extended the plastic tubing, covered the hole, and finished my watchmanly round of the tomb before picking the laser up and placing it in my pocket. Humberto returned on time, and I had another splendid evening of self-satisfaction.

At Tadwil, the Estate

Other than Ms. Elsinger, everything was going as planned. Soon Ms. Elsinger would also go as planned, but not quite yet. I spent the day double-checking all the lab equipment. Everything was ready. The side rooms, too, were in order, awaiting their occupants. When night came, I made another foray into the hillside of the tomb.

Love That Cemetery

If all went well, which it should, this would be the final time that I would have to play the grave robber. I brought LAUGH, of course, but this time I also had another special tool. After LAUGH penetrated the exterior of the coffin (it took only three seconds), I turned it off and withdrew it. This time it didn't even get hot, but nonetheless I placed it on the ground as I had before. I once again extended more plastic tubing into the ground tubing, through the tubing in the concrete cage, and then into that tiny additional space in the coffin wall.

The next step was one of the most important. In the late twentieth century, when all manner of surgical procedures were miniaturized, one of the benefits was the creation of small—microscopic, actually—cameras and surgical cutting tools. I had managed to combine the two instruments so that they both fit into a space slightly smaller than my one-inch drill hole through the hillside, cage, and casket. I needed the camera device because I did not want to get my little "pound of flesh"[39] attached to any fabric from the casket lining or from Lincoln's clothing. Because of the long time the body had been in the grave, I did not know how much of the fabric might have disintegrated and become chemically and organically confused with his flesh. The camera would project its picture to my spectrometer watch.

I fed it through slowly, watching all the time for my progress on the special timepiece. Going through the long ground section took time, but I had to go slowly. I did not want to damage any of my precious equipment. When I got to the cage wall, there was a slight reverberation. Fortunately it was only the metal casing brushing the concrete lining, but with the ultrasensitive equipment, it sounded more severe.

The camera made its way into the casket itself. Now, no one had seen Lincoln's body since that 1901 reburial. (I still curse Robert Lincoln for making this so difficult.) Anyway, at that time it was observed that Lincoln's gloves had disintegrated, as had the flag that had been draped over his body. A slight greenish moss had grown on his clothing. There was no way of knowing how much of that might have continued to thrive or might have died away with the passing of years. Likewise, Lincoln's face, it was reported, had become somewhat bronzed in color,[40] probably a result of the reaction of his facial tissue to the initial bleeding after

---

[39] Actually I would need only a half gram, or a section of flesh about five cubic millimeters.

[40] It was something like the color of the Lincoln penny. Now isn't that a fine irony?

being shot. At any rate, in 1901, those present affirmed that this, indeed, was the sixteenth president of the United States. The last witness to that exhumation did not die until the middle of the twentieth century.

The delicate part of my work now took my full attention. I would be somewhat tardy in my rounds, but I could write that up as having taken time to check out a disturbance in the cemetery and report it as chasing some teenagers off the property. It was a most believable possibility.

I wanted a small section of Lincoln's skin. The hands, as I mentioned before, might have been compromised by the deteriorated gloves. I did not want any fabric mixing with the tissue sample. It, too, could be a source of contamination. In 1901 Lincoln's body was still quite well preserved. The long funeral train ride from Washington to New York, New York to Chicago, and Chicago to Springfield (and all points in between) required a rather frequent reembalming of his corpse. What might have happened in the intervening years was speculative at best, but I would take my chances.

The microcamera, with its tiny LED light, showed the face of the great man. The boring had been accurate. My equipment came through the plastic tubing at the center of his cheek, just a fraction past the beard line. I made the incision ever so carefully, the camera reliably relaying my progress. When I had the small piece of tissue safely on the microscalpel, a tiny trap door enclosed it, cutting it off from any possible contact with clothing, casket, concrete, or dirt. It was a pure sample. I would not even need all of that to extract the DNA I required, but I had decided to take more than enough so that I would not have to repeat this process in the future.

I carefully withdrew the instruments and placed the tissue sample just as carefully in a small petri dish. I placed the instruments, along with LAUGH, in my coat pocket. Then I very carefully pulled out twelve inches of the tubing, cut it off, and pushed it back into the bore hole. I filled in that twelve-inch-by-one-inch hole with soil and plugged the all-but-invisible opening. Everything looked just as it should.[41]

---

[41] In 1985, Robert Todd Lincoln Beckwith, the last known living descendant, passed away. Anyway, his DNA would not have been useful in bringing this Lincoln back.

When Humberto picked me up that evening, he noted my rather pleasant and talkative self. I told him that I had enjoyed the evening immensely because I had chased off some would-be vandals and saved the Lincoln tomb from desecration. Now, Lincoln did not mean much to Humberto—not much more than he meant to those Chinese diplomats back in Washington, DC, at Ford's Theatre. The deed was done.

I continued working at the cemetery for two more weeks. I did not want to stir up any kind of suspicion—just in case. My caution proved unnecessary. I submitted my resignation, citing incipient arthritis. The damp environment of the cemetery at night was making me ill. There was even a party thrown for me by the daytime crew, who knew I was very dependable and had made their work easier.

CHAPTER 8

Springfield
or
A Personal Interlude

Well, you might recall that way back at the beginning of this saga, I told you that I was born on July 5, 1996. I also told you that I would get back to the significance of that date later. (Not that its being the day I entered this world isn't enough!) You see, it is also the day that someone or something else entered this world. That something would be the infamous Dolly, the cloned sheep. Yes, from the time I learned about how auspicious that date was, I have been captivated by the notion of cloning: particularly human cloning—not just the cloning of some dumb sheep.

A common dictionary definition of cloning (yes, dictionaries are still around, but not in written form; they are part of the cybermemory implanted at birth) is "The process of producing similar populations of genetically identical individuals."

In biotechnology, the field that I have been working with, cloning, in simple terms, is the process used to create copies of DNA fragments. This is also known as molecular cloning. (It is from the Greek word κλών (klōn), which means "twig." You see, in horticulture, it is possible to recreate a plant from its twig, which contains the essential ingredients for replication.

Human cloning is considerably more difficult, although it utilizes many of the principles of what we will call simple cloning, which is like the cloning of Dolly. Simply put, it is the recreation of a human being. Early in the scientific discussion, the morality of such an action was a topic of great debate, especially after Dolly's appearance in this world. The United Nations (before its dissolution, of course) outlawed human cloning. Amazingly, world scientists observed the ban. The punishment for getting caught was death by biopsy. That is the reason for all my secrecy. The efforts to use fetal stem cells proved successful, despite the objections of several religious groups. By our time in history, many of the diseases that ended human life in prolonged suffering had been relegated to the past. It is reproductive cloning that is my interest. I was not concerned with somatic cell nuclear transfer or pluripotent stem cell induction. That was too limiting. That had been done. I wanted the whole enchilada!

Now, ever since 1996, another happy coincidence involving that auspicious year, a college in Beloit, Wisconsin, has issued a list of things that its incoming freshmen would either never have heard of or taken for granted. Among the items on the list for "our class"—those born in 1996 and most (not as bright as I) who entered college in 2014 at the usual age—included things like Hong Kong having always been part of China. This year's list, for those entering college at the usual age, would have included there being no known deaths from Parkinson's disease, ALS, or SIDS. Those things were eliminated worldwide. They would also not know a world in which there was a United Nations (dissolved in 2027) or a single president for the United States (the triumvirate of ancient Rome was reinitiated in 2032: a leader for internal affairs, one for external affairs, and one for space-time continuum affairs). But I digress. Back to July 5, 1996, and Dolly.

Scotland, that wild part of the British Isle that the Romans so feared, was Dolly's birthplace. The scientists at the Roslin Institute in Edinburgh brought her about. Dolly's existence was exciting for the scientific world and problematic for the moral world—and people like Madison.

The procedure used for Dolly will be the foundation of the procedure I will use for Abraham Lincoln. Dolly had three females involved in the creation process. One was for the egg, the other for the DNA sample, and the third was the "birth mother," who carried the experiment to term.

The process for cloning Dolly was a simple (I use the term loosely) somatic (Greek for "body") cell transfer. The cell nucleus from an adult specimen is transferred to a developing egg cell whose own nucleus has been taken out. An electric stimulus is used to blast the hybrid cell. Once it develops into a blastocyst, it is transferred to the surrogate mother. (The blastocyst is the initial stage of reproduction that ends up producing the embryo.) Dolly proved that a cell taken from any part of an adult mammal could be used to produce (reproduce) a whole specimen.

Sadly, Dolly died rather young for her species. She developed arthritis, but only after giving birth to a number of offspring. She was only six years old. Her species usually lives twice that amount of time. Could the dissonance between her life span and her expected life span have been caused by the age of the animal whose cell was taken? Scientists argue about it to this day, but that problem will not play a significant role in my work. My intention is to reanimate DNA that has been dormant for almost two hundred years. If anyone can do it, I can. I take some inspiration from the experiments in northern Spain in which an extinct (but only for a decade) species of mountain goat, the Pyrenean ibex, was successfully cloned but lived only a short time. However, that gives me hope. Two thousand nine was eons ago, and we have come a long way since then.

In schematic form, this is my plan, based on Dolly's creation/ animation.

Nucleus Donor + Lincoln DNA

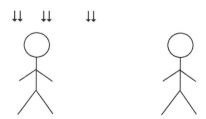

Surrogate Womb = Lincoln Redivivus

So, you see, I have a great affection for July 5, 1996, my birthday and Dolly's birthday. You can also now figure out why I needed the blood and tissue samples in order to proceed with my scheme to bring the great Abraham Lincoln back to us. This is no reanimation of dead material, such as that in Mary Wollstonecraft Shelley's *Frankenstein*. Nor is it a resuscitation, such as what Jesus did for Lazarus. This is something completely new: the cloning of a human life—and what a life at that!

CHAPTER 9

Springfield
Or
Long Nights in the Laboratory
(And Some Naughtiness as Well)

My hands are scrubbed. The computers are on. I love these new machines. For generations, one could dictate text to them, but now it is possible to think text into the systems. Those little implanted microchips are a wonderful invention.

The screens show that everything is ready. My next great challenge lies before me: I am going to clone Abraham Lincoln. The cloning science itself is not so difficult. Dolly proved that. The moral issues—well, I don't give a rat's ass about those. (How big is a rat's ass, anyway?)

The challenge—and subsequent contribution to science and to history—before me is to expedite the growth process of the cloned person. Dolly went through normal gestation. I don't want to wait that long to see if my theory will work. There are risks involved, I know, but they are calculated risks, and the risks aren't threats to me. The biggest danger is that I could use up the genetic material I have so cleverly purloined. I have kept it safe in a vault whose temperatures and humidities match those of the display case at Ford's Theatre and the coffin at Oak Ridge Cemetery. I will use only a part of the material just in case I need to reconfigure my work.

Now, the ethically queasy folk might think this is a terrible thing to do. Frankly, I think it is marvelous. I also think it is quite ironic that I am using tissue samples from Abraham Lincoln himself. He was instrumental in the middle of the Civil War in founding the AFIP Tissue

Repository (now part of the Army Medical Museum) on the grounds of Walter Reed Hospital in Washington, DC. So, you see, I think old Abe would approve. At any rate, I hope to find out soon.

Being Ready

I knew that as soon as I had the genetic programming ready, I would need, and I wanted, a human female to carry the artificially created gene to term. I surely was not going to take out an ad in the paper. I had another idea! Remember that wretched nurse who paddled my behind at my birth, Margaret Tompkins? I was going to use her womb for the gestation of Abe. All I have to do is remove the nucleus from the egg before implanting the cloned DNA. Nowadays a first-year medical student could do that.

She never left New Jersey. Finding her was just as easy as finding that dreadful mohel. Anyway, I digress.

I flew in my new jet-assisted hover car to New Jersey and called Ms. Tompkins. Someone as dreadful as her never could get married. I got in touch with her through the hospital's cybercommunications line. I told her that I was Seymour Flywheel, a lawyer for the law firm of Flywheel, Shyster, and Flywheel.[42] I told her that she had inherited a small fortune from Dr. Evanston Friedman, an actual local doctor who had really recently died. He had done work at the same facility she worked at, so she was somewhat familiar with him. No matter.

She stated that she recalled working with him when she was a young nurse.

"Oh, yes," I replied. "He never showed much emotion, but he was very fond of his nurses. After his wife died and they were childless, he wanted to thank those who had assisted him in his long career. You are one of those honorees."

Ms. Tompkins answered, "Oh my. Oh my.[43] What do I need to do?"

---

[42] I presumed that someone as pedestrian as Ms. Tompkins was unfamiliar with the early-twentieth-century radio show featuring Groucho Marx and his brother Chico.

[43] Evidently her vocabulary was rather limited.

"Well, Nurse Tompkins, I am staying at the Plentiful Arms. I can meet you in the lobby, and I will show you the will and the papers you need to sign to obtain your inheritance. Please be sure to bring two forms of identification, including the license for your microchip."

"Yes. Oh Yes![44] I can be there at seven."

"That would be fine. See you then."

I had a few hours to waste, so I went for a walk and let my scheme take more solid form in my mind. I decided to go the simple route. I would watch her leave after our meeting, see which hovercar was hers, and have a hovertaxi follow her. It was all too easy.

She showed up on time. She was wearing practical black walking shoes, a gray dress that fell well below her knees, a nurse's pin on her coat lapel, and a hat. A hat! Women hadn't worn hats in fifty years. To say the least, she was amazed at the $1,474,384 NAD that would be transferred to her bank in the morning after verification of the signatures. I ordered a cup of tea for myself. She wanted some celebratory champagne, which was fine with me. After she left, I followed. It was easy tracking her to her residence in the hovertaxi. I walked around a bit after getting dropped off by the hovertaxi. I needed this to look plausible. I pounded on the door, using the old-fashioned brass knocker. She was a bit surprised to find me at her door.

"Oh, Mr. Flywheel! What a surprise! Please come in. What can I do for you?"

She was wearing the same drab clothing as at the hotel.

"Well, Ms. Tompkins. Please do not tell my superiors, but I forgot to have you sign the release document that frees us from any further obligation to you regarding this estate. All you have to do is sign this paper and I will be out of your way."

"Oh, of course! Would you like something to drink since you came all this way?"

"Why, yes. A cup of tea would be nice."

"Then I will join you. I shouldn't have any more champagne! Ha ha!" (Ha ha, indeed!)

---

[44] How prosaic!

Margaret Tompkins brought in the tea on a simple wooden tray. The teacup was not Wedgwood, but it would have to do.

"Oh, Ms. Tompkins, I really would like a cube of sugar for my tea."

"Of course," she said. When she went off into the kitchen, I plopped the dosage of my own concoction of benzodiazepine, a powerful sleeping agent, into her cup. It would have her sleeping in half a minute.

She returned with the sugar, and I stirred it into my cup. As I lifted it up, I said, "Here's to you, Ms. Tompkins, and to many happy days."

"Why, thank you," the fool replied. She sipped her tea quickly and within the minute was sound asleep.

She hadn't had time to tell anyone about her fortune. I cyberstole the combination to her hovercar, stuffed her in the back after dosing her with some more sedatives, and used her car to return to my estate. Before we took off, however, while stuffing her into the back of the hovercar, I swatted her ample butt.[45]

When we arrived, I had Humberto and Isabella assist me in moving her to one of the prepared rooms in the barn. We used the special outer door so they could not see the lab proper. When they had left, I secured her to a comfortable reclining chair and left. Then I sent Humberto by commercial hovertaxi to New Jersey to get my own vehicle. It was too nice to leave behind. (Speaking about behinds, did I tell you I swatted Margaret Tomkins's in revenge?)

I returned three hours later, through the lab entrance. She was coming out of her drug-induced sleep. I introduced myself, using my true name. I was wearing my lab equipment, not the three-piece lawyer outfit of the previous evening. I also told her the truth about what was going to happen. I told her that I was in the process of cloning Abraham Lincoln and that, in order to complete my little experiment, I needed some special feminine assistance. I needed her womb. I explained to her what an honor it was, etc. Then I told her that she would have free use of the room and its considerable comforts, and that if she behaved, I would even let her outside occasionally. (This was a bitter lie.) I focused on

---

[45] The wheels of justice grind exceedingly slow, but they grind exceedingly fine. Or what goes around, comes around. Or what's good for the gander is good for the goose.

what an important role she would be playing in the history of medical science and told her that I had kept her in mind since my own birth. (She knew me by reputation.) The dolt was actually honored at this opportunity. I told her that her meals would be delivered daily, plus a snack, through the turnstile built into the thick wall of the room. She could order anything she wanted; she was just to leave a note the night before with her requests. (I figured the more content she was, the more chance of success I would have for a healthy Abraham.) Then I told her that when the project was over and the baby had been delivered (by Caesarean section), she would be free to go or to join me on the triumphant tour, showing off our success. (This, too, was a bitter lie.)

All this served to calm her down. I released her restraints, and she simply sat back, smiled, and actually thanked me for the privilege!

Now, Back to Work

My adrenaline was running off the charts. I needed to be careful but also quick. I entered all the existing data into the system by using the telepathic codes I had invented. I double-checked the condition of the tissue sample. It turned out I didn't really need the dried blood sample after all; however, I kept it nonetheless, after performing cross-tests between the tissue and the blood to make sure the DNA markers were the same. They were. Well, even though it meant a lot of wasted evenings at Ford's Theatre, it also meant they had been telling the truth about the display of Lincoln's clothing. This was a rare example of government honesty in any time or place!

I made sure Tompkins was well taken care of. She had plenty of food whenever she wanted it. She could view a preselected grouping of entertainment features that I allowed into her microchip's entertainment function. No news, of course, was allowed. She was amazingly content, the chump (or is it "chumpette"?).

The lab was humming at full capacity. I had the formula for the cloning, thanks to Dolly and the work of Group Four in Washington. My actual contribution to this whole secret effort was to create a genome accelerator. This had never been done before. It hadn't even been attempted. In fact, it had not even been thought about. Its purpose was to affect the genetic process in such a way that it would not take a full nine months for the human gestation period to take place. I was also concerned that I did not want to wait around for decades for Abraham to become sufficiently mature so that I could engage in meaningful conversation with him. And I couldn't wait to show him life some two hundred years after his assassination.

The challenge was to use a PCR (polymerase chain reaction) in order to amplify a targeted area of the DNA sample. I had collected the DNA template (thanks to the cemetery), two primers, and a Taq polymerase at the ideal temperature of 70 degrees Fahrenheit. A little more challenging was collecting the deoxynucleoside triphosphates—the building blocks of DNA strands. The buffer solution was easy enough to concoct (which is needed to provide a life-sustaining environment for the genome). Likewise, creating the monovalent action potassium ions was simple chemistry. A harder decision was the choice of trivalent cations (manganese ions). Usually a gentle Mg^{2+} is sufficient, but I wanted to accelerate development, so I used Mn^{2+}. Then I elevated the level of acceleration to Mn^{3+}.

The purpose of the polymerase chain reaction is to amplify a single copy of a gene. It was developed way back in the 1980s, but my work has advanced it considerably. The thermal recycling, cooling and heating, helped to melt and replicate the DNA. It took a bit of time to isolate the necessary Taq bacterium (*Thermus aquaticus*), but I did it. I melted the double helix, lowered the temperature, and then used the resulting DNA strand for the polymerase amplification.

I had a choice to make among the variations of the PCR technique, but I ended up preferring electrophoresis combined with a helicase-dependent amplification. I thought the hot-start method a tad reckless.

Each process was done at a different temperature (centigrade measurement). Schematically—simplified—it looks like this:

1. Denaturation (Ψ)
then

> **2. Naturation (ξ)**
> then

>> **3. Elongation (Ξ) = Voila! Abe!**
>> **(Quid Erat Demonstratum)**

The science was done. The formula was complete. I took a day off, went out on the *Mary Todd* a bit, and then went to the university and conducted one of the international seminars. I still had to keep up appearances. I also had to continue making Claudia Elsinger look a tad off balance. I once again arranged the chairs so she would be next to me. Unfortunately, Madison, ever infatuated with the knowledge—not with me—sat on my other side. Claudia's frequent contributions showed her genius, but she also kept looking at me for approval. How adolescent of her. The session went a bit long, since the clocks were adjusting to Astral Time at this season of the year. Half of the contributors were rising early to participate even though it was only three in the morning or earlier in their astral zones.

When the session was over, I went home, had a good dinner prepared by Isabella in the state-of-the-art kitchen, and prepared for a good rest before the next day's work.

Now, Here It Comes!

Early the next morning, I put on my best lab coat, the chalky white one with my name in gold embroidery. I made sure the exterior doors to the barn were shut, locked, and alarmed. At breakfast that morning, I intercepted Isabella on her way to deliver breakfast to Nurse Tompkins. I dusted her scrambled eggs with a sleeping potion that looked like pepper. It was an ancient but effective formula. I needed her to be unconscious for about one hour. I dosed her with enough for a two-hour rest, just to be sure.[46]

Once she was snoozing comfortably, I moved her bed (a hospital bed on wheels) into my lab. With extreme care, I removed the wonderfully prepared genetic compound that would become Abraham Lincoln from its incubator. I kept it in the sterile saline solution and kept it covered. No time for contaminants now!

I looked at innocent Ms. Tompkins. Then I remembered her slap

---

[46] The potion is an old shamanic mixture of two portions of chamomile, two portions of poisoned flour, two portions of sleepshroom, and one portion of triturator of arsenic.

so many years ago. For the fun of it, I slapped her butt again. Then, ever so carefully, I removed the genetic compound from the petri dish, extracted a single egg, and then implanted it back in Nurse Tompkins's womb. When she wakes up, she won't know anything happened. I will tell her, however, that the procedure has taken place and that she needs to take care of herself more than ever. That also means I have to take care of her more than ever.

I moved the hospital bed back to her room. Ninety minutes later, my motion detector indicated that she was stirring in bed. I went into the chamber, and we had a very pleasant conversation. Or at least I did.

"Margaret," I queried, "how are you feeling?"

"Well, Dr. Bauer, I feel fine. Just a little drowsy."

"Well, Margaret, I want you to know that this morning I performed the procedure we had discussed. I did not want to let you know ahead of time, because you don't need any extra stress. You are now carrying a cloned human being. I want you to take every precaution. If you feel any symptoms of the pregnancy, let me know immediately. Just push your buzzer. If you need or want anything, let me know. I will be monitoring your food and weight, as well as performing ultrasounds for the baby. The ultrasounds now aren't like those from the days when you were in the delivery room. The needed images can be taken by a medidrone. You won't even know when it is happening. That way, again, your stress will be minimal. Do you have any questions?"

"Well, one right now: How long will I be here? At least nine more months? Will I be taking care of the baby after it's born?"

"Now, Margaret. That's more than one question, but I'll answer you anyway. You will be here about three more months. Part of the experiment is to accelerate the whole gestation process and then the growth and development cycle of the newborn into adulthood." (This was true.) "Yes, of course you will be the primary caretaker of the child." (This was a bitter lie, but why upset her?)

The next day, I checked in on her. She was sleeping happily and cozily. I went to the university and shared a cup of tea and a scone with Madison. During our conversation, I was able to direct her into my "Elsinger plan," but she, of course, did not know that.

"Madison, dear," I said, "Have you observed at all how Claudia's behavior is increasingly inappropriate? It seems to me she centers more upon my person than the discussion. I am getting very nervous around her. While her academic work is top-notch, I really am afraid her personality is disordered."

"Well, yes, Anton. I have noticed this. Each time we have an international session, I have made it a point to be there, even to get physically close to you to see what her reaction might be. Trust me; as a woman, I can see that her interest is not platonic. Not at all. What do you want me to do about this?"

"Well, I do feel sorry for her, her having lost her sister and all. And she is a splendid student. She catches on quickly. Her expertise is growing, and I hate to upset that progress.[47] Let's see what happens over the next few weeks."

"That's fine with me," Madison replied. "Would you like some more tea?"

"No thanks. I need to get back to Tadwil, my estate." And with that, I left.

Growing Abe

I checked in on Margaret. She was awake and looked bored.

"How are you feeling today?"

"Oh, Doctor, I feel great! Do I have that glow of pregnancy yet?"

(Actually she did. I think the accelerator was working.)

"Margaret, dear, you look fantastic. I will get some new clothing for you. You will be putting on weight as the pregnancy progresses. I'll get a catalog ordered for your microchip download mechanism. Let me know whatever you want."

"Oh, Doctor. You are so good to me. Thank-you."

"You are welcome. I'll return tomorrow to see what you want."

I did return the next day. She already had a visible baby bump. I wouldn't be getting those new clothes any too soon. She gave me her order. It was modest. I took the liberty of getting Isabella to order everything three sizes larger than Margaret thought she would need.

---

[47] I lie really well, don't I?

The clothing was delivered by hovercraft the next day. Margaret was thrilled and modestly waited until I left the room before she changed into her new Hawaiian-style, loose-fitting, flowing, multicolored shift with various flowers on it. (I believe such dresses are called muumuus.)

I went back to the laboratory and worked at planning another international seminar.

The following day, I was too busy to see Margaret, but Isabella told me that she has been ordering great quantities of food. It was healthy food, thank goodness, but it was a lot of food for someone her size to put away. I decided to look in on her. I couldn't believe what I saw. After just a few days, she appeared to be five months pregnant. She was a bit alarmed at her size and the quickness with which she had grown that much, but I assured her it was all according to plan. (It was actually going much quicker than I expected.) We did another sonogram and MRI, and sure enough, the little boy was, after just three days, the equivalent of a five-month-old fetus. I told Margaret to take it easy, not get excited, watch her diet, and try to walk around as much as possible. She readily agreed.

I now placed another surveillance chip in her room. I wanted to make sure she wasn't doing anything that could possibly harm little Abe. He had a tough enough time getting born the first time around in the primitive setting of rural Kentucky. Now, with the most up-to-date equipment, science, and me, he had a much better chance at the outset of his life. I looked in on Margaret with increasing regularity. I thought I might be hallucinating or experiencing an exaggerated form of hope, but she was visibly bigger, growing literally by the hour! I went back to the sonogram. The baby was now at twenty-six weeks. Like the original Lincoln, this baby was long and seemingly undernourished—way too thin for my likes. I would have to check even more frequently.

A few days went by as normal: time spent at the university, a faculty dinner honoring me, another international seminar, more plotting against Claudia, and more suggestions to Madison about Claudia.

It was that evening when I was watching the monitor that I could see something was amiss. I hated to admit it, but yes, something was going terribly wrong. Margaret began moving back and forth in great discomfort. The baby in her womb was growing exponentially. Every minute was becoming the equivalent of another twenty-four hour day. She looked, from the belly down, like the fat lady at circuses of old. Her upper body was as thin as ever. Only the reproductive organs were swelling, but they were swelling horribly. She began to scream in agony. Had the birth process already begun? I recalled that large babies tend to come a little early. Abe was long, but not large. What was happening?

I wanted to maintain my scientific objectivity. There was nothing I could do to help Margaret. All I wanted to do was to observe, and observe I did. Her writhing was frantic, and her screaming was like a chorus of wailing banshees. Her uterus was expanding quicker and quicker. I thought for a moment that Little Abe was going to come into this world like the alien in that twentieth-century film with Sigourney Weaver—*Alien*.

She screamed one more time, and then she exploded. *Kaboom! Kerfluee!* Both the fetus and Margaret exploded into little red blood-and-flesh parts that flew all over that room. There was nothing left to identify her or the baby. Something, indeed, had gone horribly wrong. Before I could find out why the accelerator, which I had so carefully prepared and programmed, had malfunctioned, I had to clean up this mess. Well, not me. I called my faithful retainer Humberto and explained that there had been an accident in the guest room. Now, Humberto suspected that all was not kosher at Tadwil, but he was making a good living, and the work was easy. I asked him to get Isabella and commanded the two of them to clean up the mess. It took hours. I ordered them to incinerate everything in the room: all the flesh, all the supplies—everything. "No digas a nadie si valoras tu vida."[48] That was my instruction to Humberto, who repeated it to his wife.

The room looked like the hallway in the home of the dead meth dealer that Jesse Pinkman was supposed to clean up after in an early episode of that wonderfully naughty hit twenty-first-century TV program *Breaking Bad*. Instead of following Walter White's instructions and using plastic as a disposal instrument, the dope thought he knew better and used a bathtub. The acid ate through the body all right, but

---

[48] "Tell no one if you value your life!"

it also ate through the bathtub and the floor of the bathroom, causing the tub and its human slime contents to fall into the hallway below.

This wonderful duo did not complain. They performed marvelously. They scraped and clawed at every centimeter of the mess, disposed of the slime,[49] and then, as per my instructions, disinfected the room and repainted it. In twenty-four hours, it looked as good as new. I, on the other hand, did not feel as good as new. Failure was something unknown to me, and I had to discover what had gone wrong. I went back to the formula for the genetic cloning. It was fine. Then I looked carefully at my notes for the accelerator. Could I have made a mistake?

---

[49] Good-bye, Nurse Margaret. Good-bye, Baby Abe.

C H A P T E R   1 0

A Personal Interlude, Some Introspection, and a Trip to London

I double-checked the figures again. And again. Then I saw what happened. I had projected my mental model onto the wall of the laboratory. The wall was white and normally served quite well for my mental projections. I normally don't need or use that extra measure, but this project was so important that I wanted everything to be as secure as possible. And that was my mistake. My eidetic memory, as usual, had served me well. It was the projection that had failed me.

I studied it twice over and saw the discrepancy between what was in my brain and what was projected on the wall. It was a small number—just a small number. If you recall, I had set the acceleration formula to Mn^{3+}, which should have been a safe enough increase in the acceleration. The problem was that when I looked at the formula on the wall (instead of trusting my brain), I read Mn^{8+}. Instead of 3^+, I had used 8^+. Each of those components had been exponentially ten times greater than the written number (this saved a lot of zeroes in the math). No wonder Margaret and Little Abe exploded.

Well, there was a conclusion I did not want to make. My eyesight was beginning to go awry. I did not want this to become general knowledge. (Yes, pride goeth before a fall, and all that.) I did the only thing I could do. I needed to keep this quiet. No one, of course, would know about Margaret Tompkins or Little Abe, but I did not want anyone knowing I had any kind of physical malady.

I called my good friend Percival Pettigrew, the eighth earl of Upton, just outside London. Percival was one of those aristocrats who felt an obligation to the hoi polloi for his good fortune. He had studied medicine, specializing in ocular surgery. We had met many years ago when I was lecturing in London. He was an avid student, and we became friends—or as close to friends as I have.

"Anthony, old chum," Percival said upon answering, "good of you to ring me up. What can I do for you?"

"Percival, to make it short, I think I need to take advantage of your expertise, but of course the utmost discretion and secrecy must be guaranteed."

"Of course, of course. When can you get here?"

"I'll take the next astrojet over. I can be there in the morning."

"Splendid. Splendid, old man. I'll have Wilkins pick you up at New Heathrow and bring you to the estate. I have everything here I'll need."

"Many thanks, Percival. See you soon. Cheerio!"

I took the astrojet from New O'Hare to New Heathrow.[50] I arrived at dawn the next morning, and Wilkins, as promised, met me and took me to Upton Castle. The British also have hovercars, but of course they propel them on the opposite side of the skyway.

Upton Castle had been in Percival Pettigrew's family for four hundred years. It was one of only two such buildings that did not have to scratch the tourist market to survive. Ever since the success of Downton Abbey in the early twenty-first century, most of the estate owners made whores of their property. Not so the Pettigrews. The estate was enormous—the size of a small county in the United States. Like my estate, a river ran through it—the Avon. The castle itself was built in the 1600s on property given to the family almost a century earlier by Henry VIII. It had been enlarged and modernized frequently.

Percival's lab was up to date. He also maintained an office in London where he offered his skills free of charge to London's destitute. Britain's socialized medicine had long since collapsed, and the state of health care there was hellacious. Fellows like Percival saved many people from miserable chronic illness. No one wore eyeglasses anymore. The medical sciences that surrounded ocular phenomena had long since been able to work wonders through painless processes.

---

[50] These are both the largest astrojet facilities in the world. I expected delays, but none occurred.

When I arrived, Percival asked how soon I would like to have him examine me. I told him that time was of the essence. I went to my suite of rooms on the third level, using the grand staircase to ascend. Two hours later, Wilkins came to take me to the medical office. It had once been the chapel for the estate. Its windows alone were worth a fortune, having survived Cromwell's "eccentricities." I sat in the exam chair, and Percival, dressed in sterile white medical gear, flew the optical drone in front of my face.

"Hmm," he said.

"What's up?" I asked.

"It appears you have the beginning of a senile cataract. It is nothing serious, but it would make your vision a bit blurry. Does that correspond to the reason for your call?"

"Yes, Percival, it does. What can be done about it?"

"The procedure originated in Baghdad, in the medieval medical schools of Islam. Of course, it was primitive. There was no sedation. But the surgery was effective. It has been obviously improved upon over the centuries. I can do it immediately, and within ten minutes your eyesight will be perfectly normal. I'd suggest a good nap afterward, and then this evening we'll have a splendid dinner to celebrate your good health. How does that sound?"

"Yes, let's do it. Thank you."

"My dear friend, it's already done. The drone was programmed to clear the cataract with optical laser adjustment. I still suggest you take that nap. I'll have Wilkins fetch you at seven. You will find a dinner jacket in your room closet."

"My dear friend, how can I ever repay you?"

"Anton, you know well that is not necessary. That's what friends are for. See you later. I'll have a pleasant surprise or two waiting for you."

I went back to my suite, slipped into an airfoam robe, and took my nap. At six thirty, Wilkins knocked to ask whether I needed anything. I told him I would be ready at seven. I showered and dressed in the perfectly fitted dinner frock that Percival had provided.

I could hear the sounds of voices from the main hall. There was also lute music. I entered, and there were five other guests present.

"Anton, dear Anton," said Percival, "allow me to introduce you to the other guests. Dr. Anton Bauer, this is William V, king of England; his wife, Queen Katherine; and their first child, the heir apparent, Prince George. Sadly, Charlotte, 'the spare,' is off on a goodwill trek to New Australia."

I bowed profoundly and expressed my surprise and appreciation for the evening's company. William had become king after the rather short thirteen-year reign of his father, following Elizabeth II's sixty-eight years as queen of England. This royal couple had captured the imagination of the world at their wedding in the early years of the twenty-first century and had continued to do so ever since. Never had monarchs been so outdated or so beloved. Interestingly enough, there had been a London play in the earlier part of the century, when Elizabeth II still reigned, about an aging Charles finally getting the throne. The play, *Charles III*, proved to be somewhat prophetic in the strange actions of this aged monarch. He even stormed Parliament, threatening, as was his royal right, to dismiss it. But enough of that.

Wilkins led us to the splendid dining hall. It had a table for fifty persons, but only the required number of place settings was used—thankfully all at one end of the table. Percival offered King William the head of the table, but he declined and said he preferred to sit next to his wife, so Percival took the place of honor. William and Kate sat across from Prince George and me.

William was wearing his red military tunic. Despite his baldness, he looked young and dashing. Kate was wearing a simple but elegant straight-falling gown of pale blue organdy. She wore a small tiara encrusted with sapphires and diamonds, and a solitary brooch that matched the tiara. George wore an ordinary evening jacket with his prince of Wales insignia prominently visible on the lapel.

The other two guests were waiting for us in the dining room. They were longtime friends of mine—at least I actually did have some. Angus and Fergus MacDougall had been students in China when I was there. If you can, imagine what their Mandarin sounded like as it was spoken through their thick Highland brogue!

I embraced them warmly. I assure you I do not do that often. Angus and Fergus were brothers. They looked like twins but actually were a scant eleven months apart in age. Both still had unruly shocks of blond-red hair that were beginning to grow appropriately gray at the temples. We had become friends in those days in China, and young as we were, despite the ever-present danger to Westerners, we had a great deal of fun wreaking havoc whenever we could. We got away with all of it. Perhaps that's where my penchant for intellectual mischief originated. At any rate, it was a welcome surprise to see them after so many years.

The table was delightful. I knew it would be. The first course was light pigeon porridge. This was followed by trout almandine. The trout had been caught in the River Avon that afternoon. Splendid silver fish forks, shaped like fish, were our utensils for that course. Seasoned vegetables followed this, then a potato-crusted rutabaga and a splendid piece of venison (also from the estate) covered in a delightful light burgundy reduction. Of course, an appropriate wine accompanied each course. Dessert was simple—a baked Alaska, in honor of the American guest. (Thank God there was no haggis, despite the presence of the MacDougalls.)

When the meal was over, we retired to the salon for cognac and cigars. Normally this was only the domain of the men, but since Queen Kate was the only woman, she joined us. She *really* joined us. I was slightly amazed when she lit her own cigar, put it in her mouth, took a small puff, and then slyly extinguished it.

"Well, I had to be part of the action, didn't I?" she stated. "Don't tell, now!"

We talked about politics, of course. The king was preoccupied with the every-century-or-so desire of the Argentines to return the Falklands (the Islas Malvinas, as the Argentines say) to Argentine control. We also spoke about the new pan-Arab league forming in the Middle East and the recent economic slump that China was experiencing. Then the talk turned to my work. Now, William was an art scholar who later changed his course to the pursuit of geography (oh well), but he did show interest and knowledge in my work. I told him a bit about genetic mutation and genetic manipulation. He followed quite well and then quipped, "Well, old sport. Wouldn't it be something if you could clone one of my ancestors—perhaps Henry VIII or Elizabeth I?"

"Your highness," I replied, "that kind of science is generations in the future." (I can lie to royalty as well as to peasantry.)

"Pity. It would be so interesting."

As the chimes rang the eleventh hour, Wilkins brought the queen's wrap. We all promised to meet again, perhaps in the States. Just before leaving, William turned to me, pulled a sword off the wall in the foyer, and asked me to kneel. He then said those famous words: "Sir Anton, I dub thee a knight of the realm."

And now I was nobility too! Sort of. At least a little bit. I really didn't care, but it was nice of him. They departed.

To my delight, Angus and Fergus were also staying at Upton. I would have time to catch up with them in the morning. I went upstairs happy.

Breakfast was served in a smaller salon, but it was exquisite. Wedgwood china and Waterford crystal graced the table at breakfast—a sign that some semblance of elegance remains in the world. Percival did not join us. He had to go to London early, so it was just the three of us: Fergus, Angus, and me.

We reminisced about the days we had shared in China. A great deal of laughter filled the salon. As a final course of small scones with clotted cream was served, we became silent. That was always a dangerous sign for us. We were thinking, which was what we did best. And when we all grew silent, we knew there would be trouble.

Angus inquired, "Anton, are you thinking what I'm thinking?"

Fergus responded, "You know we all think alike at these times. The question is, what prank are we going to create?"

I responded quickly, explaining that I hadn't much time before I had to return to Springfield to work on my project, but mostly to be present at the university for the final lecture of my commitment. I said nothing of my recent failure.

Fergus was always the naughtiest of our troika. It was no surprise, then, that he came up with the prank we would enact. With each of us taking his own part, we could do it that evening after dinner. We had all day to prepare.

Percival joined us for dinner—another great repast. He did notice a certain atmosphere in the room that was lighter than that of the evening before, but he ascribed it to our being less anxious without the royals about. Little did he know.

After the customary cognac and cigars, we retired to our individual rooms at nine o'clock. One hour later, we met in the foyer of the castle.

We told the evening watch that we were going into London to catch a late play and would be back very early in the morning. He was kind enough to summon a hovertaxi for us, wondering a bit why we were dressed rather commonly for an evening in the capital city.

The hovertaxi dropped us off at Victoria Station. We asked it to return for us in four hours. That was sufficient time to make believable our story that we had gone into London to watch the late play, have some drinks, and return at a reasonably calculated hour. From Victoria Station, we took the short stroll to Kensington Gardens. A few people were still walking its paths, but all were heading out. We imitated their example; however, we veered in, left the walkway, and proceeded through the trees using an old-fashioned GPS to guide us. We did not want to attract any attention by using light.

Then we found the famous statue of Peter Pan in Kensington Gardens. The history of the statue was part of our fun. It was literally placed in this spot on the path during the night of May 1, 1912. No one knew it was coming. It was a surprise gift from the Scottish author of *Peter Pan*, J. M. Barrie. Barrie had composed an announcement about the statue's appearance in the *Times*. It read as follows:

> There is a surprise in store for the children who go to Kensington Gardens to feed the ducks in the Serpentine this morning. Down by the little bay on the south-western side of the tail of the Serpentine they will find a May-day gift by Mr J.M. Barrie, a figure of Peter Pan blowing his pipe on the stump of a tree, with fairies and mice and squirrels all around. It is the work of Sir George Frampton, and the bronze figure of the boy who would never grow up is delightfully conceived.

There it was—the surprise statue that has delighted anyone familiar with the various incarnations of the original story of Peter Pan.

Now, Fergus and Angus, like that famous author, were also Scotsmen and were very familiar with the work of Barrie as well as with the famous statue. It would soon be tampered with—not badly, but it would be fun. Here is the plot:

The J. M. Barrie Peter Pan statue in Kensington Park
(photo from ThinkstockPhotos.com; used with permission)

Angus had brought along all the preparations needed to conduct water from the nearby pond to the site of the statue. It wasn't too far. The swans and ducks and geese would be a nuisance to work around, but the Scot was intrepid. He set the pump in and then dug a narrow and shallow channel from the pond to the base of the statue. Naturally it had been raining in London, so the ground was soft and easy to work with. He covered up the telltale signs of the trench by tamping the grass back into place and then dropping enough goose poop around to discourage any immediate investigation. This only took him about half an hour. He was well prepared.

Fergus contributed the next part of the adventure. It consisted of connecting the pump hose to the rear end (literally) of the statue and running it through the middle of the bronze so that it could not be detected. This involved the work of tipping the whole cursed thing carefully on its side in order to access the bottom. It was the most dangerous part of the endeavor. We could have ended up breaking the statue or ourselves. Fortunately we knew that once the park closed, there was only a sporadic drive-through by the park constabulary. We had another hour to finish the project.

Once the statue was tipped, it was easy to thread the hose through the hollow interior of Peter's body. We should have become colonoscopists! Next Angus used a laser (I'm not the only one who knows about these things) to cut a small opening in front of the statue, and he inserted a small bronze tube through the front of Peter's frock. It looked like— well, you know what it looked like.

Then we placed the statue back in place, retreated through the trees to the pond, turned the control of the pump on, and voilá, we had *Peter Pan Pis*, a delightful copycat of the *Manneken Pis* in Brussels. (The term is Marols for "little man pee.") The statue of the little boy urinating is a bronze, originally by Hiëronymus Duquesnoy the Elder, around 1618. Other pranksters in history stole the original. Then it was returned, stolen, returned, stolen, etc. The current public statue is a copy erected in 1965, and the original is at the Maison du Roi / Broodhuis. All sorts of delightful stories surround it.

The Manneken Pis (Brussels, Belgium)
(photo from Thinkstockphotos.com; used with permission)

My special contribution to the effort, besides assisting with the physical work, was to send an announcement to the *Times*—a mockery of the original one from 1912.

That statue had sat there gloriously reigning for some 150 years. Well, there would be a new surprise for the children of London in the morning. As I have reported before, newspapers have long disappeared from the earth, but the morning after our stunt, all of London read the following in the cybernews:

> There is a surprise in store for the children who go to Kensington Gardens to feed the ducks in the Serpentine this morning. Down by the little bay on the south-western side of the tail of the Serpentine they will find the May-day gift by Mr. J. M. Barrie, the figure of Peter Pan blowing his pipe on the stump of a tree, with fairies and mice and squirrels all around. It has been anatomically corrected. It is the work of brilliant vandals.

We returned to Victoria Station with playbills confiscated by Fergus. From there we hovertaxied back to the castle, were warmly greeted by the night watchman, and went to our rooms.

We gathered for a final breakfast, thanking Percival profusely. He was apoplectic about the cyberheadline regarding the vandalism of the famous Peter Pan statue. We all expressed our surprise and dismay, commenting that we had been in London ourselves last evening and had had no idea anything was amiss. In fact, the morning crowds at the statue were enormous, and little boys in particular were delighted.

After breakfast, Angus and Fergus and I said a cheerful good-bye to one another. I again thanked Percival for his hospitality and his medical assistance. He promised to keep in touch and, of course, to keep the medical procedure unknown.

Wilkins took me back to New Heathrow.

I had new eyes and a new title, and I was ready to begin anew as well.

CHAPTER 11

Back to Springfield
or
Back to the Drawing Board

My homecoming wasn't exactly what I had expected. All over New O'Hare and all over the university and all over Springfield, there were huge posters announcing,

"Welcome Home, Sir Anton Bauer"

My trip had been a secret—a private affair. I was astonished at all this publicity. I was angry about it as well. Fortunately a little quick research revealed what had happened. It is evidently a necessity of royal protocol to announce the creation of new knights of the Realm. Despite the privacy of Percival's estate, William V was obliged to make known that there was now another important person in the kingdom. (Oh, the joy of thinking I'd joined the ranks of Paul McCartney and Elton John!)

The cyberpress, that ever-invasive nuisance, had seen the announcement in the palace news release. Fortunately as well, it was reported that the reason for my very secret trip to England was precisely to receive this honor. There was no word of my little ocular problem. So back to work I went.

I took a day to reorganize the laboratory. I was especially eager and careful to make sure that the transmorgrofier was sterile and ready to make another attempt at the cloning of old Abe. I got all the necessary chemicals measured out and then poured that mixture into temperature pods specialized for each one. I checked on my wonderful DNA sample from the cemetery. All was ready except one thing: I still needed another womb in which to implant baby Abe.

The solution to that one was easy. I had to return to the university for a final lecture. That had been my agreement, after all. And who was there, literally with bells on, but my little nemesis Claudia Elsinger. I plotted my plan.

As you likely recall, I had made it known to Madison that young Ms. Elsinger, as bright as she was, seemed to have a strange infatuation with me—dangerously so to my reputation and my person. I was going to take advantage of that little seed and allow it to grow into a magnificent lie.

Shortly after I arrived, I went to see Madison. I told her that I was relieved this was the last session, as much as I enjoyed them. (I lie. I lie. I lie.) Then I mentioned my ongoing reservations about Ms. Elsinger. Madison responded, "Oh, after tonight that shouldn't be a problem. She is not a matriculated student here. She was only here for your lectures."

I smiled and said, "Oh, Madison, my dear. You have greatly relieved me."

Meanwhile, I knew Claudia was making her way to the lecture. I had given Humberto, now an increasingly important co-conspirator, all the instructions. As soon as the session began, he was to go to Ms. Elsinger's apartment, find her suitcase, and pack a suitable number of items to make it look as though she left in a hurry. Then he was to leave a note: "To Whom It May Concern: I have been invited to Dr. Bauer's estate and will return to collect the rest of my possessions before the end of the week." It was left on her cyberscroller, visible for all who might poke about.

The presentation went well. The students were attentive. I was enjoying my little ploy to the end. After the session we had a little gaudy—an academic tradition of celebration. I provided white wine, red wine, coffee, and tea. I also provided a catered high tea, claiming it was all in celebration of my knighthood. Proper finger sandwiches, scones with jam or clotted cream, and savory pastries were all available. The students stayed longer than I would have cared, but they were having a good time. Claudia, naturally, hovered close by. When things finally wound down, she offered to clean up. The university maintenance staff would do that, of course. The students left. Madison noticed that Claudia, as always, stayed behind "to converse." When I was alone with her, I asked what her plans were. She responded that she would be going home for a bit and then preparing for her job as tenure-track professor of microbiology at the University of California–Berkeley. I congratulated her and asked if she would like to continue our little celebration. I thought she'd pop a blood vessel her response was so enthusiastic.

"Oh, Professor Bauer, you finally noticed," she said.

"Yes, of course, my dear," I replied. "But with all the other students about, I was not able to follow through. Please forgive me."

"Forgive you? I don't need to forgive you. I want to thank you. Where should we go? Do I need anything?"

"Claudia, darling, why not freshen up a bit. We may be up late."

"Perfect. My apartment is only ten minutes away. I'll be back within the half hour."

"That would be fine. It will give me time to pick up my final papers and say a formal good-bye to Madison … I mean Professor Jeffries. Be back here in a half hour, please."

"Oh, yes. You bet."

I then said to myself, "How can someone that smart talk that stupidly?"

Claudia left. I made my way to Madison's office, as I said, to offer my final farewell and a word of (insincere) thanks. I added, "Madison, I'm sure that you saw the continuing strange behavior of Claudia Elsinger. I must admit I will be glad never to see her again."

"Yes, indeed. You have been more than patient with her. I can understand your thoughts. I only hope her clingy behavior won't spoil your opinion of an otherwise stellar academic experience."

"Not at all. Again, my thanks, and good-bye. Oh, by the way, please use my salary to fund a worthy student. I really don't need the money."

"Anton, you are more than generous. Thank you very much. I will assure you, however, that Claudia will not get that burse. Since she is a guest student, here only for your lectures; you need not worry at all."

We both smiled. We each nodded toward the other. Madison sat down, and I left her office. There was fun afoot tonight!

Meanwhile, Humberto was waiting for Claudia to return to her apartment. Just as she approached the door, he fired a dart drone at her. Its effect was immediate, and she collapsed silently in front of her door. Humberto quickly picked her up and carried her to the hovercar and then collected me. We returned to the estate.

Now everything was once again ready. Claudia was in the renovated chamber in which poor Margaret once resided. When she awakened, she was startled to see where she was. I knocked gently and entered. Just as with Margaret, there was now no reason not to tell the truth—well, at least part of the truth. I explained the nature of my study and easily convinced her that I was thrilled someone who understood not only the science but me as well would have a chance to partake in history. The trollop was delighted.

Again, as with Margaret, I outlined the parameters of her role. She would be able to order her favorite foods, as long as they were "baby healthy." Entertainment would be provided for her, but she would have no access to cybernews. Nothing could interfere with keeping her emotional quality in the highest form. There must be some motherly instinct that I don't understand, but, just as Margaret did, she asked if she would be able to participate in Little Abe's weaning and growth. I assured her that was the singular reason I had selected her for this honored role. (I lie. I lie. I lie. I also prevaricate.)

The next day dawned. I was up early and in the lab. I told Claudia that today would be the day that I would initiate the genome sequence, create the reconstituted DNA of Abraham Lincoln, and implant the results in her womb. I told her nothing of the accelerator piece. The transmorgrofier was ready. I did inform her not to be alarmed at the rapid progression of the pregnancy. I also made sure it would not progress as rapidly as had Margaret's. Once again I dissembled and told her this was natural in cloning. I had the formula written large on a separate paper, projected again on the wall, and in my mind. I would not repeat that mistake. The symbol Mn^{3+} was firmly planted in my mind as the procedure went ahead.

All went well. The willing but unsuspecting participant was in perfect health. I removed a healthy egg and took out its nucleus. The DNA protocol was followed precisely, and the impregnation was successful. The acceleration rate would be proper. One month of pregnancy would take one week. If all went correctly, after the birth, the resulting Abe would advance to childhood, adolescence, and adulthood at a quick but safe pace. The rate would be one year per day, in fact. Then, at Lincoln's death age, the mature Lincoln would stop accelerated growth. Now came the inevitable waiting that accompanies any pregnancy.

A Child Is Born

Everything went well. Claudia bore the normal symptoms of pregnancy well. Instead of the tawdry novels that Ms. Tomkins enjoyed, she requested good scientific reading. I allowed soft music, all of which had been composed before Lincoln's demise, to play in the room. She was a contented mother-to-be. My time spent in teaching had given me the opportunity to plan this well. Little Abe came into the world on February 12, 2062. It would have been his 254th birthday. The birth went easily—much more easily, I suspect, than his original birth in a shabby, dirty, dark log cabin.

I had Isabella take the infant to another room in the barn that had been carefully prepared for his arrival. Its interior had been completely redone to mimic the log cabin of his birth. Despite the acceleration process, dealing with a child was going to be a challenge. Isabella learned to cook the simple fare of rural mid-America. She used modern equipment in the house and brought the food to the barn/lab. She also served as his wet nurse as long as that was necessary. Given the acceleration, it lasted only a few days.

You might wonder what became of Claudia. Well, you know, don't you? I summoned Humberto after the birth while Claudia was resting and recuperating in her own chambers.

"Humberto, por favor, cavar una tumba, una profunda, en el bosque del Oriente." [51]

"Sí, doctor Bauer. Tomaré profundo."[52]

"¿Sabes qué hacer entonces?"[53]

---

[51] "Humberto, please dig a grave, a deep one, in the east woods."

[52] "Yes, Dr. Bauer. I will dig it deep."

[53] "You know what to do, then, don't you?"

"Sí, doctor Bauer, regresará y conseguir cuerpo de esta Claudia que nunca verá otra vez."[54]

"Gracias."

While Humberto went to dig the grave, I went to visit Claudia. She was a bit woozy but was able to carry on a conversation. She said she would like a little milk to drink, and I happily obliged. Of course, there was an extra ingredient in the milk, and after drinking it from a splendid Waterford glass (the Lismore design), she laid back and expired. I had no further use for her; nonetheless, I had seen no need to cause her additional pain.

Humberto returned a little scraggly from his digging and took Claudia away, "never to be seen again."[55]

Two days later, on a cold and snowy February morning, I received a call from Madison. I had been expecting this; I just did not know when it would finally come. She detailed to me that Claudia Elsinger's room was now to be given to another student, but Claudia still had property in the room and had left the strange note about accompanying me for further scientific education. I assured Madison that this was news to me and that poor Ms. Elsinger, as we both knew, was rather delusional. The end of the experience must have been too much for her, and her mind snapped. I assured Madison that I would call her and the authorities immediately if my staff or I saw any indication of her at Tadwil. Madison was well satisfied with that response. I had set the scheme up carefully, and it now paid off. I was free from any commitment or encumbrance to pursue the next phase.

---

[54] "*Si*, Dr. Bauer. I will return and get Ms. Claudia's body, and you will never see it again."

[55] I hoped.

C H A P T E R   1 2

The Growth, Education, and Demise of Lincoln II

Claudia was out of my life and out of the way. Little Abe was developing along the timeline I had set for him. Isabella did a great job with him those first days. By the morning of February 15, he was already the equivalent of three years old. She stopped being his wet nurse. I also saw that I could not let her have any further contact with him. It was not because she was doing anything wrong, but she was doing something that was not acceptable. He was beginning to speak, and her accent (she was from the Dominican Republic) was beginning to show in his speech. I could not have that. I explained the problem to Isabella, who understood, although she was unhappy not to have further contact with this special child. (She did not know who he was.)

I'd had Humberto do some work before his birth on the room Abe II would have in the barn. The interior was much larger than that of any log cabin Lincoln knew, but the rest I could take care of. Humberto had placed a plank wood floor over the cement floor. The walls were without windows, which wasn't all that unusual in log cabins, but Humberto also used logs hewn from Tadwil to line the walls of the special unit. All the observation equipment was so surreptitious that even bright little Abe would not find it. He wouldn't even know to look for it, or what it was should he find it.

A small chimney was erected against the west wall, which was an exterior wall. We actually converted it into a working fireplace. We installed some crude wood shelves, a bed with a straw mattress, a rocking chair, some oil lamps and candles, and a little box of sweets that Abe could partake of at his leisure. I knew he would not have had that in his first incarnation, but sweets always make little boys more cooperative.

On his seventh "birthday," I took him outside. Fortunately, I had taken the reality of leap years into consideration when timing Abe's growth.[56] The old Victorian home, while huge, would have been a familiar architecture to him. The barn, likewise, looked authentic on the outside. The woods that surrounded the place were just like the woods of Kentucky and Indiana of his youth and the area surrounding New Salem, which he knew as a young man. On that auspicious day, February 19, we went down to the river. I showed Little Abe how to toss pebbles into the water and skip them. We had contests to see who could get the most jumps. He always won. I could tolerate that because I had no great use for athletics.

On his eighth "birthday," I introduced him to books. I had a McGuffey reader from the nineteenth century, a Webster dictionary, and a Bible.[57] I taught him the alphabet and some perfunctory words. He caught on quickly, and I learned just as quickly that he was not so much learning as he was remembering. A kind of puzzled smile of recognition often lit up his visage.

On the morning of his ninth "birthday," he was melancholy. It was February 21. That was part of the Lincoln personality, of course, but I had to think about what could be causing this rather sudden change of mood. He wasn't uncooperative, but there was no enthusiasm in his conversation, no hearty appetite—a complete change of personality, actually. Then it dawned on me. Something was working deep within his memory. He had been nine years old when his birth mother, Nancy Hanks died. That embedded memory was working its way to the surface. It was so clear; this was truly an amazing person. I addressed him about the situation.

"Abe, what's wrong?"

"Doc, somethin' is moving inside me. I remember somethin' terrible about today."

---

[56] In his lifetime, there would be fourteen leap years. His first was 1812, and his last was 1864. Twelve others would fall within the other years.

[57] Yes, I know that the McGuffey readers weren't published until 1841, but there were no other textbooks around that I could use. The content and tone would be familiar to anyone with some education from that period. The history of the McGuffey readers is a topic worth pursuing in its own right.

"Abe, I think you know that we are living in a rather unusual environment. There are not many other people around, as you have noticed. I want to tell you something now that might bother you deeply, but I want to tell you the truth." (I would not persist in this, as you can surmise.) "Abe, you were nine years old when your ma, Nancy Hanks, died of the milk sickness. A lot of people did at that time. Your aunt and uncle died too. You were fortunate to survive."[58]

"What about my pa?"

"Your father survived also, but he was never the same. You'll understand better in a few days."

"I remember my pa," Abe said. "He was a tough man. He was tough physically, and he treated me tough. He did want me to learn, though he didn't give me much time to do it. I never made him happy, and he always made me work. In fact, I think it was around this time he began to rent me out to local farmers to work for them. I did the work. Pa got the money."

"Abe, you are correct. I want to assure you that part of your life won't be repeated. I will never make you work, and I will never take your money."

By his tenth "birthday," he had mastered the McGuffey reader and was moving through the Bible. I also recalled a favorite of his— *The Pilgrim's Progress,* by John Bunyan.[59] Between that and the Bible, he mastered a kind of biblical cadence that became his trademark in speech and writing. He made good use of the dictionary. As during the first time around, he sat by the fire to read at night, his lanky legs and bare feet kicking in the air behind him. I did not yet want to introduce him to anything modern. I wanted to make sure he was developing in a timely way. There were no school systems anywhere yet at the time of his youth. That would be the invention of Horace Mann and other New Englanders. Rural education was a slipshod affair. Towns

---

[58] The milk sickness was a real disease that plagued pioneer areas in Kentucky, Indiana, and Illinois. It was caused by drinking milk from cows that had grazed on white snakeroot, which grew in abundance in shady places. It was especially attractive to cows when the long, hot summers dried up the regular grass.

[59] Published about two hundred years before Abe's birth, this book is still a classic.

were fortunate to have someone with the equivalent of an eighth-grade education to teach their children. Attendance was sporadic. Farm chores, weather, and disinterest by parents and/or students played major roles in disrupting any kind of organized education. It was a marvel that Abe learned what he did the first time around. His self-motivation was amazing. He insisted on mastering anything he attempted.

Something else happened on this tenth "birthday." In our calendar, of course, it was only one day later, but in Abe's development, it was another calendar year. It was 1819, the year after his mother's death, but the sullenness was gone and a sense of mischief and relief marked his attitude. His father had not waited long to remarry. He needed someone to care for Abe, his sister, and, of course, for Tom himself. (Abe's little brother, Thomas, died in infancy in Kentucky.) Tom married Sarah Bush that year, and Sarah's support and affection for Abe would be a major formative factor in his life.

It was becoming clearer and clearer that Abe wasn't really learning. He was remembering. In the end, that made this all the easier an endeavor. I had Humberto move the old car from the garage (the car I used to go from the road to the house for visitors). He converted that garage into a stable, and I purchased two beautiful stallions—one for each of us. We began a daily ride. He was an adept horseman. Each day after the ride there followed a very cold, brief swim in the morning in the river, reading and riding in the afternoon, more reading, and eating, eating, eating. He did remember that he had been kicked in the head by a horse when small, but this didn't deter him in any way whatsoever. Nor was he hesitant to jump into the river, even though he almost drowned in a creek when a boy.

He was also growing taller and stronger each day. His legendary height could have been problematic, but Isabella was handy at lengthening pants and shirts as necessary. I was careful to get rough homespun fabric for his clothing, including his underclothing (aka skivvies). I didn't bother with shoes for Abe. He would have outgrown them every day. Besides, boys in rural Kentucky and Indiana did not have shoes. Frequent bathing was unknown to them. In fact, had there been bumper stickers in those days, his would have read "The barn is my aromatherapy." He truly enjoyed our morning dip in the Sangamon.

It was still quite cold, but that didn't bother either of us. A quick swim from shore to shore and we were out and quickly sitting next to the fire in his room. He loved to chat and argue. I knew enough about him that I realized his arguing was not just adolescent rebellion but a genuine skill he was already honing.

After lunch he would read and then go to the forest around the estate and chop wood. His skill at this was legendary, and it was a marvel to watch him work at it. Any task he was asked to perform, he did obediently. I suspect his strict father had instilled that virtue in him, and now it was playing out in a new time and place.

Abe was doing so well that I wanted to reward him. I had Humberto search for an authentic Bowie knife. The history of the knife is interesting of its own, and Abe knew it well. Although designed by Rezin Bowie in 1830, it was the exploits of his brother Jim Bowie that brought fame to the knife. The story was well known throughout the nation. Jim Bowie, it seems, was prone to fighting. Once, while a second in a duel, he was stabbed in the sternum with a sword. The sword broke off, and Bowie got up, finished off his opponent, and then removed the broken sword from his chest. The knife grew in fame and popularity. It was long enough to be effective as a small sword (epee). It was incredibly sharp and also wide enough to function as a sort of hatchet. Both Union and Confederate troops treasured it, although it was more popular in the South. By the end of the Civil War, however, the fixed bayonet had replaced the Bowie knife as an essential tool of soldiering.

I presented the knife to Abe, who glowed with appreciation. He would carry it with him on his daily jaunts into the forest surrounding Tadwil. I was glad I could make him so happy.

His diet began as an imitation of early nineteenth-century food. In his childhood, there had been just enough food. Now there would be plenty, which would be a new experience for him at that age. There were a lot of stews made from vegetables grown on the estate. The meat was chicken or venison or opossum (The sacrifices I make for science!). As a child, he would have had bear meat, but no bears have lived around Sangamon for over a century and a half. For sweets there were molasses cookies; for drink, water and watered-down beer. By time he was fifteen days (years) old, I began to introduce him to a bigger variety of modern foods. Isabella did a wonderful job of smoothly making the transition, never giving up completely on the old, and not overdoing the new. Abe appreciated the variety.

By his twenty-first birthday, he had reached his legendary height of six feet four inches. In the middle of the twenty-first century, that would be rather standard height for a man. For someone from the middle of the nineteenth century, he was a giant. He was as thin as the rails he split. He ate voraciously but never put on any weight, probably because of his incredible metabolism and capability for hard outside work.

He would return to the fireplace every evening to read. English classics like Shakespeare delighted him. I also got him the first book published by Charles Dickens, *Sketches by Boz*. I know it wasn't published until 1836, when Lincoln was a little older, but the adherence to a strict timeline was becoming less and less necessary with this very bright boy. Soon I would give him Twain's first book, *Jim Smiley and His Jumping Frog*. It was a collection of the articles Twain had written while still in Missouri, including one called "How to Cure a Cold." Abe laughed long and hard at the antics narrated in this tale. I had taken a chance with it. It was actually published the year Lincoln was assassinated, 1865, but I had torn the copyright page out of the book. Abe loved good humor.

He was curious, of course, about what he was doing here. He was also ambivalent about the tug between this new life and his memories of his former life. His curiosity was welcome. I hedged my answers, though, because I needed to control his development. As you know, truth, for me, is somewhat pliant.

He still had no idea that almost two hundred years had passed since his death. I wanted to keep it that way for the time being. I did get some more history and politics for him to read, always being careful to remove any copyright pages.

A few other days gave cause for some concern. On his thirty-fifth "birthday," he contracted malaria, but it was a mild case. It returned again in his fortieth year (on the fortieth day, that is). That same thirty-fifth year, he got frostbite on his feet. That had happened historically, so I determined he was of full stature now and got him several pairs of shoes and boots. There was no way to duplicate the exact fashion or material of his day, but he either didn't notice or didn't mind. He was grateful for the comfort.

There were a couple more dates of deep melancholy for Lincoln. By now I was able to anticipate them and knew to leave him to his own devices on those days. On his forty-first "birthday," his son Edward died (1850). A year later, his father died, but this did not much affect him. There had been no strong bond between them when Abe left home. On his fifty-third birthday, there was the deepest depression of all, tied to the death of another son—his beloved Willie. (His stepmother, Sarah Bush Lincoln, would outlive him, dying in 1869.) The other times of deep depression were related to two women in Lincoln's life: the death of his first—and possibly only—true love, Ann Rutledge, in 1835 (Lincoln was twenty-six); and the cancellation of his engagement to Mary Todd in 1841 (Lincoln was thirty-two).

On his fifty-fourth day, he took curiously ill. Some research showed that Lincoln had actually contracted a case of smallpox shortly after delivering the Gettysburg Address. What could have been a medical calamity in 1863 was certainly not so now. Lincoln overcame the disease then, but it took some time. I gave him some strong doses of simple over-the-counter drugs to reduce fever and itching. They were not available in his time, but in only three hours the telltale fever left and the mild rash that had appeared on his face and arms went away.

On various days, Lincoln suffered from an almost clinical depression. His mood turned somber and dark, and he was uncommunicative. I connected these days rather loosely to the constant flow of bad Civil War news that he had received almost hourly while president. He stopped joining me for a daily swim, but he did still enjoy his horse riding and hiking—probably a throwback to his days in New Salem spent walking around the county, or his rides around Washington during his presidency.

His interest in political works was acute, and I supplied him with history as well, including anything in print that I could find. It is increasingly hard to find that outdated mode of communication—like trying to find Edison Victrolas. I gave him everything up to and including the Gettysburg Address, as well as items about the rather neutral initial public reaction it received at the time.

There was one major concern that the scientist in me wanted to investigate. Lincoln's large stature and rather strange body have always provoked all kinds of speculation throughout the decades following his death. For some reason, this came to become a discussion of some deeper interest in the 1960s and 1970s. A Dr. Abraham Gordon proposed in 1962 that Lincoln had Marfan's Syndrome. Marfan's Syndrome is a genetic disease—hence my curiosity in it. It has some rather unhappy characteristics that affect the body's connective tissue. Growth and development are part of the biological role played by connective tissue. Was Lincoln's strange size and shape the result of this disease? The protein that makes up the foreign element in the connective tissue in Marfan's Syndrome is fibillin-1. An abnormal increase in this component of the growth gene increases the transforming growth factor—beta. This increase causes strange growth patterns. It can vary from person to person with the affliction, affecting heart, lungs, blood vessels, bones, and skin. The growth factor protein is known as TGF-β. The discovery of DNA (deoxyribonucleic acid) was a major scientific breakthrough in the last century. Along with proteins and carbohydrates, DNA (a nucleic acid) is essential for life. Johannes Niescher in Basel, Switzerland, did the initial work around the time of Lincoln's original life. James Watson, an American, and Francis Crick are considered the true discoverers of DNA. They were awarded the Nobel Prize for Physiology and Medicine in 1962. Maurice Wilkins was also part of the team that received the award. But enough biographical history.

Medical researchers and Lincoln biographers disagreed about whether or not Lincoln actually had Marfan's Syndrome. There were those who wanted to conduct DNA studies to see whether or not they were correct. It never happened. (Such a study had to wait for me and my clandestine nocturnal obtaining of Lincoln's DNA to conduct the test.) The disease was not known (had no name) in Lincoln's time, and anyone left untreated, even now, seldom lives into late adulthood, as Lincoln did in the nineteenth century. Other more recent "scientists" suggested that Lincoln had multiple endocrine neoplasia (type 2B). One in particular, Dr. John Sotos, proposed this because of Lincoln's body shape (Marfan), large lips, and constipation (a chronic problem for Lincoln). He took "blue mass pills," which actually contained mercury, as a therapy for that condition. These pills, which he considered a necessity, also affected his humor, making him "cross." Again, his life into mature adulthood rules against his having the disease. Most people died in their midthirties if they had that condition. Only DNA testing could prove one or the other or neither to be the reality.

Well, guess who had DNA? And guess who was going to test it and find out? I thought I'd use the dried blood sample I had purloined from Ford's Theatre. I would have to reconstitute it, following the procedure created in 2052 by Samuel A. La Croix. First I had to separate it from the cloth on which the bloodstain had been residing for many years. That involved the careful scraping away of the blood mark from the pant material with a scalpel. The miniscule flakes of dry blood were gathered in a petri dish as they fell from the pants. From there, I took the sample to the solution that La Croix had discovered. I saw nothing wrong with his work, and so he saved me a great deal of time in reconstituting the blood into a usable DNA sample.

With the sample in hand, I continued my work. The same chemical formulae that you have already seen could be used for this process as well. The heating and cooling were soon finished, and by evening's end I had the useful DNA protocol to submit for microscopic examination. Fortunately we scientists no longer need squint into little pieces of glass. The analysis is done by computer programming, part of the Astral Comp System (ACS) developed in 2059. This is somewhat similar to the cloud storage from earlier in the century. Everyone had access to certain parts of its genius. I had developed a special section that only I could use. It would take seconds to find out whether or not Lincoln had either of those genetic afflictions. He, of course, had never heard of genetics, much less DNA. I wouldn't tell him a thing, but this would make an interesting appendix to the final report on my project.

Tick. Tock. Tick. Tock. The waiting is always interminable, even if it is just a few minutes. I reminded myself of some time jokes to pass the restless anxiety: "Once there was a dumb blonde who asked a man what time it was. The man responded, 'Why, it's four forty-five.' 'That's strange,' answered the blonde. 'Every time I ask someone what time it is, I get a different answer.'" "That boy is so dirty; the only time he washes is when he eats watermelon." (Following is the last one, honestly, and it is an actual quip of Lincoln—the kind of joke that made Lincoln popular with his peers.) "For a wedding present, a man gave his son $200. Two weeks later, he asked his boy, 'What did you do with the money, son?' The boy responded, 'I bought me a watch.' 'A watch!' shouted the outraged father. 'You shoulda bought yourself a rifle!' 'Why a rifle, Pappy?' asked the startled boy. 'What fer?' The father replied, "Magin' that some night when you comes home and you finds your wife sleeping with anudder man. What'cha gona do? Ask him what time it is?"

Analog time has been long forgotten. Everything needs to be digital now in order to function in our society. Analog instruments simply could not compete. How can an analog device measure Planck time?[60]

Oh, I have another time story—a true one. I was the main speaker at the 2047 conference on Theoretical Physics and Genomic Archetypes, held in Washington, DC, at the Astro-Star Pavilion. I was coming down from my room, feeling quite smart in my new Saville Row suit that I had purchased on a visit to my friend Percival Pettigrew. The elevator door opened, and two workmen were standing there with a dolly. Strapped to the dolly was a grandfather clock. I looked at them and quipped, "Wouldn't it be easier to wear a watch?"

Of course, "tick-tock" is now a sound that does not relate to anyone born in the last twenty years. It's like speaking about eight-track tapes to anyone under ninety. (A few cuckoo clocks and sonorous grandfather clocks remain, but the skill for making new ones is lost.)

Well, enough of that. The results are in. Lincoln definitely did not have multiple endocrine neoplasia type 2B. That was rather well suspected and opened no new avenues of research. But the results did indicate—not prove, but indicate—that some of the Marfan's Syndrome factors were present in his DNA. Well, that will make for some interesting continuing research later on.

---

[60] The smallest measure of time, according to quantum theory. It is the time needed for light to travel in a vacuum a distance of 1 Planck length (named after Max Planck). Planck time (t_p) is equal to the square root of hG over $c^5 = 5.39106$ $(32)x^{10-44}$s. It is too complicated to relate all this to attoseconds at this time. One needs to understand dimensional analysis and gravitational constants to delve further into this.

Truly, tempus fugit.[61] It was April 9, 2063, or day fifty-six (and year fifty-six) for Abe. He was a fully mature man, though he lacked the presidential beard. He was still very thin, for at this point he had lost his beloved Willie, had been commander-in-chief of the Army of the Republic, and had seen the nation through the Civil War. All the reading material I gave him led up to that fateful night of April 15, 1865.

I asked what he remembered of that evening. His mind was keen, and he remembered wanting to relax a bit and take Mary out for the evening. It was Good Friday, according to the Christian reckoning. The war had just ended, and they thought a comedy would be just the thing to lift their spirits, so they agreed to go to Ford's Theatre and see the popular play *Our American Cousin*.[62]

They arrived and took their seats in the Presidential Box, appropriately done out with banners in red, white, and blue. Lincoln recalled dismissing his bodyguard for the night and enjoying the play as Mary nudged him in the moments he nodded off and began to snore. He remembered laughing heartily at one of the lines and then having a severe headache. That, of course, was caused by the fatal shot from John Wilkes Booth. Lincoln's memory ceases at that moment.

Now it was my turn, indeed my duty, to fill in what had happened in the 198 years that had passed since that event. I asked Abe if he were ready for a rather remarkable journey into the future. He assured me he was. I knew he was, too, because he was so bright and so curious.

I was honest with him at first. I began by narrating in broad strokes the events that had brought him back to life. He said he never knew much about medicine or science but was not surprised there had been considerable advances. He expressed regret that none of this miracle medicine had been available to the soldiers who were so badly injured in battle, or for his two boys, Eddie and Willie.

I wasn't sure how much or how fast to inform him of all that history. There were the events, the people, and the technology. I asked him

---

[61] For those who don't know Latin, "Time flies."

[62] This three-act play premiered in New York in 1858. It actually continued to be popular until the end of the nineteenth century, despite its connection with the Lincoln assassination. Written by an Englishman, Tom Taylor, it is the account of a boorish American who goes to England to claim an inheritance.

straight-out, and he said that I should just do my best and he would ask questions and read to fill in any gaps.

It was at that point when—how can I say it—an obtuse spirit entered me. I was thrilled, of course, that the experiment of bringing dead DNA into existence had been successful. I was more than thrilled that the recipient of this scientific advance was someone so prominent. However, despite all that, something made me want to hurt him. Oh, physically I could have. I was much stronger and much healthier, even though older, than fifty-six-year-old Lincoln. The war years had worn him out. His duties kept him sedentary, other than some horse riding and his walks to the War Office to get the most recent reports.

I wanted to be thorough, but I wanted to be mean. I asked Abe if he would mind it if I took the evening off to prepare, and he was most gracious. I asked Isabella to bring him a twenty-first-century dinner instead of the simple food he had been eating. Even in the White House, despite Mary's prodding, his diet had been simple. This evening he had his first taste of blanched ostrich (healthy, you know), organically raised asparagus (braised, not boiled), a baked potato, and raspberry tiramisu for dessert.

The next morning, we went for a ride around Tadwil. He looked quite calm and content. The evening before, I had given him some very comfortable contemporary clothing. He was a bit puzzled at it initially, but after he put it on, he knew it was a considerable upgrade even from the material and style of a president in mid-nineteenth-century America, much less a rural farmer.

After the ride, we returned to his "cabin." Some time before, during the second pregnancy, I had Humberto relocate the old outhouses closer to the barn. Lincoln would not have known modern plumbing, and I wasn't about to introduce him to it. For nights, he had the customary chamber pot. Humberto kept the outhouse clean. Isabella had the unhappy duty of seeing to the chamber pot. (I gave them a raise.) I still did not want him to see the lab. He would have been overwhelmed. I had Humberto bring us some cider (yes, the hard stuff), and we sat down in rocking chairs. I began my narrative.

"Abe, you know that you have a lot to learn and catch up on. As I speak, there might be terminology that you are unfamiliar with—words that came into being in the many decades since the assassination. If that happens, just stop me and I will explain in further detail to the best of my ability.

"The story is not going to be a happy one. I want you to know that from the get-go. I have brought with me, just to start on a lighter note, an instrument that was invented in the last decade of your life, the 1860s, and became an indispensable tool in business and then in personal life until the 1980s, when even newer and better technology took over. It is called a typewriter. It is actually a sort of miniaturized moveable printing press. Let me show you how it works.[63] In fact, Abe, the person who used the machine was called a type-writer, because instead of using quill and paper, the writer used the type machine."

I brought in an old Sholes and Glidden typewriter, the first with the still familiar QWERTY keyboard. I inserted a piece of paper and began to type the beginning of Abe's famous Gettysburg Address. He was a bit startled when the carriage first reached the end of line and the bell sounded. It took him by surprise. He asked if he could try it. His hands were big and, of course, not used to the keyboard, but his initial effort wasn't bad:

> hullo my nname is abrahamm lincolnn annd i amm
> thee presidennt of the unnited states of ammerica i
> emmphasize the word unnited

His large hands dwarfed the keyboard. For some reason, his index finger pecking away at the keys kept hitting the letters *n* and *m* repeatedly. Capitalization and punctuation were understandably beyond that initial effort, but he was delighted.

"Abe," I said, "I will leave this with you, and you can have fun with it whenever you want. I promise you, things even more interesting are coming your way."

---

[63] Efforts at the creation of a type writing machine took place simultaneously in Europe and the US. The first real workable model was made in Milwaukee, WI in 1868 by Christopher Latham Sholes, Carlos Glidden, and Samuel Soule. They sold their patent to Remington and Sons, the makers of sewing machines.

It was a manual typewriter. Even many children in the last half of the twentieth century never saw a manual typewriter, but only electric ones. I wouldn't even bother Abe with an electric one, since there was no electricity here. The new power systems were not compatible with electric plugs. There were no outlets.

"I thank you, kind sir," replied Abe.

"Now, to get back to the events after your assassination. At 10:20 p.m., Booth entered your box at the theater. Immediately after the shot rang out, Mary screamed. You slumped over. Your companions that evening, Henry Rathbone and Clara Harris, tried to help you and Mary, but then pandemonium swept through the theater as John Wilkes Booth—yes, the great actor Booth, your assassin—jumped over the rail to the stage below and shouted "Sic Semper Tyrannis."[64] He also broke his leg in the fall. Soldiers ran up the stairs to the Presidential Box and saw you slouching in the chair. Mary continued her screaming. The soldiers carried your body across the street and commandeered a civilian home there—the home of William and Anna Petersen, directly opposite the theater.[65] The address was 516 Tenth Street. You died there on Saturday morning at 7:22 a.m. The Petersen family and others assisted as they could. Physicians were brought in, of course, but there was little to be done. In fact, one probably did more damage than good by trying to locate the bullet by sticking his finger inside the wound in your skull. Abe, since that time, medicine has learned a lot about what are called germs and bacteria and infection. No physician today would do such a thing without protecting the patient and the physician with very thin gloves." (I didn't try to explain rubber or elastic to him at that point.)[66]

"You can imagine the chaos that took place as word got out. Huge throngs of people gathered in the streets. Your son Robert was summoned from the White House, where he was staying. Mary actually had to be

---

[64] Please tell me you don't need a translation.

[65] Later almost two dozen men would claim to be the ones who carried his body across the street.

[66] Yes, I know—Charles Goodyear had made great strides in creating and perfecting vulcanized rubber in the 1840s, but that crude process is far removed from the modern product.

physically dragged from the room because she was so hysterical. Tad was at the National Theatre with his tutor. The play there was *The Great Oriental Spectacle of Aladdin*. Someone ran down the aisle and told Tad's tutor what had happened. He grabbed Tad and rushed back to the White House. Soon the rest of the audience would hear the announcement.

"Robert heard the commotion on the streets outside the White House. When he heard its cause, he rushed to Ford's Theatre and then to the Petersen House across the street."

(All of this is true.)

"Telegraph offices that morning began to send the word around the country. Naturally, the South also got the message. The transatlantic cable, that new line from Newfoundland to western Ireland, carried the news to Europe. It took only minutes instead of a week and a half to get news of your death to the Continent."[67]

(All of this is true.)

"The soldiers carried your body out of the house and onto a hearse that transported it to the White House. I will let you read more of the details for yourself, even though it might be a very difficult experience. To summarize, though, there was a great funeral procession; a train took your body from Washington back to Springfield for burial. It would take some two weeks before you were placed in the ground. It would take even longer before a permanent resting place with Willie and Eddie would be constructed.

"What about Mary?" he queried.

"She died in 1882, but I will get to that eventually."

(All of this is true.)

Lincoln rocked back and forth quietly for several minutes. He repeated what he had said earlier about remembering only laughter and then a great headache. I asked if he wanted me to continue, and he did. This is where the obtuse spirit took over.

"Very well, Abe. Again, I will let you read the details in other sources. I just want to provide you with an outline of events. Now, stop rocking a moment. I want you to know that this is the year 2063."

---

[67] Ironically, Lincoln was the first president to receive a transatlantic cable.

Lincoln's eyes grew large. He looked both sad and startled and then asked me, "How can this be?"

I replied with a little truth. "Abe, science has moved at an incredible pace since your death. I will teach you more about all of this in due time. Just please trust me; it is the year 2063, and you are very much alive, and very much the same Lincoln that you were on the night of your assassination.

"Now, to get back to the history. You know all too well that you had enemies in abundance. There was always fear for your safety. As the night and following days went on, more information came forward. John Wilkes Booth did not act alone but was part of a cabal that was intent on disrupting the Northern victory. A man named Lewis Powell killed Seward, your secretary of state. He stabbed him with a knife. Another conspirator, George Atzerodt, broke into the room where Andrew Johnson was staying in Washington. He shot him, just as you were shot, only in private rather than in public. Grant and his wife, Julia, did not join you at the theater, even though you had invited them. He would have been killed there as well. Instead he and Julia were ambushed while taking a Friday-evening carriage ride in the area of Soldiers' Home."

(None of this is true.)[68]

Lincoln's face became pallid. He stopped rocking. His sad eyes misted.

"So much death," he said. "So much suffering. It never ended, did it?"

I continued. "Sir, it gets worse. Do you want to hear it, or should I stop for now?"

"No," he said. "I have always been a believer in truth. Keep on going. I will let you know if or when it becomes too much."

"Okay," I responded.

Lincoln interrupted. "Please, don't use that word. It has Democratic undertones for me."[69]

---

[68] I enjoyed an exquisite irony in lying to Honest Abe. By the way, the origin of the epithet "Honest Abe" is unclear. Some state it comes from his clerking days in New Salem—perhaps specifically from his inclination not to charge poor clients.

[69] Lincoln was correct. "OK" has a confused origin, but in the 1840s it had already become a standard part of vocabulary in the United States. It was probably part of

"Understood," I replied. "In the next days, as the nation—that is, the North—was preparing for your funeral and literally stopped all activity out of shock and mourning, your political enemies, including those within your party, were already conspiring to take harsher measures against the South than you had ever thought of. 'With malice toward none and charity for all' did not sit well with those who stood to profit from Reconstruction or whose hatred for the events of the past four years could not be assuaged.

"However, before they even had a chance to act, other realities came to light. Now, Abe, this is going to be hard. Your wife, Mary—and I know you loved her dearly, but you asked about her, and you asked for the truth—your wife, Mary, was acting throughout the entire war as a Confederate spy. You know she had been accused of this often enough, but you thought it impossible. Her family supported the South. Her half-brothers were southern soldiers. One blood brother was a surgeon for the Confederate Army. Whenever she could, she would listen in on cabinet meetings; and in your own private discussions, she encouraged you to confide in her. She would then write out the messages in a simple code, and her maid, Elizabeth Keckley, would sew them into her dress. When the maid left, the message left with her in her dress, and she went directly to spies who would forward the messages by telegraph to Lee and Davis."

"Oh Mary, Mary," said Abe, "how could you? I remember that night, sir. When we were at the theater, she was holding my hand. Mary quipped, 'What will Miss Harris think of my hanging on to you so?'"

I replied, "She won't think anything about it."

"I thought the horrors of the war were over and that Mary and I could relax and preside over a difficult but joyful rebuilding of a united country."

"Sir, that is a noble thought. However, as you can see, it was not a sincere one on her part. Her encouragements to you to retain McClellan

---

newspaper humorists' abbreviations for phrases, such as GT for "gone to Texas" or OK for "oll korret." Remember, spelling was not yet standardized. However, for Lincoln the interruption was prompted by the use of "OK" in reference to Old Kinderhook, Martin van Buren, the eighth president. It was easier to say "Vote for OK" than for folks to pronounce his Dutch name. But I digress.

despite your growing hesitation over his lack of action—all that, sir, was part of the plot to slow down the Union Army and give the South time to strengthen itself and to forge European alliances. Mary's histrionics were part of her personality, but they were also part of her plot. She was able to play her role very well.

"Now, sir, you know better than I do that your son Robert was not enamored of you. His mother's insistence that he not serve in the Union Army had more than maternal love as its motivation. Robert, too, was a Southern sympathizer. Just before war's end, when you did let him serve, you arranged for him to be an aide-de-camp for Grant. All that did was bring him closer to the information table. In the evenings, he would ride into the Virginia countryside and share final war secrets from the White House with Lee's spies. Mary and Robert knew all the assassination plots. They did not know the details, lest they accidentally divulge them to you. Sir, do you want something? Do you want me to stop?"

"Give me a moment," said Abe, "And give me some of that cider, please."

More silence ensued. Abe took a great swig of the hard cider. He finally said, "You know, I never really liked McClellan. I felt it my duty to support him, however. I always wanted to give a feller a chance. I recall finally saying this to some visitors in my frustration: 'For organizing an army, for preparing an army for the field, for fighting a defensive campaign, I will back General McClellan against any general of modern times. I don't know but of ancient times, either. But I begin to believe that he will never get ready to go forward!'"

"Allow me to continue, sir," I said. "Since you were dead and Andrew Johnson was dead, the next in line for the presidency was the speaker of the House, Schuyler Colfax. He was given the oath of office on Easter Sunday. It had taken that extra day for the scope of the plot to be discovered. Salmon Chase, in the almost fully completed Capitol Building, administered the oath.

"Meanwhile, Davis and Lee were active. They called back all their troops, most of whom had not yet gotten far on the journey home. They took what was left of the rail lines in the South and gathered individual armies around New Orleans, Saint Louis, Vicksburg, and Charleston. With the telegraph sending their messages so quickly, it did not take but a few days. With the northern leadership in disarray, they easily retook these commercial cities. They telegraphed to Europe and asked for military and economic aid. England, France, and Spain all responded. They had been waiting for this opportunity. Within two weeks, millions of dollars of gold and silver were coming westward across the Atlantic, along with tens of thousands of soldiers and hundreds upon hundreds of ships. It took about ten days to cross the Atlantic.

"The Spanish armies found easy collaboration with the Texans and reestablished Texas as part of Mexico before your funeral cortege reached Springfield. In the north, French forces were given free travel down the Saint Lawrence. Their troops found little resistance as they moved along the great rivers, from the mouth of the Mississippi to Saint Louis, and then to New Orleans. Those areas are now New France.

"The British were the most eager. Their double defeats in the War for Independence and the War of 1812 made them more than savage for revenge. They blockaded Boston Harbor. Ships from the South could take the much-wanted cotton to Europe. In early May, the same time as your official funeral in Springfield, the British had conquered Boston, New York, and Philadelphia. The Union armies were too dispirited and disorganized to resist.

"All that remained to be conquered was the Capitol itself. From the south, Lee led his army into the city. From Philadelphia, General Gordon Upscott led the British into the city. From the west, Commander Jean LaGrange led the French through the areas of Illinois, Indiana, Kentucky, and Ohio. The victory was complete.

"On May 31, 1865, Salmon Chase was hanged as a traitor. Schuyler Colfax escaped the city and was never heard from again. That same day, Jefferson Davis took the Oath of Office as president of the "American States." Lee was his vice-president. Your son Robert was named secretary of state and later, in 1884, was elected president on the new Confederate Party ticket. Edwin Stanton, who was with you at your side when you died, was also a traitor. His craving for influence and power overcame him. He wasn't trusted at first, but he had so much information about the reconstruction plans that he was given a special post as secretary of reconstruction. He also oversaw the writing of a new constitution. Jefferson Davis's first action as president was to make sure a sufficient number of troops were stationed in major southern cities, and then he annulled the Emancipation Proclamation. Mary returned to her family in Kentucky, and later, a few years before her death, Robert would have her committed to an insane asylum."[70]

I was out of breath. Lincoln was so pale I was afraid he would faint or have a heart attack. I said, "It is time to stop. This is enough for now. How we got to the present can wait for another day. We have time."

Abe said, "Kind sir, truth is a hard mistress. I thank you, though, for being honest with me. I know I was referred to as Honest Abe during my lifetime. You can be referred to as "Honest Anton." (I almost felt bad.) "Sir, you are correct. It is time to stop and give me some time to pull all of this together. Can we meet again in the morning—after our customary ride?"

"Of course, of course," I said. "Rest. If you need anything, ring the bell. I will have Isabella bring you some food."

"Thank you, kind sir." I left the room. I always used the exterior exit when coming and going from Abe's room. A false panel led to a small concrete divider between the lab and his room, but I saw no need to use it this evening.

Sometime During the Night

It was my custom to have Humberto monitor Lincoln for two hours after I spoke with him. Every evening, after our chats, Lincoln would sit by the fire or at the table, reading. He did this again on the evening of our historical conversation. This evening he followed his habit but ended a little sooner than usual. He went to the typewriter, which Humberto thought a good thing. By midnight, Lincoln usually retired, and so did Humberto, as he did this evening. All was a semblance of normalcy.

Perhaps I should have known that the great melancholy that tended to overtake Lincoln might manifest itself after my prevaricative revelations. But I didn't.

---

[70] Of all the above, only the commitment of Mary to the asylum at is true. She was sent to Bellevue Place, an insane asylum, in Batavia, Illinois. She would be there a scant four months before her sister took her into her care back in Springfield.

At five in the morning, when Humberto began his work for the day, there was a solid, insistent pounding on my door.

"¡Doctor, Doctor. Ven pronto! Es el Señor Lincoln. La cinta de la noche demuestra algo terrible. Rápido. Rápido."[71]

I was a light sleeper. I slid on a pair of trousers, a casual shirt, and some slippers, and together we ran to the barn. I used the exterior entrance to the "Lincoln Room." A most unpleasant sight greeted me. Lincoln was lying in his bed in a pool of blood. His treasured Bowie knife (I should never have given it to him) was jutting forth from his chest. He had jammed it into his heart, up to the hilt.

I instructed Humberto to shut the door, stay in the room, and touch nothing. The bed was a mess. I took the secret door into the lab and gathered a half dozen glass vials and a petri dish. I immediately collected vials of blood, and I made a triangular incision in Lincoln's breathless chest, ten centimeters by ten centimeters by ten centimeters. I would have all the Lincoln DNA anyone could possibly want. I would not have to generate it any longer, but if I chose to do this again, I only needed to work with the accelerator.

Then I instructed Humberto to undress Mr. Lincoln and burn the clothes, mattress, and wood bed. Then I told him, as he began nodding in anticipation, "Humberto, cavar otra tumba, nueve metros pies de profundidad y siete pies de largo. Hacerlo cerca de la otra."[72]

"Sí. Sí. Immediatamente."[73]

Humberto, that faithful retainer, went right to work. He undressed the corpse of Lincoln and placed it in a large canvas bag. He got the old Trabant to drive into the woods, where he dug the grave near that of the unfortunate Ms. Elsinger, the surrogate mother of the second Abe. He destroyed the clothing and the bed and returned to ask if there was anything more to do. I told him that tomorrow he and Isabella should clean the room completely and sanitize it; and then, in the next week

---

[71] "Doctor, Doctor, come quickly. It is Mr. Lincoln. The night tape shows something terrible. Hurry! Hurry!"

[72] "Humberto, dig another grave, nine feet deep and seven feet long. Dig it near the other one."

[73] Really? Can't you figure this out?

or so, he should build a replacement bed and refurnish the room—just in case.

While Humberto was taking care of business, I sat down in the rocker. I needed to ponder the meaning of all this, although the meaning was really quite obvious: my lies had driven an already melancholic, depressive man to the edge, and he had jumped over it. I wasn't completely surprised that it happened—only that it happened so soon. I really thought I'd get the chance to remake history. I was actually disappointed I wouldn't get the chance. It was while rocking that I noticed the paper in the typewriter. I went over to see what it was, because I knew it had been left empty. Then I saw his note. There was no question it was his; no one else was ever in the room, and it was filled with the typos that were characteristic of his first efforts with the device.[74] This is what I read:

Here where the lonnely hootinng owl
sennds forth his mmidnnight mmoans
fierce wolves shall oer mmy carcass growl
or buzzards pick mmy bonnes

nno fellowmman shall learnm nmy fate
or where mmy ashes lie
unnless by beasts drawnn rounnd their bait
or by the ravensn cry.
yes i've resolved the deed to do
annd this the place to do it
this heart Ill rush a dagger through
though i inn hell should rue it

hell what is hell to one like mme
who pleasures nnever knnew
by friennds connsignned to mmisery
by hope deserted too

---

[74] No capitalization, no punctuation, double *m*'s and double *n*'s.

to ease mme of this power to thinnk
that through mmy bosomm raves
ill headlonng leap fromm hell's high brinnk,
annd wallow in its waves

though devils yell, annd burnning chainns
mmay wakenn lonng regret
their frightful screamms, and piercinng painns
will help mme to forget

yes imm prepared, through enndless nnight
to take that fiery berth
thinnk nnot with tales of hell to fright
me who amm dammnn'd on earth

Ssweet steel Comme forth fromm your sheath
annd glistnninng speak your powers
rip up the organns of mmy breath
annd draw mmy blood in showers

i strike it quivers inn that heart
which drives mme to this ennd
i draw annd kiss the bloody dart
mmy last-mmy only friend

It was still in the typewriter, and therefore, sadly enough, unsigned. Only Lincoln could have written it. He was the only one in that room. It certainly wasn't written by Humberto. What is really interesting is that this piece of work (see appendix A) was an unsigned poem published in the *Sangamon Journal*. This was a small quarto published by the Whigs in Springfield. Lincoln was a Whig in 1838 when this was published, some three years after the death of his beloved Ann Rutledge. William Herndon (1818–1891)[75] was Lincoln's Springfield law partner. After

---

[75] Herndon's biography is not a reliable source of history. His prejudices and self-aggrandizement make it so.

Lincoln's death, he made money by giving speeches about Lincoln and becoming Lincoln's first official biographer. He might have been the first to claim that Lincoln had written this poem. It has always been debated. That Lincoln had these words stored in that vast mind of his and wrote them out before his own actual suicide should end the discussion. But could I ever tell anyone?

Indeed, perhaps in the end the dagger was his only friend. He is said to have spoken to Mary on the day of his assassination about an image of his death and a funeral in the White House. She quieted him quickly, superstitious as she was; or knowing that a plot was in the air, she played her role perfectly.

Well, what can I say? If you are expecting some kind of apology, stop waiting. In the end, this is my thought about the matter. As Flip Wilson, the famed black comedian of the last half of the twentieth century said when taking on his cross-dressing role as the saucy Geraldine, "The devil made me do it!"

CHAPTER 13

Hiatus
(Again)

Well, what to do now? Humberto diligently worked at getting the "Lincoln Bedroom" back in order. He did a fine job recreating the simple cabin bed. The clothes had been destroyed, which is too bad, since they were difficult enough to come by. I asked Isabella to make more of the same. (You getting any ideas?)

Every vestige of Lincoln II was gone, except for my vials of blood and two grams of flesh. I no longer needed the patch from the Lincoln clothing purloined from Ford's Theatre, but I kept it. Nor did I need the hard-to-obtain flesh sample from the actual Lincoln corpse, but I kept it too. I now had enough DNA material to make an army of Lincolns. Imagine that! Imagine the debating society it could create—not to mention the confusion. One living Lincoln would have been enough to confound the world, much less a whole platoon of them.

I took some pleasant days sailing on the *Mary Todd* up and down the Sangamon River, and I also spent time in the laboratory making sure everything was in good order. I performed a few minor experiments. Nothing, of course, would equal the DNA accelerator. I took sufficient pieces of it out of the lab and hid them in the woods. I needed a vacation, but on the off chance that someone got into the lab, I didn't want this precious machine compromised. I made sure the DNA samples were safely stored in a double safe in the cement wall of the barn. (Robert Lincoln isn't the only one who can use concrete to hide things.)

I asked Isabella and Humberto when they would finish their tasks. They said one more week should be enough. *Perfect.* I phoned my old friend Percival and asked if I might stay a bit with him. I needed a break. As always, he was most gracious. I also asked if he would once again get those scallywags Angus and Fergus MacDougall to come and visit. He knew it would be a fun time. I still had lots of money rolling in from my book royalties, but I wanted to make my European visit as credible and as profitable as possible. I contacted some lesser peers at the Sorbonne, the Madrid Institute of Science, the Hebrew University, and the Bonn Society of Mensa (Tisch Gemeindschaft von Bonn), the equivalent of the US Mensa Society. Those lectures would give me good public exposure again, not to mention over a million NAD.

I asked Humberto if he and Isabella would like a little holiday. They were thrilled. I asked them to determine where they would like to go. I would pay for their time away as a reward for their faithful service. After all, cleaning up human slime and outhouses and digging graves is not fun work. They reported back to me in two days that Isabella would love to see her homeland again. *Perfect.*

I would miss Tadwil. It was a comfortable and beautiful place, but I had to get on with things. I arranged for the pair to take me to New O'Hare and told Humberto that he and Isabella could use the hovercar for their journey. It would save them a lot of time from traveling on public conveyances, and Humberto was a master at the controls of the hovercar. I helped them plan a route and get the necessary clearances for them to use the hoverspace internationally. Again, all their papers were in order, since I had been careful about hiring people who were here legally under the Obamagration Act.

It was midsummer, a perfect time to escape central Illinois and its heat and humidity. The barn/lab was secured, as was the house. I made a final check on the "cemetery"—all was well—and we were set to go. I didn't need much luggage, since I wanted to get some new clothing at Harrod's or my favorite shop on Savile Row.

Humberto dropped me off and then left for his vacation with his wife. Perhaps I should say "Unsuspecting Humberto dropped me off and then left for his vacation with his unsuspecting wife." You see, I had two problems. The first is that by this time they both knew too much. Faithful retainers that they were, that was a chance I was not willing to take. Secondly, Lincoln was always a bit confounded by them. I don't know if he had ever seen a Hispanic person (how politically correct!).

He was in New Orleans once in his youth, but the population there was still heavily French.

Lincoln only knew of household help that was black, either enslaved or free. White-gloved, high-mannered attendants would have been part of his life after moving to Springfield and settling down. His wife's home, as well, would have been staffed with black servants. It was the same for the White House.

Two hours into their journey it happened. I had rigged the hovercar with subsonic explosive devices. It would burn at a slow deflagration rate and thus attract minimal attention. For the fun of it, I used the studies of Frederick Augustus Abel. He developed nitrocellulose in 1865, the same year as Lincoln's assassination. I thought that rather poetic. The original molecular formula was simple enough:

$$C_6H_9(NO_2)O_5$$
$$C_6H_8(NO_2)_2O_5$$
$$C_6H_7(NO_2)_3O_5$$

Almost two hundred years since its invention, it would take a long time for investigators to figure it out. It ceased being used in the 1930s. Its combustion point was a handy 160–170 degrees Celsius. That is the temperature of the exhaust system of a hovercar after approximately three hours of flight. Sulfuric acid acts as a catalyst to produce $NO+2$ (nitronium ion). Electrophilic substitution at the C-OH centers of the cellulose triggers the reaction

Ka-boom! (But not said too loudly). Somewhere over the Appalachian Mountains of western North Carolina, the hovercar exploded and evaporated, and with it went Humberto and Isabella. (If anyone were watching, he or she would think the hovercar was a falling star.) I will miss them, but not a lot.

On to London and Some Fun

I decided to deliver the lectures before returning to London, thinking I might as well get the work out of the way. I used the same text for each presentation: "An Analysis of the Diodical Indices of Polychromic Genetic Mutations." It was a profitable success.

I was embarrassed when I landed in London. The airport personnel rolled out a red carpet, and over the speaker system a voice announced, "Their royal majesties, King William V and Queen Katherine, joyfully announce the arrival of Sir Anton Bauer. All hail!"

Everyone looked around, and there I was. Frankly, this "sir knight" greeting business is getting tiresome. Well, I waved to the crowd. Thankfully I always dress to the nines when I travel.[76] These days the flight from Berlin to London took only half an hour. I suppose the king was just trying to be gracious. Later I learned that upon the first return of a knight of the realm, such an announcement is customary. It won't happen again.

In London, at New Heathrow, I was met by Percival's new manservant. He was a solid soul, some six feet two, like myself, and dark complected. He introduced himself as Omar O'Malley, manservant to the Earl of Upton. Once inside the hoverlimo, he closed the partition and we took off for the estate.

After the initial greetings, I asked Percival what had become of Wilkins. He told me that Wilkins had reached the age of sixty and that, in the family tradition, he was rewarded with retirement and given a house in the village to live out his years. More interesting was the story of his new man, Omar. Omar was the product of a Muslim Lebanese mother and an Irish Catholic father. They had met while representing their nations' interests at the Second Pan-Arabic Peace Summit some thirty years ago in Baghdad. Omar was the product of their love.

"Percival, he looks quite handsome—a bit like a Circassian soldier of old," I commented.

"Yes, quite. He is very dashing. He is obedient, has learned how to anticipate my needs, and is even quite helpful at the clinic. More and more of my clients speak Arabic. He is able to assist with the translation of their problems and my advice to them."

---

[76] Interesting. No one has the slightest idea where this phrase originated, yet it is very popular. Some say it took nine yards of cloth to make a coat. Other ideas abound. Oh well. It's not that important.

"Quite fine. Are the boys here yet?"

"Yes, they arrived about two hours ago and are resting and cleaning up. Might I suggest you do the same? Dinner will be at 20:00 hours in the main dining room. Without the royals here tonight, we can be quite relaxed and informal. We'll start with preprandials at 19:00 hours."

"Splendid. See you then."

I went upstairs and found the same wonderful bed and robe and took a snooze. At 18:00, Omar came to assist me. He had a choice of casual evening wear for me. I chose the gray shirt, blue blazer, and deep blue trousers. I had my own shoes.

When I got to the library, Fergus and Angus were already there. I poured myself two fingers of Tio Pepe, and we sat down and chatted like it was just yesterday. The meal was served on time, and it was as delicious and decadent as every other meal I ever had at Percival's. The soup was potato leek. The items had been grown on the property. The fish course was a lightly breaded haddock in cognac sauce. The entrée was pheasant stuffed with chestnuts, again all from the property. Dessert was, to my great surprise, bananas Foster. It seems that Percival had visited New Orleans a few months ago and had tasted that wonderful dessert at Brennan's. It was absolutely delightful. I am so glad that the great old restaurants are maintained someplace in the United States.

Protocol demanded that we share the obligatory cognac and cigar after dinner. I recalled the queen lighting her stogie and stifled a smile. We chatted until late in the night. On the way upstairs, I said to the boys, "Percival is going into London tomorrow to work at the clinic. Why don't we hitch a ride and see how our little project is doing?"

(Kensington Park officials, of course, wanted to correct the anatomical insult we had inflicted upon Peter Pan, but popular opinion and the crowds of money-spending tourists and Londoners alike made them change their minds.)

We woke up early, had a splendid breakfast of trout, soft-boiled eggs (again all from the estate), and toast and marmalade.[77] Then we joined Percival and Omar and went into the city. We were dropped off at the

---

[77] It was, of course, the finest Dundee marmalade.

entrance to Kensington Park, the entrance opposite the palace. I then told the boys what we were going to do.

"Walk with me, boys. Look casual and try not to stare or dawdle when we get near the statue."

"What's up?" they asked in unison.

"Well," I replied, "remember the ad placed in the cybernews announcing the 'new gift' to Kensington Garden?"

"Of course," said Fergus. "It was a wonderful prank."

"Well," I replied, "I placed another ad in last night's final edition. Take a moment now and summon the copy on your own microchips."

They both chortled loudly as they read the note:

PEOPLE OF LONDON:
Recall the notice in this paper last year:

There is a surprise in store for the children who go to Kensington Gardens to feed the ducks in the Serpentine this morning. Down by the little bay on the south-western side of the tail of the Serpentine, they will find the May-day gift by Mr. J. M. Barrie, the figure of Peter Pan blowing his pipe on the stump of a tree, with fairies and mice and squirrels all around. It has been anatomically corrected. It is the work of brilliant vandals.

Well, here is an additional notice for your further delight:

The donors of the newer version of the Peter Pan statue (now aka *Peter Pan Piss*) announce a contest. It will take place tomorrow morning promptly at 9:00 am. Every boy of London, aged ten to twelve, is invited to a pissing contest. Whoever can match the angle, arc, and volume of Peter Pan's toilet will win a prize of 10,000 New Pounds Sterling.

The boys were actually choking they were laughing so hard. We made our way to the edge of the crowd of about three thousand youngsters and parents and other observers. No one, fools that they are, bothered to note that no mention was made of who was giving such a preposterous award for such a pernicious act. As the clock came closer to the appointed hour, we observed moms and dads forcing their boys to drink water, soda, and even beer, all in an effort to make the urge stronger. The park police hadn't sufficient notice to deal with such a crowd. Little boys were jumping about, eager to relieve themselves, while parents continued to force them to imbibe. (Oh, did I mention there isn't a public toilet for a half-mile in any direction?) The hour came and went. The boys were desperate to relieve themselves, but no official showed up to conduct the contest, much less offer the reward. By ten minutes after the hour, the boys were crowding around the duck pond and disappearing into the shrubbery. Parents scolded their offspring for "not holding it," while park police gave up any effort at trying to control events. Meanwhile, the three of us stood far off, smirking at the whole event and holding our guffaws deep inside, and then casually we made our way to Speakers' Corner while frustrated parents corralled their young charges.

Back at the estate that evening, the cybernews was filled with comment on the latest outrage against this famed London monument. Percival joined in the lamentation, never connecting the first assault and this one to the visit of Anton, Fergus, and Angus to his property at the same time as both incidents.

Two days later, we said our good-byes once again. There was quite the chance that we would never see one another in the future. It was a sad moment for us all.

Omar took the three of us to New Heathrow, the boys headed north to Scotland, and I myself headed west to America, to Springfield, to Tadwil, and to plan my next move.

CHAPTER 14

Third Time's a Charm

I returned to New O'Hare, and wouldn't you know it—more cheers and shouting awaited me. I wondered if this arrival nonsense was ever going to end, but then I realized it wasn't for me. I was both relieved and disappointed. It was a cheer for the fresh cybernews that the Martian crew, launched eight years ago, had returned safely. It takes about one year each way to cover the precarious distance. We all knew that the landing had gone well and that the experiments and discoveries continued to be remarkable. Two astrocosmonauts were left behind while another crew had been launched, not knowing if the original group would make it back. These were brave people. The returning spaceship, *Inter-Mars* (it was an international crew) had just landed safely in Western China.

The first thing I did was once again go to the laboratory and check everything out. All was fine. I retrieved the parts of the accelerator from the hiding spot in the woods and reassembled the mechanism. The birthing room was ready for another occupant. Abe's log cabin mockup awaited. The grounds had gotten a little run-down with no one to care for them. The house was fine, if not a little dusty. It looked just as it had the day Humberto, Isabella, and I left it.

I made it known in the local cyberpress that I was looking for domestic help. Of course, all kinds of applicants came forward, but I recalled the minor difficulties I'd had with the Hispanics and Abe. The hiring laws forbade specifying gender, race, nationality, or religion, but I knew what I was looking for. I needed a black couple.

It took several weeks before the right pair showed up. They were identical twins, in fact. Darius and Darren Didymus were my new servants. Darren took care of the domestic chores. Darius would replace

Humberto. He demonstrated skill when we went shopping for a new 2063 hovercar. It wasn't much different from the previous model. I got this one in jet black. I moved the brothers into the housing formerly used by their deceased predecessors. I dutifully explained what I expected of them. In the ensuing weeks, they proved a good hire. Darren was an excellent cook. I gave him recipes from the 1800s, and he delighted in duplicating them with the closest ingredients available now. Darius got the property in good shape.

Now I needed another womb. Where to find one? I certainly could not place an advertisement for that—not that someone wouldn't do it. Surrogate parenting is very popular now. I knew only one woman who might be able to help me, but I was not sure how willing she would be. I took my chances and called Madison.

"Madison, Madison. It's me—Anton."

"Oh, Anton," Madison replied, "it is so good to hear your voice. I've been following your European lectures. It seems everything was a great success."

"Indeed it was. Madison, I am calling for two reasons. The first is this: I am wondering if anyone has ever heard from Ms. Elsinger?"

"No, Anton. Nothing. It was certainly a strange experience. I hope she is well and getting some assistance. If she had applied for any scientific job, though, I'm sure she would have used the university as a reference. We've heard nothing."

"What a pity. Problematic as she had become to me personally, she was an able scientist."

"And the second reason might be?"

"Oh, yes. Madison, while I was away, I had a lot of time to ponder our conversations—you recall—on the ethics of genomic medical science. I would like to continue those discussions if you are interested."

"Yes, I would be most interested. Just to see you again would be wonderful. To continue those talks would be a bonus."

"Tell you what. I'll send my chauffeur to the university tomorrow about 4:00 p.m. You can come here to Tadwil, my estate. We can have a little discussion and then a splendid dinner. My chauffeur's brother is a splendid cook. Bring a light wrap. We can take a spin on the river on my houseboat before dinner."

"That sounds perfect. I'll be in front of the Science Building at four, prompt."

"Splendid," I said. "I cannot wait to see you."

This was the truth, of course; I could not wait to see her. As I mentioned before, she was easy on the eyes. Now I needed to find out more about her ethical stances. You do know what else I am up to!

The Next Evening

Darius picked up Madison, and she was ready on schedule. I knew she would be. Darius brought her to the front door. I met her there. She looked splendid. She was wearing her hair a little differently. The Betty Boop style that was popular almost 150 years before was the newest style craze. She wore a lavender skirt, fashionably long, and a loose-fitting satin blouse of pale, pale pink. Her earrings, which she never wore in the lab, were two simple gold columns on each side. Her necklace matched the earrings—a pair of tiny, gold columns cascading down her lovely front.

"Welcome to Tadwil, Madison."

"Tadwil—what does it mean?" she asked. (She had probably searched her language memory and come up empty.)

I explained the origin of the term and its Lincoln reference. I then escorted her through the house. She marveled at the tasteful combination of the very up-to-date mixed with the mid-Victorian. I told her how I had found the place, sketched the broad design lines, and left the details to others. She was most impressed.

We walked down the path to the Mary Todd, which was moored at the pier and ready to go. Darren had stocked the small refrigerator with a variety of beverages and had prepared the most splendid hors d'oeuvres. On his homemade crackers there was a variety of foie gras, lox with capers, and a homemade marmalade. There was an assortment of nuts as well. I asked which beverage she would prefer, and she asked for a red wine. I always kept a variety of wines and the appropriate stemware for each one. She marveled at the splendid Waterford Lismore glass.

"Perfect," I said. Now Madison, if you will allow me, I will pour the wine for you; but I would like to spice it up a bit with a topper of champagne. I know that doing this drives the oenophiles crazy, but it's quite good."

"Please. I trust you."

Fool. "There you go. Cheers!"

After sipping a bit, she relaxed. As we navigated the Sangamon, I risked everything. Well, almost everything. I had decided to tell her the truth. Just not all of it.

I revealed my fascination with the genome project, which was no surprise to her. She was delighted and declared me a hopeless romantic when I told her of the connection between my work and my birthday, shared with the infamous Dolly.

I then told her of my research into the regeneration of DNA of the deceased. At first she thought this was disgusting—a kind of Ed Gein grave robbery.[78] I assured her that it was nothing of the sort. She knew that my kind of research in the last half century had helped to eliminate a great deal of disease. Leukemia was no more. Nor were ALS or Alzheimer's. I then told her of my plan to clone Abraham Lincoln. She hiccupped a bit at first and spilled a splash of wine, but then she just looked at me.

"Anton, that is almost preposterous, except if anyone can accomplish it, I suspect you can." (She did not know, of course, that I had already done it—twice!)

"Well, my dear, let me continue to explain." I told her that I did not dig up the dead, which, strictly speaking, was the truth. I then took the first great risk of the evening and told her of the robbery of the bloodstained clothing from Ford's Theatre. The caper still made the news occasionally. The Washington, DC, police would follow up on leads (planted by you-know-who) claiming that they were about to nab the culprit. There was egg on the police department's face when they came to realize that they were about to arrest one of the three presidents for

---

[78] A notorious serial killer in Wisconsin in the 1950s. He exhumed bodies from the local cemetery and then used the bone and skin to make furniture for his home. The Hitchcock thriller *Psycho* may have been based upon his actions. There was a popular joke at the time: Why didn't Ed Gein succeed at farming? Because he only had a skeleton crew.

the crime. Madison had a good laugh at that. I was glad she shared some of my antinomian tendencies.

"Anton," she said, "this puts everything in a different perspective. My ethical objections dealt with the general use of DNA investigation on living people, not on the deceased. Given, especially, the sources of your DNA, the moral issues take on a whole different aspect. I would have to think about it more carefully, but initially I have no objection to this. In fact, I find it fascinating."

I was relieved to hear her say this. Otherwise, frankly, I would have had to kill her.

"Let's head in," I said. "I'd like to show you my lab before dinner."

After docking the Mary Todd, we walked back to the house and then followed the gravel path to the laboratory. She was amazed at the quality and quantity of equipment in what looked, from the outside, like an old barn. She puzzled a bit about one piece of equipment—the genome accelerator. When she asked what it was, I told her. (Again I kept the death option open on my end.) I asked her to come with me to the house for dinner, where I would continue my probing.

Dinner was excellent. Darius served. The soup was watercress and chestnut (all items grown on the property, of course). The salad was a simple mix of hearts of palm with fruit bits and raspberry vinaigrette dressing. The main meal was ostrich stuffed with quail, with a light frizzle sauce of the pan juices served as gravy. The vegetable was eggplant with a tomato parmesan sauce. A small serving of new potatoes buttered in rosemary rounded out the meal. The dessert was a chocolate lava cake. All was served on the splendid Royal Doulton china that Percival Pettigrew gave me on my sixtieth birthday. It had been in his family for over two hundred years. Madison was duly impressed by the meal and the dishware.

"Is everything to your liking, Madison?"

"Anton, this is superb. I have never had such a splendid combination of tastes. Is this Royal Doulton, by chance?"

"Yes, it is. I am impressed that you recognize it." I told her of its provenance, and she was all the more impressed. She admired the hand-painted periwinkles.

"Madison, I would like to explain a few more things to you." *Here comes the big one!* "My work is really quite advanced—well beyond the planning stage. I am ready to use the Lincoln DNA to clone him, but, as you know is the case in cloning, I need an egg that I can denucleate and a uterus in which to grow the implant. My dear, I can think of no one more qualified than you."

Madison blushed, then paled, and then blushed again. She looked at me, and I thought, *Uh oh. The jig is up!*

"You know, Anton, I think we make a good partnership. Tell me more."

I explained everything about the process, even the genome accelerator. I knew that if she backed out now, she would become another member of the cemetery club. To my satisfaction, she showed intelligent and deep interest.

"Madison, let's go back to the lab," I said. "I want to show you two more things."

We walked off our meal a bit. It was dark now, and the moon was casting wonderful Halloween shadows through the bare autumn trees. We entered the lab, and I explained the genome accelerator and how the pregnancy and subsequent growth of the cloned Lincoln would take place. I showed her the comfortable room that would be hers during the pregnancy, should she wish to stay here. I would actually give her that option. Then I showed her the "Lincoln Room"—that replica of a pioneer log cabin. She continued to be impressed.

"Madison, I want to time the birth of the clone to the actual date, next February, of Lincoln's birth—the twelfth. That means that the egg must be dealt with and implanted by next Wednesday. Are you sure you want to do this?"

"I have no doubts."

"Good! Would you like Darius to take you home? Of course, you can say nothing about this. When the birth takes place, you will be an integral part of raising young Lincoln, even though he will grow and mature physically and intellectually at the rate of a year per day." (I had learned from the other two mothers that these maternal concerns must be addressed.)

"Yes, I would like to go home, but have Darius pick me up the evening before the procedure. I will have time to clean up a few things up in the lab and to pack some items."

What she did not know was that the chocolate lava cake contained yet another microchip, this one the size and shape of a small crumb of chocolate. This would keep tabs on her whereabouts as well as record her conversations. It would attach itself to the front of her stomach lining and transmit to me in the lab. If she said or did anything that endangered the project—well, you know what would happen!

But she didn't. She was true to her word—truer than I ever am to mine. I did, though, actually plan to have her help in the raising of young Abe and then, when the time was right, to share in the scientific acclaim. I must be mellowing in my old age.

I reminded her about the acceleration process—that one month of pregnancy would take one week, and then, after the birth, young Lincoln would develop at the astonishing rate of one year per day. She said she understood. I asked her to get a wardrobe together so that near the end of the pregnancy she could stay at Tadwil, in the specially prepared room. I did not want to confine her to that room too far ahead of time, as I had done with the others. She was a willing colleague. She was also intelligent enough to know how to take care of herself during pregnancy.

On December 12, 2062, Madison showed up for the procedure. You've read it before, so I won't detail it all over again. Everything went smoothly. She stayed the night in the laboratory dorm. By morning she was doing fine. She asked if she could return to her own home. I reminded her of the conditions of our agreement and of her delicate condition. I didn't want anything to jeopardize this birth—not that I didn't have plenty of DNA to work with, but I really wanted this one to work.

Over the New Year holiday, she returned for a week. It was too cold to take the houseboat out on the river, but we sat on that wonderful Victorian wraparound porch and talked about all kinds of things. She had been doing a lot of homework on Lincoln, which I appreciated. I reviewed for her all that she could expect after the birth, reminding her *ad nauseam* of the quickness of Lincoln's growth once back in this world. We took a little field trip to Oak Ridge. We went during the day so the work crew was busy elsewhere and not in the tomb itself. I was a little concerned about bumping into my old boss while this beautiful woman was with me, but it was January, and he was on vacation in a warmer climate. Madison knew nothing of the small borehole in the hillside, much less the assault upon Lincoln himself, and I didn't tell her. My little marker was still in place! I guess the grounds crew isn't very attentive.

As the weeks went on, her baby bump became prominent. She wore the right kind of clothes, loose but elegant, so it took some time for people to notice. At the end of January, she announced to her faculty and staff that she was pregnant (which was obvious) and that she was serving as a surrogate mother (which was the truth). Surrogate parenthood had become quite standard by now. (Ah, how the mores of society change!) This worked out splendidly. Everyone smiled at her and wished her well.

Two days later, Madison called me. She was flustered, angry, and scared. I asked what the problem was, and she responded, "I think someone broke into my cyber records. The red flag alert was on this morning."

Now, ever since the invention of computers and the subsequent cyber-systems, there have been those who are thrilled to circumvent the law and steal information, money, and/or identities. This was a major problem at the beginning of the twenty-first century. By 2025, Congress and science cooperated, and the results were remarkable. Cybercrime of any sort was a federal offense. The crimes could now be tracked easily and the offenders caught and punished. The quantity of cybercrime decreased some 85 percent, a remarkable figure. Because the detection systems were absolutely foolproof, there was no need for a trial. Guilty was guilty. The perpetrator was brought before a special cyber council magistrate. The prosecutors showed their evidence, and the punishment was the same for everyone: exile to Predison without parole.[79]

---

[79] "Predison" is a syneresis of the prefix "pre" and the name "Edison." The name was chosen in honor of the prolific inventor Thomas Edison. Nothing can be found in Predison that came into existence after Edison's first major invention, the phonograph, in 1877. If Predison's inhabitants want music, they have to create it. There is only candlelight or kerosene light. Heat was found in Predison by gathering firewood. Water is drawn from wells. You get the idea. It is a dire place and is best avoided.

Predison was a part of northwestern New Mexico and northeastern Arizona—some of the most inhospitable turf in the United States. That is why it had been given to Native Americans as reservation land. Once again the federal government broke treaties, but the tribes were pleased to receive the substantial financial settlement and relocate in other states of their choice. Many chose Hawaii.

The land, several million square miles, was marked with simple wooden fencing. Underneath the fencing, however, was a perimeter of detection devices. Any prisoner who attempted to cross the boundary line was instantly tased, rendered unconscious, and then picked up for return to the center of the settlement. The microchips planted in their brains, for most of us the source of knowledge and memory and communication, were altered upon sentencing to alert guards to the attempt to escape. Any second attempt resulted in immediate execution by a cyber-generated heart attack. After the first two years, there were no more escape attempts. The power of the system was well known and feared.

I thanked Madison for the call and told her not to worry. Sometimes government agencies prove worthwhile. I contacted the CCC, the cybercrimes constables, and informed them of Madison's concerns. It took only minutes to track the intrusion. It was no one less than Dr. Wilson Adamson, the chancellor of the university. His plea was that he simply was searching for some record to indicate who the actual parents of his pregnant, now-on-leave superstar department head might be. It made no difference. I phoned Madison.

"Madison, we know who the culprit is. It was Dr. Adamson."

"It couldn't be. He has always been my friend and supporter."

"Well, that might be the case, but he claims he was curious and used his executive power at the university to check your database to see who the actual parents of your baby might be. Was there any written or stored record of this, Madison? It's important, you understand."

"No! Absolutely not! I understood from the beginning what our agreement was and what the gravity of this decision entailed. He would have found only mathematical formulae and my class lecture notes. There was never anything personal in my data accounts."

"Well then, we can both breathe easier. You know, of course, Adamson's destiny.

"Yes. And he deserves it," Madison said.

"Well, do relax now, and keep in touch. All is well."

As the pregnancy acceleration was in full swing, she wisely took the second semester off and asked if she could stay at Tadwil. I was more than willing. She showed up on February 1, radiant. I gave her a choice of Caesarean birth or natural birth. She chose natural, which I thought she would. There was only a little over a week to go now.

Meanwhile I had instructed Darius and Darren about our visitor, a friend who was having a surrogate baby and would be staying with us. I said she was a scientist, which was true, and would be staying in the guest room in the lab rather in the house so that she could have quiet but also have access to scientific materials and the splendid cyberlibrary if she wanted. I also instructed Darren to get recipes for mid-Victorian pioneer food, as Isabella had done before. He was up to the challenge, and in the evening we tasted his handiwork. He could make possum taste like pheasant under glass.

Madison was getting bigger and was getting anxious. I was getting anxious as well. On the morning of February 12, 2063, Abraham Lincoln III came into this world. As with his predecessor, he was long and thin—very thin. But a child of that era would have had a struggle to survive. The birth left Madison exhausted, so I took little Abe to the "Lincoln Room" and had Darren watch him. I had told the boys about Madison's pregnancy—not everything, of course, but only that a friend of mine was embarrassed at her situation and wanted to have the baby in private. I lied and told them that the log cabin mock-up was her idea, part of an experiment in US history. They asked no questions. Darren had prepared formula (which young Lincoln would not have known) and enough baby food of the era to keep him healthy as his growth spurt began.

That night Darius came to my door, not unlike Humberto. "Dr. Bauer, Dr. Bauer, come quickly! Something is wrong with Ms. Madison."

I thought I was dreaming—déjà vu—but there was Darius. I put on a robe and slippers, and we made our way to the lab. Darius had been watching the surveillance monitor, not so much to spy on this cooperative beauty as to make sure she was resting and recuperating after the day's hard work.

She was not doing all right.

"Anton, Anton," said Madison. "It hurts. I am bleeding."

And she was. Copious blood was on her nightgown and the bedding. She was in a panic.

"Madison, I am going to call a hoverambulance. It can be here in minutes."

"Please, hurry. I'm so scared."

I didn't call the ambulance. Not yet, anyway. I knew it would arrive too late. There was too much blood, and the monitors showed she was failing quickly. I watched from the monitor in the lab as Madison's color faded and her heartbeat alternated between going wild and almost stopping. She gasped a final, desperate catch of breath, and then the monitor showed that she passed away, a victim of Abraham's childbirth pangs. I was genuinely distressed. I had looked forward to working with Madison and young Abe, but at the moment I had other things I had to take care of.

I instructed Darius and Darren to carry her body to the ladies' salon in the house and to lay her out on the Victorian fainting couch. Then I had them take the sheets and dab spots on the fainting couch with blood, a lot of it. Then they were to burn the sheets and get them out of sight.

I did call the ambulance then, and it did arrive in moments. I explained to the EMTs that an associate of mine had volunteered to be a surrogate mother. She had come for dinner but in the middle of the meal began to have severe cramps. I told them that she was only five months pregnant, which to anyone thinking in normal pregnancy terms would seem accurate. I had to have a good story for the university crowd, you know. This timed out fine. I told them that she had had a miscarriage. When they asked where the fetus was, I told them that the servants had taken it away from her just before she passed away. There was enough blood to convince them that something radically wrong took place. As they must, they tried to resuscitate her, but it was no use. After a half hour, they stopped, put their equipment away, and brought in a body bag. While they were carrying her out, I asked, "What about the fetus?" One of them responded, "Well, the child is not alive. Have your people do whatever. It's really not our problem. As the old saying goes, 'Not my circus, not my monkey.'"

I thought that was a tad callous, but I was also relieved. Meanwhile, Darren was taking care of little Abe in the "Lincoln Bedroom." He was doing fine. Pity, though. In a way, this made four birth mothers he'd lost.

The memorial service for Madison was held in the university auditorium. The full faculty and staff were present, as were several thousand students. Scientist-peers from institutions all over the country showed up as well. Just as with the memorial service for the students in Washington, I was asked to address the mourners. I did so eloquently but briefly, taking a cue from Lincoln's own unwritten handbook of public discourse. My sentiments about missing her were genuine, but science must go on, and so must I.

CHAPTER 15

Raising Abe III

Well, here we go again. I could repeat verbatim all the experiences that took place in those early weeks with Abraham II, but why waste the space? If you have forgotten, just turn back to chapter 12. Everything went according to the same schedule with Abraham III. He had his melancholy days and his high days in the same pattern as Abe II. No surprise there. I interacted with him in the same way as well. His days passed in a sequence of growing, reading, cutting wood, riding, swimming, and hiking around the grounds. I did explain to Abraham III that he was free to go about the fenced-in property but was never to leave it. Recall that I had the perimeter circled with an underground electrical fence system to deter trespassers. It worked the same way on the other side. I did, one night, plant a microchip in Abraham's head while he was sleeping. I had riddled his cider with a potent agent that would knock him out long enough for the procedure and its short recovery time.[80] I did not have the microchip programmed fully with all the knowledge that could have been held in it. I did not want him to know everything yet. I did program it to cause great pain should he ever transgress the property boundaries. He never experienced that pain, however. He was a very obedient boy. I planted the chip in the exact same place where the bullet had entered the original Lincoln's head.

As before, I marveled at how quickly he could learn things, which I figured out last time was actually Abraham remembering things he had learned in his first incarnation. Because of this experience, I did make some changes to his education, giving him more to read than the

---

[80] I used benzodiazepine (colloquially known as BZD). The core chemical structure is the fusion of a benzene ring and a diazapene ring; in short, it is a knockout drug.

standard books available in his day. He delighted in fiction, in Aesop's fables, and in anything with humorous stories. His own well of great stories was deep as an adult. He started putting those things together in his boyhood by careful observation and memorization and adding his own personal touches.

Likewise, I decided that I would begin bringing him into the present sooner than I did with Abraham II. When Abraham III was twenty years old (twenty days with us in this new form), I sat down with him in his room.

"Abraham," I began, "I know you are a bright and a curious young man. Look at how fast you are growing. You are already six feet four inches tall and as skinny as the rails you split."

"Yes, I know. And I have so much energy. Thank you for the books."

"Now, Abraham, I would like you to call me Anton. That is my given name."

"Very well, Anton. And you can call me Abe."

"Very well. Now, Abe, I think you know there are some strange things going on around here. I want to assure you first of all that you are absolutely safe. No one is going to harm you. In fact, everyone is here to help you. That includes Darius and Darren. They are trusted workers. They are our butlers."[81]

"Very well. Very well. But what is it you want to tell me?"

"It's a long story, Abe. It will take days, weeks even, but that's fine. I think you know that you live in a very remarkable time in history. Look at all the inventions you've seen: the telegraph, the steam engine, the cotton gin, the locomotive and rail travel. I ask you to trust me now. Many years have passed since that time. You will understand better as the days go on. I just want you to know that there have been many, many more incredible inventions. I brought with me one of them. It is called a typewriter. Instead of having to use a quill and paper to record your words, it is possible to use this machine. Let me demonstrate it for you."

---

[81] Lincoln had taken to wrestling with the brothers, who were just slightly shorter than he was. The original Lincoln wrestled a great deal in his youth, especially while living in New Salem. Once, in Beardstown, Illinois, in 1832, on a bet, he was thrown by one Lorenzo Dow Thompson.

I put a piece of paper in the old manual typewriter—the same one Abraham II had used to write his suicide note. I typed out the phrase "Four score and twenty years ago" and then asked Lincoln to do the same. He stated that it sounded vaguely familiar, and then he sat his tall frame down at the desk and typed "four score and twennty years ago." The similarity to Abraham II's errors was remarkable and encouraging, if not eerie. Once again his large, ungainly hands spread over the QWERTY keyboard. The ability to use punctuation would come in time, as would a mastery over the double letters and capitalization. I told him that I would leave the machine with him so he could practice using it. I could hardly wait until he used dictation and thought transfer on the newest computer systems!

"Excellent," I said. "You will have plenty of time to learn how to use it. There are other machines as well." I had Darius bring in an old Edison phonograph, the kind with the thick records and the windup handle on the side with the large cone-shaped speaker.

"This is called a phonograph. The name means 'sound writer.' This large plate is called a record. You place it on here, like this, wind this crank, and place this mechanism with the little needle on the record; and now listen."

In the old scratchy tones of those original Edisons, the sound of Stephen Foster's "Old Folks at Home" (aka "Swanee River") began to play. It was composed in 1851, so Lincoln knew it in his original life. Abraham was fascinated by it. He walked all around the machine, studying its various parts. Obtaining it had been quite difficult, as so few of these are left. I didn't want to show him the most up-to-date items yet. They would be beyond him. When the song was finished, the needle kept playing at the end of its track until I lifted it back to the small stanchion that held it. I had only a couple of other records with music that would have been familiar to Lincoln. That collection included Civil War music, such as "We Are Coming, Father Abra'am,"[82] "The Battle Cry of Freedom,"[83] "When Johnny Comes Marching Home

---

[82] 1862, James Sloan Gibbons and Luther Orlando Emerson.
[83] 1862, George Fredric Root.

Again,"[84] "The Battle Hymn of the Republic,"[85] and, to boot, "Dixie."[86] It wasn't much of a repertoire, but it was all that I could find (that Darren could find) for that old machine. Abe quickly learned how to make the machine work and asked if he could listen to the music again. I told him he was free to do so and I would leave him for the day to entertain himself with the phonograph and the typewriter

He spent that afternoon and evening listening to the records over and over again, with that strange old music coming out of that strange old machine. He sang along a bit as well. It was not a pretty sound. Abe sat at his typewriter and typed out the words of the songs, still missing punctuation and doubling the *m*'s and *n*'s.

I let a few days pass before I continued moving him along into present reality. On day twenty-three (year twenty-three), he was quite excited. It was the year he invented a device to lift boats over shoals when they got stuck in the river. He had been working on a flatboat, taking items to New Orleans, when his boat got stuck. He successfully created the lift that freed the boat.[87] Now he was at the age where he lost Ann Rutledge. I sat with him a bit on that glum day but again left him to his own devices. I made sure he had a good meal that evening—one of his favorites: roasted bear meat.

Instruction began again. He caught on to the technology quite readily. His clothing, up to now, had been period clothing supplied by Darren, who was as handy with a needle and thread as the late Isabella. As with Abraham II, he had grown quickly. Now he had shoes, several sport shirts, sweaters, pairs of trousers, and several coats and various jackets. I explained that style had changed over the years, and while it was not as decorative as clothing had been, it was more comfortable. He readily agreed. The modern fabrics and styles suited him just fine.

He read a lot of law books, and I took another risk. One of the great writers of legal fiction in the twentieth and twenty-first centuries was

---

[84] 1863, Patrick Sarsfield Gilmore.

[85] 1862, Julia Ward Howe.

[86] 1860, Daniel Decatur Emmett.

[87] Lincoln would be the first and only president to get a patent. He made a model of his invention but it was never produced. In 1849, years after the event, he received US PATENT #6469.

John Grisham. I explained this to Abe and told him that there would be references in these books that would puzzle him, but I added that in time he would understand. I invited him to just enjoy the stories. He did. He had never seen a paperback book before. It would be some time before I'd introduce Abe to the current use of microchips in order to read whatever he desired.

The years (days) that made up Abe's travels about the circuit passed quickly and without event. He continued to read voraciously and to enjoy every chance to be outside. He particularly liked riding. We took to doing it as a routine every day.

On his fiftieth birthday (day fifty), I mentioned that in the eighteenth century, fifty was the average lifespan of the American male. Of course, there were fewer and fewer of those men around in his original lifetime because of the great number of deaths during the Civil War.[88]

By his own age of fifty, Lincoln had served as a lawyer and a congressional representative, debated Stephan Douglas, married, had children, and buried one son. He inquired about Mary, but I didn't want to say anything yet. I told him we would come back to that, and we would. (This was a rare moment of truth, but this time it was easy being truthful with this man.) We went through the years of his life in Springfield. He delighted in telling how, after he had been gone for some weeks on the circuit, he would come home to an irate Mary who had been trying to control her very obstreperous boys. Lincoln spoiled his sons terribly, perhaps as a reaction to his own hard boyhood. His law partner would complain that when the boys were at the office, all they did was cause mayhem. Mary would actually chase him down the street in Springfield while brandishing a broom. What a sight—the tall Lincoln running with that strange, awkward gait and laughing as he fled from the squat, rather rotund Mary.

Lincoln was fifty-one when he was elected president. He had enemies on every side: within his own still-new Republican Party, in the Democratic Party, and certainly from Southern partisans. It was

---

[88] Some 620,000 persons died in that war, almost 2/3 of that number from disease, the rest from war related injuries. There were 360,000 Union dead and 260,000 Confederate dead.

time to get serious with Lincoln. We sat down again on the Victorian porch at Tadwil. He had moved out of the log cabin room now and was getting accustomed to the hybrid experience that was my home. He relished every convenience—especially our modern toilets and full-body showers.

"Abraham," I said, "you are doing so well. I have the deepest respect for you, and I want to continue to help you find your life in this new world you are encountering. Now, you will have to continue to trust me even though some of the things I will say to you will continue to sound outrageous—insane, even. The first is this: I am a scientist. Science has come a long way. Trust me when I tell you that it is now the year 2063. Yes, over two hundred years have passed since you were elected president. Now there are three leaders for our American nation. The task just became too much for one person to master. It is based on the ancient Roman system of the triumvirate. So far it has worked quite well, but you know what your world was like as president. The three work in Washington, DC, in the same White House that you occupied. There are still wars, but now they are fought by flying machines. Spies still abound, although much of it is now 'machine driven' rather than risking people in the field. There are now fifty states in the Union. The Kansas-Nebraska Act, the Missouri Compromise, and so on, were important parts of your political world. Now they are history. Those areas are called the 'heartland' of America. They produce food for the country and for the world.

"You might have noticed when you go outside that it is quite warm for Springfield in March and April. For some time now, the machines that we created in the last one hundred fifty years wreaked havoc on nature. The average temperatures rose several degrees across the globe. We have learned how much we rely upon all parts of the earth and how interdependent we are. The leaders of the world have slowly come to realize that without universal cooperation, any part of the globe could perish. The economies of the world are intertwined. It is not just cotton from the South any longer. Wood fires do not supply our heat, and gas lanterns do not give our light. The energy resources we need are created by harnessing wind vectors and using machines that capture and store natural energy and convert it into something useful. We have done the same with the power of the sun. Manual labor still exists, but it is rare. Only those who choose it need work at it. Most citizens are able to support themselves from their own homes on machines something like your typewriter but more advanced. Let me show you one."

Once again I skipped any information about the electronic typewriter. Cell-powered machines were the norm. I showed Abraham a twenty-first-century tablet—still a primitive machine compared to today's thought processors. He caught on quickly and enjoyed asking questions to the machine. When he asked what the year was and the response came back 2063, he smiled. He knew I was either telling the truth or I was a magnificent conjuror. (Ahem.)

We went through the years of the Civil War, again allowing a day of melancholy for the death of Willie. The next day, we chatted about Robert. Abraham explained that he did not have as favorable a relationship with this son as he would have wished. He did not want to be like his own father: strict, overbearing, demanding, and uncommunicative.[89] However, Robert did not respond to Abe's overtures. A kind of jealousy took over him with the birth of each new sibling. Lincoln, rolling around on the White House floor with Tad and Willie, was too undignified for Robert. Robert also wanted desperately to serve in the military, but Lincoln followed Mary's protestations and kept him out until the very last weeks. Robert resented Lincoln for this, even though he was receiving a splendid Harvard education in the meantime—something Lincoln could not have even imagined.[90] I tried to cheer him a bit.

"Abe, I know that you and Robert did not share an ideal relationship."

"He seemed more of a competitor to me than a son," Abe replied.

"You should know, though, that he went on to do some very fine things with his life. Like you, he became a lawyer. Like you, he served in the federal government. He was secretary of war from 1881 to 1885

---

[89] In fact, Lincoln did not attend his own father's funeral. His stepmother, Sarah, outlived them both.

[90] Lincoln's formal education in a classroom totaled less than twelve months. The schools were primitive frontier places, and students recited their lessons out loud; hence, they were referred to as blab schools. His last school was in Indiana, and his attendance there lasted only a few months.

and also served as the US ambassador to the Court of Saint James. In these capacities, he did you proud. But there is some bad news also. Your son Tad died at the age of eighteen. That means that Robert was the only one of your children to actually live into adulthood. He survived well into the twentieth century, not passing away until 1926. He is buried at Arlington Cemetery."

"Arlington? That name sounds familiar to me, Anton."

"Yes, I thought it might. You knew it as Arlington House, the residence of General Robert E. Lee and his wife. Then, in the middle of the war, you had the government purchase the property because there was great need of more burial space for Union soldiers. Over the decades, it has become one of the largest military cemeteries in the world and probably the most famous. Your son, because of his service in the Union Army and the federal government, is buried there. So, too, are other political leaders and some presidents.

"Here is a photo of Robert in his late adulthood. The photo is from 1922. Robert is on the far right. Next to him is the sitting president of that time, President Warren Harding, and at the left is former president Taft. You were president number sixteen. Taft was the largest man ever elected. He was president number thirty-one. Warren Harding, in the center of the photo, was president number thirty-four. You will be glad to know that both were Republicans."

"Well, I reckon that Robert is a most distinguished looking person."

"That he was. He was always a handsome boy. Here is his photo as you remember him. Quite the handsome fellow, wasn't he?"

His moods these days shifted according to the contemporaneous activities of the Civil War. There had been no telegraph in the White House, so Lincoln would hike to the War Department every day to read dispatches. When a battle had been won, he was ebullient and told stories, to everyone's delight. When news of defeat came, he sulked off or rode in the woods. There is some debate about the name of Lincoln's horse in Springfield: "Bob" or "Robin" or "Old Bob" or "Old Robin."[91] He was often comforted in the White House by his cats. In fact, he would feed the cat Tabby at the table. Mary complained about this, but

---

[91] An 1864 fire in the White House stable killed his horses and Tad's ponies.

he responded, "If the gold fork was good enough for Buchanan, I think it is good enough for Tabby."[92]

"Can I ask you a question, Abe?"

"Of course. Ask anything." He then added with a chuckle, "I always tell the truth, you know!"

"Abraham is a great name, a noble name, and a biblical name at that. Was your family religious?"

"Anton, I cannot say that we were. I certainly cannot say that I was. I found many a truth in the Bible and was greatly moved by it, and I believe deeply in the Divine Being, but church—no. Church was not really a part of my life. When I was a young'un my folks occasionally went to a Baptist Church. In Springfield I would find myself upon rare occasion in the Presbyterian Church, but no, I never officially belonged to any church. They all seemed a bit too keen on having a corner on the truth and on God for my liking."

"Yet you have this great biblical name. Next to the character in the Bible, you are the most famous bearer of that name."

"As I understand it, I was given that name in honor of my pappy's grandfather, the original Abraham Lincoln. He was killed by Indians in 1786."

"I know you had no middle name. Today everyone has at least two middle names. In your time, it was something reserved for the aristocracy or the arrogant."

"Anton, there ain't much different between them two."

"Oh, I know. In fact, in later wars, when soldiers were drafted and asked their middle names, if they didn't have one—which was still rather common—the government gave them a name, or at least a middle initial."

"Well, I'm glad to see they got somethin' free for all their trouble," he said with a smile.

"Abe, I've never seen you smile!"

---

[92] As a child, Lincoln had a dog named Honey. In his Springfield days, the family dog was Fido. When the Lincolns were moving to Illinois (1830), Honey jumped off the ferry into the Wabash River, breaking through a thin layer of ice. Abe jumped into the water and rescued the family pet.

"Well, I laugh a lot, actually—usually at my own stories! In all those photos, you never see me smiling because we had to sit absolutely still. No movin'. It would ruin the photograph. Brady was a tough taskmaster on that one, let me tell you."

"Thanks. That makes sense. I have a copy of one of his photos. He was very courageous and original in documenting the Civil War. Wait 'til you see how we take photographs now."[93]

"Show me. Please."

I showed Abe a photo from Mathew Brady and then took his photo with my eyeblink computer cyber system. It projected automatically to Abe's microchip.[94]

"It's been a long day, Abe," I said. "You've seen a whole lot of life in just a few hours. Let's have a little nightcap and then retire. After our swim and ride tomorrow, we can begin again."

"Ah, a little schnapps, as the Germans say!"

"Exactly! Name your poison!"

"What?" Abe looked startled—frightened, even.

"I apologize. This is a phrase that simply means you have the chance to state your preference of beverage."

"I am used to conspiracy theories and the constant danger of assassination."[95]

"Yes, I apologize. Now, what can I get for you?"

After sharing two stout snifters of Kentucky whiskey, we retired for the night.

---

[93] There is no known photograph of Abraham with Mary Todd Lincoln.

[94] Mathew Brady—only one *t* in his spelling. Brady died indigent.

[95] Two known attacks are recorded: There was a carriage "accident" on July 2, 1863, in which bolts had been loosened in the presidential carriage. The horses bolted when the carriage came loose. Abe was not in it, however, but Mary was thrown against a rock and injured her head. In August of 1864, while riding around Soldiers' Home (the summer presidential retreat), someone shot at Lincoln, putting a hole in his hat.

Day Fifty-Five

Lincoln had been a marvelous companion. The growth accelerator was almost near its term. Tomorrow would be "assassination day." I wanted to use this last day of normalcy and predictability as profitably as possible. We got up early and rode through the woods. Lincoln finally asked when he might be able to leave the property. I thanked him for his cooperation and told him I thought that day would be coming shortly.

After our ride, we took a quick swim in the Sangamon River. Darius brought breakfast to us on the *Mary Todd*. Lincoln knew I named the pontoon boat for his wife. Other than that initial question some time ago, he had yet to ask about her, which I found curious. During the night, I programmed his microchip with a great deal more technology. He was fascinated by it, and I wanted to wait until day fifty-six to continue the historical sagas and then see where we might proceed. I had taken a genuine liking to him—a respect and a liking.

That day we covered the invention of the telephone (none of the originals are available, and phone lines, those ugly blights on the environment are long gone). All communication by this point was based on satellites and microchip implants. We looked at photos of original phones and switchboards, and we then quickly moved into the cell phone era, which was succeeded by the smart phone, which was finally taken over by the implanted microchip. All one had to do was think "Call so and so" or "Call number such and such," and it happened. The microchip also allowed face time technology. The person called appeared in front of the caller's eyes in real time. There were few secrets in this brave new world.

Next came a discussion of the development of the automobile. I brought out the old Trabant, that miserable East German excuse of a vehicle. Lincoln was astonished at it. I let him drive a bit (within three minutes, he wrecked the gear case—understandably), and I finally had him cease when he kept yelling "Whoa, whoa" to the vehicle. We went from there to images of limousines and luxury cars and finally the last of the old fossil-fuel vehicles. I had Darius bring the hovercar around. If someone's eyes ever bugged out of his head, Lincoln's did when this machine silently landed in front of us. He asked if he could control it, and I truthfully told him he would need some time. I did have Darius take us for a spin—just a low hover over Tadwil. I wasn't sure Abe was prepared for more of modern life than that. I took a sneak peak at the "cemetery" in my woods. It looked undisturbed—safely overgrown, in fact.

We took a lunch break. The brothers brought out a fine picnic for us. The day was so splendid that we ate on the porch. There was lemonade, croissants with jam, various sandwich meats, and a variety of bread and rolls. Then I introduced Lincoln to the hot dog.[96] It was a gourmet hot dog, of course, using pork and beef from our local farms. He rather liked it, dipping one end in the catsup[97] container, a splendid Waterford dish, and chewing it with gusto. He did not like sauerkraut and avoided it after his first taste.

We took a brief siesta on the porch swings. Darius brought out some more lemonade and some sugar and cinnamon cookies, still warm from the oven. We continued our session. From the automobile it was a small step to talking about war machinery. The cannon, of course, was the dread instrument of the Civil War. Submarines had been around in Lincoln's time. He laughed when he recalled how the Confederate sub, the *Hunley*, sunk a Union ship but then caught fire itself and sunk because it was too close to its target.[98] The size of World War

---

[96] A German immigrant sold this European treat at Coney Island for the first time in 1870. It did not exist in Lincoln's original lifetime.

[97] A recipe for catsup (ketchup) was first printed in the United States in 1801. Americans rather liked it, even though it would take another generation or two before they trusted eating tomatoes raw. Lincoln delighted when I told him that a (Democratic) presidential candidate was married to the millionaire heiress of a company that began some of the first mass public production of the product (Heinz). The boys, of course, made their catsup from scratch, from tomatoes grown on the estate.

[98] Submarines were considered illegal. There isn't much known about their development in the United States because records were destroyed after the Civil War, as inventors feared strong retribution. One sub inventor, a Frenchman named Brutus De Velleroi, made a sub called *The Alligator* for the Union. On a census form, when asked his occupation, DeVelleroi responded "natural genius." Truly, he is a man after my own heart!

II submarines amazed him, as did the reality of the two great world wars. He asked how often the United States had been at war. The sad response was the truth. We were almost always at war. We reviewed the instruments of war, spending quite a bit of time on the atomic bomb and then the use of drones, which he could understand a bit because of his experience in the hovercar.

He shed tears during my recital of the events of the Holocaust and the ongoing struggle for land and water in the Middle East. The newest hope was the Pan-Arab Republic, which has brought some semblance of calm to the area. The Communist era fascinated the historian in him. He was aware of Russia only as a great Imperial power that stretched from Europe to Asia but was far away. He likewise was amazed to learn that China, that exotic land so far distant, had become the dominant military and economic power on the world stage. In fact, he was astonished to learn about the world stage and how communications keep us instantly informed of anything, anywhere. I charged up his microchip to store all this information.

In the later part of the afternoon, I took him to the lab. He had seen the old log cabin mock-up, of course, but now he saw the full glory of a modern scientific laboratory. It was here that I taught him a quick history of energy, the Edison lightbulb,[99] and the use of electricity in the twentieth century and early twenty-first century. I showed him the pollution that resulted from the quest for oil, as well as the wars fought to maintain control of the world's natural resources. He was cheered to learn that his secretary of state, William Seward, had engineered the purchase of the vast territory of Alaska in March of 1867. While the initial thought of over $7 million made him blanch, I told him that on any given day, for well more than a century, that dollar value of minerals and oil poured into our national coffers.

Should I tell him now about space travel? Is he ready? It is getting dark out and it is almost dinnertime. I will wait. Tomorrow will be an

---

[99] In his memoirs, Edison recalls selling campaign materials on trains for the Republican Party, which was urging Lincoln's election. Edison was only thirteen at the time. (See Emil Ludwig, *Abraham Lincoln: The Full Story of Our Martyred President* [Boston: Little, Brown and Company, 1929]).

auspicious day. For supper we had a beer cheese soup, vegetable medley, a baked potato with sour cream and chives, and pullet au champignons. For dessert we had a simple chocolate cake with vanilla ice cream. After a little brandy, we retired. Tomorrow was going to be an auspicious day. (Oh, I already said that.)

Day Fifty-Six

Well, once again, tempus fugit. It was April 9. The year was 2063, or day fifty-six (and year fifty-six) for Abe. Like Abe II, he lacked the presidential beard. (More about that later. For the time being, I wanted him to look unlike all his famous images).

In the morning, we followed our usual routine—a ride in the woods and a swim. We had another splendid breakfast on the *Mary Todd*: country-fried steak; scrambled eggs; and thick, juicy bacon, washed down with apple cider made from our own trees and a rich chicory coffee with whipped cream.

"Abe," I said, "today is one of the most important days in your life and in the life of these United States. The fourteenth of April was a Friday—Good Friday, to be exact—in the 1865 calendar.[100] It was the fifty-sixth year in your life. I want to ask you a very difficult question, and these next hours might be hard for you. We will go at whatever pace you require. Let's walk up to the porch. Darius will have some lemonade and sugar cookies for us—and something stronger, too, should you require it."

I asked Abe to think about what he remembered of that evening. As with Abe II, he remembered wanting to relax a bit and take Mary out for the evening. The war was over, and it was time to breathe again. Robert did not want to join them. (No surprise there.) He recalled that they took a carriage to the popular Ford's Theatre and planned to see the play *Our American Cousin*. He recalled the patriotic banners in the

---

[100] Time is still recorded in the Gregorian system for popular use; however, since 2050 all time has been measured in astral units as well. Other cultures maintain their own time systems (e.g. Koranic time, Coptic Time, Jewish Time), but all also refer to Astral Time, the new universal measure.

theater and the acknowledgment of the crowd, relieved that the long war was over and pleased to see their commander-in-chief. Ulysses and Julia Grant were also invited, but they couldn't make it. (More about them later.) Instead the Lincolns were joined by another couple—Clara Harris and her fiancé, Henry Rathbone.[101]

Lincoln again recalled enjoying the play, but nonetheless Mary had to nudge him several times when he fell asleep and began to snore.[102] (How unpresidential!) Lincoln said he laughed out loud at several of the scenes and recalled laughing heartily before suddenly succumbing to a terrible headache. After that, the memory of Lincoln ceased to recall anything. That, of course, was because of the fatal bullet wound. This was where the genome accelerator was programmed to cease functioning.

Now, the last time around, this is where the obtuse spirit entered me and I began to invent a false history regarding subsequent events. As you recall, all of that culminated in the suicide of Abe II. I was not in such a foul mood this time, and I really wanted to see where my scientific work might lead, so I determined to be absolutely truthful with Abe III. (Well, as you know, truth with me is somewhat elastic.)

I told Abe about being carried across the street to the Petersen House and how his son Robert was summoned from the White House.[103] I conveyed to him how Mary kept going into hysterics and had to be removed from the bedroom. Soldiers were summoned to keep the crowd out of the house and under control because word of the event spread quickly. The streets around the theater were packed with the curious, both friend and foe of Lincoln. I narrated how Booth jumped to the stage, injured his leg in the fall, and shouted the infamous words "Sic semper tyrannis."[104] I spent a few moments reviewing Booth's escape

---

[101] Rathbone was stabbed by Booth during the assassination. His arm bled, and he collapsed at the Petersen House shortly after crossing the street from the theater.

[102] It's easy to understand why—he was sitting in a rocking chair and was very relaxed. This chair is now in a museum in Detroit, Michigan. Lincoln had seen Booth perform once on stage at Ford's Theatre, on November 9, 1863. The play was *The Marble Heart*. Booth had the lead. Booth's familiar presence at Ford's Theatre made it possible for him to gain entrance that fateful night.

[103] See chapter 12.

[104] These are three of the best-known words in American history.

plan; how he got caught, cornered, and shot; and how the others of his cabal failed in their efforts to assassinate Andrew Johnson and William Seward. When I finished the tale of the conspirators, ending in their hanging, Abe was pale and breathing deeply, but he asked me to continue. (One difference between the historical Lincoln and the new one was that the new one was not thin and drawn of visage. Quite the opposite, he was at a proper weight, alert, and strong in every way. I take full credit for that.)

I told him that at the Petersen House, many politicians began to show up, demanding to see for themselves. Among them was Edwin Stanton. I reviewed how the physicians kept removing blood clots from the wound, draining it, and, by probing the wound with bare fingers, probably making matters worse. In addition, some of those present began to cut small locks of Lincoln's hair for souvenirs.[105]

"Abe, you died the next morning, Saturday, April 15, 1865, at 7:22 a.m. You were only fifty-six years old—the age you have achieved as of today. You might want to know that one of the attending physicians was a Canadian-educated black surgeon.[106]

"Now one hundred ninety-eight years have passed since that event. I'd like to take a moment to let you ponder all this, and then we can continue. To help you, I have a little gift for you: your favorite poem—'Mortality.'"[107]

---

[105] Yes, it's true. Read David Chambers Mearns's *Largely Lincoln*, chapter 3, "The Scalping of Abraham Lincoln." In 1905 Teddy Roosevelt wore a ring with a lock of Lincoln's hair to his inauguration. The ring was a gift to Roosevelt from John Hay, one of Lincoln's secretaries. At his autopsy, physicians were amazed at the muscle quality and bone structure of the dead president (*sic*, Army Assistant Surgeon Edward Curtis. Others say it was Joseph Barnes.) By the way, I know that the Dallas Heritage Auctions House in early 2015 sponsored an auction of Lincoln items from the collection of Donald P. Dow. One of these hair samples and a bit of linen from the deathbed, with Lincoln's blood on it, were among the items that brought in tens of thousands of dollars. Needless to say, the folks who bought these items had no idea what could be done with them in the right hands. They need now to check their vaults!

[106] Anderson Ruffin Abbot.

[107] The author is William Knox, a descendant of Scottish reformer John Knox. Lincoln began to memorize it in the 1830s, during his melancholy days in New

I told him I would leave him on the porch for a bit to consider all that he had just learned. The accelerator had run its course for Abraham III. From now on, everything would be tabula rasa for Abe.[108] We would write the next chapters of his life together, if he allowed. I went inside, and he remained on the porch, slowly swinging back and forth, humming unknown melodies as the spring breeze blew quietly past.

At three I went back out. Abe was still in the chair, dozing lightly. I shook his shoulder and inquired whether he needed or wanted anything.

"No. No thank you, Anton. This truth is very sobering. I appreciate the truth, you know. And the poem—the poem is very comforting. It always has been for me. I read it first after Ann's death. Death seems to be my constant companion, almost my shadow self."

"Abe, there is much, much more to learn. You are a fast learner, and more importantly, you know how to put a perspective on everything. You incorporate it into yourself. You are a truly wise man, and I don't bestow compliments readily."

"Thank you. Where do we go from here?"

"I would like to take a little time yet today to go over what developed immediately after your death. I think you need to hear it today in order to keep a sequence of events in order. Then, as the next days go on, we will proceed with more of the last two hundred years of history. I will always provide you with other materials to research and to fill in the blanks spaces, and I will always be ready to answer your questions.

"You asked about Mary. As you might imagine, Mary was not mentally able to do much. Her wailing at your passing—well, you heard it often enough in your family home and the White House. Immediately after your death, Stanton is reported to have said, 'Now he belongs to the ages.'[109] Your body was taken back to the White House and placed in a casket on a hastily constructed funeral catafalque after the necessary medical procedures and cleaning took place. You might be interested in

---

Salem. See appendix B for the text.

[108] Latin for "A blank slate."

[109] Some sources say he uttered the words "Now he belongs to the angels." Whichever is true, it is a noble statement.

knowing that that funeral catafalque is still in the Capitol and has been used for the deaths of other great leaders.[110]

Your funeral took forever. Pardon me for being so bold, but the whole nation wanted to take part. There was a long vigil in Washington, DC. People lined up for miles to pass your open casket. Then a great funeral train left Washington for Philadelphia, New York, Chicago, and finally Springfield. It was opened many times so that the crowds could view their murdered leader. Once it reached Springfield, your casket was placed in a temporary resting site and moved a number of times over the years until a final mausoleum/tomb that was considered adequate and grand enough for you was completed. There were difficulties with all of this, and in 1876 someone actually tried to steal your body and hold it for ransom. The FBI foiled the plot. A quarter of a century later, in 1901, your casket was opened for a final time and was then, at Robert's instruction, encased in walls of cement about ten feet thick, never to be tampered with again.[111]

"After the assassination, when she had recovered a bit, Mary and Tad spent some time in Europe. Mary, as you know, was always a spender. When you died, your estate was valued at about $85,000, a considerable sum in those days. However, you naughty lawyer, you did not have a will!"

"Oh, Mary and money!" said Abe. "What headaches she gave me. She thought she was clever and was hiding the great amounts of her expenditures from me, but the staff was loyal to me. I knew everything. It just wasn't worth stirring up that hornets' nest with her."

"Well," I continued, "after Europe, your son Tad died in 1871. He was only eighteen. His death was probably due to tuberculosis. Robert and Mary did not get along. She grew increasingly erratic. Despite getting a government pension, for which she fought hard and won, she would walk around Chicago with thousands of dollars sewn into her gowns. Robert was trying to establish his own reputation as a lawyer,

---

[110] It has been used for presidents Garfield, McKinley, and Kennedy, among others notables.

[111] Well, almost never. I did not tell him the details of my work at Oak Ridge Cemetery.

and Mary's behavior was possibly dangerous to herself, so he had her committed temporarily to an insane asylum.[112] With her sister assisting, Mary managed to get out after only a few months and went to live with her sister in Springfield until her death in 1882. She is buried in the same mausoleum as you are, along with Willie, Eddie, and Tad. We have already spoken about Robert and his personal successes. He had three children, but his son, named after you, also died young. It seemed to be the fate of Lincoln men. So you had some grandchildren, but all their issue have now passed away, and there is no blood relative of yours left in this world."

Lincoln stopped rocking, and again I asked if he wanted some alone time. He said that would be fine and that he would join me for dinner. That evening we ate late, about eight. We ate simply: some tomato soup, some slices of sourdough bread and cheese and German sausage, lots of cider, and ice cream for dessert. (He needed something good at this point.)

"Anton, I believe you," Abe said. "As I told you, after my headache, I remember nothing. You are telling me, I believe, that I was quite dead and now am quickened?"

"Yes. Exactly. It is the year 2063, as I told you. You have seen many of the technological and scientific developments that have taken place in all these years. There is much, much more, but I don't think this late hour is the time to discuss it. Let's continue in the morning."

"I understand and I agree. Good night, Anton."

"Good night, Mr. President."

Day Fifty-Seven

Abe retired to his new room in the mansion, and I retreated to my study. I wanted to think through clearly what to tell him, how to tell him, how much to tell him, and so on. I did not want another Abe II on my hands, although with the truth, the real truth, he seemed to comprehend and accept it all just fine.

The next day, it rained. A late spring thunderstorm threatened to

---

[112] It stood at Bellevue Place in Batavia, Illinois.

spawn a tornado. Abe sat on the porch and watched until the wind blew the rain too hard and he began getting wet. I invited him to come with me to the barn-become-laboratory. I began to explain to him how he came back into existence. I didn't focus on too much technical detail; in fact, I avoided it altogether. It would have been beyond him. He said he never knew much about medicine or science but was not surprised there had been considerable advances. He expressed regret that none of this miracle medicine was available to the soldiers who were so badly injured in battle, or for his two boys. (Abe II had said the same. There was a remarkable consistency to this man as well as to the revivification experience.)

I showed him the various devices that were part of my scientific work. Just in case, I once again had dismantled and hidden sections of the accelerator. That was my real contribution to this effort. I informed him that his prior body, indeed, was still in its coffin in the mausoleum at Oak Ridge Cemetery. I also assured him that this new body was his, truly his, and that he was truly himself, 100 percent, and no other. I made a cursory report to him about medical science since his time: the awful realities of the Civil War battlefield and its primitive medicines, the discovery of x-rays, the great contribution of the Scotsman Alexander Fleming and his discovery of penicillin, and the eradication of polio, measles, chicken pox, mumps, diphtheria, whooping cough, and most forms of cancer and diabetes. He was astonished at the possibility of limb replacements and organ transplants. He joked that he had suffered with bad feet most of his life and wouldn't mind a new pair. I told him that the kinds of shoes made now, which he was wearing, eliminate virtually all foot pain and podiatric disease. When I told him that most people born in this century would live to be one hundred, he asked if he would make that century mark. I told him truthfully that I rather doubted it since the building blocks of his physical life were given to him in the nineteenth century. He just nodded. I was glad, relieved even, that he accepted his new life with such calm.

That was a long day with a lot of education. The next day was much the same. We reviewed US history in some detail and world history in general as it related to our own national interests during the decades. There would be plenty of time for him to catch up on details, should he be interested. I told him how his successor, Andrew Johnson, was a leader almost doomed to failure from the beginning. The opportunity to take advantage of a true leadership void gave many of Lincoln's foes the opening they needed to try to reverse his policies—especially his promise of charity and common sense in the work of reconstruction. He was appalled at what happened to the South and amazed that it was almost a century later, under the Civil Rights Act of a Texan-become-president, Lyndon Johnson, that at least in law (but not always in peoples' hearts) the African American people of the entire United States gained equal rights and the right to vote. (In his lifetime, Lincoln had also advocated for women to vote. He would have been a favorite during the suffrage era.)

He was thrilled that Grant became president but saddened by the corruption that surrounded his administration. He was very much taken by the whole saga of Teddy Roosevelt. The First World War saddened him, and he had an admiration for Woodrow Wilson and his peace efforts. He didn't quite grasp the way that the world was already at that time becoming more and more interdependent and why we had to fight on foreign soil. The Great Depression saddened him deeply, but he commented that life for most Americans then was rather like the simple life he knew until his maturity as a politician and lawyer. World War II brought similar questions to his mind about the role of the United States on the world stage. That so many lives were lost and that the theaters of operation were so vast staggered him. He had a lot of respect for the presidency of Franklin Roosevelt. I played several of Roosevelt's speeches for him, especially his first inaugural address, which includes the famous line "The only thing we have to fear is fear itself."[113] He also had an admiration for the tough-minded spirit of Harry Truman. I asked if he thought he would have dropped the atomic bomb in order to end the Civil War, had such a device been available. He just looked at me and asked for another glass of cider.

He enjoyed listening to the speeches of John Fitzgerald Kennedy but did not think too highly of his wealthy background and aristocratic companions and ways. He was, however, deeply saddened at the image

---

[113] The speech was delivered in 1933, during the worst days of the Depression.

of the assassination of another young US president, and he felt especially sorry for his wife and children.

The 1960s fascinated him. The kinds of political activism that characterized the era cheered him. It was a republic at work, in his opinion. He laughed at the hippie movement and caught on quickly to the problems that the drug culture would produce for the next three generations.

The Vietnam War was another question mark for him. It was obvious that the idea of fighting on such distant soils continued to be puzzling, but he was beginning to catch on to the way the world was shrinking. I tried to avoid the technological pieces that were part of these decades, wanting to save them for another day. We went over the brief presidencies of Richard Nixon and Jimmy Carter. He couldn't believe an actor was elected president when we reached Ronald Reagan's eight years. (Lincoln knew only of stage acting. I had not shown him film yet.) He was unimpressed with George Herbert Walker Bush and disgusted at the behavior of Bill Clinton, although he saw that his administration was relatively effective.

I stopped there for the day. We had a nice dinner on the *Mary Todd*. The rain had stopped, and the spring smells were almost intoxicating. Fish were actually jumping in the river. Darius and Darren made walleye encrusted in potato, fresh asparagus with Hollandaise sauce, and a light dessert of small pieces of fruit flamed in cognac.

Day Fifty-Eight

Day fifty-eight dawned picture perfect. Birds were chirping, rabbits were chasing about the yard, and the morning dew was melting away as the sun rose. We breakfasted on the porch. I asked Abe if he slept well, and he responded that indeed he had. I asked whether he was ready for another day, promising it would be a little less intense—a bit of a breather. He appreciated that.

We returned to the laboratory. I had Darius obtain some films from the twentieth and early twenty-first centuries. They had all been transferred to the newest microdigital projection format, but the stories would be interesting. I began the day's instruction with a catch-up of the Industrial Revolution; the South retained much of its agricultural economy while the North invested fully in technology. Great factories were built. Immigrants from Germany and Ireland and Italy continued to pour into the country at the Eastern Seaboard. I showed him a photo of the Statue of Liberty and the famous poem at its base. Lincoln was very moved but at the same time understood that there would be tensions between these newcomers and those who had been part of the nation's founding experience. I showed him photos of New York tenements—homes to the Irish, Italians, and Jews. I also showed him images of Alabama cottages where black people—free but economically and politically subjugated—lived in crowded, fearful places.

He loved the invention of the airplane and said he would like to ride in one. He was disappointed to learn that they no longer existed. Ever since the outlawing of fossil fuels in all but the most backward parts of the world, airplanes weren't flying. The hover industry, using vector power, had taken over.[114] I showed him those early films of the Wright Brothers' adventure at Kitty Hawk, then the development of passenger planes, jets, and finally spacecraft. He watched the famous film of Neil Armstrong exiting his spaceship and setting foot on the moon. He asked to see it several times. I told him about the recent return of the Mars crew. He was slack-jawed, marveling at what had been accomplished. I had Darius bring the manual typewriter out and then showed him how computers had developed.

I then asked him to touch the top of his head, slightly to one side. He winced. I explained to him, "This is the spot where the bullet entered you on April 14, 1865. It is sore now because a few nights ago I implanted in your skull one of the microchips that every child now receives at birth. I have controlled the type and amount of information

---

[114] This, in fact, was a source of my fortune. I invested heavily in it when younger. This and my invention of the fibertron made me a billionaire several times over. Fibertron replaced plastic. With the increase in the mean temperature because of fossil fuel emissions (finally proven and accepted in 2045), the production of all plastics was universally outlawed. Among other things, landfills were spontaneously combusting as the hotter weather cooked the plastic waste of the twentieth century.

available to you, but soon you will be caught up. I didn't want to give you everything too quickly."

He reached up and touched his head again. Again he gave a slight wince. He just looked at me. I told him that this was enough for today's new information but that we could now have some relaxation and fun. It was raining again, so we couldn't ride or swim, but I had a number of classic films that I thought he would enjoy and would fill in some of the empty places and answer some of his questions. The boys joined us.

First I reviewed something he was familiar with—photography. Then we quickly went to more sophisticated and quicker cameras; the toy darling of the twenty-first century, cell phone cameras; how our friend Edison had invented moving pictures, and the advent of sound in film. I also introduced Abe to popcorn.[115] He loved it smothered with melted butter (not a butter substitute but the real thing). I also gave him his first Coca-Cola, but he didn't like it and asked for some cider. (My kind of man.) We spent the afternoon enjoying ourselves. Now, you know, I don't ever actually enjoy myself, but this I was enjoying. Abe was great company. We watched *The Wizard of Oz*, *Gone with the Wind*, *How the West Was Won*, *The Birth of a Nation*, *My Darling Clementine*, *Duck Soup*, *Lawrence of Arabia*, *Jaws*, *Psycho*, *Schindler's List*, *Ben Hur*, *The Grapes of Wrath*, *The Maltese Falcon*, and *All Quiet on the Western Front*. We ate a lot of popcorn, took a few breaks in between films, took a couple of naps, and very much enjoyed watching these classics. No one wanted to take a long break or have a big meal, so I had the boys introduce Abe to another couple of American standards- licorice whips, nachos and cheese, and pizza. He loved it all. His appetite was good.

I asked whether he was ready to quit, but he said no. "One more please."

I thought carefully about it. There were thousands to choose from, but I selected two more. We watched Henry Fonda in *Young Mr. Lincoln*

---

[115] Popcorn has been around in various ways for hundreds of years, but the kind we know and love was popularized by Charles Cretors in 1885 with the invention of the kettle popping machine. Although movie theaters now have completely new technologies for showing their creative efforts, any theaters that want to make money still appeal to the American nostalgia for the smell and sound of popcorn in a theater. By the way, all this creativity took place in Chicago.

(1939). Abe asked whether or not he really sounded like that. I said, "No!" Then we watched the last film, the 2012 *Lincoln*, starring Daniel Day-Lewis and Sally Field. It is hard to imagine what it must be like to see yourself portrayed by others and to see your story told in ways that aren't quite what you remember—and Abe's memory was prodigious.

At the end of our marathon, he sat back in his rocker. Furrows knotted his forehead as he rocked slowly back and forth, poured another cider, and said, "Thank you. This is remarkable. I need to sit a spell and ponder all this."

I left him to his own devices for the rest of that day. He asked later at dinner if he could see more of such wonders, and I assured him that he could spend the rest of his days doing so without watching all that had been filmed, be it comedy, tragedy, history, or science fiction. He did say he didn't particularly care to see any more films about himself. Filled with popcorn and cider, our dinner was hot dogs and potato chips—and more cider. Then we sank into a well-deserved sleep.

The Next Day

Lincoln was a sponge when it came to learning history. He could not get enough of it and could not get it quickly enough. After our usual routine, we sat on the *Mary Todd*. It was rocking gently in the morning, providing a soothing, calming feeling. I began where I had left off.

"Abe, the growth of wealthy nations in Europe and our own great wealth in the United States were accompanied by many social problems. Within our society, there was increased poverty despite the great wealth. There were problems with new addictions. Just as you knew alcoholism, and it is still with us, there came new ways to get peoples' money and to make their lives miserable: the creation of artificial medicines called drugs. Used with proper medical direction, these were marvelous balms for human ailments, but in the hands of the unscrupulous, they became the scourge of our people—especially young people. It continues to this day.

"Besides this, there were groups of anarchists, as you called them, or terrorists, as we call them. They are dedicated to the destruction of those things that they do not have or do not approve of. Most of their activity is directed against innocent civilians. It is a new type of warfare. On September 11, 2001, three attacks were launched against the United States by terrorists from the Middle East, from countries that did not exist in your time. Airplanes flew into the great Twin Towers in New York, instantly killing thousands of people. Another plane flew into the military headquarters in Washington, DC—a building called the Pentagon after its architectural shape. Hundreds died there. Another plane, which was aimed for the White House, was taken over by the passengers when they realized what was happening. It crashed in a field in Pennsylvania. The United States realized that it was vulnerable in all ways and in all places. A huge effort was made to try to secure our citizens both here and abroad. (I showed him historical news clips of those events.) This effort continues to the present day. Ground wars were launched in the countries thought to harbor the terrorists or to pose a threat to our allies or us. Those wars ended, finally, in 2020, but the global effort to keep fighting these kinds of insurgencies continues.

"Great strides were made in the 2020s. Under the leadership of Germany, Great Britain, China, Russia, and the United States, a new map was drawn in the Middle East—a map that respected the ancient tribal boundaries and leaderships that have held sway in that part of the world for thousands of years. While not perfect, it is the first time since the fall of the Ottoman Empire there was some kind of stability in that part of the world. It was far superior to the quick initiative of the group called the United Nations after World War II.

"It was during that time as well that the federal leadership in the United States came to understand that it was unrealistic and counterproductive to expect one person to oversee the administration of government. It just became too complex. That was when our current system of a triumvirate was created. It is not perfect, and the struggles to amend the Constitution to bring it about were formidable, but I don't think anyone would choose to do otherwise. In fact, only Russia and China still operate with only one leader, and the administrations of those countries are floundering."

"This is all remarkable. It is a lot. It is sad and hopeful all at the same time. Anton, I have some questions."

"Shoot!"

Lincoln blanched and looked quickly left and right and asked, "Where? Where is the shooter?"

"Abe, relax. It is just a colloquialism meaning 'proceed.'"

Lincoln sat there, and a smirk appeared on his face. He slapped his knee with his right hand and guffawed, "Gotcha!"

Indeed he did. His great sense of humor was revealing itself.

"I do have some real questions," he said. "First, when can I leave this property? I am beginning to feel like a hog in a gunny sack."

"Of course. Let's take just a couple more days to learn and relax. Then we can leave. I would prefer that we do so somewhat secretly. You will learn and see and experience much more if you can remain anonymous for a while. I thought perhaps we could begin with New Salem, Chicago, and then Springfield. Is that acceptable?"

"That would be great. Second question: Can you bring Tad back to life?"

"Abe, that is not possible." (I lied here. I just didn't want to do it. At least not yet.) "The process that made your new life possible was a once-and-for-all event. That is why I chose carefully whom I would use for this experiment."

I reviewed for Abe my time at Ford's Theatre as an usher and the bit of bloodstained clothing that I "borrowed." I told him that it was the availability of the much-needed blood that made this experiment possible and that to attempt another redivivus I would have to dig up dead bodies. I assured him I could not participate in such an activity. It would be macabre. It would be unethical (shades of Madison, not to mention hypocrisy!).

"I see," said Abe. "I understand. I don't grasp all the science of it, but I respect your expertise and your moral posture. But it would have been nice. I do so miss my boys. My third question: Can I watch another moving picture?"

I smiled. "Of course. I'll have Darius get something for us to eat, and then we can spend the rest of the day relaxing. By the way, Abe, have you noticed you don't need your blue pills anymore?"

"Yes, I was wondering about that. It's wonderful not having to take those wretched things."

"Well, science, medicine and health have all progressed. I think that the diet you are now observing has taken away your illness."

"Just another thing for which I sincerely thank you, kind sir. Now, let's watch those moving pictures!"

We settled in for an afternoon of Laurel-and-Hardy films. Abe's laughter at the slapstick was contagious, and we had a splendid afternoon. The next days passed with lots of review, discussion, political opining, and movie watching. Finally I thought we were ready to go off the property and see what might happen.

CHAPTER 16

Stepping Out

Abe had been very patient, but I could see signs of restlessness. He had stayed on the estate now for quite a time since he reached that most special fifty-sixth day/year.

He enjoyed his riding, his wood splitting, his reading, and our evening conversations, but he was too intelligent to be coddled much longer. Months passed.

It was a Wednesday afternoon when I finally asked him, "Abe, would you like to start venturing out into the wider world?"

He replied, "Sir, I would very much appreciate that."

I responded, "Very well, then. Tomorrow we will take our first adventure. You have learned well how much the world has changed since 1856, and the world right around us is no exception. Rural Illinois is still quiet and beautiful. To be honest with you, I don't think we should go too public yet.[116] I have an idea that I hope you will find acceptable. Let's get up early and ride to New Salem. It is only about eight miles from here, and we can get there and back in a long day. I'll have the boys pack some lunch for us."

"Anton, that would be thoroughly enjoyable."

Stepping Out to New Salem

That night I asked the boys to get the horses ready and to prepare a picnic lunch for us. Early the next morning, just at the break of dawn, we ate a hearty breakfast of flapjacks with maple syrup (yes, from the estate), bacon (yes, from pigs from the estate), and dark, rich coffee

---

[116] Honesty—a rather rare occurrence for me.

(Jamaican Blue Mountain Coffee). A hearty side dish of grits topped off the meal.

We walked to the garage (which had been converted into a horse barn), and the boys were there with saddles on the horses and two rucksacks of vittles. I asked them to surprise us with the meal, knowing they would be clever.

We took a slow trot down to the Sangamon River. I thought it would be safer to travel off the road, where many rural equestrians still enjoyed their leisurely rides. There were horse trails through the woods as well, but they were often populated. It was a time of day when we ought to be able to remain relatively unseen.

The rising sun filtered through the trees. Mourning doves announced our intrusion, and an occasional fox peered out from a lair to see what the commotion was. The river was rather low that season. There had not been much snow or rain in the winter or spring months. All of this was the aftermath of climate change. The trail was quite dry, but hard-compacted, so there was little dust getting kicked up by the horses.

I had wanted to wear a "riding to the hounds" outfit given to me many years ago by Percy Pettigrew, but it would be a tad ostentatious in Sangamon County. Instead I wore riding boots, a pair of old jeans (hard to come by in my closet), a red-checkered flannel shirt, a heavy sweatshirt bearing the logo of Oxford University (which read '*Dominus Illuminatio Mea*'), and a hunting hat.[117]

Abraham, at my continued request, had not yet grown his beard back. Two generations ago, his height would have proved a visible liability to any hope for anonymity, but by this time most adult men averaged six foot three to six foot four, so Abe would not stand out. I had obtained some old clothing from a resale shop in Springfield so he would have suitable attire for the adventure—nothing too extraordinary. The last thing I wanted was publicity. It was not yet time for that. This outing was a favor to Abe. There was, of course, the possibility that he would try to escape from me. I hoped his integrity would prevent that, but one can never be too careful. Before retiring that night, I programmed his implanted microchip so that if he ever got more than twenty feet

---

[117] The logo's text means "God is my light."

away from me, he would suffer a debilitating headache and collapse. (Fortunately, it proved unnecessary. He was truly a man of his word.)

I had obtained a pair of nonprescription sunglasses for him, thinking that they might add to his anonymity, but he looked too ridiculous. Instead we arranged for a rather large, floppy hat that cast a shadow over his face. He only had to have it on if he wanted to, other than when we were at New Salem itself.

He was rather proud of his outfit: heavy boots of tooled leather, baggy black corduroy pants, a loose fitting flannel shirt (Republican red), a jacket with a removable liner, and, of course, that hat. All of this was worn over his comfortable, familiar skivvies.

We did have one minor, interesting comical incident. The pants, obtained at the same retail store as my outfit, had a zipper. Abe had never seen a zipper before and didn't know what to do with it.[118] He asked me for help, but there was no way I would do anything other than demonstrate on my own pants how the zipper worked. Zippers, you see, were still fashionable in this day and age. For a time, a return to the button fly made a hit, but it could not compete with the incomparable reliability of the zipper.

Once shown how to use it, Abe enjoyed pulling it up and down a few times. Finally, when I showed him the jacket with the removable liner, he moved from his pants to the jacket and toyed with the zipper all during our ride, an enormous smile illuminating his face.

The morning air was invigorating. The horses were eager to stretch their winter muscles as much as Abe was eager to stretch his mind.

---

[118] Elias Howe, the man who invented the sewing machine, patented a clumsy initial form of the zipper in 1851. He called it an "automatic continuous clothing closure." In 1893 Whitcomb Judson introduced a more contemporary form of the zipper at the Chicago World's Fair, but it did not catch on (get the joke?). In 1917, one of Judson's employees, Gideon Sundback, perfected the zipper as we know it. It still did not become popular. In 1923, Goodyear introduced a new winter overshoe and called the useful fastener "a zipper." We have had the term ever since. It took the French, of course, those connoisseurs of fashion, to proclaim it acceptable. That was 1937—and the rest is history.

Speaking of patents, Abe used to enjoy visiting the patent office during the Civil War. His usual companion was Tad.

We made our way along the narrow trail, following the contour of the meandering river. Property owners along both shores had long since allowed the public to have access to this bridle path.

Abe held the reins of his horse in one hand and joyfully pulled his jacket zipper up and down while whistling a tune unknown to me. For my part, it was a splendid day, and seeing Abe so happy made me actually feel some giddiness. All was going well.

We were set to be at New Salem by late morning. We stopped once to give the horses a chance to drink from the river and to give us a chance to relieve ourselves of the morning's coffee. Abe stayed within the prescribed distance and came back with a big grin on his face. That man really liked zippers!

Lincoln the Surveyor—Statue at New Salem State Park
(photo by the author)

We sat under one of the great hickory trees and opened our rucksacks to see what the boys had prepared for us. We pulled out some beef jerky—a great trail snack. Abe started to go to the river to get a drink, but I had to warn him away from that water. Great strides had been made in cleaning up the environment, but drinking water from a river outside of a protected national park was an invitation to disaster. It was not so much a problem for the horses or wildlife but remained hazardous to people.

I pulled out a styrothermos—one of the lesser inventions of the century, but it kept hot things hot and cold things cold. We drank the mineral water the boys had provided. I could hardly wait until Abe saw a drinking fountain at New Salem!

We mounted again and led the horses through the brush along the narrow trail. No one else was out, which made the going easier and relieved me of the worry that someone might recognize Abe. It would be difficult enough at the state park known as New Salem. I would try to keep him away from any prying eyes. We trotted a bit, and then, when the park was in sight, I asked Abe to stop for a moment. I had to give him a little history lesson before we got to New Salem. We stopped about a half mile from the park. While the horses drank more refreshment from the Sangamon River, I took time to chat with Abe.

"Abe, do you remember much about New Salem?"

"Oh, yes indeed. It was a rather typical pioneer village. It was unusual only in that there was only one so-called public house. The rest was the usual assortment of small business places. It was not a farming village but a want-to-be town. The founder was James Rutledge. I think he came there around 1828 and built a gristmill.

"I had a lot of jobs there, like a number of fellows my age. I think I was twenty-two when I left home and moved to New Salem. We were young men about town, eager to make our mark on the world and to find our way to fortune. I worked hard there doing a little bit of everything. I tended a store. I partnered in a store. I was a boatman and, for a bit, the postmaster. To be honest, I wasn't much of a success at any of those jobs. Somewhere in there I even became a soldier, fighting in the Black Hawk War. Actually, I never even fought, but I was elected leader of the squad, probably because the other soldiers knew they would be able to get away with a lot with me in charge. It was a motley group, but I enjoyed it all."

Indeed he did! While he was not a success at business, he was a success at people. Everyone liked Abe. It was during these years that he garnered the material for his famous stories. That man could entertain. In the early part of the twenty-first century, he could have made a success of himself as a stand-up comic.

"Abe, tell me more." He was eager to continue.

"Well, I once went on a flatboat down the Sangamon to the Mississippi, all the way to New Orleans. That was the first place I ever saw a slave market. I knew better than to say anything in that place, but I certainly took a lot of time over the years remembering the misery of those people.

"I left New Salem in 1837. It was clear I wasn't going to do much there that I hadn't tried already. I took my chances and moved myself to Springfield. It was nearby. It was busy. It was already the state capital. I had my eyes fixed on becoming a lawyer, and I did so. Can we go on now?"

We saddled up again and continued. We followed the trail along the river. Fortunately the folks at the park are accustomed to an occasional equestrian visitor, so no one thought twice about the two tall men hitching their horses to the old post.

We climbed up the riverbank near the site of the gristmill. A highway from the earlier part of the century marked the other side of the river, its concrete ribbon scarring the countryside. Abe looked about slowly, intently. He was puzzled.

I queried, "What's wrong?" (I knew, of course, what the problem was. The village was a reconstruction. It was rather accurate; only someone who knew firsthand what was originally there would notice. Abe noticed.)

He responded, "I feel like I am in a dream. Everything looks familiar, yet different. For example, the cooper shop looks just fine, but everything else is just a little strange to my eyes."

Bull's-eye! He had it exactly. The cooper shop had been moved away and then moved back to New Salem. Every other building was a reconstruction, and Abe caught on immediately.

We walked along the paths, which had been worn down by tourists. It was a quiet day, and we avoided the visitor center. Abe would go into a house or a shop and just stand there looking, taking in, and remembering. Now he became the teacher. (I didn't need to be taught, but Abe needed to teach.) He went on about families he knew and families whose lives he had shared, just as he had shared space at their tables. Tales began to spill out of him, and a vivid portrait of pioneer life sprang out of his words. We toured the whole site and, as I mentioned, carefully avoided the visitor center. A few other folks wandered about, chatting loudly and only glancing at the world that helped to create the man Abraham Lincoln, who was touring, incognito, in their midst.

Abe said, "You know, I am surprised that anyone bothered with this place. I had only been in Springfield about three years when everyone left New Salem. The Sangamon just wasn't big enough to handle steamboats, and that was the up-and-coming mode of conveyance for people and for trade. I thought everyone would forget about the place."

"Abe," I said, "people did not forget about you. None of this would be here if it were not for you. Anything that was part of your life became a part of your heritage and your myth. You will see more of that as time goes on."

Well, not everything in pioneer days was fun.
(photo by Misty Garfield)

"Anton, a favor, please. Can we go to the Old Concord Burial Ground?"

I knew why he wanted to go there. He wanted to visit Ann's grave.

Biographers of Lincoln have argued for more than fifteen decades about the exact relationship that Abraham had with Ann Rutledge. She was the daughter of James Rutledge, one of the founders of New Salem. There was no kind of photography yet, so no image of her exists. No known portrait exists either. In pioneer Illinois, even boys seldom attended any kind of formal school, much less girls. Lincoln himself is an example of that reality, so it is all the more remarkable that Ann did attend classes in the small school established in New Salem by Mentor Graham.

Lincoln boarded at the Rutledge tavern. Ann, despite being very young, was often its hostess and caretaker. No doubt she saw this tall, angular young man sitting near candle and kerosene lamps, reading books about the law. She was engaged, sort of, to another. John MacNamar had started another general store in the town, and in 1832 he left to visit his family in New York. Ann corresponded with him, but eventually things went silent and she never heard from him again, so she turned her attentions to young Lincoln. Exactly how deep their relationship went will never be known—except now Abe himself can tell us and unravel one of history's secrets.

"Abe," I said, "Ann Rutledge was buried, as you know, in the Old Concord Burial Ground, but long after your own death, her body was moved to another place in Petersburg. In 1890 her body was exhumed and placed in a new grave. There is an old marker at the original site, but I think it is Ann you wish to visit, not a piece of stone. Am I correct?"

"Yes. Let's go."

We walked back down to the river. It was not a far ride to Petersburg, so I suggested we eat a little something first, but Abe demurred. I understood. He was anxious. Our ride was silent. Abe was deep in thought. We followed the Volksmarch Trail as far as we could. Once we were just outside Petersburg, I suggested we tether the horses and continue on foot. Unlike the state park, horses in Petersburg would be out of place, even though the town was small. Abe agreed. We walked about a mile and a half into the town and then up to Oakland Cemetery.

It wasn't a large cemetery, and it would have taken a while to find that special, single grave, but Ann's grave was fenced off, and there was a granite monument marking it. It was badly weathered but legible.

Fenced area marking the grave of Ann Rutledge, Oakland Cemetery, Petersburg, Illinois. (photo by the author)

Abe stood quietly in front of it for some time. I did not disturb him. He went closer to the granite marker, which had been weathered by time and was covered with moss, and read the inscription, which includes lines from Edgar Lee Masters.[119]

---

[119] Yes, this is the same Edgar Lee Masters who penned *Spoon River Anthology*. He is another biographer of Lincoln. His book *Lincoln: The Man* is quite unflattering. At one time he was a law partner of Clarence Darrow. He was born in 1868 and

Out of me unworthy and unknown
The Vibrations of deathless music
With malice toward none and charity toward all
Out of me, forgiveness of millions toward millions
And the beneficent face of a nation
Shining with justice and truth
I am Ann Rutledge who sleeps beneath these weeds
Beloved of Abraham Lincoln
Wedded to him, not through union
But through separation
Bloom forever, oh Republic
From the dust of my bosom.

Abe rubbed away the moss, as much as possible, and ran his hand over the chiseled letters over and over. I think he was memorizing the words—some of them, of course, his very own.

We left that place of quiet and retraced our steps through the town and back to our horses. It was midafternoon, and we needed to begin our ride back. We alternated our pace, cantering a bit and trotting a bit, and then, when Tadwil was in sight, we galloped. The horses loved it, and I think it gave Abe a bit of therapy for the emotion of the day.

I knew Abe was prone to melancholy, and this was one of the kinds of events that could well trigger it. Unknown to him, I had the boys always placing small amounts of Zimopro in his food. It is a form of antidepressant similar to the more primitive drug Prozac. It kept Lincoln in balance, and I didn't worry so much about Lincoln III's fate matching that of Lincoln II.

I told him that I would respect his need for privacy and would have the boys deliver some corn chowder, muffins, and coffee to him in about an hour. Myself—I was famished and ate roast squab stuffed with apricots, grilled cauliflower with brown butter, and a stuffed baked potato.

The next day, Abe was up at the usual time; and after some morning

---

died in 1950. He is buried in the same cemetery as Ann Rutledge—Oakland Cemetery in Petersburg, Illinois.

exercise, we met on the porch of my house. I figured I might as well be as direct with him as possible. I boldly asked him about Ann Rutledge. He settled back in his rocker, took a long swig of lemonade, and began speaking.

"I did love her. She was pretty and had blue eyes and auburn hair. She had a great laugh, which she bestowed most graciously upon me, especially considering my attempts to woo a girl were as awkward as my dangling limbs.

"She was intelligent—especially gifted at arithmetic—and she liked to read. Books were scarce in New Salem, as you might imagine. If either of us got one, we shared it—except the law books. She took little interest in that.

"She was a tiny thing, especially compared to me. I'd guess she was about five foot two or three, surely no more. We made an odd couple when we walked together through the village. Tongues wagged, of course, because she was more or less betrothed to John MacNamar, but there was a kind of inverse ratio of her greater attentions to me as the attention from him diminished. I might well have married her, but as you know, she died. The typhoid got her, like it got many of the people of Illinois in the summer of 1835. She struggled to overcome it, but there was so little of her to begin with. She died on August 25, 1835, a mere twenty-two years old. I sulked for a long time. She was the second woman I loved who died; the first was Nancy Hanks, of course—my maw."

"Abe," I asked, "did you ever stop loving her?"

He answered, "No. Not really. Oh, don't get me wrong. I loved my Mary dearly. I truly did. She could be a challenging and difficult woman, it is true, and I was always faithful to her, but I never forgot that sweet little Ann of New Salem."

The truth is that Lincoln went into a severe depression at Ann's death. It was the first truly public sign of this part of his personality that would haunt him throughout his life. Mentor Graham, the schoolmaster of New Salem, helped him through the event when Lincoln admitted he was contemplating suicide. Supposedly Graham said, "God has another purpose for you."

A later biographer of Lincoln quotes longtime friend of Lincoln

Isaac Cogdal. Supposedly, after Lincoln was first elected, he asked Abe about Ann. As a close friend, he would have known something about their relationship. Abe is reported to have responded thus: "It is true-true indeed I did. I loved the woman dearly and soundly: she was a handsome girl-would have made a good loving wife ... I did honestly and truly love the girl and think often – often of her now."[120]

The depression was real enough. There is conjecture that the "poem" that Abe II left in the typing machine had actually been composed by Lincoln several years after Ann's death—a sign of just how long his melancholy stretched.[121]

I took a bold step and asked Abe whether or not he actually was the author of the lamentation. He just looked at me, smiled, and then turned away, lost in his own thoughts.

I told him about the controversy over the relationship, especially the writings of another longtime friend and his law partner, William Herndon. Herndon wrote that Lincoln never got over Ann and never really loved Mary.

Abe responded, "It is true that I never got over Ann. There was always a place for her in my heart, but not in my life. Mary and the boys and the Union were the centers of my life. William never liked Mary, and Mary never much took to William either. I suspect the animosity was mutual. Perhaps with me out of the picture to make any corrections, he took advantage of the situation in order to hurt Mary. Leastways, that's what I suspect."

With that he took another swig of lemonade and rocked back and forth on the porch with a knowing Mona Lisa–like smile on his face.

Our first venture turned out just fine.

Stepping Out to Chicago

The next morning, we met on the front porch. It was a cloudy day, promising some much-needed rain. A light wind was blowing, and the smell of the rain perfumed the air. We had a little coffee (actually we had

---

[120] Donald David Herbert, *Lincoln* (New York: Touchstone, 1995), 57–58.

[121] The text of the poem is in appendix A.

some chicory coffee—a blend sent up from New Orleans) and reviewed yesterday's activities. Abe was deeply grateful for the chance to stretch his legs and his mind and his memory. He asked when we might go out again. I told him that if he'd like, in two days' time we could go to Chicago. I thought it would be a little safer trip. Abe had been there frequently during his political career, but there were none of the more deeply personal experiences of his life attached to a Chicago visit, as there had been in New Salem.

I had been making more and more information available to him, and he absorbed everything he read. He preferred reading to the visual experiences that dominated education in the present, a sign of his long-ago background. I gave him a lot of material on the history of the United States. I did make available an ancient edition of D. W. Griffith's *The Birth of a Nation*, that provocative early commentary on American life. He had already seen the film; now he wanted to read the book. Abe was appalled in reading and viewing to see what had happened to the South in the aftermath of the Civil War. The reconstruction plans that he hoped to make a reality in his second term never happened. Instead, the worst took place. The lack of civil rights and of human decency, and especially the activities of the Ku Klux Klan, deeply disturbed his moral compass. He knew that reconstruction would not be easy, and just as war plans were complicated and controversial, so would the rebuilding of the South take twists and turns, but he never foresaw what did take place and continued to take place legally into the middle of the twentieth century and morally still occurred.

His curiosity was insatiable. I charged him with taking in more on the civil rights movement, including viewing *Mississippi Burning* and reading the speeches of Dr. Martin Luther King Jr. [122] Those concerns were the meat of our discussions during those days. He was amazed that the Democratic president from the South, Lyndon Johnson, was the outspoken advocate and muscle behind the legal changes that marked

---

[122] The great text of Dr. King's speech should be read in the context of Lincoln's amazement at the lack of progress that had been made in the century since his assassination.

life in the 1960s and 1970s. He had little time or sympathy for the hippie movement—a phenomenon beyond his comprehension.

Along with the civil rights information came all the history of the presence of the United States in Southeast Asia. He understood the controversies about policy because he had endured much of the same during his years in office. He was amazed at the energy of young Americans and their commitment to causes, but he was deeply saddened again by the development and growth of the drug culture that plagued the country as well during those heady years.

"Abe," I said, "Would you like to go to Chicago on our next outing? We won't be able to do it horseback. Even in your previous life, you wouldn't have done that. We can take a hovercar. It will be easier and will save a lot of time. You surely know that the Chicago of 1860 and the Chicago of the 2060s are considerably different. I will show you a print that advertised the first Republican National Convention.

He asked for some money since we were going "to town." I had to laugh. Up to this point, Abe had neither needed any money nor asked about it. Well, that had to come to an end. I wanted him to feel some independence. I took time to explain a few things to him.

"Abe," I explained, "first, you will be honored, I think, to know that on the centennial of your birth, the US mint issued a penny coin with your image on it as a way to honor you. The penny stopped being used in 2020, as its value was so immaterial, but collectors keep them. Let me show you one."

I went into the armoire in the women's parlor, opened the middle drawer, pulled out a framed set of the now useless coins, and extracted a shiny Lincoln penny and handed it to him. It was a 2009 issue—two hundred years since his birth and one hundred years since the first Lincoln penny.

He held it as if it might explode. Then he turned it over in his large hand several times, his head tilting to catch the image of his face from every angle. A great smile broke out, and he chortled, "Well, at least this ugly face of mine was good for something! And you said that the penny was worthless!" He laughed up a storm.

"Well, Abe, there's more!" I said. The US Department of the Treasury also decided to put your face on a five-dollar paper note. Those, too, are now collectors' items, but in its time, it filled many a pocket."

I handed him a five-dollar treasury note. This, too, he examined carefully, stretching it out and viewing it from both sides.

"I hope," he quipped, "the fellow who drew that image didn't get hanged!"

I explained to Abe how the modern currency system worked. One has a bank account inscribed in the microchip implanted in the head. The banks keep track automatically of earnings and expenditures. When someone wants to purchase anything, one simply imprints an index fingerprint on the seller's device, whichever form it might take. I wanted to place some money into Abe's account, since he had none, so our conversation continued.

"Abe, I think we will have to invent a pseudonym for you. It is too soon in our adventures to let you use your real name. Your face, even without the beard, is sufficiently famous to have you "come out" before the world is ready. Someone once told me that the best way to do this is to take the name of your first pet as your given name and the street where you grew up as your family name."

Abe started to laugh, slapping his knee, guffawing, chortling, chuckling, roaring, howling, and in general cracking up.

I summoned all my immense intelligence and asked, "What's up?"

He said, "Oh, Anton, if we do that, I would be Honey Backwoodsfarm!"

"You're right!" I said, and I joined in the merriment.

"How about this—we'll take your wife's maiden name, Todd, and join it to the street in Springfield where you lived. That would make you Todd Jackson; it's an altogether acceptable name."

Abe thought that was just fine, and so we prepared for our next outing. I made a deposit of $500 NAD into the new account of Todd Jackson, and we were almost ready to go.

I showed him the pictures of Chicago then and now.

"Are you sure that is the same view?" he asked. "It can't be! How do they make those buildings so tall? Well, I reckon with everything else that has happened in two hundred years, this is possible, but it stretches my mind. Yessir, it stretches my mind."

"I know. The Chicago that you knew has been rebuilt many times.

Much of what you might remember—virtually every building—was destroyed in a great fire in 1871. It had been an unusually dry summer, and most of the structures, public and private, were timber-framed—ripe fuel for a fire. Strong winds helped to create a kind of fire swirl, a tornado of fire, that ravaged the city. About three hundred people were killed, and miles and miles of the growing city were destroyed. The fire raged for two days, and it was so hot that it took weeks before some areas cooled down enough to be investigated. About one hundred thousand people were left homeless. As bad as it was, that same day there was an even worse fire about three hundred miles north of Chicago, in rural Wisconsin. A town named Peshtigo was completely destroyed. About fifteen hundred—a conservative estimate—lost their lives. Chicago, however, being a much more prominent place, got all the publicity.

"No one knows exactly how the fire actually started, but some enterprising journalists capitalized on the anti-Irish, anti-Catholic sentiments of the time. The street where the fire originated, De Kovan Street, was typical of Chicago at the time. Homes had barns. Barns had animals. A reporter named Michael Ahern sensationalized the story by reporting that there was an occupant of De Kovan Street, one Catherine O'Leary—quite an Irish name, don't you know—whose cow kicked over a kerosene lantern and started the blaze. Decades later, he admitted his lie.

"At any rate, the Chicago you saw doesn't exist anymore. Only a few buildings, constructed after your first lifetime, survived the fire, but Chicago played a major role in your political life, and you should see a modern city.

"You are getting used to your posthumous fame, I think. You will be pleased to know that one of your greatest biographers was an Illinois native—a poet named Carl Sandburg. He lived in Chicago and wrote for Chicago newspapers, but he is most famous for his volumes on your life and a poem about Chicago published in 1916. Let me read it for you."

> Hog Butcher for the World,
> Tool Maker, Stacker of Wheat,
> Player with Railroads and the Nation's Freight Handler;
> Stormy, husky, brawling,
> City of the Big Shoulders:

And I continued to the famous ending:

and Freight Handler to the Nation.

"That is not the kind of poetry that I am used to, but I understand it. I like its rhythm and its sassiness, and I can understand that description of Chicago. It could have been Chicago in my time."

"Indeed, it could. Now, I have some clothing for you to wear for our outing. And yes, I made sure it has plenty of zippers! Chicago is a huge city—a busy city. Most people will pay no attention to you. They are too concerned about getting to where they want to go to offer much attention to strangers. The hovercar is ready. Let's go."

I had the boys drop us off at the hoverpad on the lakefront. Once known as the Magnificent Mile, that area has only the Chicago Water Tower remaining. It had been redeveloped in the 2030s into a huge park. The efforts to bring green back to cities had worked. The great shopping areas ceased to exist over the early decades of the twenty-first century as people worked more and more out of their homes on the succession of data machines that were invented and reinvented in the tech labs of the world. "Going shopping" did not mean leaving the home. Shops became redundant. Dwellings were now all west of the Chicago area that Abe knew. I told him that Mary had lived here in Chicago with Tad for some time but the home had been destroyed in the great fire. Robert had lived here too, practicing law, but any building associated with him was also no longer to be found.

We walked along the parkway, Abe taking those great, loping strides afforded by his long legs. I didn't have to struggle to keep up, but it was a pace most people did not use. I cautioned him to slow down lest the curious get too close.

We walked south, toward the Chicago Art Museum, which was still home to one of the most prestigious collections of art in the United States. I asked if he wanted to go in, but he said Mary would enjoy something like that, but not him. So we continued south, moving slowly over the paths toward the lakefront. When we got to the Field Museum, I asked if he wanted to go into that hall of collections. Always well done, it had expanded over the decades and now rivaled the Smithsonian for its collections. I knew it would have enough material in it to keep Abe fascinated as well as to continue the effort to catch up to the current decade.

Chicago, which once hummed with human traffic, vehicle traffic, and the screech of the elevated train, was a quiet city now. Noise ordinances and the development of quieter and quieter machinery made it so. All this made our march to the Field Museum all the more pleasant. One could actually hear birds chirping in the trees and the waves of Lake Michigan breaking on the beach. It was a thoroughly splendid day.

Abe asked if he could pay the cost of admission, now $30 NAD. He was eager, I knew, to try his luck with this newfangled way of handling money. At the entrance, he pressed his thumb against the screen. Nothing happened. I reminded him that it was his index finger that opened up his account, so he touched the screen again and pushed the number two for the quantity of tickets, and he was asked by the machine whether or not he wanted a paper receipt. He answered no. A chime sounded twice, indicating the transaction had been accepted, and we were on our way in.

Fortunately, the museum's directors saw the wisdom in continuing the "great hall" theme of exhibitions. The hushed echoes of voices and the sense of the millennia hung heavy throughout the buildings.

We took our time, stopping to see Sue the *Tyrannosaurus rex*, a popular leftover from earlier in the century. Abe also enjoyed the Egyptian section. He had never seen a mummy before. He recalled some press about the discovery of the Rosetta Stone, but it didn't affect his life any. Egyptology was in its infancy during his lifetime. He had learned about the Rosetta Stone when Jean-François Champollion announced his successful interpretation of its inscriptions in 1822. I projected into his microchip images of the King Tut exhibit from the Egyptian Museum of Antiquities in downtown Cairo.[123] He was awestruck at the richness of it all. He had no interest in the Oriental exhibits but lingered for a long time in the African Hall. I think he wanted to learn as much as he could

---

[123] That poor place is still advertising that it will be moving to a newer, larger, cleaner facility in the near future. It has been doing so since 1985. I suppose in a land where time is forever, they can get away with such a thing.

about the culture that was disrupted by the slave trade he so abhorred. I could see his melancholy beginning to return, and so I suggested we stop for a little lunch.

The museum had a splendid buffet-style cafeteria. While it was not my kind of meal, I knew it would be a novelty for Abe, so we walked to the cafeteria, and Abe's eyes lit up when he saw the bounty that was available. As a child, something like this would have been beyond his wildest imaginings. Even as an adult—a prosperous one at that—the sight of so much food would have astonished him. And now it did.

He walked along the serving line, which was protected by those filthy "sneeze guards." He wanted a little of everything, but I convinced him a smaller portion would suffice. Abe selected a cheeseburger, fresh fruit, and a slice of good old American apple pie. I followed his lead. Once again, he was thrilled when he was able to use his fingerprint to pay for our meals. The place was busy—so busy that no one paid any attention to two old, tall men engaged in animated conversation at a corner table.

I said, "Abe, you can see it would be easy to spend a week touring this place. There is one area, though, that I would like you to see before we leave. It is the section that deals with the development of the United States in the decades after your presidency—the Wild West. Are you up to it?"

"Sure. My belly is full, and my mind is filling up as well."

So we left the cafeteria and headed to the area with some of the oldest exhibits in the museum. These were the dioramas that had been created by Carl Akeley. Akeley invented the concept of the diorama—the lifelike posing of animals and people in the contexts of their own environments. They look primitive now by the standards of the day, but in their time they were quite the thing.[124] These dioramas have been augmented by newer interactive technology. Virtual reality is the key to much of the educational process since the demise of traditional schools.

---

[124] Akeley made his name as curator of the Milwaukee Public Museum in the late 1800s. An English teacher in that city would give as an assignment the charge to go to the museum and question the guard on duty as to whether or not the large stuffed elephant at the top of the entrance stairs was "the Akeley Elephant."

Abe stepped into one of the machines and was mystically transported to Custer's last stand. He played through the whole scenario—a half-hour of trying to stay alive while surrounded by Sioux warriors. As with other new experiences, he came out with a huge grin on his face.

"Well, Anton, that was really something! You know, I never really liked George Custer, but let's keep that our little secret."

The only area we did not delve into was space exploration. I thought it better to give him a little break at this point and not enter into an entirely other realm of knowledge without some background. Even Abraham Lincoln can absorb just so much at one time.

I suggested we stay at the famous Palmer House. The original burned to the ground in the Chicago Fire only a few weeks after it was finished. It was a classic hotel that deliberately maintained a nineteenth-century front-parlor atmosphere. We got adjoining rooms and met for dinner at seven. Lincoln wanted another cheeseburger, but such was not on the menu of so prestigious a hotel. Instead we settled for roast duck with apple-orange sauce, potatoes Lyonnais, pickled beets, and baked Alaska for dessert. Again he delighted in using his index finger to pay for the dinner.

A Slight Detour on Stepping Out

The next morning, we awakened refreshed and well rested. We had breakfast in the small coffee shop: eggs Benedict, a rasher of bacon, hash browns, and good, rich, dark coffee. (Abe had quite the appetite yet always remained rail-thin.) I told him that I had a rather special plan for the day—a little detour. I asked if he had ever heard of Racine, Wisconsin. He was familiar enough with Wisconsin because of his service in the Black Hawk War and political campaigning there. It was still Michigan Territory at the time of that war. Lincoln had served in the militia for less than half a year in the spring and summer of 1832. He had been in Milwaukee, Beloit, and Janesville on campaign stops.

"Oh, yes. I remember it well. I never actually fought in that war, but I was a soldier in it. I made many friends and, frankly, got a lot of stories out of the experience. One time a Potawatomi Indian stumbled into our camp. The others assumed the man was a spy and readied their muskets to shoot him, but I stood between them, and the Indian and knocked their rifles up. I guess I've always had some kind of inner sense of fairness. What I remember most, though, is the gruesome task of burying the dead. We would come upon the site of a battle, and the fallen were all about. Our soldiers, to a man, had been scalped; a patch of red about the size of a dollar coin glistened in the sunlight, which made the scene all the more obscene.

"There was one other reason I remember that place. I had my horse stolen there! It was at a small place named Cold Spring. I wanted to get back to New Salem and to campaign, but someone stole my horse and saddle during the night. Horse thievery was a capital punishment in those days. My friend and I had to walk, canoe, and then walk again to get home. Yes, I remember Wisconsin all too well!

"Well, Abe," I said, I remember reading about that event. The place we are going to is just north of Chicago. The city came into its own after the Black Hawk War. You would be proud of it, because it was one of the stops on the Underground Railroad. The people of Racine were avid abolitionists. They also believed strongly in good education and founded one of the first public—that is, free—high schools in the United States. But it isn't for any of those reasons we are going there. After your assassination, your wife and Tad moved there briefly. Mary had hoped to enroll Tad in one of the schools in Racine. Tad and Robert had gone to Washington to testify in the trial of John Surrat, one of the plotters of your assassination. It didn't work out, and Mary returned to Chicago before beginning her sojourn in Europe, but the people of Racine, always good citizens, built a statue in her honor. It is located on the main street in downtown Racine and is probably the only statue in existence of the two of you together. You are seated, and Mary is standing, In fact, Mary exceeds your natural height in the statue; she is seven feet tall! By the way, it seems that your noses have been the targets of vandals over the years. The last time was back in 2009, coinciding with your two-hundredth birthday. It was a coincidence, perhaps, but ever since, security cameras have been protecting the area in East Park.[125]

---

[125] The statue was crafted by Frederick C. Hibbard of Chicago. He used models of the couple from before the presidency, wanting to depict them without the cares

We stood in front of the statue for some time. Then Abe slowly circled the work, examining it from every angle. He returned to where I was standing facing the statue and proclaimed, "Mother would be right proud of this. She looks content—regal, even. She was fussy, you know, about always looking good. It cost me a fortune, even though she thought she had hidden those expenses from me. Mrs. Keckley kept me informed all the time."[126]

"I'm glad you approve, Abe. I thought it would bring a happy memory to you. Let's get back to the hovercar now and head home. Are you ready for some of the boys' home cooking?"

It took only forty-five minutes to make the trip. Abe and I napped while the boys prepared our dinner, a feast of crown roast pork, gravy, whipped garlic potatoes, and rutabaga. For dessert we had another baked Alaska. Abe was amazed at this culinary treat.

The next day, we just sat on the porch, enjoying the sun and some summary conversation of the previous days' adventures. Abe did not think much of modern Chicago. He was, naturally, amazed at the size of the place; but with little there from his time remaining, it was all quite alien to him. He liked the visit to Racine much better.

Abe was getting to like these forays into reality, and I was glad. I was afraid he might prefer to be reclusive after all that had happened to him. I told him that we could make another trip in a day or two, perhaps to Springfield, if he felt up to it.

"A capital idea," he responded, grinning widely at his joke.

We Step Out to Springfield

In the next few days, Lincoln read all he could about Springfield, his old stomping grounds. He read about his home becoming not only a tourist attraction but also a shrine. He followed the events of his funeral with quiet determination, frowning often, smiling a bit, and frequently stopping to ponder what he was reading. I told him we could go anytime he felt up to it but that we would once again have to be somewhat coy

---

of that office. It was dedicated on July 4, 1943.

[126] Mrs. Keckley was Mary's maid.

about our presence. He understood and agreed. He wasn't ready for personal publicity yet. He was still catching up on almost two hundred years of reality.

He was a historian by nature. He sat on the rocker, recalling those early, heady days in Springfield. He mentioned that it was originally called Calhoun, after John Calhoun. It was settled by the typical pioneers of the era: farmers on the outskirts and traders and trappers making their way through, selling their goods, staying on to enjoy other human companionship after months in the wilderness, readily available food, and real beds. (It was the custom for gentlemen in a hotel room to sleep two to three to a bed with strangers.) By 1820 the first house was constructed, and in 1839 it became the capitol of Illinois. Lincoln had been living there for some two years when that happened, and he took a bit of pride in stating that he and some of the other "young bucks" were responsible for the honor.

I had the boys prepare another light lunch. I did not want to have to sit still in a restaurant in Springfield, Illinois, with Abraham Lincoln. It would be dangerous to his anonymity. Once again we did our best to get Lincoln dressed in some modern clothing, making him inconspicuous. He was still clean-shaven. I hoped it would work. I kept the boys on alert to come and fetch him if anything went wrong.

We took the hovercar, and the boys dropped us off near the Old Capitol Building. Abe recognized it immediately, even though everything around the place was new. Springfield still had a bit of a nonurban air about it, even though it tried hard to be cosmopolitan. We walked through the city. Vehicle traffic—that curse for some 150 years—no longer existed. What had been streets were long ago converted to broad pedestrian malls. It was quite a change from the mud streets and raised sidewalks of the 1800s.

Groups of children on school tours crowded around the open areas. Fortunately, like students of any era, they paid little attention to the adults, being much busier trying to cluster in their own groups. Students never change. Anywhere, anyplace, at any time, they are loud and obnoxious and travel in groups. We strolled over to the office that Lincoln had shared with his partner, William Herndon. Abe stood across the street from the office, looking up, looking down, and looking up again, lost in a fog of his own memories. This was the place where he had made his reputation. It was the center of his political life. Important as all that was to Lincoln, it was most important as the place where he would escape with his boys and let them run wild, pulling books off the shelves, spilling ink, creating a general pandemonium—all of which he loved deeply. If he ever disciplined his children, it was a well-kept secret, much to the consternation of his law partner and of his neighbors.[127]

View of Jackson and Eighth Streets
(photo by the author)

---

[127] Himself a sprite by nature, Lincoln and Mary both indulged their children after Willie's death at age four. Herndon, that would-be biographer of Lincoln, betrayed him greatly in his writing. His own poor opinion of Mary Todd prejudices his account. He even went so far as to suggest that Thomas Lincoln was not truly Abe's father but that Abraham and Jefferson Davis, unknown to each other, were half-brothers!

I knew that the visit to his home would be difficult. He had last seen it when he left Springfield for Washington in spring of 1861. The street had been both maintained and reconstructed to reflect a typical mid-Victorian, middle-prosperous American scene. Gaslights still burn here. Streets are cobbled. Lincoln's neighbors' homes are marked, but the most famous, of course, is the house at the corner of Eighth Street and Jackson.

Lincoln, the rising political star, purchased the home, and then he and Mary expanded it to accommodate their growing family and the need for this prosperous gentleman to have a proper place to entertain the many favor-seekers and political wags that helped to create his presidential candidacy and his legacy. After Abe's departure from Springfield, no Lincoln would ever live in the house again. After sojourns in New York, Chicago, and Europe, Mary Todd Lincoln could not bear to return to this place, so she took up residence with her sister who had preceded her in coming to Springfield so very long ago. The short walk from the office to the house was a familiar one to Lincoln. When the evening meal was ready, Mary would send one of the boys to fetch her husband. Work and people were always on his mind. He had no sense of time whatsoever. On his walk home, he would stop and visit with neighbors, chat politics with anyone who would listen, and tussle with the children in the neighborhood. It was a perennial frustration for Mary, but she knew it was part of her husband's way of life. Whining, cajoling, teasing, and threatening did nothing to deter Abe from this habit.

The home still bore the simple nameplate on the front door: "A. Lincoln." As we got closer and closer to the house, he slowed his loping gait and then stood silent across the street, once again completely absorbed in his own memories.

What was he picturing in his mind's eye? The boys playing in the large backyard? The neighbors gathering to wish him well as he and his family left Springfield? Did he see Mary chasing him down the street with her broom, excited and overwrought as always? Did he remember the smoke-filled meetings in the parlor? The antics of wrestling with the boys on the floor? Did he see himself rocking on the porch, a shadow of recent weeks at Tadwil? Irritating Mary by walking about in his shirtsleeves? He would not say, and I would not ask. We walked around the block, giving Abe a view of the property from all angles. The carriage shed was still in back, as was the outhouse. He wanted to enter the home, of course, but I advised we wait until another visit. I could see the toll this was taking on him, and we had another stop to make before returning to the estate.

Front view of the Lincoln home, Springfield, Illinois
(photo by the author)

"Oh, Anton!" said Abe. "The times we had in that house. Are you sure we can't go in?"

"Yes. It would be a great risk. There are too many people in the crowd right now. But we can return another day, when there aren't so many students about and perhaps nearer to closing time, when we might be the only ones about. I can tell you, though, that some of the furnishings inside are authentic. They are your property. Other items were brought in to make the site as authentic as possible. You cannot imagine the curiosity that people have about you, Abe. If you ran for president now, you would be elected in a heartbeat. You have been good for the economy of Illinois! Back in the days of fossil-fueled vehicles, in Illinois, the license plates were inscribed with 'Land of Lincoln.'"

I wanted to go to Oak Ridge Cemetery next. It would probably be the hardest part of Abe's reentry into the world of the living. I could have ordered a hovertaxi, but there was too much danger of connecting the house to the cemetery and to the tall passenger, so I signaled the boys to come with our own hovercar. They met us two blocks east and then took us to the cemetery entrance. I knew the place inside and out, of course, from my time as a janitor and guard there. It was getting near twilight, and the main gates would soon be closed. I knew that the guard would begin inside the monument and then make his or her way through the cemetery and end up at the office. We would have about one hour to ourselves. I explained this to Abe as we made the journey. I lied (imagine that!) and told him that a friend of mine is the director and gave me a key because I wanted to come and pay silent homage to Lincoln.

When we arrived at the gate, the hovercar stopped and we got out. The first key worked fine, with the gate creaking in an appropriately cemetery-type fashion. We walked down the long road.

Abe stopped and looked. "All that for me?"

"Yes, Abe. You were first buried in a holding grave on the backside of the hill until the monument was finished. Then your coffin was placed in a location of honor, and a large stone memorial marker was placed over it. Mary, Willie, Eddie, and Tad are also buried inside.

"It is a magnificent structure. It is almost one hundred twenty feet high and made of granite. The statue shows you holding the Emancipation Proclamation. The eagle has broken chains, the chains of slavery, in its beak. The statues represent the army, the navy, the artillery, and the cavalry; all of them served in the Civil War." We went around to the back of the monument to view the holding tomb.[128]

---

[128] This vault was the resting place for Abraham, Eddie, and Willie beginning in December of 1865. At his burial on May 4, 1865, Abraham and Willie's bodies

"You'll like this part, Abe. You see the great sculpture of your face? People believe it is a form of good luck to rub your nose! You will see another work by the same sculptor in later travels."[129]

Abe quipped, "Well, then I guess it's a good thing it was a big one!"

Borglum sculpture of Abraham Lincoln, Springfield, Illinois, Oak Ridge Cemetery
(photo by the author)

---

were placed in a public holding vault. The monumental tomb would not be used until September 19, 1871.

[129] The bronze bust of Lincoln was made by Gutzon Borglum—the same man who blasted the images of Washington, Jefferson, Lincoln, and Roosevelt at Mt. Rushmore, South Dakota. The marble original of this bust is in the US Capitol Building in Washington, DC. Borglum used the 1860 Volk life mask of Lincoln and photographs to create this masterpiece.

Then I told him the story of the grave robbers. He got quite a bit of enjoyment out of that and even said he wished they had been successful. He thought it would have been delightful to be part of a prank even though he was in the state of death. Then I told him about the rebuilding of the monument to make its foundation more solid and how Robert had his coffin encased in concrete. (I did not tell him about my escapades in that place, but while approaching the monument, I saw that my little marker was still in the ground. My secret was still safe.)

I took the key and opened the side door that leads inside. The lights are always on. Abe walked in slowly and saw the huge cenotaph that marked his burial place. I told him that the actual casket was several feet from the marker and deep underground. While he stood there, hands clasped behind his back, he looked at the flags and the inscription. I narrated the story of the funeral train and the outpouring of devotion and love that followed it every mile.[130] I also told him that Mary did not attend the funeral. Her mental state was far too precarious. As far as anyone knows, she never came to the place except in death to join her husband and sons.

Many people visit family cemeteries and see the markers of their own burial spot, but as far as I know, no one before ever stood alive looking at a marker with the dead body of the very onlooker underneath. This was a historic moment on many levels.

A low whistle came from Abe as he circled the cenotaph a second time. Then he walked over to the markers for Mary, Willie, Eddie, and Tad and slowly moved his hand over the etched words, tracing them carefully with his large fingers. His head bowed deeply again and again. I did not want to interrupt his reverie, but the time for the watchman's first round was quickly approaching. I did not want to get caught here, especially if the watchman were someone I had worked with during my previous nightly escapades.

"This is like a holy place," said Abe. "I don't want to leave."

"I understand, Abe. I understand. However, it would be better to leave before anyone sees us here. It could be very dangerous for us

---

[130] More about that later.

both." (I included "us both" because Abe would have shrugged off the personal danger). "I promise you we can return here."

"Thank you. I want to go home and spend some time pondering all of this."

We exited the tomb and walked quickly to the front gate. Just as I closed the gate and locked it, I saw the watchman come hurrying out of the office. He must have heard something. Fortunately the boys were there with the hovercar, and we took off immediately and were home in moments. That evening, Abe wasn't particularly hungry, but I had the boys take him a cheeseburger—a big one—and some coffee. For me, the day was another triumph, and I was hungry. I sat down to a late meal of venison stew (all the ingredients having come from the estate) and a fine bottle of Chateau Latour, 2001. I am not one to drink a lot of wine, or anything too alcoholic for that matter, but when one drinks, one should drink the finest. The current bottle was in our great cellar. I sat out on the porch, finishing a third glass of this fine beverage and pondering our little steppings out. It was all going better than I could have programmed. Oh wait! I did program it!

CHAPTER 17

Road Trip

Abe traveled well. He responded to new stimuli and old memories with a balance that, frankly, amazed me. I did want to take a few days of respite before moving on in our adventures, so I invited him to stop on the porch after his morning stroll through the woods and to chat. I knew it would be interesting. I would also let him think he was assisting in planning the next phase of his introduction to the twenty-first century and his new life. The details would come later.

That evening at dinner, I had a lot more to discuss with Abe. We had our usual splendid repast. Darius brought in an almond soup, dressed Cornish game hens with a plum reduction sauce, yams, a steamed broccoli head, and a variety of petits fours for dessert.

During the meal, I asked Abe if he remembered the poet Walt Whitman (1819–1892). He responded that he was indeed familiar with the man. His verses, Abe said, were very controversial.[131] Abe said he had not only read some of the poetry, which to him seemed to sound a bit of a biblical cadence,[132] but also that he had found it challenging.

"Well," I said, "Abe, after your death, Whitman wrote a poem about you. It is not as 'modern' as his other poems, but it is famous. Many a schoolboy has had to memorize it over the years."

"Well, then, I would like to hear it. I know that Whitman worked in an army hospital during the War Between the States. He seemed to support abolition, but sometimes he also seemed to back away from it,

---

[131] Whitman's use of free verse and implicit sexual themes made his book *Leaves of Grass* one of the most controversial topics of discussion among the intelligentsia of the day.

[132] Lincoln freely used images and cadences from the Bible. Ironically, Whitman based his own meter on much of the same.

but he was a Unionist through and through, as far as I know. Let me hear that poem."

Since I was one of the schoolboys who had to memorize the work, I began:

1

O Captain! my Captain! our fearful trip is done;
The ship has weather'd every rack, the prize we sought is won;
The port is near, the bells I hear the people all exulting,
While follow eyes the steady keel, the vessel grim and daring:
But O heart! heart! heart!
O the bleeding drops of red,
Where on the deck my Captain lies,
Fallen cold and dead.

2

O Captain! my Captain! rise up and hear the bells;
Rise up—for you the flag is flung—for you the bugle trills;
For you bouquets and ribbon'd wreaths—
for you the shores a-crowding;
For you they call the swaying mass, their eager faces turning;
Here Captain! dear father!
This arm beneath your head;
It is some dream that on the deck,
You've fallen cold and dead.

3

My Captain does not answer, his lips are pale and still;
My father does not feel my arm, he has no pulse or will;
The ship is anchor'd safe and sound, its voyage closed and done;
From fearful trip, the victor ship, comes in with object won;
Exult, O shores, and ring, O bells!
But I, with mournful tread,

Walk the deck my Captain lies,
Fallen cold and dead.

Abe remained silent for some time, his head tilted slightly to the right, his eyes closed. The quiet endured until finally Abe spoke: "A poem, written about me. Me, dead. The ship of state moving on. Loss and gain. Suffering and victory. It is quite an elegy, is it not, Anton?"

"Yes, indeed. It was written shortly after your death. Whitman wasn't so sure about your leadership initially but came to appreciate it greatly. Whitman was always adding to that great work *Leaves of Grass*. This poem was added as well. It was originally published in pamphlet form in a collection of war poems called *Sequel to Drum-Taps*. That work included another poem about you, but it is less famous. The title is "When Lilacs Last in the Dooryard Bloom'd." I'll have Darius get it immediately. It's quite long, so I will let you read it in your own time later.[133] Its style is more in keeping with the Whitman free verse. Now let's finish our dinner, and afterward we can talk about another outing.

We ate in monastic silence; only the occasional clank of silverware against plate or spoon stirring cream into the coffee interrupted our mutual hush. We met in the library, as usual, for some libations and discussion.

"Abe," I said, "how would you like to go on another outing? I was thinking we could continue to use your relative anonymity—which, by the way, I continue to appreciate but promise not to perpetuate. I was thinking of a little visit to the East Coast, to places familiar to you—specifically New York and Washington. Then, if you'd like, we can venture to Europe. We could go to Rome or Paris or Madrid. Whatever you would like. I have some friends in England who would delight in meeting you, and they are completely trustworthy to keep our little secret."

"I believe I would enjoy that very much, Anton."

"Very well, then. Let's plan on leaving Tuesday. I know that we invented a new identity for you and it worked well, but I am afraid I am the agent of trouble this time. If I travel under my known

---

[133] See appendix C.

name—especially to England, where I am a knight of the realm—there is bound to be publicity. Let me work on some new identities for us. It shouldn't be too difficult. We won't need them until we plan to leave the United States, so there is plenty of time to work on that. By the way, I got you some new traveling clothes. I hope you like your new look. And Abe, I think once again it would be better if you remained beardless."

Abe sighed deeply and said, "I suppose."

New York

Our first stop was New York. Lincoln was familiar with it, as he was with Chicago. There was virtually nothing of mid-nineteenth-century New York remaining. Lincoln found the congestion and volume of people overwhelming. He had read a great deal about the events of 9/11 and wanted to see the memorial. So we went there. Abe, in his traveling gear, did not stand out among the hundreds of tourists at the site. We also whisked ourselves up the express elevator at One World Trade Center. Lincoln liked speed, and the ride was exhilarating for him. He also wanted to see the Statue of Liberty.[134] He had read about this famous gift from the children of France and stood for a while in front of it, reading over and over the famous inscription—another poem memorized by generations of schoolchildren.

The New Colossus
BY EMMA LAZARUS

Not like the brazen giant of Greek fame,
With conquering limbs astride from land to land;
Here at our sea-washed, sunset gates shall stand
A mighty woman with a torch, whose flame
Is the imprisoned lightning, and her name
Mother of Exiles. From her beacon-hand
Glows world-wide welcome; her mild eyes command

---

[134] The sculptor was the Frenchman Bartholdi, and the engineer was Eiffel, of tower fame.

The air-bridged harbor that twin cities frame.
"Keep, ancient lands, your storied pomp!" cries she
With silent lips. "Give me your tired, your poor,
Your huddled masses yearning to breathe free,
The wretched refuse of your teeming shore.
Send these, the homeless, tempest-tost to me,
I lift my lamp beside the golden door!"

The wave of immigration that ignited the fervor of the masses had begun during the Lincoln presidency. The burden of dealing with the Confederacy, though, took away his attention from the reality of the tens of thousands of new citizens arriving on the Eastern Seaboard. The main issue was whether or not to trust the Irish- and German-speaking immigrants as fighters for the Union.

"Tis a mighty thing, isn't it, Anton? Powerful. And a mother to the nation. I know it was a gift for the Centennial of the United States. I am proud that my humble efforts as president kept that Union together so this monument to human courage could stand through the ages with integrity."

"Indeed," I said. "That it is. Our nation owes much to your wisdom and courage."

We took the typical tourist excursion, disappointed only that we could not get into the uppermost region of the great lamp. The view over New York was spectacular. I had one more stop I wanted to make while we were in this area.

We went to Riverside to see the tomb of Ulysses S. Grant. I explained to Abe the great controversy over whether his burial place should have been in Washington or here, but Julia Grant insisted that this was her wish, and finally a decision was made and the funds were raised and the tomb was erected.[135]

Abe commented, "Grant was a true man's man. A soldier's soldier. If only I had put him in charge of the Grand Army of the Republic at the

---

[135] Recall that Mary Lincoln also had to tussle with bureaucrats about Abe's final resting place. Some wanted Chicago or Washington DC. Abe had been clear long before his death: Oak Ridge Cemetery outside of Springfield.

beginning, maybe that horrible war could have ended sooner. I always wanted to give him the chance, but I also needed to show my support for McClellan. That was one of my big mistakes. I remember one night when I traveled out to Antietam after the battle there. I asked a friend who accompanied me as we looked over the encampment, 'What is that?'

"'Why, Mr. Lincoln,' he answered, 'that is the Army of the Potomac.'

"'No,' I quipped. 'You are wrong. It is General McClellan's bodyguard.'" Abe laughed uproariously, slapping his sides. "You liked that one, Anton?"

"Yes," I said. "It is a clever response."

"Well," said Abe, "I've got another. It was the night after the Battle of Bull Run. All kinds of fools came in to offer their explanations of what had happened at the battle. 'Ah, yes,' I said. 'I see. We beat the enemy and then ran away from him.'"

Again he roared at his own cleverness. Well, I knew that he had a great deal of respect for Grant and for Julia Dent, Grant's wife. In fact, they had been asked to accompany the Lincolns to the theater that fateful night. I took a chance and said, "Abe, do you know who is buried in Grant's tomb?"[136]

He looked at me quizzically and stated, "Why, Ulysses Grant, of course!"

"No!" I retorted. "No one is buried in Grant's tomb. He isn't buried at all, but is above ground in that sarcophagus."

For a moment Abe looked stunned, and then he burst out in laughter again.

"Oh, Grant would love that! Maybe not Julia, but Ulysses would, no doubt!"

We spent the night in Manhattan after a splendid dinner at Patrick's, the world-renowned restaurant now located in the former rectory of Saint Patrick's Cathedral, New York. It is the only place in the Western

---

[136] Popular culture attributes the joke to Groucho Marx, comedian of the mid–twentieth century. In his radio program *You Bet Your Life*, he would ask the question and accept the real answer or the usual answer—Grant—so that contestants would all go home with some prize.

Hemisphere that makes a proper Irish soda bread and corned beef and cabbage.

On to DC

Abe stayed up late into the night, reading some of his favorite humorous material. The episode at Grant's tomb had stirred his old sense of humor, and he wanted to entertain himself. We got microchips of the material—no easy endeavor. I could hear him from the room next door, guffawing as he enjoyed the humor from his time in history: stories from *Quinn's Jests, The Facetious Man's Companion, Flush Times, The Nasby Papers,* and *Hood's Poems*.[137] I only hoped I wouldn't have to listen to all of it the next day.

The hovercar ride to DC would take only a half hour. Getting permission to fly over the Federal Area is difficult, but the boys knew how to use my true name. We were able to land on the White House lawn, courtesy of the triumvirate. The boys explained that it was a bit of an emergency trip and I wouldn't have time to meet with them, but they also said I extended my deepest thanks for their courtesy.

We went first to the White House. Despite landing inside the perimeter gate, we went outside the gate, with the rest of the tourists. Abe marveled at how good the old place looked. Unlike his time, great lawns and gardens now surrounded the building. The muddy streets of Civil War Washington were long gone, and the whole city, at least the federal area, looked worthy of the title "National Capital."

We walked around the property as much as security would allow. Then we went inside for the famous tour. The so-called Lincoln Bedroom was not on the scheduled tour, but I called upon Bradford Carpenter, an old acquaintance of mine who happened to be related to the chief White

---

[137] It is reported that once, Lincoln was so moved by the caricature in one of the stories that late at night he came to his secretaries, John Hay and John Nicolay, to show them the image—*An Unfortunate Bee-ing*. Hay reported that while Lincoln was laughing at the book, they had to restrain themselves from laughing at him, with his short shirt loose about his long legs and looking very much like the tail feathers of an ostrich. Also serving as secretaries to Lincoln were William O. Stoddard and Edward Neill.

House usher. He explained to his cousin that two important visitors, great professors of history, were in the White House and would much appreciate a special favor. Since the triumvirate was busy in other parts of the building, we were quickly escorted to an elevator and taken to the second floor. When I explained to Abe the fuss and bother over the wealthy, the famous, and the infamous getting to sleep in the Lincoln Bedroom, he stifled a guffaw. He knew well the political motivations behind such favors but whispered a truth: "I never slept there. That room was my office." I didn't want to burst his proverbial bubble, so I feigned surprise.[138] I thanked Bradford's cousin, Beauregard, and we took our leave.

Abe wanted to go to the theater. He remembered taking a carriage there that fateful night so long ago. I could well understand his interest in the theater, but I "honested up" with him and revealed my hesitation; there were crowds there, and the multiple images of Abe in every corner could make it difficult to maintain our safe anonymity. Reluctantly, he agreed. We walked around outside, enjoying the view of the Washington Monument and the Capitol Building.

Abe marveled at the Washington Monument. In his time, it was just a stump, about half finished. Funds for the completion of the great obelisk had run out, arguments over who controlled its construction derailed work, and the lead-up to and aftermath of the Civil War caused work to cease from 1854 to 1877. It was finally finished in 1888. Over the decades it has seen internal improvements. The strange earthquake of 2011 threatened to topple the great edifice, but the damage was repaired and it has been open to the public ever since.

We took a hovertaxi to the Capitol Building. It was the Frenchman Pierre L'Enfant who laid out the city streets, all of which radiate from this building. Work was begun during the presidency of Thomas Jefferson. As more and more states were admitted to the Union, the building was no longer large enough to accommodate the increased number of representatives, senators, and their assistants. Two great wings were added, but that made the original dome look misplaced.

---

[138] See my comments on the Lincoln Bedroom in chapter 4.

A larger one was built to replace it, but the work was not yet done for Lincoln's first inauguration.

The dome was strengthened in the early part of the twenty-first century, the work being finished in 2017. It has stood the same since, with, of course, considerably modernized conveniences and securities.

Lincoln, of course, recognized the building immediately and was awed at the pleasant, familiar sight. Although those who inhabited its halls during his tenure were often at odds with him, it was one of the few things in the city that was familiar to him.

From the Capitol Building, we took another hovertaxi to the Lincoln Memorial. I gave Lincoln a short tutorial on the building, knowing that he would be both overwhelmed and humbled at the sight. It was only two years after the assassination that a sculptor tried to immortalize the sixteenth president. A small statue by Lot Flannery was erected in front of the District of Columbia City Hall in 1867.

It was universally agreed that a more fitting memorial was appropriate, but it took decades for Congress to finally allocate funds and agree on a location and a design.[139] Many thought the Greek temple motif was far too exalted for the man born in log cabin. Obviously, the temple motif won. Ground was broken on February 12, 1914. It would take eight years to complete, but finally, on May 20, 1922, President Warren Harding dedicated the Memorial. Seventy-eight-year-old Robert Todd Lincoln stood next to him on the platform. Abe's eyes began to water as he heard this story. He was equally moved when he remembered that the bill that bore his image (the old US five-dollar bill) and the reverse of the copper penny both bore images of the memorial.

As he has done before when confronted with images of himself and his legacy, he just stood there. He looked down at the ground. Then he looked at his own huge hands and held them up as though comparing them to the colossal hands on the David Chester French statue. As with the White House, we walked slowly around the entire structure. The crowds of tourists were unaware that the great man himself was in their midst. He returned to the front of it and again bowed his head deeply—whether in thought or in prayer, I don't know.

---

[139] A camel is a horse that was designed by a committee.

The Lincoln Memorial
(photo from Thinkstockphotos.com; used with permission)

I have become sensitive (yes, even me) to Lincoln's moments of silence. I have sufficient respect for the man not to interrupt him in these moments. In the distance, he saw Arlington Cemetery, which in his time was the property of the Custis-Lee family. Congress appropriated it as a cemetery for the Union dead. As they say, the rest is history. However, Lincoln wanted to visit two graves: that of his only son to survive into adulthood, Robert Todd Lincoln, and that of assassinated president John F. Kennedy. We took a tram to the entrance and shuffled about in our incognito ways.

On our way, I narrated the story of another president and the Lincoln Memorial. "During the turbulent 1960s, during the equally turbulent presidency of Richard Milhouse Nixon (president thirty-seven), the nation was in turmoil. An unpopular war was still raging in Vietnam. (He remembered the country as Siam and recalled the gift of elephants that King Rama IV wanted to send to him; it took a bit of diplomatic maneuvering to reject the gift.) Social unrest, the hippie movement, and war protest all brought people to the streets. On the afternoon of May 4, 1970, US National Guard officers opened fire on unarmed protesting students at Kent State University in Ohio. Four were killed. Many others were injured. In a surprise move, Nixon had his valet, Manolo Sanchez, leave with him from the White House on the night of May 9. They drove to the Lincoln Memorial, and he spoke with students who had taken shelter there. Like most of your successors, he had a great admiration for your accomplishments and for your person. He is said to have recorded in his diary part of the inscription from this memorial: 'In this temple, as in the hearts of the people for whom he saved the Union, the memory of Abraham Lincoln is enshrined forever.' Other presidents studied your biography and had paintings of you hung where they could reference them in times of the incredible stress that defines that high office."

"Hmm" was his only response.

We went first to the grave of JFK. The story of this young man's presidency did not much impress Lincoln, but the reality of his assassination, a fate they shared, brought a different kind of bond than any of us could imagine. Again he stood there, quietly letting his thoughts roil through that great mind.

Robert's burial place was up the hill from the main entrance of the cemetery. I chose to take him there last. The day was taking a toll on him; I could tell. Robert was buried here with his wife and his son, Abraham Lincoln II. Lincoln was a little chattier here. His relationship with Robert had not always been a happy one. He commented that he was deeply honored that Robert named his only son for him, and he said that his father's heart and his Christian heart understood quite thoroughly the well of grief that Robert must have known at his young son's death. It was all too common an occurrence in the Lincoln family.

"Anton," he asked, "What of my family? Who is left? Where are they?"

I stood silent for a bit, for the story is a sad one. "Abe," I said, "No one is left. There is one person who lived in Florida—a lawyer, by chance—who claimed to be Robert's great-grandson through marriage, but the man he claimed was his father had a vasectomy and could not have produced the child. He was an illegitimate son of the man's third wife. Let me transfer the family tree to your microchip so you can see for yourself.[140] Of course, of all the Lincoln children, only Robert lived into adulthood. Of Robert's two daughters, only one had children. I am truly sorry, Abe."

"Well, it's not your fault, but it is rather sad." He stood before Robert's tomb for well over an hour, his hand nervously running through his hair and often holding his forehead, which was furrowed in what had to be deep sorrow.

"Abe, are you tired? Can I get something for you?"

"No, I am doing fine. I am pleased that one of our children was able to survive and make a notable contribution to our country. I am sure I was not the most available or best of parents, especially for Robert, but I loved him. I truly did. I tried to arrange the best for him, even though he fought me on those issues so often. Anton, there is one more place I would like to go today, if we could."

"Of course. Where?"

To my amazement, he wanted to see the burial place of his killer, John Wilkes Booth. He knew the story of Booth's escape from Washington, the massive manhunt, and Booth's eventual entrapment and death at the Garret farm, between Port Royal and Bowling Green, Virginia. It was April 26, 1865, ten days after the infamous deed. I had Darius bring our hovercar around. I wasn't sure how this was going to play out. I don't much like things that I cannot control, but it was one of the few requests, odd as it was, that Abe ever made of me. So I instructed Darius to take us to the cemetery, outside of Baltimore.

He dropped us off at the entrance. The Booth family had a large plot in the cemetery, but I explained to Abe that John Wilkes Booth's burial place had never been marked. There was far too much fear that there

---

[140] Cf. footnote 127.

would be vandalism or a theft of his body. Abe understood. We found the family plot with the marker.

Once again Abe stood still for a long time. He had known Booth and his brother, Edwin. Their fame matched the notoriety of film stars of later ages. He remained still—as still as the small obelisk that marked the spot. He shook his head left and right and then up and down. Again he looked at his feet. He shook his head again. Then he stood up straight and addressed the monolith in a clear voice: "I forgive you."

I guess when Lincoln said, "With malice toward none and charity for all," he really meant it.

Darius and Darren came with the hovercar and met us at the cemetery entrance. It had been a long, interesting, cathartic outing. We hovered to Tadwil, arriving late in the evening. Once again this man revealed that his greatness was not the stuff of legend but a strength of character that is a rare reality among the human race. The boys prepared a light snack of lemonade and finger sandwiches, and then we retired, all of us wondering what might happen next.

CHAPTER 18

Reverie

Anton Bauer Comments

Abe spent the hours of many days on the front porch of the Tadwil mansion, rocking back and forth ever so slowly and ever so deliberately. Sometimes his eyes were shut as he made the monotonous movement. Back and forth he rocked, in the rhythm of the pendulum of a grandfather clock. He wasn't sleeping; one cannot rock and sleep at the same time. Other times he looked far out into the distance—perhaps into the past, or maybe into the future. I never disturbed him when he was in one of those somber moods. I made sure the boys silently put out some sugar cookies for him as well as some lemonade or hard cider. The choice was his. He liked them both. I had no idea what he was "a-ponderin'," as he liked to call it. Even mid-twenty-first century science could not yet read a person's mind.

Abe, Rocking on the Porch and Thinking to Himself

I like these quiet mornings. One thing—this new world is so noisy. The sound of the machinery is often overwhelming to me, and I need to close my eyes, my ears, and my mind against it. How can they stand it? Anton said it used to be even worse. At least here, on this estate called by that silly name Tadwil, I can escape. It is quiet here. Then again, the escape is purely emotional, not spatial. I don't know if I could actually escape this place and the clutches of that strange man, Sir Dr. Anton Bauer.

He has been good to me, I must admit. I lack for nothing except the freedom of movement that I granted to the black people in 1863. Isn't this a predicament; the Great Emancipator is himself a captive! O Lordy, what a world!

I feel good. I truly do. In fact, I don't think I ever felt so healthy in all my life. The food is abundant and well prepared. I even appreciate the efforts to duplicate my former diet. It's not quite the same, but very close. I certainly do not miss those little blue pills that I had to take. In fact, I've had no medication whatsoever, not even for a headache, other than that small bout of illness I dealt with that day in this new life that included Gettysburg. One thing I am right proud of: that battle and that address at Gettysburg erased the Mason-Dixon Line! In all the reading I've been doing, I learned that my Emancipation Proclamation finally became the law of the land with the passing of the Thirteenth Amendment.

I do enjoy walking. The area around Anton's estate is filled with splendid woods. I have made a number of trips so frequently that I have created some footpaths. It is much more pleasant to walk this way than it was to pace the halls of the White House during the tensions of the Civil War. And this modern clothing—I wear comfortable, warm clothes on these walks, although I kind of miss my shawls.

Isn't that odd in its own right? I have no emotional headache in dealing with the war and no personal headache in dealing with Mary and Robert. Oh, I do miss them. I surely do. But I do not miss the constant tension they brought with them into my presence. No headache! Yet the last thing I truly remember from my previous life is laughing loudly and then suffering a terrible, terrible, searing headache. Then blackness. Oblivion. And then, like Lazarus, I was called back into this world.

And what a world it is! Strange machines have replaced horses and oxen. They are fast; I admit that. In my former world, we thought a train speeding at thirty-five miles per hour was about as fast as a human would ever travel. Now, in minutes, we cover the distance it took days to traverse. I rather like it, truth be told. I appreciate the horse that Anton got for me. I still enjoy riding, even though I am limited to the boundaries of this estate. I have never pushed to leave without Anton taking the initiative. I don't really trust him very much, as he is so eccentric, but I also have to admire his intelligence. He did bring me back and has been nothing but solicitous of my welfare ever since. Yet

I still feel there is much more going on with me, around me, than I can grasp.

Oh, Mary. Oh, Robert. Oh, Tad. Oh, Willie. Oh, Eddie. I do miss you so. I had many companions in my life, and many were boon companions at that, but you were my family. We lived together. We ate together. We played together. We mourned together. I do so miss the nonsense of those boys. Their antics kept me young, and they promised never to tell Mary that I instigated most of their recklessness. I did not want those boys to fear me or to loathe me the way I did my own pa. He had two good wives and a dutiful son, but he never knew it. Honestly, I don't remember a compliment or kind word ever escaping his mouth. He never understood my love of books. Even if it was midnight and I was reading by a slim candle, he complained of the waste of the candle and the loss of energy that could be used the next day in work. I stuck around with him as long as I could. I felt terrible sorry for my step-ma, Sarah. For her sake, I stayed there longer than I should have. I didn't want her to be alone with that man, but I could take it no more. It was time to strike out and see what I could do in this world. I did love the adventure of it all.

I was lonely during those first months of my new life away from Pa and Sarah. I enjoyed the tavern companionship in New Salem and soon learned that I could spin a tale that caught everyone's ear. People paid attention to me. People liked me. People trusted me. I did my best to maintain that trust—so much so that I was encouraged to become an elected representative of those fine people. And then I met Ann. Oh, Ann, I never forgot you. I loved Mary, I truly did, but no one ever gets over a first love. Had you not gotten sick and passed, I am sure that you would have been the mother of my boys. I don't know what else of our destiny would have been different. I might not have gone on to the presidency, but I know that we would have been happy together. Perhaps New Salem would be a prospering city instead of a park if we had stayed there and woven our destinies together. Well, I guess we'll never know.

So it is lonely here, like the loneliness of New Salem in those first months. I see only Anton Bauer and his two slaves, although he assures me that "people of color," as they say now, are not slaves. He calls them butlers. True, they do come and go more than I do, but they do ever'thing he bids without question. I am glad, though, that they are such fine cooks. And they seem to like me.

Well, I think back on the days long gone. I spend my time on this rocking chair, going back and forth, back and forth; it is not unlike the life I lived—and live now. I go back and forth, figurin' what has happened to me, what has happened to the world, and what will become of me in this new life.

I have truly enjoyed some aspects of all this modernity. I am always comfortable. The clothes are remarkable, even if the fashion is so very different. And I love those zippers! What a great invention. Anton has made sure I have all the zippers I want in my clothing. I used to keep my notes in my top hat. Now I keep them in all my little zippered pockets. He has assured me that I could keep everything in this object he calls a micro-cheep, but I prefer my pockets and hat.

But what does he want of me, this Sir Dr. Anton Bauer? He has been, I think, quite thorough in educating me about all that happened since that April night in 1865. It is nearly impossible to believe that almost two hundred years have passed since then, but they have. I've studied the history carefully. The supply of information is without end. I am not surprised at the endless wars that have plagued this human race of ours. Our lesser angels are always at play. And the weapons! The inhumanity of those weapons!

Of my successors, I admire Theodore Roosevelt the most. He was a bold man. Unlike me, raised in poverty as I was, he was born to privilege, and he used his resources to help the common man. I think a lot of Woodrow Wilson also. It seems to me he was the first president to really deal with the bigger world. His hopes for peace remind me of my quest for a resolution of the War Between the States and the hatred and prejudice and selfishness that engendered it. And that other Roosevelt—Franklin. I was president a little over four years. It was easy to see what domestic and international headaches did to that man, but he, too, worked for the benefit of those who most needed government's ability to assist. So I also learned that three others were assassinated. The successor to that popular fellow Kennedy was a good president. I respect that second president Johnson for codifying into the national laws the very programs that I had hoped to establish with my version of reconstruction a hundred years before. I was flabbergasted to find out that a black man became president of these United States earlier in this century. The very thought of it in my first time on this earth would have bought a one-way ticket to an asylum. The poor fellow had a devil of a time with it. No wonder they now have this strange system of three presidents. Such a complicated world! Perhaps the remote quiet of this place is a secret blessing and I should just appreciate it.

Oh, Mary! You should see the fashions of the day. Most of these women would have been arrested for wearing what they wear—or don't wear! What a far cry from the styles that you so loved—and spent so much money on! Yes, I know all about your expenditures. Mrs. Keckley reported regularly to me, even though you never knew it. I could not bring myself to stop you from buying clothes and items for the White House, even though I knew that it was politically unwise and it was making us candidates for the poorhouse. That's how much I loved you, Mary. I could not have stopped you any more than I could have stopped the boys from their shenanigans! You would love, though, how easy these fabrics are to care for. They have machines now that make clothes clean without even using water. It is a marvel. I do have a suit like the one I wore to the theater that night. I must say, I think I look dashing in it, if "dashing" is anything I could ever say about myself. I recall one time being called two-faced by a political opponent. My response was, "Sir, if I had two faces, do you think I would be wearing this one?"

(Abe chuckles to himself for a few moments.)

Oh, my boys! Remember how you loved to speed around the White House in a wagon drawn by the old goat? You wouldn't believe the toys that exist now. The best ones still involve wheels and balls, but there is so much more! You can pretend any reality you want and play in it: ancient Greece, Colonial Boston, or even the stars. It's called virtual reality. Anton has introduced me to it, and it is fun. I like to make believe I am Julius Caesar, except his end was all too close to home for my comfort! People still read about him, still enjoy the great work of Shakespeare about him, and not long after we all left this world, archaeologists uncovered the actual ruins of ancient Rome. Maybe I'll get there someday in this new world.

You boys would also love the flying machines. These mechanisms have actually gone to the moon and back, and just recently one of these returned from Mars. I am not joking. Human beings from our world have actually gone to the moon and to Mars, walked on those heavenly spheres, and returned here to tell about it. Maybe I'll get there too in this new world.

Zippers, boys. You would love zippers. Imagine going to the outhouse and not having to fuss with all those buttons. Imagine this: there are no outhouses! You'd think the world would stink afoul, but there are new inventions that take care of all that quickly and cleanly. What a world this is! You boys used to overturn the neighbors' outhouses. I am sure you would find some way to upset the order of things today as well.

But the history. The history reads as it did in our time. Adventurers, yes. Exploiters, yes. Explorers, yes. Thugs and tyrants, yes. They are still about. I guess no matter how much all this technology advances, our human selves are much unchanged. It is so sad. I weep. There have been some great heroes also. A man named Martin Luther King Jr., a great preacher, brought to life the effects of my Emancipation Proclamation, only to be martyred. It seems there are always those who don't want truth to be spoken. In the Good Book, that was usually the penalty for telling the truth. Those crusty prophets and the blessed Jesus know all about that. There was another fellow I admire too. He was from India. I remember England had made it part of its Empire, but people everywhere want freedom to determine their own destinies within the framework of their own cultures. A man named Gandhi led nonviolent peaceful demonstrations against the British. Many of the demonstrators were killed, but eventually the great British Empire had to yield to the power of the personality of a man clothed in a small loincloth. Then he, too, paid the martyr's price for his godly actions. Such a sad pattern history has imposed upon us.

(Abe stops rocking for a while and takes a long drink of lemonade. He downs four of the Linzer Tart sweets the boys brought out, pours another glass of lemonade, and goes back to his reverie.)

I am fascinated by all that has happened in these scores of years. The technology alone is a wonder. This nation, my country, fought so hard to preserve itself and has been the leader of the world in many things.

It learned the use of power and exercised it both frivolously and wisely throughout the world. The social causes that were part of the mid-nineteenth century have their modern equivalents. "My people" would be shocked to learn that white Christian Americans are a minority. The majority of people are now either black or brown. They hold the high positions in education, government, and social society. While Germans and Irish and Italians were streaming to the East Coast during my first life, now it is Canadians seeking refuge from their great civil war who come south. The borders were walled off and then sealed with thermal ray detection in the 2020s. The birth rate was so high that it made no difference. Anglo citizens had fewer and fewer children while the others propagated. China, which was supplying rail workers in my first time on this globe, has become the greatest economic power in the world, but its own population's needs continue to outrun production. The same is occurring in India. The poverty levels in those places match the disparity of economic well-being that characterized twentieth-century America. Well, it has all come a long way from the era of King Cotton. As technology advanced, the need for manual labor diminished. Those skilled at repair began to take control over the intelligentsia. This world is becoming a bit like one of the cinemas that Anton showed me—a fun and interesting piece called "Wall-E."

I do love all that cinema. Anton has showed me how it developed from the staccato black-and-white initial films to the way I can download the desired programs into this computer chip in my head. I especially like the historical movies. The westerns I can't stand. That was not the West of my time or the decades following. Then there is that chap Walt Disney, whose reinterpretations of history for popular consumption have done such a disfavor to generations of Americans. It was all good for the economy but bad for truth. I especially loathe what he did to Dan'l Boone. As a Kentucky native, I know the stories and the truth. The man was no giant among men. He was, in fact, on the short side, even for those days. Boys, you would have liked to watch those stories. I can only imagine the games you would invent afterward, to the consternation of Mary and all the neighbors. My neighbors put up with a lot from those boys—and from Mary too. She could level them with her tongue in a trice.

It is beautiful out here today. I like listening to the river flow. Maybe later I'll hike through the woods. It brings me great peace. I have learned how close these treasures of nature all came to extinction in the last century and a half. The battle between conservationists and plutocrats was a civil war of its own definition. I cannot imagine the sad state of the country's waterways throughout all those years. We could drink without hesitation from any stream or jump into any body of water to refresh ourselves. It took a lot of courage for the first triumvirate to stand against the wealthy, but it worked. With the industrial controls in place and the use of solar and wind sources of energy, the great polluters lost. It took riots and prison time for those who tried to escape the regulations, but that is one place where this modern world, always on someone's watch it seems, took care of itself. The trillium—which bloomed around Kentucky, Indiana, and Illinois in my first life—has become the symbol of the movement. Anton's woods are filled with the flower.

I have enjoyed our little outings. If modern Chicago is indicative, the other great cities like Boston and Philadelphia must be equally impressive. I'm not sure I like all this, but I cannot deny it is impressive. Buildings stretching into the sky defy gravity, it seems to me. Anton showed me the scenes of the destruction of the two great towers in New York on what is still referred to simply as 9/11. Those symbols of American prowess are all over the world. While our world was a bit on the stinky side from the presence of horses and their by-products, the pace of this contemporary world is dizzying. Perhaps that's why I so enjoy just sittin' here and rockin' and thinkin'. My mind can race on and on, but my body knows some rest.

Anton has told me that we will soon make another venture into the wider world. I have cooperated with him in every way—at least so far—and hope that his tutelage of me will soon be over. I am itching to do more than keep learning—not that I mind that, but it is becoming stifling. I do wonder what that man's plans are for me. Hmm.

(Abe is suddenly distracted by a noise from the river. He has never seen any other people on the waters that run through Tadwil, and then he sees what it is: it is just the twins mooring the *Mary Todd*. He pours another lemonade and eats a couple of Victorian sponge cakes, wipes his mouth with his shirtsleeve—how Mary hated that—and continues his pondering.)

Oh, Joshua. I miss you too. I will never forget your kindness. When I was newly arrived in Springfield, you took me in. Free. I shared a room with you above your store. Oh, the stories we told one another. And the secrets we confided to each other. In every way, you were my brother. Oh, I hardly remember my blood brother, little Tom. Little Tom, you died when you were only three days old. I was only three years old at the time. I didn't understand much of why Ma and Pa were so sad. Pa carved a small coffin for you and buried you near the Knob Creek farm. He even scratched the letters T. L. into a small stone to mark the spot. It is one of the only times I saw Pa quiet and sad. So Joshua, you became my brother. I wish you had stayed in Springfield. I remember visiting you and your family at your Louisville home in 1841. I broke off my engagement with Mary Todd on what should have been our wedding day. You left that same day. I soon felt that same darkness taking over me that had descended into my soul when Ann died. I stayed there with your family in Louisville about six weeks. Your mother gave me a Bible—the Oxford edition of the great King James. She told me it was the best cure for the blues. I didn't read it right away, but when I started, I was faithful to it. Joshua, you and I disagreed about slavery, but it never came between us. I even offered you positions in my administration, but you turned them all down. Oh, how I would have loved to have you around in those terrible days of the war.

I remember your great house. Some say it was based on a design by Thomas Jefferson, who was close to your grandfather. It was a magnificent building. I don't know how you could have left it for the wilds of Springfield, but like many young bucks, we wanted to strike out on our own. We talked into the night. We talked all day. We shared every thought we had. Your older brother James was a lawyer. I spent many an hour in Louisville talking with him. He lent me books to take back to the house and read. I read everything I could. I always did. I wish you had accepted one of my offers. Your brother finally did and became my attorney general, but it wasn't like having you around. I saw slaves there. Joshua, you and your family owned slaves.

Now Joshua, thinkin' 'bout you makes me think on my boys John

Hay and George (John) Nicolay. They were like more sons to me: so loyal, so dutiful, and so hard-workin'. Oh, Mary, you always gave them a hard time. I think you were jealous of them. I don't know if they ever fig'rd out that I learned their nickname for me—'The Tycoon" or, on some days, "The Old Tycoon." Well, I was nothin' of the sort, but I enjoyed their company—'specially on those late nights during the war when I paced the halls of that great White House.

I used to like wrestling. Oh, I haven't done it at all recently. I know that I am too old, but when I was a young man, in New Salem, I would take on anyone and usually win. A few of the days (which were actually years in my developing stage), I did wrestle with those butlers. I usually won, too! All that rail splitting finally paid off. I've been doing a lot of walking and riding on this estate. It doesn't wear me out, but I am probably too old to get winded and not worry. Most people in my time didn't live to this age, much less enjoy the kind of health I now possess. I haven't seen a doctor yet, but I have the feeling I am being monitored. That's all right with me; I enjoy feeling healthy and carefree.

But how carefree should I be? It's not like me to sit so quietly so long. I enjoy it; I truly do. But there's got to be more to this new existence than catching up on ten score years of history. I wonder what kind of freedom I actually have. Can I make plans, or are they all being made for me? I don't talk out loud to myself. I have a sense there is someone listening—like the spies in the White House, I guess. That's why I like sitting here on the porch and rockin' and thinkin' and plannin' and ponderin'.

And I ponder on. Here I am, at comfortable rest, but I cannot help but think of the years of that horrible war. How often did my soldiers ever get the opportunity to rest? There was always some intrigue: struggles among the leaders, dispirited soldiers, sickness in the camp, lack of food. Supplies were bartered and bargained and purloined. There was the presence of spies—from both sides. Yes, those soldiers deserved their time to rest too.

The situation in the camps was horrible, even when it was good. There was rain, mud, dysentery, homesickness, and desertion. I always did my best to pardon the deserters, even though my cabinet advised me to the contrary. How could I blame a young man for running from the horrible things he saw and would ne'er forget? I was always proud of Mary for visiting the hospital camps around Washington. She did it at great risk to herself. Our enemies were everywhere and would not hesitate to do her harm. But she went out day after day, whenever her delicate constitution allowed. She saw the agony of young men maimed forever in body and soul, yet she had her charm and was able to bring them a moment of encouragement and some cheer and thanks for their service. That was my Mary! Oh, Mary! What things have happened to me since that evening at the theater! Now you are the one who is gone, and it is I who lives on. And I wonder, given this new condition of mine, how I will live on. And for how long? Will I vanish from this mortal coil once again? Through a repetition of violence? Through sickness? Through old age? Maybe Anton knows, but if he does, that sly devil doesn't give out much information of that sort. He is good with the data of history but silent on the plans for tomorrow.

Well, what am I to do? I enjoy these quarters and the intellectual company, and the outing was an adventure. It was difficult and draining but so very good for me. But now, here I sit: thinkin', dreamin',mournin', wonderin', hopin', worryin', rockin', plottin', plannin', watchin', dozin', wakin', livin', dyin,' reasonin', discernin', swayin', shakin', grievin', lamentin', viewin', observin', seein', calculatin', preparin', arrangin', pretendin', breathin', and rememberin'. All this while I sit here, day after day, trying to figure out what might come next. What would I like to do next, had I a choice to make?

I reckon for the time being I will let things just be. I'll let Anton lead the way so long as that way seems to do no harm to me or to others. I could write a book; seems everyone does that. But these days, the idea of a book, that wonderful weight of words in hand, doesn't seem to exist anymore. But I could do that. Much of what I've read about me needs some clarification. Maybe I'll do that. Or maybe not. Depends, I guess. Meanwhile, I will keep rockin' and thinkin' and rememberin' and plannin'.

Here comes Darius. It must be close to dinnertime. I've spent the whole day out here on this porch, in the sunshine and the evening shadows.

***

Darius picked up the tray holding the lemonade and noticed the cookies and other sweets were gone.

"Had a nice day, sir?" he asked solicitously.

"Yes, Darius. Yes indeed! A very fine day," I responded.

"Shall I accompany you to dinner? We are having a Creole feast tonight: crawfish, shrimp, hominy grits, and gumbo. We've even made some mint juleps to go with the feast."

"Thank you, Darius. I will go with you."

And thus ended another day for Abe III.

CHAPTER 19

World Travelers

And thus two new people were born into this world—or at least into the world of bureaucratic autocracy. I took the name Drako Dorolex. Abe became Oskar Pferdbein. I loaded our microchip accounts with plenty of funds using our new names. We would need a quantity of new American dollars for our trip. Fortunately, this currency and the new yuan[141] were the most accepted currencies in the world at this time. And with the help of the boys navigating our private hovercar, we set out on our newest adventure.

Abe and I had talked about travel to Europe. He had never done it in his first life, and now it was so easy that I thought he might enjoy seeing some of the sites he had read about as a young man and in his new state of life.

I asked where he would like to go. The incognito status of the beardless Lincoln was still a necessity, but he didn't mind. He rather enjoyed using the new laser-shaving technology. It beat all the cuts he got using and reusing old razors. Even the professional barbers had rather primitive, but sharp, implements of the tonsorial arts.

"I think I would like to see London," said Abe, "even though the British were not particularly helpful to me during the War Between the States. They were good to Mary, I believe."

"Splendid, old fellow. I know just the place we can stay."

I explained my friendship with Percival Pettigrew as well as those two rascals Angus and Fergus MacDougall. I did not tell him about our adventures in Kensington Park. At least not yet.

"Any place else you would like to visit?" I asked.

---

[141] Henceforth "NY."

"I have read so much about Rome and its senate, its dictators, its emperors, its legal system, and its wonderful ruins. I would very much like to see all that. I've also read that the cuisine in Italy is superb. I am eager to try it firsthand."

"Splendissimo! I know some of the best restaurants in the city. They are not necessarily the most famous, but they endure because they are so good. In fact, I've never had a bad meal in Rome. As long as we are there, would you like to see the Vatican? Perhaps I could arrange a private meeting with the pope. After all, if I ask him to keep our audience sub rosā, he will have to oblige that promise of secrecy."[142]

Abe looked at me with utter disdain. I was amazed. I had never seen such a cross look on his face. He actually stamped his foot on the floor and said he had no interest in meeting the king of Rome.

I tried to explain to him that much had taken place—as he usually understands—in the many decades since his original life among us. I inquired about why he was refusing to do this. Most people would give anything to meet the saintly Pope Augustine.[143]

---

[142] Although the origins of the phrase are debated, there is a general agreement that the phrase "sub rosā" or "under the rose" dates back to ancient Egypt and the god Heru-pa-khered, who came into Greek and Latin culture as Harpocrates, who was a god of silence. The earliest statues of this Egyptian god were figures of a youth with his finger toward his mouth. This was later misinterpreted as a gesture for silence. If discussions at table were to be considered privileged and secret, a rose, either painted or real, was hung from the ceiling of the banquet hall, hence the term "under the rose" / "sub rosā."

[143] Starting in 2013 with the election of the Argentinian Jorge Bergoglio, the successive popes have all come from outside of Europe. Bergoglio, aka Francis, was followed by the Panamanian Adelmo Escueda, who took the name Oscar in honor of the martyred saint Oscar Romero. He served from 2022 to 2035. He was succeeded by the Filipino Tadaashi Yokomto. He served from 2035 to 2049 with the papal name Antonio, chosen to honor the first Filipino cardinal of universal influence, Luis Antonio Tagle. Antonio was followed by the brief reign of Francis II, whose birth name was Nadir Hadawi. He had been the patriarch of Jerusalem prior to his election and served from 2049 to 2052. The current pope is the Ethiopian pope Augustine. Born Dubaku Qaeschaun, he selected the name Augustine in honor of that famous North African prelate, Augustine of Hippo.

"Absolutely not. I am not the least bit interested, and I refuse to accompany you, Anton, if you insist upon this."

"Please, could you do me the favor of explaining a bit what your objection is? I will certainly honor it, but it would be helpful to understand your reasoning."

"Of course, Anton. As you know, I consider myself a Christian gentleman. I read the Bible. I know the Bible quite well. But I have never been enamored of the internecine argumentation that characterizes organized Christianity. I am not anti-Catholic. I am not a Know-Nothing. But no matter how saintly or how smart these popes are or have been of late, I have an experience and a knowledge of two of them that have forever set me against dealing with them."

"Well, I find this very interesting. Would you please detail this a bit?"

"Gladly." He took a couple of deep breaths, apologized for his outburst, and then continued.

"First of all, I think you know that I agonized over the whole experience of the War Between the States. Part of that agony—and I do mean agony—was the thinking I did about the Emancipation Proclamation. You know well how difficult it was to come to that conclusion and then to effect its promulgation. Well, recall I am quite a student of history. In my work to prepare the proclamation, I did a great deal of reading about slavery in different times and in different places. I know there were slaves in the time of the Bible and that there were slaves throughout the known world, but in my research I was astonished and disgusted to learn that one of the popes, a so-called religious leader, an Italian fellow—of course—who had the name Nicholas V, sanctioned slavery, even giving the right to traffic in human lives to the Portuguese."[144]

Abe continued, his voice rising in volume and pitch as he spoke.

"Then there is that arch-scoundrel Pius IX, who was pope during

---

[144] See the papal bull *Romanus Pontifex*, issued by Nicholas V in 1455. While a patron of the arts and an architect of the Renaissance, he was a man of his times when it came to the dominance of Europe in the world. During his reign, the Byzantine Empire came to an end. He sanctioned the capture and forced conversion of the "enemy of the faith."

the time of my presidency. I wrote to him asking that he make the Archbishop of New York, John Hughes, who was a strong abolitionist, a cardinal. He didn't do it. Then I found out that he and Jefferson Davis were communicating. That pope even sent Davis an autographed photo of himself. He called Davis 'The Honorable President of the Confederate States of America.' Maybe he was just being polite, or perhaps he was misinformed, but that man did not understand our struggle and did nothing to advance the cause of the Negro ... Oops—now you always say 'African American.' I know that the nation was rabidly anti-Catholic, but a leader who claims to speak for God should have had more interest and more courage. Why, after the war, Lee even said that the pope was the only European leader to recognize the Confederacy![145] There you have it, Anton. Those are my reasons for not wanting to deal with the leader of the Catholics. I am not anti-Catholic, I stress, but for the time being, I prefer not to traffic with such an organization."

"Very well, Abe. I do think you would find that things have changed under the last half-century of leadership, but I respect your feelings. We will not attempt to visit the pope. If you would like, though, we can visit the monuments of the ancient Romans."

"That I would enjoy very much. Thank you. Anton, I think these last comments were rather severe. Let me lighten things up a bit with some humor—if you'll allow it."

"Be my guest!"

"You can imagine that during the war there was a great need for secrecy. I guess government has always been obsessed by it, but in times of war it is paramount. Well, one evening at the telegraph office, I got word that a fleet had been readied and sent out. Its destination,

---

[145] The historicity of this is somewhat suspect, but it is bandied about as a possibility. After the Civil War, the letter became the foundation for Congress to pass a bill forbidding diplomatic relations with the Papal States (later Vatican)—a reality that continued until the appointment of Francesco Satolli as an "apostolic delegate" after a deal worked out between Pope Leo XIII and President Benjamin Harrison. Then, in 1984, full diplomatic relations were established between the Vatican and the United States during the presidency of Ronald Reagan. Archbishop Pio Laghi was the first nuncio to the United States. (See *A Plea for the West* by Lyman Beecher.)

of course, was top secret. One of the regulars who inhabited the place, and I suspect was a Confederate spy, sidled over to me and very quietly asked, 'Where has it gone?' I leaned into him and whispered gently into his ear, 'It has gone to sea!'" With that, Abe slapped his thigh and laughed out loud. The tension had been resolved with some of his typical humor.

"That's a good one! And true besides. Let's begin planning in earnest tomorrow."

Preparations

Preparations for European travel were not as difficult as they used to be. The quickness of the hover transports allowed one to arrive quite refreshed instead of dragging. The use of Astral Time also assisted. I wanted Darius and Darren to join us. I thought they might enjoy taking a little holiday at Percival's Upton Manor and spending some time with Percival's manservant, Omar O'Malley. They could barter in trade secrets, not to mention gossip behind our backs. (Little did the twins know, though, that every bit of Percival's place was as security endowed as Tadwil.) As usual, I got the lab cleaned and the transmorgrofier and accelerator dismantled and well hidden. I talked to Abe about British history since his last stay among us. He was amazed to find out how the great British Empire—upon which, once upon a time, the sun never set—had diminished. We reviewed a number of tour options and decided to spend just a little time in Rome and then spend a leisurely holiday in Merry Olde England. Darius and Darren made more leisurely clothes for Lincoln—concentrating, of course, on zippers. I wanted to be back by November of 2064 in order to show Lincoln a few more places in the States. During this time away, I would also have the leisure to figure out how to introduce Lincoln to the modern world. While he remained gentlemanly and polite, I could tell that he was itching to exercise some independence. Likewise, I was beginning to feel ornery, and when I begin to feel ornery, that obtuse spirit enters me, and when that obtuse spirit enters me, people tend to die in strange ways.

We loaded our own new hovercar with our belongings and cleared all the necessary licenses and permissions for the international trip, and then I let the boys take turns at the controls as we departed for our European holiday. It would take about four and a half hours to make the journey from Springfield to Rome. Once in Rome, we would have to use local transportation, since the old, narrow lanes of the city, carefully preserved, were too narrow to fly the hovercar hither and thither.

On the trip, we had some wonderful snacks that the boys concocted, most of them consisting of sweets and beverages. International law was very strict about alcohol consumption, so we limited our drinking to lemonade and hot tea (a good way to prepare for England, where the barbarians put milk into their tea).

On the way, Lincoln entertained us with more stories. "Once there was a man who was a-pestering me to make a friend of his a brigadier general. Now, I was the commander-in-chief, so I could make the nomination and my choice and command would be followed. I said to him, 'See here. You're a farmer. Suppose you had a large yard full of all sorts of cattle—cows, oxen, and bulls—and you kept killin' an' sellin' an' disposin' of the cows and oxen but takin' good care of your bulls. By and by, you would find you had nothing but a yard full of old bulls, good for nothing under heaven. Now, it will be just so with the army if I don't stop making brigadier generals!'"

We all chuckled, and Abe, of course, chuckled the loudest, including his characteristic knee slap. Well, we deserved it; we had encouraged him, I guess, so he continued.

"We did a lot of talkin' about issuing greenbacks. Now, of course, with this newfangled new American dollar and the money put away somewhere in your head, you might not find this humorous, but the discussions went on forever. Finally it was determined that we would, indeed, begin to issue greenbacks. Well, then the argument broke out over whether or not the motto on our hard currency, 'In God We Trust,' ought to be used on the greenbacks as well. It was tedious, and the contentious cabinet could not decide. After listening to this discussion for longer than I wanted to, I inquired if perhaps the motto should not be from the Bible itself: 'Silver and gold have I none; but such as I have, give I thee?'"

Abe sure knew his Bible.

Roma

We arrived at Rome's Hoverport in the early hours of the morning. It was much closer to Rome than the old Fiumicino Airport. Once again, I thought Abe would like a train ride, so we took the local from the hoverport to Stazione Termini in the city. From there we took an old-fashioned horse-drawn cab to our hotel, the Hassler, which overlooked the Spanish Steps. It is still the finest hotel in Rome. I knew that Abe and the boys would love the Italian cuisine. We had a single room for Abe, another for me, and a double room for the boys. Abe was still amazed that two or three people weren't sleeping together in hotel beds, as had been the custom in his time. Ah, social progress!

Abe was completely incognito. No one cared about the Didymus twins. I caught a few glances on our stroll for dinner, but that is to be expected, since my photo appears in almost every scientific cyberjournal in the world. We headed toward the Trevi Fountain. People still toss coins into the fountain, but now they have to make a withdrawal from their cyberaccounts at the kiosk nearby in order to get cold, hard coins for the tossing. We made the obligatory stop, tossed our coins, and headed toward my favorite place to dine in Rome—Ristorante Abruzzi, near the Piazza dei Dodeci Apostoli. I didn't care what they ordered for their *secondo*, but for all of us, the pasta carbonara was a mandatory first. We dined splendidly. The setting was simple. The restaurant was family owned and operated, and after our three-hour meal, we took a casual stroll through the night streets of Rome. We didn't get back to the hotel until late, but the next morning we could sleep in—and we did.

Our time in Rome went smoothly and quickly. As per Abe's rather adamant instructions, we avoided Saint Peter's Basilica, the Vatican, and most churches. (The boys did go to the Vatican Museums, however.) We did see the usual tourist things: the Flavian Amphitheatre, the Arch of Constantine, the Arch of Titus, and the various forums. We also spent a great deal of time at the Piazza Navona.[146] Of course, we had some of the famous chocolate tartufo from Tre Scalini. Abe could people watch

---

[146] The Flavian Amphitheater is known to most people as the Colosseum.

safely. No one recognized him.[147] Both the native Romans and tourists alike were more interested in the sites than the people around them. Abe, on the other hand, loved watching the people. Like all tourists, we walked and walked and then ate more of the wonderful cuisine of Rome.

Among other places, we ate at Il Pompiere, Apuleius, Ristorante Musa, La Porta dei Principe, Noi Nuova Osteria, Osteria Barberini, Pipera Al Rex, Ristorante Crispi, and Il Fellini. To put it mildly, we were well fed. Fortunately, the walking through the Roman streets and the time hoofing through a plethora of museums helped to keep us in shape. None of us minded our pedestrian efforts.

Lincoln spent an inordinate amount of time walking about "The Italian Wedding Cake," the monstrous shrine to Italian unification, the Risorgimento. The shrine to Victor Emmanuel II was built to honor the first leader (king) of a united Italy since the sixth century. Perhaps it was the fact that these Italian efforts were contemporaneous with Lincoln's own efforts to reunite his own country that made this place so interesting to him.

I did talk Abe into going into two of Rome's churches. I knew he would appreciate seeing the magnificent *Moses* by Michelangelo. He would have to miss the *Pietà* since he refused to go to the Vatican. We spent the better part of the day in the area of San Pietro in Vincoli.[148] At least from this one masterpiece Abe got a feeling for the splendid skills of that Renaissance master.

The other church we went to confirmed a bit of Abe's opinion of organized religion. I insisted that we visit the Capuchin Boneyard— the crypt of several small chapels of the church of Santa Maria della Concezione dei Cappuccini, on the Via Veneto. It is not far from the Piazza Barberini and its magnificent fountain. The walls of the crypt are lined with bones from the skeletons of deceased Capuchin priests and brothers. I, of course, enjoy its macabre power to shock. The boys enjoyed it too—perhaps a little too much.[149]

---

[147] For whatever reason, Rome is one of the only major European cities that does not boast a statue of Lincoln.

[148] "St. Peter in Chains."

[149] More on that later.

We also took several side trips to the usual places: Orvieto, Assisi, Florence, Venice, Milan, Naples, and Pompeii. We ate just as splendidly. We ended our weeks in Italy by spending a few days at the beaches along the Adriatic. Abe knew how to swim and enjoyed his time frolicking in the water, as did Darius and Darren. For my part, I observed, I read, and I plotted.

Arrivederci, Roma!

Well, all good things come to an end, and I had promised Percival that we would arrive at his place sometime near the end of October 2064. We returned from the beach area near Sperlonga. We spent a few more days in Rome eating, imbibing, and then preparing for our next leg of the journey.

We were well rested, well tanned, and well fed. It pays to travel first class. Abe was happy to see the places he had read about all his life, and he thanked me for the opportunity. He also made a point of thanking me for not making him violate his own religious sentiments. I was fine on both counts. The boys, likewise, were quite grateful.

We returned to the hoverport, got our own vehicle ready for travel, and settled in for the half-hour trip to England.

London and Its Environs

Once in British airspace, we were obliged to stop at New Heathrow. All of our papers were in order. (Recall that for traveling we used the names Drako Dorolex and Oskar Pferdbein). Once at Upton, we could resume the use of our real identities. The boys were able to use their own names. We finished the immigration and customs procedures and returned to our hovercar for the five-minute trip to Upton.

Upton Adventures

I asked Abe to wait a few minutes in the hovercar while I took the boys with me into the mansion. Percival was thrilled to see me again. It was a mutual feeling. I introduced him to Darren and Darius, and in turn

Percival introduced them to Omar O'Malley. He used the title "valet" for Omar. I had used "butlers" for the boys. Omar invited them to follow him to the room they would share in the west wing of the mansion, closer to the kitchen. They would have a lot in common to discuss. I had suggested to the boys that they might learn a few things from Omar. Percival had done likewise with Omar. Great minds, and all that!

Once they set off, Percival and I went to the library. Besides the tremendous collection of cybertomes, he actually had real books, including some incunabula from the Middle Ages.

"Percy," I said, "I have another guest. I know I told you I would be arriving with three other persons. I want to talk to you a moment before I bring him into the residence. As you know, I have been dealing with stressful and secretive affairs for some time now. I am grateful to you for your hospitality when I needed a little respite from those endeavors. Well, the next guest is the product of all that scientific work. Now, I know that you will keep my secret, Percival. It is vital for the time being. The moment to make this announcement to the world has not yet come. I need just a little more time. Can I rely upon our friendship and your discretion, old friend?"

"Most certainly, old chap. Now, my curiosity is piqued. What is this great secret?"

"Well, you know I work in genomic physics. I have had many successes, all of them trumpeted as triumphs, but this one is the best of all. I won't go into the details of the science; it would bore you and delay meeting your guest. I have worked with the science of cloning in great secrecy—not the cloning of farm animals and lower primates, but the cloning of human beings. Percival, I have cloned Abraham Lincoln!"

A furrowed brow appeared on Percival's face. A slight tilt of his head indicated disbelief. But he knew I would not deceive him. He recovered from his shock at my words and declared, "Well then, bring him in!"

I went out to the hovercar and fetched Abe. In one of our many conversations on the porch at Tadwil, I had told him about my rare friendship with (rare in its uniqueness and rare in my admission to having a friend) and rather frequent visits to Percival. I assured him that our little secret would be safe until we were ready to make it public in the relative near future. He unwound himself from the hovercar. (He contorts into strange positions to make himself comfortable.) Percival came out the great walnut front door with the gold lead–inlaid coat of arms of Upton. He stretched out his hand and looked up. (Of course.)

Sir Percival Pettigrew," I said, "I would like to introduce you to Abraham Lincoln, sixteenth president of the United States of America and recently returned from the dead."

"It is a pleasure, sir," said Percival. "Welcome to my humble home. It is not the White House, but I think you will find it comfortable."

"It is my honor, sir, to make your acquaintance," said Abe. "Anton speaks highly of you. I am looking forward to my time in your country and our visit to your home, although in the prairie where I hail from, we would not call this humble. However, I remain your servant, Abraham Lincoln."

"Splendid, splendid," said Percival. "I will take you to your rooms myself. My valet, Omar, might suspect something, but he is the picture of discretion. He knows to be—as, I suspect, do Darius and Darren. And without your characteristic beard, I don't think anyone in England will recognize you readily. I think your secret will remain safe as long as you wish."

"Thank you, Percy," I said.

"Thank you, Sir Pettigrew," Abe stated.

"Please just call me Percy."

"Fine," Abe replied. "And you can just call me Abe."

With that we went to our quarters in the east wing—the rooms that overlooked the lake. Abe asked whether or not he would be able to go swimming and if Percival had horses.

I guffawed. "Abe, you can swim in the lake. You can also swim in the indoor pool that you will find just off the Billiards Room. Likewise, there are plenty of horses. Some are steeplechase champions.[150] Just let Omar know, and he will prepare one for you. Percy and I will probably join you as well, if you don't mind.

With that we retired for a bit of a nap until dinner.

---

[150] So called because of races in the countryside that used church steeples as markers for the route.

At 6:30 p.m. sharp, Omar knocked on our doors, informing us that dinner would be served lakeside at seven thirty. It would be an informal meal; no dinner jacket was required.

We met in the Great Hall, and Percival joined us for the quick stroll to the lakeside gazebo. The picnic area was the size of a small park. The boys and Omar were already there, but naturally, they would eat separately from us.

Dinner was delicious, as always. Since it was informal, there was only a soup course and a main course, followed by dessert. The soup was cream of mushroom, made with a duck consommé. The main course was typically British—more something that the lower classes would eat, but it was, after all, informal. We had chips and kippers. When Abe took a drink of his beer, he made a sour face. I quickly leaned over to him and whispered, "Sorry. I forgot to tell you that the British like their beer at room temperature."

"Well, I'll finish this one," he replied, "but I want no more."

Dessert was a medley of peach, pomegranate, and blueberry sorbets. After the meal, we strolled around the lake. As the sun began to set, we headed back for the "humble home."

I asked Percival if we could go with him into London in the morning. Abe was eager to see this famous city. Percival said that he had planned to go to his eye clinic.[151] He said that all four of us could accompany him in his hoverlimo. Omar would navigate, and we would have the whole day to ourselves. We were told to be ready to leave by 8:00 a.m. We returned to our rooms at Upton and took our rest for the night.

In the morning, we were casually attired. Abe was getting used to the informality of this new life, even though he understood there were occasional events that would require more formal attire. The boys were excited because I had loaded $500 NAD each into their cyberaccounts. I suggested that they go to Savile Row and splurge. They did like to look good—though for whom, I don't know; I didn't let them far from Tadwil. Omar dropped Darren and Darius off in the Mayfair District. He dropped Abe and me off at the entrance to the Tower of London and then took Percival to his clinic. We would rendezvous later for the return trip.

---

[151] See chapter 13.

Once again, Abe did not stand out in the crowd. His disguise, his beardless face, and the interest of tourists in the sites rather than the people kept him safe from inquiring eyes.

We spent a great deal of time at the infamous Tower of London. Abe had heard about it and how it had been used at the whim of various monarchs. He commented that it was exactly such unbridled power that caused the colonies to revolt against the British. The sad tales of Henry VIII's revolving wives, of dissenters (both loyal opposition and genuine enemies), and of the general public held captive here in this dank, dreary place saddened him deeply. I could see one of his melancholy moods beginning to descend upon him, so I suggested we go to Westminster and to Buckingham Palace.

Decades ago, the Tube, London's famous underground transportation system, was rebuilt. Its ancient tracks and cars had become dangerous. The new system was virtually silent, for—yes—it hovered as it made its way through the labyrinth of routes. We didn't even have to "mind the queue" to get in. Microchip implants both paid the way with automatic deductions from our accounts and also made sure we were not on any of the Interpol (yes it's still around) wanted lists.[152]

Once at Buckingham, I thought for only an instant that it might be fun to visit with King William and Queen Kate, but then I recalled we were journeying about under our assumed identities and that using my pull as a knight of the realm would not work. We walked about the outside of the castle and played tourists as we watched the famous changing of the guard.[153]

Once again Abe commented about the size of the residence and compared it to the White House, which by comparison was quite modest.

---

[152] Remember, we are traveling under the aliases of Drako Dorolex and Oskar Pferdbein.

[153] I reminded Abe that the United States was now doing something similar at Arlington National Cemetery. He commented that he remembered when the North purchased/commandeered the property as a burial place for Civil War dead. He did not know that the government was subsequently sued by the Lee family and the Supreme Court returned it to the family, who in turn sold it back to the government. The signing of the new deed took place in 1883. Robert Todd Lincoln represented the government at the signing.

We walked over to the Parliament buildings. Parliament had been a nemesis of the Founding Fathers of the United States and did not do much better for the Lincoln presidency. Lincoln lectured me about the relationship between the Confederate States, the United States, and Great Britain. While the official British government position was one of neutrality, the British upper class favored the South. Trouble erupted between the Union and Great Britain when shipbuilders took advantage of the South's need for warships and built several for them. Later, after the war, those shipyards would pay a fine to the United States.

The current Parliament buildings were constructed around the earlier medieval ones. A fire in 1834 destroyed much of the medieval complex, but the "new palace" followed the form of the old. Its centerpiece is the Elizabeth Tower, known more commonly as Big Ben, after its largest bell.[154]

The structure is located officially in Westminster, of the famed abbey. Westminster Abbey's true and full name is the Collegiate Church of Saint Peter at Westminster. Once a cathedral for London, it is now a royal peculiar, meaning that it is under the direct control of the sovereign. (Only the British!) King Henry III began its current incarnation in 1245. We marveled at its size and spent considerable time walking about its many famous tombs. The most ironic of all the tombs is that of Elizabeth I and Mary I, the half-sisters whose political and religious sentiments were at odds with one another; now they rest here together. In fact, the inscription over the shared tomb reads, "Regno consortes et urna, hic obdormimus Elizabetha et Maria sorores, in spe resurrectionis."[155]

Well, it was a long day, but we enjoyed the touring. I enjoyed it all the more since no one recognized either of us. We communicated with Omar, who picked us up just a short distance from 10 Downing Street. He already had Percival and the boys, so we headed back to Upton. There we ate another informal lakeside dinner and retired.

---

[154] Pity that people don't do their homework and know these things.

[155] "Consorts in realm and tomb, here we sleep, Elizabeth and Mary, sisters, in hope of resurrection."

Shenanigans at Night

Unknown to me and unknown to Percy, our three trusted menservants, it turned out, had ideas of their own. Actually, those ideas were somewhat after my own heart; however, I cannot take any credit for them. It was completely their idea.

It seems that each of them alone, much less together, had a mind for mischief. It actually wasn't mischief quite as much as it was crime. All those evenings during which I thought they were sitting in the servants' dining room relaxing or playing cards, they were actually plotting some adventure of their own. Word of the Peter Pan desecration had buzzed around London and its environs for some time. All kinds of copycat thugs attempted to make their own news. There had been yet more efforts to steal the Crown Jewels, to blow up Tower Bridge, to dye the Thames Irish green, to flood the Serpentine, and to steal the statue of Lord Nelson from Trafalgar Square. My personal favorite was the attempt to manipulate the temperature controls at Madame Tussaud's Wax Museum to a degree so hot that the famous statues would melt. None succeeded. All the conspirators, in each instance, were caught, tried, and now reside in various London jails.

This cabal planned to succeed where others had failed. The omnipresent security cameras around London—much refined since their initial appearance at the beginning of the twenty-first century, and widely distributed since the defacing of the Peter Pan statue (ahem)—made such crimes absolutely foolish. But fools learn slowly. The three collaborators knew better than to try something in London itself, so they looked for other significant national treasures upon which to wreak their havoc. They settled on Stonehenge, that structure of stone that has stood in one form or another in Wilshire (near Salisbury) since 3,000 BC.

Percy did not know that Omar had a background in civil engineering. I knew that Darren and Darius were bright, but I had underestimated them. The trio, combined, was almost as bright as I am. I never suspected anything from them, however.

They traveled together one day to Dartmoor National Park, that repository of Bronze Age life on the British Isle. They wandered through

Wistman's Wood. There Omar inducted them into the beliefs and rituals of the Neo-Druids. After their return, in their evening sessions over the next few days, they plotted the assault. Every other day, one or the other took off. I presumed my butlers were going sightseeing, and Percy surmised that Omar was about business for Upton. Well, sightseeing they were a-going; however, the main intention was the accumulation of data to assist their project. They had to make sure that the national park grounds surrounding the stones would be secure. Oddly, there were no guards. I suppose the idea of stealing the stones would be preposterous. Defacing them was another matter, and motion detectors were active twenty-four hours a day around the perimeter of the stones themselves as well as in the grassy areas around the monoliths. Any movement heavier than a rabbit's would trigger an alarm that would bring the Wiltshire sheriff to the site, along with local officials of New Scotland Yard. The site, you see, was now owned by the Crown.

Besides the discussions about their dastardly deed, there were discussions of religion. Darren and Darius were members of a newer Baptist sect that had gained popularity in the United States in the last century. Omar, however, belonged to the Neo-Druids, a kind of smorgasbord of religions centered around the ancient Druid rituals (such as people thought they were) and newer age beliefs (focusing on environmentalist concerns and a "philosophy of theology"). Omar and his coreligionists had been bounced from the site several years earlier, and they never forgave the Ministry of Tourism for that excommunication. They were always seeking some form of revenge. These three figured a way not to tread upon the property and alert any authorities. All the security precautions were aimed at ground assaults on the site. No one ever thought of an air attack. I have to admit, they did their homework. The famed monoliths rested on an ancient foundation of Cretaceous chalk.[156] This rock is a soft, porous limestone. For a more visual concept, the White Cliffs of Dover are of similar composition.

---

[156] This is the vestige of biomicritic debris from the Cretaceous age (approximately 145–66 million years ago. One might call it part of the primordial ooze. This period was followed by the more famous (made that way, unfortunately, by late-twentieth-century films about dinosaurs) Jurassic period.

The boys had done a splendid lithostratigraphic study of the site. They knew that the night sky over the site was unprotected. They spent several nights scouting out the adventure. By means of GPR (ground penetrating radar, a popular tool in modern archaeology), they were able to discern the substrata upon which the famous stones rested. The result showed geophysical images that were then used to seek weaknesses in the ground substrata. They never had to set foot on the ground itself because the use of air-launched antennae fit perfectly in their air spy system. They were never detected. Any military radar would have missed them, since by using hovercars, they could literally fly under the radar. Their study revealed to them the berms that formed outer, but underground, circles around the plinths. They simply had to attack that weak strata of support, and like Jericho, the walls would come a-tumbling down.

The next phase of their destructive scheme was to create thousands of flea-size drones containing powerful sound amplifiers; with these they could generate the kinds of sounds that trigger avalanches.

The night of their deed fit perfectly into Omar's Neo-Druid religion. They selected October 31, 2064—All Hallows' Eve of that year. Since many in the country were observing the feast, revelry all over was at fever pitch. Percy, Abe, and I, being far too sophisticated for such shenanigans, went to bed early. Given the immense length of the approach to Upton, no trick-or-treaters were expected. First, though we shared a wonderful port.[157] The threesome took one of the larger hovercars from Percy's estate. It was comfortable enough for the three of them. The flight would be only about a five-minute adventure. Their drones easily fit into a specially made cargo net that would deteriorate as it fell, thus releasing the sound bombs on the soil supporting the great Stonehenge. (Oh, if only those ancient Druids could see this!) In the event that anyone happened to be in the area of the monument, that person would simply think he or she was being attacked by midgies.[158]

They left Upton at 11:00 p.m. Midnight would have been a better

---

[157] Taylor's Tawny Port, one of the best; it is always aged at least ten years.

[158] A slang term for a tiny pesky insect, neither mosquito nor fly, that seems to prefer human nostrils as a target.

time as far as the Neo-Druid was concerned, but they knew the witching hour itself might be a dangerous time to be about. They would be back well before then. They flew illegally low (presuming the constabulary would be busy with revelers on the ground and not too concerned about aerial anything). Once at Stonehenge, they made a quick circle of the site, double-checking their calculations. Omar flew the hovercar, and as they made their second circle around the park, Darren and Darius threw out bundles of drones—one bundle every five seconds—for a total of fifteen sacks of drones with twelve hundred drones in each sack. They would hit the ground at perfect intervals, each sack deteriorating as it landed. By time they were finished, with the sacks falling according to the law of gravity, accelerating at the rate of thirty-two feet per second per second, the first wave of subsonic explosions began to blast the atmosphere. They did not look back to see their handiwork. It was wiser and more expedient to return to Upton. So they did.

Meanwhile, the ground began to tremble as the ancient limestone foundation was shaken apart. Seismologists as far away as India recorded the event, thinking it was an earthquake. But it wasn't. It was the foundation of Stonehenge imploding. The great plinths that had stretched across the top of the support stones for thousands of years began to sway and then toppled. The upright stones fell into each other. Disarray was the order of the day.

The next morning, the cybernews carried the report of the destruction of the great English treasure Stonehenge. Percival was beside himself. I was too, to an extent; for a change, I actually had nothing to do with such an incident. Percival ranted about it and then projected the cybernews onto the breakfast room hall. King William V had been informed of the tragedy. Was it vandalism or a terrorist attack or an act of war? Opinions multiplied. The cybernews reporters all tried to outdo one another with theories. Archaeologists, seismologists, historians, and the "maddening crowd" all gathered at Stonehenge to see the destruction and to assign blame. All the while this was occurring, the three guilty parties were standing at the side table, waiting for us to ask for more breakfast (quail eggs, bacon, pomegranate juice, and coffee with freshly made rolls). A scene of the destroyed national treasure was projected on the cybernews. I looked at Darren, actually wanting a little more pomegranate juice and coffee. As the image came into clearer focus, I saw the slightest upturn of a smile on his lips. He saw me looking at him and resumed his staid footman's face, but at that moment, I knew. Oh, I didn't know the details, but I knew. And when I looked back at Darren I raised my right eyebrow ever so slightly in a questioning manner. Darren, in turn, gave the most imperceptible of nods. Then I was sure I knew. And Darren knew that I knew. And I knew that Darren knew that I knew. (Oh, enough of this epistemological malarkey.) I said nothing. Secretly I was actually rather proud of their accomplishment, but I also made a mental note to keep myself wary of those two once we were home.

Our Holiday Winds Down (Sort Of)

During the next few days, Abe and I spent time at the lake and riding about the extensive grounds. He spent hours going through Percival's library, picking out volumes to read at the lakeside gazebo. Even though he now had access to cyberinformation, he still enjoyed the old, familiar way of holding a book and reading. I really can't blame him. He particularly enjoyed reading Churchill's *My Early Life*, *The Gathering Storm*, and *History of the English-Speaking People*. Lincoln wanted to get more information about Henry Lord Temple, the third viscount of Palmerston, who was prime minister during his presidency, but the fellow's accomplishments were not noteworthy enough for Sir Percival's collection of history volumes. General histories of the era had to suffice.

After these weeks of relaxing, we went on tour again. We did a lot of the usual, traveling to Hampton Court, Windsor Palace, Eton, and Stratford-upon-Avon, and even making a day trip to Edinburgh.[159] He wanted to see Holyrood Palace (and have high tea) and Edinburgh Castle. For a little diversion, I took him to the Blair Street Underground Vaults. That piece of eighteenth century Scottish history is entertaining, if nothing else. We also stopped at the Lincoln Monument on the famous Princes Street.[160]

---

[159] When we visited Stratford-upon-Avon, Abe made clear that he knew his Shakespeare!

[160] The granite-and-bronze piece was sculpted by George Bissell. It was unveiled on August 21, 1893. It was the first foreign statue to honor Lincoln.

Lincoln Monument on Princes Street, Edinburgh
(Photo by the author)

We returned to UPTON and then spent another several days walking about, riding, and swimming. During this time, the boys were spending a great deal of their energy and money buying new clothes and learning new recipes and new behaviors from Omar. I was glad they were enjoying themselves and equally glad they were leaving us alone. I thought they would, but one never knows about servants! The image of Darren's smirk is implanted in my remarkable mind.

Our time in Great Britain was coming to a close. There were still a few things that I thought Abe would enjoy, so we once again took the hovercar with Omar and Percival into the city. We got off at the Clinic and summoned one of the great London traditions, now modernized—a hackney cab. Once they were fossil fueled, like all other vehicles, but since 2045, while continuing the classic black cab look, they are now hovercars—which the British, in their inimitable way, have nicknamed "hovvies."[161] Hovvy drivers must still possess the famous knowledge before they can receive a license.

I summoned a hovvie, and we took off for Kensingson Palace and Gardens. We strolled around for a while and then went into the palace itself. In one of the sections of the palace open to visitors, there were several large display cases. Inside of one was a letter written by Abe to Queen Victoria, expressing his sympathy at the death of her beloved husband, Prince Albert.[162] On April 29, 1865, a still-grieving queen would return the kindness and write a note of sympathy to Mary Todd Lincoln.[163]

After a light lunch of fish and chips from a vendor on the grounds, we took a stroll. I told Abe that there was something I really wanted to see. I explained in summary fashion the story of the *Peter Pan Piss* and the fun cooperation of my Scottish friends Angus and Fergus. He looked at the statue intently, and then once again that famous guffaw emanated from him as he slapped his side. He was vastly amused at the prank and said his boys would have absolutely loved this. Then he

---

[161] Pronounced "hōōvēēs."

[162] Francis Albert Augustus Charles Emmanuel was originally from Saxe-Coburg-Sallfeld in Germany. His family had long-standing connections to the British royal family. He died December 14, 1861.

[163] The original is in the Library of Congress.

surprised me. He asked if the two of us might pull something off before we left. Given the state of the land after the Stonehenge incident, and given that a third insult to the prized Peter Pan during another of my visits would be suspicious, I explained that I thought it wiser not to do anything at this time. Abe was saddened by this, but he understood.

We returned to Upton in a hovvie and then had another informal dinner at the lakeside gazebo. Although we had had fish and chips for lunch, we had another fish dish for supper: swordfish in a cranberry-champagne sauce, more chips, and beer. Percival had relented and refrigerated Abe's beverage. Dessert was a chocolate cake with apricot sorbet.

Our time abroad had been spectacularly successful. Abe enjoyed seeing the sites and roaming about incognito. The boys had forwarded home their many purchases and had gotten along famously with Omar. They shared recipes and, I suspect, stories about their employers. I only hoped that they hadn't gotten too many recipes for English food. Even though Percival's table is a delight, I preferred the cuisine of just about any place else. Percival informed me that our second-to-last evening would be graced with some dinner guests. There was a couple from Northumberland, the duke and duchess, who had been very generous to him in assisting the establishment of other eye clinics throughout the realm. They were on their way to London for a week of theater and had asked if they could stop by to say hello. Well, Percival could not let them come and go so quickly. He was ever the gentleman. I expressed some concern about others meeting Abraham. He assured me that I needn't worry. Besides Abe's incognito beardless self, Percy said, "That couple is extravagantly rich but as dumb as rocks. They inherited their titles. They could never have earned them. In fact, the only way they could raise their IQs would be to stand on a chair."

Well, this is unusually candid criticism from the gentleman Sir Percival Pettigrew, so I knew they shouldn't be a problem. Nonetheless, I warned the boys, who were prepared to protect Abe as though their own lives depended on it. (They did. I never told them about the fate of Humberto and Isabella, but they suspected I was not someone to trifle with.)

Percy asked if I would mind if Darius and Darren assisted Omar as footmen for the dinner. They would be dressed in the formal attire of the Edwardian era. I assured him that as long as they got to eat, there would be no objection. Percy went on to say that the couple tended to talk and talk and it would be difficult to bear them. He asked me to please put up with them for the sake of the clinics.

I thought to myself, *Well, who am I to judge?*

The eight o'clock formal dinner hour arrived. The company had not. Percy was agitated, and the repast was cooling. Finally the couple contacted Upton and said that they had been delayed and would arrive later the next afternoon. Percy and I had our formal attire on, but the boys and Omar had not yet gussied up, so we ate together in the servants' quarters off the kitchen. Actually, I was a bit relieved I did not have to meet the chattering couple, but the next day we would not be so fortunate. After eating, we retired.

The next morning, we spent some time together reviewing our visit. I asked Abe if there might be anything else he would like to do before we left. He said no and added that he would enjoy spending some final time in the magnificent library.

Well, the next afternoon, true to their word, the guests arrived. They might have been wealthy, but the hovercar they used was one of the original models, not the refined elegance to which I have become accustomed. They actually sounded the horn on the old vehicle. In their childishness they had equipped it with an old Klaxon from the beginning of the fossil-fuel Model T Ford days. I could not believe what happened next. We were lined up outside to greet these guests. The chauffeur descended from the front and went to open the doors for his employers. The first thing out of the car was a man dressed in an old military uniform, complete with the bicorne hat of days gone by. He looked the fool, but then again, Percy had warned me. All I could think of was that this person standing before me was visible proof that evolution can go in reverse. (That's quite a statement for an expert in genomic physics!) I had the suspicion that he had a Teflon brain— nothing would stick. I would soon be proven correct.

The rest of his attire was equally outrageous. He had on high boots, black, polished to the extreme. He wore pantaloons—red, with a yellow stripe running down the sides. His blouse was the eighteenth century kind, white, with puffy sleeves. Over that he wore a red yeoman of the guard's jacket with bawdy gold epaulets. In truth, he looked like a runaway actor from a bad production of *H.M.S Pinafore*! I did my best not to break out in laughter. The boys were fortunate to be in back of us. Their sniggering was audible to Percy and to me. I wanted to scorch them with a look of death, but I couldn't blame them. Omar, too, was choking as he tried to stifle a guffaw. What would the woman look like? I, too, almost choked to death when I overheard Darius say to Darren that the Duke of Northumberland ought to sue his brain for nonsupport.

Well, then the wife got out of the hovercar. When her first foot hit the ground, I thought there had been an earthquake. I was sure the rotation of the earth on its axis had been permanently altered.

One giant foot, the size of an elephant's, exited the hovercar. Then came the second. Then followed the rest of her corpulence. She, too, was attired rather strangely. She had on a tight-fitting white sequined dress with a royal blue sash.[164] The world's largest sapphire brooch was pinned to the sash, yet it was strangely tiny given the rest of her ample bosom. Her makeup had to have been applied by a blind person. A gaudy, bright red outlined her pursed lips. Eye shadow, thickly applied, gave her the appearance of one long dead. Her earrings matched her brooch, dangling from ears that matched the size of her "elephantiasized" feet. Her hat, I found out, was actually her hair, spun up a foot off her head, powdered white, with a blue-tinted ostrich plume fluttering in the breeze. It took my breath away—not because of the beauty, but because of the absurdity. It was hard to understand how Percival could actually befriend such humanoid monstrosities, but then he was always the gentleman and they were generous to his eye clinics for the poor.

The boys, of course, were not quite as composed as Percy and I were. I overheard Darius say to Darren that she was so fat it would take two trains and a bus just to get around her! Then Darren whispered back to Darius, "She's so fat that when she steps on a scale, it reads 'to be continued.'" Well, their sniggering and their comments were hilarious, and I almost bit my tongue in half to keep from laughing.

---

[164] She truly looked like two hogs in a gunnysack fighting for air!

Then Omar, to everyone's surprise, muttered surreptitiously, "That woman is so fat that when she sat on the beach, Greenpeace threw her back into the sea." Well, that one did us all in. Even Percival smirked. I had hoped, for her sake, that perhaps she was intelligent. While they were moving toward us, I asked Percival if she had any redeeming qualities. Even he said, "Sorry, old chap. She's so dumb that when you stand next to her, you can hear the ocean."

Well, isn't this going to be interesting? They approached, and Percival dutifully went up to them, gave a polite but perfunctory bow, and led them over to where I was standing. (The help, of course, does not get introduced.)

Percival said, "Sir Dr. Anton Bauer, may I present the Duke of Northumberland, Sir Tobias[165] Teitelbaum. And this is his wife, Dame Tallulah Teitelbaum."

As they stepped forward, Sir Tobias Teitelbaum shook my hand and said, "It is a pleasure to meet you. You may call me Toby."

Then his wife stepped forward and proffered her hand, swathed in a white glove with red sequins, and said, "It is also my pleasure. You can call me Tullee."[166]

I stretched out my hand to both of them and said, "It is my pleasure to meet you both. You can call me Sir Anton Bauer."[167]

Thank goodness their intellectual capacities were severely diminished. I didn't worry for a moment that they would recognize Abe standing with us. They wouldn't recognize their own king, much less a person from American history. A perfunctory introduction was made using Abe's former pseudonym, Todd Jackson. They looked up at this tall fellow who was gangly yet imposing, but they essentially ignored him. Abe breathed a sigh of relief, quickly catching on to the pathetic reality of this pair.

Omar and the boys left for the kitchen. Percival had asked if I minded if they assisted with the serving of dinner, playing the role

---

[165] Like myself, Sir Teitelbaum was obviously Jewish. "Tobias" is Hebrew for "God is good." "Tallulah" is of Irish/Gaelic origin and means "leaping water."

[166] To be pronounced "Tool-ēē."

[167] See chapter 1, paragraph 1, sentences 1–3.

of footmen. I didn't mind, but I had the courtesy to ask them if they minded. They did not. It would be fun seeing the getups they would wear and the deportment they would bear.

Percival invited us all into the small salon while the other household workers carried their considerable luggage to their rooms. I found it interesting that Percy used the small salon. This couple would never realize the insult that was being dealt to them. Truly important guests were always entertained in the grand salon or the library.

We shared a sherry or two, and then dinner was announced. (Odd, too, that Percy did not give them time to freshen up and change their attire, although who knows what they would have worn to dinner!)

I must say Darren and Darius looked quite becoming in their footmen's uniforms. The black bow ties, stiff shirtfronts, and cufflinks (gold with a cloisonné logo of Upton), made a great impression. Omar, too, with his dark Middle-Eastern looks, was quite dashing.

We did eat in the grand dining room. The chandelier cast a magnificent shadowed light. Candles on the table were placed in splendid Waterford holders. The place setting was the family heirloom set with the Pettigrew coat of arms on the dinner service and the flatware. The first course was a leek soup with small scallops. The main course was drunken beef (an English specialty) with potato dumplings and rutabaga puree. Dessert was a simple flan. The boys served with elegance and panache. I was quite proud of them. They followed Omar's lead carefully.

Unfortunately, the Teitelbaums were not persons of elegance or panache. During the meal, we all tried to keep up some semblance of an intelligent or witty conversation. Wit was beyond them. Intelligence was wanting. Abe tried out several of his standard stories. He was careful not to reveal his own identity but changed names and avoided stories that obviously had been connected to him, even though this dull couple would never have known the difference. Tullee was so dense that she probably put lipstick on her head to make up her mind.

At one point during the meal, Abe said, "I was once at a nice hotel in Chicago, and an Englishman said to me, 'I have heard with some astonishment that gentlemen in America black their own boots.' 'This is true,' I responded. 'But do not gentlemen in your country do that?'

'No, certainly not,' replied the Englishman. 'Then whose boots do they black?' I retorted."

He did not tell any of his signature stories. It was not that they would have identified him; it was that the listeners wouldn't have understood.

Percival chortled lightly. I did too. The Teitelbaums did not understand the joke. Even our footmen smirked at the mild insult to the English. I tried to engage Dame Teitelbaum in some personal conversation. I commented that her name was rather unusual, certainly for someone in the twenty-first century. While putting forkfuls of food into her ample mouth, she responded that she was not named after that city in the Colony of Louisiana; nor was she named after that red-headed, horse-headed, hoarse-speaking twentieth-century actress Tallulah Bankhead. No, her name came from a song her parents liked—"Running from a Gamble," a big hit of 2011 by Company of Thieves. Then, to everyone's surprise and horror, she began to sing it.[168] I prayed for a sudden death as she began to crow the words:

Ooh girl. Be my girl!
You know there was death in Tallulah,
Don't turn your eyes away
Ooh girl! Be my girl!
You know there was death yeah.

And on she droned. I kid you not. Neighborhood cats began to screech. Traffic on the A1 came to a grinding halt. The Waterford water pitcher on the table shattered. I was sure that we would all need ear surgery. Is there a word beyond "horrible"? That's what her performance was: ghastly, horrendous, appalling, disgusting, unbearable, repulsive. And these are the kind reviews.

Despite Abe's efforts, Percy's efforts, and my efforts, we could not get the conversation going. In fact, we rather gave up in the face of the opposition. Never before in my life have I heard human beings talk as much and as loudly and as stupidly as that husband and wife. Of the

---

[168] I use the term loosely.

two, Tallulah was the greater sinner. On and on that woman chatted, conversed, gossiped, harangued, yakked, chitchatted, jawed, nattered, shot the breeze, and literally chewed the fat. (Yes, she did!) Never before in history had someone spoken so much and eaten so much all at the same time. Her chewing was accomplished with her vocal chords in motion. Sadly, small particles of partially masticated food came flying out of her mouth with every utterance. We were all victims of the assault, but poor Abe was seated across from her. With each explosion of victuals, he calmly picked up his napkin and wiped off his face. His dinner jacket, on the other hand, would have to be discarded. No one would want to don it again.

Honestly, I hoped that woman would have a brain operation so she could change her mind! I had never heard so much about so little for so long. Her husband hung on her every word, agreeing with her about everything with the standard "Yes, darling. Anything you say, darling!" The rest of us just ate in silence. The "footmen," standing behind this pair of nimrods, kept rolling their eyes. Dame Teitelbaum managed to insult royalty, commoners, Catholics, and Protestants (remember, they were Jewish), and she even insulted Jews. She railed against vegetarians and alcoholics and smokers and the price of everything. She slighted the Irish, the Italians, the Poles, the Germans, the French, the Chinese, and then the Americans. She completely forgot that we were of that illustrious ilk.

Her husband, Tweedledum, affirmed everything she uttered. Honestly, that woman was so dumb she would dig for apples. It was all really too much. Never before had such a fine meal been spoiled by one person. I couldn't wait until we were finished. But then, as the rest of us were finishing our dessert (the simple flan—how appropriate!), Her Ladyship asked for more of the drunken beef (on top of flan!). Omar turned and fetched the silver serving tray from the sideboard and approached Dame Tullee from the right, as is appropriate. However, at that very same moment, Dame Tallulah turned to see what was taking Omar so long to give her more food. (She was like the giant plant in *The Little Shop of Horrors*—"Feed me!") As she turned, anxious for her food, she bumped the serving tray. The beef fell onto her ample bosom, down her dress front, and into her lap. As she reacted, she jerked her right arm into the silver serving fork, piercing her bulbous upper arm. She let out a screech that would shame the banshees of hell. I half expected gravy to seep out of the slight wound, but a few pinpricks of blood appeared instead.

Omar was mortified. When Dame Tallulah stood up, being gentlemen, we also arose; however, as she stood, she brought the damask tablecloth along with her, spilling plates and flatware, wineglasses and water glasses, and knife rests and candlesticks into her lap (even when she stood, part of her remained behind) and onto the floor. She turned crimson. I thought she was having a stroke, but it was just anger at the perceived insult to her personage. Percival, of course, was mortified that such a thing could happen in his dining room and to his patrons. But next Sir Tobias ("call me Toby") went to his wife. At first he took his wife's gargantuan hand and tried to comfort her. Then he looked at Omar and shrieked, "You fiend! You scoundrel! You upstart!"[169]

Poor Omar had nowhere to turn. Darren and Darius quietly tried to clean up the mixed stew that was now the vestige of dinner, but Sir Tobias Teitelbaum was not finished. He was shaking uncontrollably as he stared at Omar and said, "You Saracen! I duel you to a challenge. I mean, you to me a challenge duel. I mean, I challenge you to a duel. Swords. At dawn. In the garden."

Percy tried his best to calm his friend, but there was no balm adequate enough to assuage the cause. He pulled his sword (yes, he wore it in its scabbard to dinner) and began to brandish it, threatening all nearby with accidental decapitation.

I had the urge to practice defenestration on him! It was a scene out of a comedy of errors. Finally Omar, Darren, and Darius had the common sense to leave the room. Her Plumpness fell back into her chair, once again shaking our home planet. This time the world went off kilter, so great was the assault upon the Earth.[170] Percival asked that Abe and I be excused, and we quickly left. Then he tried to talk Sir Tweedledum out of his threat, but the man was beside himself. He finally poured a

---

[169] His vocabulary matched the era of his attire.

[170] "Off kilter"—what a strange phrase. It seems it originated in the Old English word "*kelter*," which meant "good condition" or "good health."

remaining bottle of wine that had been left on the side table over his wife's anterior. (I suspect the dress was ruined anyway). It cooled down the burn of the hot gravy and meat, and then he took his handkerchief out of his jacket's front pocket with ceremony and dabbed at the wound on his wife's arm. Mollified a bit, he finally sat down.

Percival simply said, "I think it's best that we forego cigars and cognac and retire to our rooms."

Dame Tallulah and Sir Tobias huffed out. Her stomping (or was it just her walk?) caused chandeliers to sway, vases to topple, and wall hangings to go crooked.

What would happen in the morning?

CHAPTER 20

Sometime During the Night

Well, to say the least, that was some evening. After Sir and Dame Tobias and Tallulah Teitelbaum trounced off to bed, the house quieted down. The crew of servants, ever hovering unseen in the background, went into the room to clean up the mess. Darren, Darius, and Omar sat in the servants' dining room, trying to figure out what had happened. Of course, they knew what had happened. They just couldn't believe it. How unfortunate that there are people like the Teitelbaums who give us nobles a bad name!

About twelve thirty, I heard a gentle knock at my door. I was a little surprised at this, for the Pettigrew Mansion, Upton, was always extraordinarily quiet at night. The walls and door were very thick. Heavy carpeting ran through the center of each hallway. Yet, there it was—a gentle knocking at my chamber door.

"Identify yourself and enter!" I commanded.

The serving crew called out their names, and ever so slowly the door opened. There stood Darren, Darius, and Omar, still in their footmen's uniforms but sans the white serving gloves. Not unlike Abe's dinner jacket, those gloves were now good only for the trash bin.

"Sir," uttered Darius. "We three apologize for the intrusion at this time of the night, but we could not bear the—well, pardon the phrase—low-life character of those two guests. None of us has ever seen anything like it. Omar assures us that never before have guests behaved like that in this most esteemed house. Well, Sir, we are wondering if there is anything you would like us to do about it."

Uh oh, thought I. *These two and their companion are catching on.*

I said, "Well, to quote—or somewhat quote—one of the famous

authors of this country, 'It wouldn't hurt to decrease the surplus population.' Now, good-night!'"[171]

I had no idea how that troika would interpret my words, but I was sure they got the drift. Unknown to me, besides all the kitchen/recipe/footman lessons that Darius and Darren had learned from Omar, they had also learned many secrets of the house. Now, Percy was a man above reproach, and none of those secrets were about him personally, but the house had been around a long time, and it held many skeletons. Omar had made it his mission to learn as many as possible, and he had been very successful. There were the usual scandals, of course: mistresses, young men consorting with young women, a few poisonings, and a lot of missing money and valuables. Omar most delighted, though, in the secrets of the house's architecture. Almost as in the movies, many of the paintings of royals about the place actually concealed spy holes that could be used to watch and listen to conversations. (Even sub rosā ones.)[172]

Most exciting to Omar, however, were all the secret passages tunneled into the massive walls of Upton. Most had originally been built during the time of the Protestant Reformation. The Pettigrews had been Catholic and for several generations were part of the secret resistance that offered succor to the brave Catholic clergy who dared to travel from town to town and house to house to offer Mass and hear confessions. These secret hiding places were known as priest holes, and many homes were dotted with them.[173] When it became clearly politically expedient to abjure Catholicism, the family did just that and embraced the new official religion of the realm—Anglicanism. In fact, the mansion boasts a chapel where the local Anglican clergy would come to administer the sacraments for the family. They even had their own family chaplain for over a century (but not the same person).

Well, that unholy trio repaired to the servants' kitchen to exchange

---

[171] The quotation is from Charles Dickens's *A Christmas Carol*. Dickens's phrase was actually a commentary on one of the philosophic and economic debates of the time proposed by Thomas Malthus, an early advocate of population control.
[172] See footnote 142.
[173] For further information, read Evelyn Waugh's *Edmund Campion: Jesuit and Martyr*, 1935.

many words. They came up with the conclusion (actually correct) that the elimination of that horrible obstreperous duo would not disturb my peace of mind. In fact, it would be a gift to the whole planet. Omar was concerned about Sir Percival, but these three were clever. They planned to enter the room using one of the secret corridors between the walls. These passageways were narrow, but if they went one at a time, it would work out splendidly. Sadly, forensic science was in such a fine state these days that virtually every conceivable method of murder could be ascertained. It was almost impossible to get away with murder. But, then, who am I to say that? I'd gotten away with several. (Several? Plenty!) Perhaps the trio would be successful as well.

They planned to spy through the portrait of Queen Anne that hung over the fireplace in the room assigned to Sir Tobias. Once they saw that he was sound asleep, they were going to inject him with a small but adequate dosage of air, which would offer all the signals of a heart attack. As long as no medical examiner detected the place of injection, they would get away with it. With the three of them acting in concert, two could easily hold him down (he was not the size of his wife—not even close), while the third forced open his mouth and injected the fatal air bubble into the back of his throat.

However, the spyhole offered them another method. Sir Tobias Teitelbaum used a sleep apnea machine. Oh, they were different from those of decades past. These no longer could be plugged into an electrical outlet. England, like the USA, had abandoned that mode of power in favor of the vector system. His little machine, now the size of a deck of cards, had no wires. But it still had the long, flexible hose that connected the facemask (which covered the mouth and nostrils) to the oxygen pump. Each of them saw this new opportunity, and they silently agreed by looking at each other and nodding to show that they now had a simpler, more natural way to eliminate this pest.

Omar hurried back to the servants' kitchen and got three clean sets of white serving gloves. There would be no fingerprints. They took off their shoes but not their socks. Their entrance through the closet wall would be silent and undetected. Each put on a pair of extra cotton socks over his own to lessen any possibility of DNA residue being left behind.

They carefully checked over each other using flashlights[174] and then slipped ski masks over their faces to eliminate any possibility of leaving so much as a whisker of DNA behind. The police would not have any knowledge of the secret passageways anyway.

The spy door opened quietly, as it was built to do. They moved in. By placing his hand over the metal plate that stored the power, Omar incapacitated the machine. The sound sleep induced by the product would ensure that Sir Tobias stayed asleep. Darren disconnected the flexible hose from the unit, and then, as Darius gently lifted up the head of the sleeping fool, Omar wrapped the hose around Tobias's neck twice and then pulled it tight. The action awakened Tobias, but he was powerless. In less than a minute, his struggles ceased. He had been choked to death with the very machine that was engineered to save his life. Darren reconnected the hose to the unit, and the three of them walked out. They held their heads high until they got into the secret hallway. They then hurried back to the servants' kitchen, took off their ridiculous costumes, and then burst into laughter. The trio presumed (correctly) that the coroner's verdict would be that the machine ran out of stored vector power and that in his struggles to get the mask off, poor Sir Tobias Teitelbaum choked himself to death! Was this not the perfect crime?

The three of them went to their quarters and tried to catch some sleep before their morning duties summoned them. Meanwhile, I was sleeping the sleep of the innocent. So was Abe. So was Percival. So was the she-devil from hell, Dame Tallulah "Tullee" Teitelbaum.

The Next Morning

Abe, Percy, and I came down at seven thirty for breakfast—the typically delicious and abundant English morning fare. After the previous night, we were all still rather weary, if not leery. It should have surprised us, but it did not, that Dame Tallulah had already been eating. And eating. In fact, Omar surreptitiously reported to Percival that she had already consumed a rasher of bacon; a dozen eggs, prepared in a variety of ways;

---

[174] Or *torches*, as the Brits say.

as well a quart of orange juice and a pot of coffee. We were accustomed to waiting until all the guests were at table before indulging in our breaking of the night's fast; however, Dame Teitelbaum had other ideas.

Percival, ever the gentleman, suggested that we wait for Sir Tobias to come down. And we did. And we waited. And we waited. When the grandfather clock in the room struck eight, Percival finally motioned for Omar to come over. He whispered to Omar, "Please see if everything is satisfactory with Sir Teitelbaum." Omar went off, knowing of course that everything was not satisfactory with Sir Teitelbaum. He went up the back staircase to Sir Tobias's suite and knocked gently, then a bit harder, and then quite firmly and called his name. Surprise— there was no response. Omar played the game well and knocked again. Then he entered the room and saw the corpse of Sir Tobias Teitelbaum, purple-faced, a death grimace on his lips. Rigor mortis was doing its ancient labor, and the flexible oxygen tube around his neck was already embedding itself further, as Tobias's neck was swelling because of his prone position.

Omar left the door to the chamber open and went with manservant calmness to Sir Percival. He whispered in his ear, "I think Sir Teitelbaum is dead." (Of course he knew damn well that the male Teitelbaum was no longer of this earthly coil.)

Percy exclaimed, "What? Say again!"

And this time Omar said quite audibly but still in a gentlemanly fashion, "I think there is something wrong with Sir Teitelbaum."

Percy responded to Abe and to me, "Please, accompany me upstairs. Madame, if you wish, please remain here until we have further information."

Well, there was food on the table, so she needed no convincing.

The three of us went upstairs, followed by Omar, Darren, and Darius. Percival went first into the room and saw his houseguest reposed in death. We followed, approaching the bed carefully, bent over the torpid corpse, and confirmed the reality.

"Oh, my!" said Percival. "It has been centuries since something like this happened in Upton. Omar, call the police and ask them to send the coroner right away. Anton, please, let us—Abe, you, and me—go to Dame Tallulah and tell her the sad news. She will be devastated."

I thought to myself, *She might even lose her appetite!*

While Omar went out of the room to use the cybercommunication system to contact the authorities, we three went back to the breakfast room. There, Dame Teitelbaum was sitting back on her rather large specially made chair. She inquired, "What's up?" Sir Percival sat down next to her, took her bounteous hand into his own, and said, "My dear, it seems that Tobias had an accident during the night and strangled himself with the hose from his breathing machine. The police are on the way. Let me take you upstairs, but remember: don't touch anything—especially not your husband."

Well, this is going to be interesting, I thought. It took some time for the behemoth to ascend the stairs. At the sight of her husband in bed on the other side of the room, she began to wail. (Frankly, I was afraid she would faint and fall over—with catastrophic results for the planet, not to mention the mansion and all of us standing nearby.)

She saw her dead husband; the flexible tubing was wrapped tightly several times around his neck. Tobias's face was an interesting mauve. The banshees returned as she screamed. "Murder! Slaying! Anarchists! Assassins!" (At that remark, Abraham blanched visibly, but he quickly reinstated his composure.)

She kept up the litany and added, "Murder most foul!"[175]

The constabulary arrived shortly after we finally got the grieving widow to sit on a divan in the upstairs hallway. Her sobbing and bellowing threatened the peace of the European Continent. One quick glance at her and the inspector general knew who she was and what he would have to deal with. He went to her first and offered his sympathy and then explained what he had to do: examine the body for any signs of foul play, thoroughly go over the death room, and question everyone in the house. While he was questioning the lesser servants, the coroner arrived and confirmed that Sir Tobias Teitelbaum had, indeed, accidentally strangled himself with his own breathing apparatus. Only

---

[175] For a moment I thought this poor excuse for humanity might have redeemed herself by quoting Shakespeare's *Hamlet* (act 1, scene 5: "Murder most foul, as in the best it is. But this most foul, strange, and unnatural"; the line is spoken by the ghost). However, she was referring to an old MGM film from the 1960s, a century before, a Miss Marple mystery titled *Murder Most Foul.*

his fingerprints were found on the tubing and the machine. No forensic evidence of anything else was discovered. (At this time in history, such investigations, which used to take hours, are now completed in minutes. Technology, unlike the Teitelbaums, knows of evolution.) Each of us was questioned, of course, and although there was no forensic evidence to tie anyone to this "accidental death," the police had to be thorough. Dame Tullee was regaining her strength and her voice, not to mention her appetite. She asked for something to eat and then began her harangue anew. The chief inspector had Percival sign off on the report. Efforts to get Dame Tallulah to do the same were entertaining, to put it mildly. Finally he held the pen in her hand (which completely enveloped his), and she scribbled the semblance of a signature.

Percival knew the importance of burial within twenty-four hours in Jewish tradition and so gently told Tullee that he would see to the arrangements and that if she needed anything else, she should let him know. He then had his family physician, who had been summoned earlier by Omar, inject her with a sleeping solution. It took a quart of that concoction before she finally dozed off on the divan. The elixir worked!

Meanwhile, Percival was busy with the funeral arrangements. Since they had the legal documents releasing Sir Tobias's body, he called a local undertaker. The funeral observances would take place at Upton, with burial in the Teitelbaum family plot in Northumberland the next morning. Percival also contacted a local rabbi who agreed to conduct the service. Percival even had small programs printed up with readings from scripture (naturally, the Old Testament only) and from some secular sources. He included the Mourner's Kaddish in both Hebrew and English.[176] The casket was a rubbed bronze. He would have liked to have had the Teitelbaum coat of arms on the casket cover, but time was too short.

Meanwhile, Dame Tullee was waking up. As she began to move, the house trembled with her exertions. She picked up right where she had left off, caterwauling her litany of murder, mayhem, etc. After

---

[176] The *Mourners' Kaddish* is a prayer offered at a time of grief. It affirms one's acceptance of the glory of God despite tragedy.

some fifteen minutes, she collapsed onto the divan; however, there was something new added to the litany: "Oh, Tobias, I cannot go on without you. I will not go on without you. Oh, murder! Oh mayhem! Oh, murder most foul! Dear Tobias, most certainly I cannot go on without you!"

Sadly, her implicit threats of suicide made the scene all the more pathetic, but the sentiment was not lost upon Darren, Darius, and Omar. She repeated her act continually, well into the late hours. Finally the physician was summoned again, and he sedated the behemoth with even more of the magic solution. The household retired for the evening, preparing for tomorrow's obsequies. But not all slept. The unholy trio plotted. *What have I created?* I thought. They decided that they would help Dame Tallulah (or, as they began to call her, Damn Tullee) to fulfill her wishes. The three of them, using Omar's latent skills at computer cybercrime, were able to break into Tullee's microchip and forward a message to the London and Northumberland cybernewspapers. It would appear to have originated with her. It read,

> Friends and family,
> I have no desire to continue living without my husband,
> Sir Tobias Teitelbaum. I will vanish this evening, never
> to be seen again.
> —Dame Tallulah Teitelbaum

Once again these three musketeers scurried through the hidden passageways after observing her through the spy holes in the portrait of Queen Mother Elizabeth that hung in her suite. She was quite asleep. But how would they move her? They decided that she wouldn't feel any pain with all the sedation, so the three of them rolled her bed to the double window with the lead latticework and then simply rolled her out the window.

First she fell into the hedge below, and then she rolled off the hedge and onto the finely manicured lawn. From there Omar came with one of the estate's hovercars. The three of them tied her hands and feet to the lower front and lower back of the conveyance and then firmly trussed her torso to the middle of the machine.

Omar had some difficulty getting the hovercar to rise to the legal height for travel. Darren and Darius, meanwhile, took a second hovercar and followed. The unwieldy body bumped and banged against obstacles such as trees and buildings. It was just so difficult to get the proper height. Finally Omar got to the Thames and followed its winding course into downtown London. He had pulled in a chit from a friend who worked for the London municipality and managed to have all the security cameras go offline.[177] The confusion it caused for the London Police and New Scotland Yard gave them the opening they needed to complete their endeavor. Another obstacle they had not prepared for came up along the Thames—Tower Bridge. Omar tried to maneuver underneath the support struts, but there wasn't enough room between them and the bridge proper to fly through. The boys, sans the huge and heavy still-breathing body, made it through just fine. Finally Omar took a flight risk, revved up the hovercar into its highest gear, and just cleared the struts with his pudgy payload.

Ever on the lookout for some added adventure, the boys flew their craft in circles for a bit around the London Eye.[178] Both vehicles then landed in Jubilee Gardens, between the Eye and the Thames. The threesome existed their respective machines and untied the dozing Dame. Darren and Darius then tied a two-hundred-pound weight to each of her feet and rolled her into the water. An immense tsunami-like wave resulted. It went outward from the dock, swamped the boat on the other side of the river, and even splashed against buildings along the opposite shore.

---

[177] Debate as to the real nature of this surveillance system continues. Is it an invasion of privacy, a spy apparatus, or genuine security?

[178] Built in 1999, it is still Europe's tallest Ferris wheel. It is also known as the Millennial Wheel.

The London Eye
(Photo by the author)

Unknown to the trio as they made their escape was the fact that in the various twistings and turnings of the obese woman during her flight, several puncture wounds were inflicted upon her still-living self. The blood, which was beginning to ooze from the wounds, attracted eels, specifically some very hungry predator eels, *Anguilla anguilla*.[179] The feast was a banquet of unparalleled joy to them. Thousands slithered through the water to the feeding trough of her body. This, of course, would eliminate any danger of identification. But also unknown to them was that the sudden displacement of so much water was amplified by the presence of the eels. The underwater casements, now some two centuries old, could not take the added weight of the body and the eels. They began to shift and opened up an old sewer line from Victorian times. The water from the river, of course, sought its own level and began to back up through the old pipeline. The pipes were so old that they began to fragment under the sudden pressure from so much water. As the pipes shattered, the water seeped up into the ground, making the area around the Jubilee Gardens into a swamp. With the foundation thus disturbed, the great London Eye began to rock precariously. Part of its fame was that it was supported by an A-frame brace on only one side. This was not strong enough to endure the collapsing substrata of soil, and the great wheel fell over onto its side into the garden.

News of the disaster was reported around the world the next morning, but only three people suspected its origin. Percival was beside himself. When Dame Teitelbaum did not appear for breakfast, he assumed it was because of her grief, but as the hour for the service approached, he thought someone should check on the hapless widow. I volunteered. Like Omar the day before, I rapped gently on her door, and then rapped more firmly, calling her name, even resorting to shouting out "Tullee!" There was no response. I pushed the door open and saw no one. I did see the suspended cybernote with its plaintive words. By now that note was making its way through the cybernews along with the London Eye disaster. I ran down to the breakfast hall and, with modified surprise, informed Percival that another of his guests was not to be found—and this one probably had disappeared forever.

Omar, Darren, and Darius stood at their stations, looking as innocent as lambs, but I caught a slight twinkle in Darren's eye. I truly did not know what had happened, but I knew that somehow her disappearance and the disaster at the Jubilee Gardens had to be connected. Abraham,

---

[179] Aka European eel. They can live to be eighty-eight years old.

through both of these episodes, had remained rather still—remote, even—during the events surrounding us. I suppose when one has endured the Civil War and assassination, such events are not particularly noteworthy.

Once again New Scotland Yard came, as well as the chief inspector, Clive Barrowman. They had many questions for each of us. There was no sign of foul play that could be discerned. (He never thought of looking out the window to the crushed greenery beneath Tullee's suite.) The rabbi arrived, and permission was given to proceed with the ceremony for Sir Tobias, but by now it all seemed rather pointless. Nonetheless, we endured it. Abe even looked genuinely moved as he read the Mourner's Kaddish. The police stayed for the service—not so much out of respect, but rather to attempt to ascertain whether anyone looked guilty; but the boys remained the picture of propriety.

When the service was over, the casket was loaded into the back of the hearse and a light lunch was served. In honor of Sir Tobias's Judaism, Percival had a completely kosher buffet brought in from London. Breakfast had been ruined by the disappearance of Tullee. Discussion of her cybernote was the theme of every conversation. The magistrates had nothing to conclude other than that this grieving widow had been true to her publicized word and, huge as she was, had disappeared without a trace.[180] They did cast a few glances at Abe, still known here as Todd Jackson. If Abe suspected that anything was amiss, he did not let on.

---

[180] I will never eat eel again.

CHAPTER 21

Cheerio, England; Hello Springfield

Our time in England was quickly coming to an end. Percival was absolutely distraught over the events of the past weeks. A guest died in his house, another guest mysteriously disappeared, the iconic London Eye fell into the Thames, and the ancient shrine of Stonehenge was destroyed. Like most upper-class Brits, he took these things most seriously. It showed in his demeanor. While he remained ever the gentleman, his conversation had dulled. Meals became perfunctory events rather than celebrations. Knowing what I knew (oh, here we go with that epistemological garble once again), I thought it best to get Darren and Darius Didymus out of the country. Abe, too, was beginning to itch for some new adventures. He had gone through all the tomes in Percival's library of printed books. It was also late autumn, and I wanted to return to Springfield before the snows arrived, if they would. Ever since the climate changes, one never knew what a winter, summer, fall, or spring might actually bring forth.

I let Percival know at breakfast that I thought we would be leaving within a few days. I could tell that he was genuinely relieved because of the situation, but he was also saddened because we might not see each other again. Regrettably, Angus and Fergus MacDougall never made it during our visit. How I had wished to introduce Abe to them!

The night before our departure, there was another late discrete knock upon my chamber door. "Enter!" said I. It was Omar. Now, this surprised me greatly. I was afraid he was going to deliver some bad news about Percy, but his demeanor was not sad. It was respectful and hesitant—the demeanor a valet should have.

"Dr. Bauer," he began. "I would very much like to accompany you and Darren and Darius and Todd Jackson back to the States. I have never been there, and as you know, I have become very close friends with your valets. Perhaps we could arrange some time for them to accompany me about your country. I have not yet mentioned anything to Sir Pettigrew. He has become rather sad these last days, and I don't want to cause him any further injury."

"Well, Omar, I know that you and the boys are friends and have enjoyed your outings and your time together in the kitchen. I appreciate all that you have taught them, and I am sure they have taught you some new tricks as well. I would speak to Sir Percival about this, but I have two reservations." (Actually, I had three, but I didn't want to let him know that I knew—there we go again—about his role in the decapitation of Stonehenge. I wasn't so sure I wanted him set loose in the United States with the twins.)

"My two reservations are these: in this difficult time, Sir Percival really needs your assistance. Besides your presence in the house, he has come to rely upon you for his work in the eye clinic. Secondly, when we return, we will all be quite busy getting the house and my lab up and running again before the bad weather might set in. You have never experienced a winter in the Midwest of the United States. I don't think you would find it very pleasant. However, I will speak with him about having you come in the spring. The weather is splendid then, and everyone will have a better time. I am sure that Sir Percival won't mind your absence by then. What do you say?"

Omar responded, "Well, I am disappointed, but I understand your points. I look forward to the spring and will do everything I can to assist Sir Pettigrew in the meantime."

"Thank you, Omar. Or should I say شكرا؟[181] See you in the morning."

It was a sleepless night. I didn't particularly care, since the boys would be piloting the hovercar back to London and then to the States once all the regular immigration and customs details were finished. I would have to assume the identity of Drako Dorolex again until we were in international airspace.

That morning the entire household showed up to wish us farewell. Abe was particularly gracious in greeting each person by name. Percival gave Abe a splendid going-away present. He had seen many photos of

---

[181] "Shūk'-ran"—standard Arabic for "thank you."

Abe and knew that in the colder, damp weather, Abe liked to wear a shawl, the male adornment of choice in mid-Victorian times. It was a splendid tan shawl, made from the finest cashmere, specially ordered from Scotland. It pleased Abe greatly, and even though the morning was on the warm side, he donned it before entering the hovercar.

As I shook hands with Percival, he leaned in close and whispered to me, "Please, Anton. Don't worry. Your secret is safe with me."

"Thank you. I will let you know when my covert activities will be made public."

Once in the vehicle, we took off to begin the return journey. These days much of the piloting was simply programmed into the machines, but there was always the need for the human touch. I knew that Percival would recover in due time; however, in about three months, he would again go into mourning. You see, my sleepless night was spent trying to figure out what to do with Omar. I didn't want him anywhere near Darren and Darius, much less Abe. He was a danger to me and to Abe.

I am always prepared for eventualities, as you know. I carry with me, always in disguised form, an "arsenal of assistants," should a little lessening of the population continue to be a necessity. I had arsenic. I did not want to use it in any way, shape, or form in the usual method of adding it to a beverage or food. It would act too quickly and be relatively detectable. And I would surely become a person of interest, even though I was half an ocean away by noon. No. This had to be a little subtler. With the boys leaving Upton, Omar would be the only footman left on duty. I knew that everyone would be asleep, weary from departure preparations, and wanting to be up and ready in the morning. I went down to the footmen's livery. I dusted the inside of all the white footmen's gloves with the poisonous powder.

Actually, ever since seeing the play *Arsenic and Old Lace*, I had wanted to try something like this. I had found my chance. The poison would gently, quietly enter Omar's system through the tender skin underneath his fingernails. As the weeks went on, his health would deteriorate. He would feel numbness and burning. With some luck, after removing the gloves, he might even run his fingers through his hair, allowing each blessed follicle to absorb some of the death I had planned for him. He would grow numb and begin to lose weight—maybe even his eyesight. Since the dose at each ingestion was so small, it would be a slow death, and anyone observing him would assume something else was wrong—cancer, perhaps. Finally heart failure would occur, and that would be the verdict of the coroner. It would take about two months if he served even every other evening. I would be long gone from the scene, and there would be no evidence that could be connected to me. Oh, Percy would contact me, and I would have to tell the twins about Omar's expiry, but I had come too far to do anything other than play it safe. As the tune from that British rock group of the 1980s insists, "Another one bites the dust!"[182]

Back in Springfield

It is always good to get home. Oh, don't get me wrong; I love to travel, to learn, and to teach, but coming home is always special. Abe, too, felt a genuine homecoming after his many recent travels. The twins set about the work of getting the house in order. We hired outside help to prepare the grounds for the winter. The boys went to the neighboring farms to visit the men and women who had watched over our property and animals while we were gone. They had been paid by automatic deposit into their accounts, but I insisted we be neighborly. I, of course, went straight to my lab to sterilize everything and to prepare to set up the genomic accelerator, should the need arise.

We had returned just a few days before the national celebration of Thanksgiving. For my part, it meant little, but I recalled that Abe had a hand in fixing the date for Thanksgiving on the last Thursday of November. It seems that previous to his 1863 declaration, each state set its own date for the feast.[183] A bit of chaos ensued, for it was long before the era of instant communication. Among other reasons, Lincoln did this in an attempt to bring about some kind of unity to the divided, warring nation. The South, of course, did not recognize his authority, so it wasn't

---

[182] Queen, "Another One Bites the Dust," from *The Game*, 1980.

[183] The declaration was made on October 3, 1863. After decades of lobbying for an official date, the efforts of Sarah Joseph Hale to establish a uniform date for the feast finally paid off. She is better known as the composer of the children's ditty "Mary Had a Little Lamb."

until well into the period of Reconstruction that the holiday took its present form through the entire country. I've gotten rather accustomed to accommodating Lincoln's needs, both real and perceived, so we had a bit of a celebration at Tadwil. The twins prepared a customary Thanksgiving feast, with all the elements having been grown or raised upon the property. After they had brought the feast to the table, I invited them to join us. Abe was pleased with their company and the victuals.

Another new element in the routine at Tadwil was the introduction of a daily high tea. Whenever we were at the estate at that hour, which was almost every day, the twins prepared this traditional English treat for us. We had been at Upton so long during this last visit and had so enjoyed that most civilized custom of the British that we incorporated it into our daily ritual. I admit we did cheat a bit by not having the full variety of edibles that would generally be included in high tea. Contrary to what some think, the custom of high tea is relatively new. It originated in early Victorian times, so, of course, it was "ever so proper." The break from whatever one was doing allowed time for some conviviality, not to mention a minor jolt of caffeine to make the rest of the workday tolerable until the great evening meal. I decided that we should also do our best to experiment with different brews of tea. (We would never use those uncivilized tea bags that are still about.) The varieties were legion. There were, of course, the major tea families: pu-erh, oolong, green, black, and white. Within those families, there were endless choices of specific flavors. We delighted in guessing what we were drinking on any given day. Some were smoother than others. Some were naturally bitter, while others were naturally sweet. We also incorporated that barbaric British custom of putting milk into tea. At any rate, we looked forward to our daily respite from labor.

As Christmas approached, I knew I would likewise have to do something to observe the feast. If you recall, I am not of the Christian persuasion. Abe was not enrolled in any definite confession of faith. The boys had adopted (they thought secretly) the Neo-Druidism of Omar. Nonetheless, we put up a tree, grown on the property. I insisted that any decorations be handmade or natural. We used some old German candleholders for Christmas trees that Darius found at a yard sale. When lit, the tree was quite spectacular. Strings of berries from the garden festooned the bush. We kept it up only a few days. I had insisted that no gifts were to be exchanged. No one minded. It snowed that Christmas Eve; it was the first snow in December in forty years. We determined that this natural gift was sufficient for all of us. We had a special afternoon tea on Christmas, complete with the proper finger sandwiches and so on. Dinner that evening was right out of *A Christmas Carol*. Well, almost. We had roasted goose stuffed with shrimp, sweet potato puree, acorn squash with brown sugar, and, for dessert, crepes Suzette. Abe really loved that.

As the new year dawned, 2065, I knew that there would be many changes. I left Abe more and more to his own devices and his own time. He did enjoy Tadwil and did not stray far from it. One day he did return to Ann Rutledge's grave and came back to Tadwil in a somber mood. I was beginning to think about when and how to make him known to the world. It had been some time since his "birth," and the time for his epiphany was approaching. That evening, the cybernews announced that on May 4 the City of Springfield would observe the 200th anniversary of Abe's assassination and subsequent burial at Oak Ridge Cemetery. The event would follow the same pattern as the 100th anniversary in 1965 and the 150th anniversary in 2015. The train that bore Lincoln's body was destroyed by fire in 1911, but copies of it were reproduced just for these observances. I asked Abe if he thought he was up to at least watching the events from a distance. He went one further and said he would very much enjoy watching, at close hand, his own burial. His grin betrayed his sense of humor. That decided it for me. Abe's "coming-out party" would coincide with the 200th observance of his death.

The Christmas snow soon melted. A few weeks into January, when the weather in winter used to be frigid and snow-filled, we took advantage of the climate change and went for a ride along the Sangamon. There wasn't a trace of ice on the river—not even the thin layer that sometimes appears overnight and quickly melts away. While we stopped to let the horses rest and drink from the river, I asked Abe if he thought he was ready for the next big step in his new life—to go public. He looked at me a moment and said, "Anton, I've been waiting for this moment a long time. As you know, I can be a rather patient man, but I was soon going to ask you that question. I do believe that I can handle it. Whether or not the world can is another question altogether. Do you have any ideas about how we should go about this?"

"Yes," I answered. "First, let me ask you this. You've been most cooperative in maintaining your secret identity; new names such as Todd Jackson and Oscar Pferdbein have helped. Also, your beardless face has assisted you in blending into the mid-twenty-first-century crowd. Would you like to grow your beard back? It is so very much a part of your popular identity."

"Yes. Yes. Yes. Frankly, even with the new machines you use for shaving whiskers, I find that daily routine tedious. I would much enjoy not doing that and having a beard to tug on. The distant look of Abe going into memory mode was painted across his face. His eyes grew a bit distant, and then he closed them. When he came out of his brief trance, he asked if I knew the story of why he grew the beard. I did, but I let him tell it anyway.

"Well, you see, it was like this. I was running for president in 1860 on the Republican ticket. This was a very new political party, and we were still finding our way into the national scene.[184] I was taking trains and horses everywhere, trying to get our message out to the public. I was in New York, in a little place named Westfield. I was speaking to a crowd of people there who were sympathetic to the Republican platform. A little girl named Grace Greenwood Bedell was in the crowd and later wrote me a letter telling me that I would be taken more seriously if I had whiskers.[185] Now, my Pap never had whiskers, which was quite unusual for us Kentucky backwoods folks. This was one of

---

[184] The Republican Party was founded in Ripon, Wisconsin, at a meeting in an old schoolhouse on March 20, 1854. Its original members were ex-Whigs and antislavery people who had been angered by the Kansas-Nebraska Act that repealed the Missouri Compromise. Its first motto, "Free labor, free land, free men," was coined in 1856 by Salmon Chase, who later ran for president himself and served as Lincoln's secretary of the treasury.

[185] Grace Greenwood Bedell Billings was born in Westfield, New York, in 1838. She married a Union veteran and moved with him to Delphos, Kansas. She died there at the age of eighty-seven in 1936. (See appendix E.) Lincoln was the first

the rare times I followed his example. Well, that little girl's letter got me to thinkin', and I started growing those whiskers, first on my chin and then filling in on the sides. I looked pretty good in those whiskers, I think. On my way to the inauguration, we stopped in Westfield, and I met with that little girl and asked what she thought of my whiskers. I guess she approved. I kept them, as you know. Now I will be delighted to see how it all turns out again. Thank you, Anton."

"My pleasure. Now, let's go back and get some lunch, and then we can chat further about your future.

We rode back and had a light lunch. It was actually more of a brunch, because Abe liked flapjacks with lots of maple syrup and strong coffee. We used homemade bread to sop up the syrup from my own trees. I am already looking forward to spring, when a new supply of syrup will begin to run. Fresh strawberries and blueberries, flown in from California, were served in cream as well.

Weeks went by. Afternoon teas went by. We enjoyed the game of guessing the exact type of tea that we were drinking. Some were sweet. Others were just a bit bitter. We began to chart our favorites but made sure there was something new at least three afternoons a week. It was a wonderful custom for us.

Abe's beard was coming in nicely. He looked exactly like the image on the copper penny or the old five-dollar bill. It was January 21 when I got word from Percival that his "new" servant Omar had died. (Imagine that!) He was deeply distraught. He communicated that the autopsy was not very definitive—odd in these days—but it seemed Omar had died of heart failure. No other preexisting conditions seemed to precipitate that. Percy was quite beside himself. He mentioned that in such a short time the London Eye fell, Stonehenge was damaged beyond repair, a knight of the realm died in his house, and another peer of the realm mysteriously disappeared. Now Omar was gone. I offered to come and visit a bit, all the while hoping he would say no, and he did. He was convinced that his house, like other great manor houses was cursed or haunted. I assured him that such is the stuff of superstition. I mentioned that his

president to sport a beard. Some ninety photos of him with a beard are known to exist. Likewise, forty without the beard are about.

former manservant, Maurice Wilkins, was still living out a comfortable retirement in a dwelling that Percival himself had provided. He agreed that was so. I said that perhaps Fergus and Angus would come to stay with him for a week or so, but he did not want their rather raucous companionship at this time. I ended by reiterating my offer and wishing him the best.

Now I had to tell Darren and Darius that their new boon companion would not be coming to visit. Ever. I thought it best to have Abe present as well, to act as a mediating party should the twins react in any sort of unprofessional way. I summoned them to the library and offered them a seat. Imagine—the master standing while the servants sat! Anyway, I simply told them rather matter of factly, "I have just received word from Sir Percival that his manservant and valet, Omar O'Malley, has passed away. He died yesterday. The coroner reports that it seems to have been caused by heart failure. I know that you had become fast friends and were looking forward to his visit sometime in the near future. As is the custom of the Neo-Druids, he has already been cremated, and the ashes have been buried. Sir Percival did him the honor of using the Pettigrew family plot. If you wish to take a few days off, I understand. Everything here is running well since our return from England. Abe and I can certainly manage for a few days."

"Yes," said Abe. "My sympathy to you both. We all enjoyed Omar's company and the tireless service he rendered to us. Is there anything I can do for you?"

"Thank-you for telling us," said Darren. "I think we will send a message of condolence to Sir Percival and to Omar's parents as well. We will take two days off, if you are sure you don't mind. May we use one of the hovercars?"

"Yes," Darius added, "I think a little time away would be good. We can be back on Friday evening, Doctor, if that is satisfactory."

"Indeed," I replied. "By all means, take the hovercar of your choice, but if you decide to stay away a bit longer, do let me know."

Darius and Darren said in tandem, "Thank you, sir." They exited the library. So did Abe, who was obviously upset at the news. And so did I, externally saddened but internally rejoicing because another potential enemy had been eliminated.

Two days later, true to their word, the twins returned. Abe and I had made time for several lengthy conversations about his future. I knew he wanted more independence, and I wanted that for him as well. Sort of. I was also anxious to return to my laboratory to begin working on some new ideas that came to me during our sojourn abroad.

On his "birthday," we celebrated with a great cake and homemade ice cream. Abe loved sweets. In his time, there was nothing like the variety available today. Darren made the cake, which essentially resembled an Italian wedding cake. It had six layers and was filled with vanilla and chocolate custard. Decorating the top of the cake were small bits of crushed Neuhaus chocolate arranged to say "Happy 275th Birthday, Abraham Lincoln."[186] He loved it. We sang that wretched ditty "Happy Birthday to You."[187] Abe loved this too. It is so simplistic that after the first time through, he knew it and sang it solo. It was not a pretty experience. After the cake and hazelnut ice cream, we had some cognac and then retired for the night.

I got up early, wanting to do some work in the lab before beginning what might prove to be a difficult discussion with Abe. Just before I got out of the door, Darren approached me and asked if he could expand our gardens. He wanted to grow more vegetables and increase the acreage of our already sizeable flower gardens. I was gratified that he took this initiative and told him I would place $1,000 NAD in his account to use at his discretion. He walked away quite pleased.

The next day, I told Abe that we really had to get serious about what came next. I reminded him that this spring, in 2065, there would be a spectacular reproduction of his funeral to mark the 200th anniversary of that event. He reminded me that we had discussed this and he was looking forward to observing his own funeral. His beard was ready, and all we had to do was determine how to introduce him to the world. In 1965 and in 2015, on the 100th and 150th anniversaries

---

[186] Neuhaus chocolate is some of the world's finest. We had it imported from the "home shop" in the Galleries Royales in Brussels.

[187] Abe had never heard it before. It seems that its first use was in 1893 by two sisters, Patty and Mildred Hill. The words were originally "Good morning to you." It was a simple song, easy to teach children. By 1912 the customary birthday words had been attached to the melody.

of his assassination and funeral, Springfield sponsored several days of reenactment activities. Each of those years tried to be true to the original. The 2065 event would be no different.

Although the original train engine that brought his casket cross-country was destroyed in 1911, a replica would bring a weighted casket to Springfield. A logistical headache that the original funeral organizers had to deal with was the fact that in the middle of the nineteenth century, small private lines owned most train tracks. The coordinated effort was remarkable, given the communication means of the times. The original funeral train went from Washington, DC, to Baltimore. From there it went to Harrisburg, Philadelphia (Independence Hall), New York, Albany, Buffalo, Cleveland, Columbus, Indianapolis, Michigan City, Chicago, and finally Springfield.[188] At each stop, there were thousands of people. The casket was opened, and the public could file by to view their fallen leader.

In Springfield, Abe laid in state in the Old State Capitol building. His burial was May 4. That was when his coffin and that of his son Willie were placed in a temporary receiving vault at Oak Ridge Cemetery (my former third-shift stomping grounds). Its peripatetic existence is chronicled elsewhere. Finally it came to rest permanently and unmolested (so thought Robert Lincoln) in the cement chamber in the great monument erected for the Lincoln family. This year would be much the same, but there was one added feature. Usually taking place on the Fourth of July, this year, for the two-hundredth death anniversary, there would be a contest to discover the person who could best proclaim Lincoln's Gettysburg Address. The winner would be made an honorary pallbearer. Efforts were made at all the other reenactments to find relatives of the original men who carried Lincoln to his final resting place. The contest winner would walk in front of the hearse—a carriage adorned with black ostrich plumes. In the original procession,

---

[188] Along the route, all kinds of Civil War songs were played and sung by the crowds. They included "The Union Army March," "Our Banner of Glory," "Rock Me To Sleep," "Stand Behind the Union," "The Soldiers' Death Song," "Grand Union Medley," "Hymn for the Union," "A Nation's Trust in God," "Every Star-34," "Stars and Stripes Unfurl," "Defend the Stars and Stripes," "May God Save the Union," and "Sadly the Bell Tolls."

Lincoln's favorite horse, Old Bob, was part of the spectacle. At each of these great anniversary events, there was another horse that played the part. The winning Abe would walk immediately behind that horse.[189]

I was quite frank with Abe about the possibility of his depression returning around the memorial time of his assassination. He was aware of that prospect but said the opportunity to finally come out to the public would override any distress he might suffer. I hoped that would be true. The fourteenth and fifteenth of April came. Lincoln did draw into himself a bit on those days. He spent silent hours on the rocking chair outside on the great porch that surrounded the house. He himself was wrapped in the shawl that Sir Pettigrew had given him, but he did not fall into the deep depression that I feared.

The next days went as usual as we prepared for the great event of the two hundredth commemoration of his funeral and his debut into this wider, newer world.

Funeral Day: May 4, 2065

The morning of May 4 dawned with alternating clouds and sun. Fears of rain dissipated as the hours ticked by. Thousands of people had come to Springfield for the event, joining the crowd of locals. Taverns, restaurants, and hotels were doing a brisk business fleecing people. Anyone dressed in period costume received a 50 percent discount. It was amazing to see what some people thought the mid-Victorians dressed like. The boys and I did ourselves up for the occasion too. Abe wore his customary Brooks Brothers black suit with the tall hat. (Of course, this suit had several zippered compartments hidden within.)

At nine that morning, the contest for the Gettysburg Address took place in front of the Old State Capitol building. Some three thousand people came to watch. As a nod to authenticity, the building was bedecked in flags festooned about the building. A podium was erected in front of the main doors, but again, nodding to legitimacy, no sort of

---

[189] Think about that a moment. Would you want to walk immediately behind a horse?

amplification device was allowed. Each speaker would have to project—a speech requirement that had not been seen for over one hundred years.

To our chagrin, there were about three hundred contestants wishing to compete. Given that the speech itself was only about two minutes long, we were looking at some six hundred minutes of listening to the same proclamation. Add some time for ascending and descending the stage and for introductions, and the prospects of a pleasant morning went grim. An announcement directed all the contestants to line up around the building. Then the team of judges began walking along the circular queue, measuring each candidate's height. Anyone not exactly six feet four inches was automatically eliminated. Some of the contestants had placed lifts in their shoes. Taller candidates had cheated on the height of the hat. The unwhiskered were whisked away. In his first life, by that time in 1863 when he delivered the original address, Lincoln had already become rather emaciated. Any contestants who looked too well fed were likewise sent on their ways. The remaining candidates had been reduced to a still unmanageable fifty. The team of judges made the rounds again, checking the candidates for the telltale mole on Lincoln's cheek. Historically it was on the right. Those who had pasted fake moles on the left were next to leave the contest. Finally the frock coat lengths were compared, and anyone whose coat was too long or too short was eliminated. The process of selection took almost an hour, and the crowd was getting restless and booing the hapless rejects as they trudged away. Finally there were six candidates who would have the chance to compete and to imitate Lincoln's appearance and utter those famous words. One of them, as you may well have surmised, was the real Abraham Lincoln.

Candidate one announced himself as Avery Manfield Stone. He did fine for the first sentence and then got confused and was booed off the stage. Candidate two came forward and offered his name: Isaac Frederickson. He began to recite Lincoln's rather long First Inaugural Address.[190] The judges hit their gong, and Isaac went away in shame. Four candidates were left. Candidate three ascended the rostrum and began to recite the Gettysburg Address. He did it perfectly from heart,

---

[190] See appendix F.

complete with dramatic pauses. Then the judges gonged him off the stage. Lincoln had not delivered the original address from memory. He used notes. Candidate Four got stage fright and left before performing. Candidate Five ascended. He gave his name as Abraham Lincoln. The crowd was somewhat bemused by this and waited to see what happened. He looked about the throng with nervous, darting eyes. He had seen the failure of the others and was afraid he, too, would be eliminated and be forced to make his shameful exit. He performed, however, perfectly. Each word, each pause was measured out with great solemnity. He was a true contender!

Now the sixth and final contestant, our Abe—the real Abe—went up the steps. His lanky frame ascended the platform with his customary awkward gait. *Good. Already a sign of authenticity.* It was so natural that no one could think it was rehearsed. Then he looked over the crowd and announced: "I am Abraham Lincoln, President of the United States." Some in the crowd booed at him. Others laughed. It seemed as if this Abe (the real one) were copying his immediate competitor in the contest. If skepticism had a look, it was that crowd. He took off his hat, searched in vain for the text, put his hat back on, and then pulled out his notes from his frock coat pocket, and, as you might expect, flawlessly proclaimed the Gettysburg Address. As he reached the peroration, his voice got stronger, and as it got stronger it also became higher in pitch—the exact characteristic that he was known for.

The Gettysburg Address[191]

Four score and seven years ago our fathers brought forth, upon this continent, a new nation, conceived in

---

[191] There are about five known versions of the speech, each written by Lincoln and given to friends. This is the Nicolay Version. This and others are kept in the Library of Congress. A large stone inscription in the Lincoln Monument also contains the address. Depending upon the version, the address was approximately 272 words long and lasted two minutes. The Bliss Version is better known and is the last that Lincoln himself signed. Edwin Everett's speech at Gettysburg that day, on the other hand, lasted some two hours and was 13,607 words long. (No one has memorized it.)

liberty, and dedicated to the proposition that "all men are created equal."

Now we are engaged in a great civil war, testing whether that nation, or any nation so conceived, and so dedicated, can long endure. We are met on a great battlefield of that war. We have come to dedicate a portion of it, as a final resting place for those who died here, that the nation might live. This we may, in all propriety do. But, in a larger sense, we can not dedicate—we can not consecrate—we can not hallow, this ground—The brave men, living and dead, who struggled here, have hallowed it, far above our poor power to add or detract. The world will little note, nor long remember what we say here; while it can never forget what they did here.

It is rather for us, the living, we here be dedicated to the great task remaining before us—that, from these honored dead we take increased devotion to that cause for which they here, gave the last full measure of devotion—that we here highly resolve these dead shall not have died in vain; that the nation, shall have a new birth of freedom, and that government of the people by the people for the people, shall not perish from the earth.[192]

Silence descended over the crowd. They knew something special had happened, but it was still confusing, for the two final contestants were so similar. The judges hovered together to discuss how to resolve the situation of a seeming tie.

Alex Leas, the senior partner in Leas, Leas, and Abernathy, the best-known law firm in Springfield in the middle of the twenty-first

---

[192] Gettysburg was a new military cemetery for those who had died there in battle less than five months before. The date was November 19, 1863. On the way home, after the dedication, Lincoln did not feel well. In fact, it seems, he had a minor case of smallpox.

century, had proposed a test of Lincoln trivia. Only the "true Lincoln," they hoped, would know the correct answers.

Leas spoke to the crowd. "Ladies and gentlemen, you have all witnessed a historic event in this, the bicentennial observance of the burial of Abraham Lincoln. Your judges have compiled a series of personal questions that, we hope, will help to determine who the winner of our contest is.

"I would like to begin with contestant five. Sir, what is the name of your Springfield dog?"

The man answered readily, "His name was Fido."

"Exactly. Congratulations. Contestant six, what is the name of your favorite horse?"

"His name was Old Bob," said Abe.

"Exactly. So far each of you has answered correctly. Let's try again. Contestant five, where did you write these famous words?"

"I wrote the address in the White House and edited the text on the train to Gettysburg."

"Correct again. Now, contestant six, who was the other speaker that day?"

"It was Edward Everett, sir," said Abe. "The old windbag spoke for some two hours. Frankly, I thought my razor was dull until I heard him speak."[193]

Everyone burst out laughing. The judges and the crowd began to see who was the real Lincoln. It was a comment typical of his clever spontaneous wit.

"Correct again. Let's try the next question. Contestant five, what is your middle name?"

Without hesitation, contestant five responded, "Thomas, sir. After my pap."

"Contestant six, what is your middle name?"

"Sir," said Abe, "I have no middle name. My name is simply Abraham Lincoln."[194]

---

[193] Abe swiped this line from a book of Groucho Marx one-liners.
[194] Lincoln had no middle name. Most people of that era did not.

"Ladies and Gentlemen," said Leas, "we have a winner. Contestant six, please come forward. Contestant five, please stand down."

Abraham moved forward, and as he moved, he received a raucous round of applause. Henry Trumbull, another of the judges and a descendant of the famous Illinois statesman Lyman Trumbull, took to the rostrum and said, "Congratulations. You, sir, are the winner of the Bicentennial Abraham Lincoln Funeral Gettysburg Address Competition. Now, would you please tell us your real name?"

Lincoln spoke loudly. "I am Abraham Lincoln, the sixteenth president of the United States."

The crowd again went silent. Then boos and hissing started again.[195] I began to fear for Abe. I was in the third row of listeners, and I pushed my way forward. I went up the dais and stood next to Abe. I had to muster all the voice I could, for as you recall, there was no amplification system that day.

"Ladies and gentlemen—residents of Springfield and honored guests: I believe that all of you either know me or know of me. I am Dr. Anton Bauer. Yes, the Dr. Anton Bauer whose name appears in the cybernews and who was knighted by King William V of England. As you know, not too long ago I purchased property in Sangamon County, along the river. In the several years that have passed since that purchase, I have been busy pursuing my scientific work. It involved genomic manipulation. Please listen to me. What I am about to say will offend some and scandalize others, but I am telling you the truth.[196] I have been working these many years to improve the science of genomic physics. And I have succeeded beyond anyone's imagination. Now, at great personal risk, let me begin with two admissions of illegality. After you have heard me, you can do with me as you will. I am not afraid.[197]

"Yes, I know that the cloning of human beings was outlawed by

---

[195] "Over all crowds there seems to float a vague distress, an atmosphere of pervasive melancholy, as if any large gathering of people creates an aura of terror and pity."
—Émile Zola, *The Attack on the Mill and Other Stories*

[196] As Pilate states in John 18:38, "Truth! What is that?" As you know, I have a rather flexible definition of the term.

[197] But I had the boys readied nonetheless.

the 2040 Acts of Universal Scientific Agreement. I admit I have violated that international trust. My only excuse is that I wanted to accomplish something before the science of human cloning fell into the clutches of persons or nations that would use it for harm.[198] I also want to publically admit that it was I who was responsible for the theft of a piece of clothing from the Ford Theatre Museum. I took it because I needed the actual DNA of Abraham Lincoln in order to proceed with my work. Other efforts at human cloning, as you know, involved the gruesome work of defiling corpses. I would never do such a thing! I assure you that the man standing before you is indeed Abraham Lincoln, the sixteenth president of these United States, redivivus.[199] My particular field of expertise was the development of an accelerating process by which the DNA could be engineered to revivify the dead DNA of a subject and bring it to its condition at any time of life I so determined. I decided that for Abraham Lincoln I would have the acceleration process cease to function on the equivalent of April 15, 1865, the day of Lincoln's death from the assassin's bullet. The details of the science remain secret and hidden. I do not want enemies to poach the information needed to accomplish this great feat. I will be happy to entertain questions from the scientific community tomorrow morning at my estate, Tadwil. Abraham will be there, but I want to reiterate that I will not divulge the formulas or machinery needed to accomplish this.

"Should you not trust me, should you be so bold, you may open the well-sealed grave of Abraham Lincoln, and you will notice that everything is as the last time the casket was open in 1901."[200]

Darren and Darius gave each other knowing looks. They didn't know that I saw them, but I did. Pandemonium ensued. Outraged citizens began issuing threats against Abe and against me. Others, who knew my scientific reputation, began to applaud. City police and state officials (who had come to protect the members of the Illinois legislature) finally calmed the crowd. Leas announced that whether or not this man

---

[198] See, I can still lie with the best of them.

[199] "Brought back to life." Some in the crowd looked puzzled at this reference.

[200] Well, I didn't really think anyone would do this, and they didn't. Should you be interested, there is a purported photo of Lincoln from that event taken—and later regretted—by one Douglas Crawford.

was who I claimed he was, the march to the cemetery must take place. It was already behind schedule and upsetting the carefully choreographed historical reenactment.

The hearse was brought forward, and so was "Old Bob."[201] Lincoln—the real Lincoln—took his place behind Old Bob and in front of the hearse. The pallbearers, all descendants of the original pallbearers, took their places next to the hearse. There were about five thousand men dressed in various Union soldier uniforms in the parade. Some even walked with crutches or had bloodied rags wrapped around their heads or arms to simulate battle wounds. Behind the soldiers, those citizens of Springfield and out-of-town visitors who had joined the native folk by dressing in period costume were allowed to march—not so much in precision as the soldiers, but tightly together, despite the elaborate parasols adding some danger to the endeavor. Finally a group of black citizens, representing the emancipated slaves of the South and the freedmen of the North, followed. (This was a reenactment, recall. Nowadays such a politically incorrect placement would not be tolerated.)[202]

As the procession left the front of the Old State Capitol building, it wound its ways through the modern streets of Springfield and then made its way past the Lincoln Library and then past Lincoln's home at the corner of Eighth Street and Jackson. There Lincoln himself stopped marching. It caused a brief panic in those who followed, because they had just gotten themselves into a safe rhythm of progress. He tipped his hat toward the house and gave a slight bow. After returning the great top hat to his head, he continued following the parade route all the way to Oak Ridge Cemetery. In front of the old holding vault, repaired some fifty years ago, the procession stopped. While the great throng continued to enter the main gate and circle around the memorial, another round of speeches began. (People in mid-Victorian days, evidently, loved to talk.) Lincoln waited through it all, alternating looks of solemnity and bemusement. I stood nearby, as close as I could get. When the obsequies were finally ended I had the twins pick us up in the hovercar, bringing

---

[201] "Old Bob" was Lincoln's nickname for the horse. Its actual name was Robin.
[202] The Didymus twins dutifully walked with this group.

it quickly to an open area just outside the great tomb. We were able to get out before the crowd, still divided in its opinion of the veracity of my narration and Abe's self-revelation, was able to intervene and take us away before there could be further questioning—or, worse, bodily harm.

That evening, the governor of Springfield called. So did each of the three presidents. King William called. Fergus called, as did Percival. Cybernews all over the world was buzzing with the events of the day. We were all rather tired and knew that the next days would be extraordinarily busy. The twins prepared a dinner for us: barbecued capon, cranberries, pork sausage stuffing, new potatoes with rosemary and parsley, and asparagus tips. We skipped dessert, agreeing to meet in the morning in the dining room.

During the night, there were several would-be incursions into Tadwil, but the security system held firm. There had even been three attempted escapes from Predison,[203] but as you know, those who attempted the long reach for freedom were automatically killed by microchip technology. So heinous were cybercrimes that their corpses were left to become carrion for the animals.

That next morning, there were tens of thousands of cyberinquiries into the events of previous day. I anticipated as much and responded with a mass media blast mail to state that only scientific and historical journals could present credentialed reporters or researchers and that we would do a cyberinterview. We reserved the right to maintain silence if we thought a question inappropriate or too invasive. Unknown to me, the pair of twins had stayed up quite late that night discussing the events of May 4, 2065. They were eager to participate in the cyber-conference, but they really had nothing to add, so I sent them out with another task. I had the twins patrol the property while the interviews were taking place; it was a way to get them out of the house as well as to protect us and the property against any more felonious activities. Darren stayed a little closer to the house. He could work in the gardens, especially his new ones, and keep an eye on the river and forest trail

---

[203] See footnote 79.

while Darius flitted about the property, making his rounds over and over in a hovercar.

I had invited the current governor, Amelda Khoury-Dixon (Richard Yates, Republican, was the governor of Illinois in 1865 and had been in Washington, DC, at the time of Lincoln's assassination) to be present, as well as to bring any two experts she wished to monitor the veracity of our responses. That famous machine of twentieth-century law enforcement, the polygraph, had fallen out of favor many decades ago.[204] There was just too much controversy about the true value of its results. Relying upon blood pressure changes, pulse fluctuations and respiratory patterns as a measure of truth might have been considered advanced back then, but it was no longer. For two decades now, the much more sophisticated aletheaometer was used to discern truth from lies.[205] Clever folks were able to fool the old polygraphs, but no one could fool this machine. It was connected through a cyberport to a person's microchip. It could read the microchip's memory and quickly distinguish truth from falsehood. Being familiar with the technology, that night I took my own chip out (there are about four people in the world who know how to do this) and inserted another that had no record of the several crimes connected with the return of Abraham Lincoln to this earth. Among other topics, missing from the new chip were any mentions of Abe I, Abe II, their unfortunate mothers, and Humberto and Isabella, as well as the details of the genomic accelerator. Thus I would appear truthful while being able to maintain my little secrets. I did not bother with such a change of microchips for Abe, since he was exactly who he was and knew nothing that could jeopardize him—or, more importantly, me.

---

[204] The polygraph was invented in 1921 by a law enforcement officer with a medical background and a PhD from Berkeley, John Augustus Larson.
[205] The name "aletheaometer" comes from the Greek, meaning "truth-measure."

CHAPTER 22

The Interview and Its Aftermath

The next morning came quickly. I knew it would be a challenge, but I also knew I could handle it. Reporters all think they know everything, when in fact they know very little. They certainly know nothing about the real me or the processes that I have both created and continue to create. But I had to do something the day before to rescue poor Abe. This is how it went:

A reporter from the International Institute of Science said, "Well, Dr. Bauer, your claim is remarkable. We all know, as you stated, that the science of cloning is nothing new and that your claim to have invented a way to accelerate the growth of the cloned specimen is your unique contribution. May we see this device?"

"No."

"Why not?"

"It's really quite simple and quite defendable. The device is very new, and I have not yet had it patented. I would not want the technology to fall into the hands of cybercriminal nations or unscrupulous individuals."[206]

A second reporter, this one from the *New Daily Standard*, Ontario, asked, "Do you plan to clone anyone else?"

"No."

"Why not?"

"It is really quite simple. First, I proved to myself that it could be done. That is adequate for me. Second, you can imagine the requests I would receive. Some might be a tad legitimate, but most would be aimed

---

[206] Well, this is true, isn't it? I just didn't tell the whole truth.

at sensationalism. My scientific expertise should not be misused. That would be unethical." I smirked inwardly at this.

A reporter from *Allegemeinde Zeitung* chimed in: "Herr Professor: Warum Abraham Lincoln?"[207]

"I am sure there are other historical characters worthy of the honor; however, Abraham Lincoln, though American, is recognized universally for his accomplishments, his role in history, and his personality."

A *Paris Match* reporter asked, "Mr. Lincoln, comment vous sentez vous sur tout cela?"[208]

"Well," said Abe, "I must admit I was mighty confused at the beginning. In the written notes given out by Dr. Bauer, he detailed to you the events of my reconception, my rebirth, and my rearin' into this new era. It all went fast—as fast as a bobcat with a burr under its tail!"

All those connected to the conference laughed at the typical Lincolnesque colloquialism.

Abe continued: "As the weeks and months have gone by, Dr. Bauer has reeducated me into the world, and what a world it is! I do note, though, that the remarkable technological improvements have outpaced the development of the human soul. I reckin' it has always been that way. He has taken me to many places familiar to me from my first go-round on this earth and to many new ones as well. I have actually moved among you with some degree of secrecy. My beard did not grow out until shortly before that contest yesterday morning."

A reporter from the *Beijing Express* asked, "林肯先生，你有什么计划吗?"[209]

"Well," Abe replied, "right now I just hope to get through this questionin'. After that I hope to continue my daily walks, daily study, daily tea with the professor, and my continued learnin' about this new way of life and what happened 'tween 1865 and today."

This kind of repartee continued for three hours. When it was finished, Abe and I were exhausted; however, the press conference served its purpose. I begged a little time to rest (during which I replaced

---

[207] "Why Abraham Lincoln?"
[208] "Mr. Lincoln, how do you feel about all this?"
[209] "Mr. Lincoln, what are your plans?"

my own cyberchip into my head). Then, as was our custom, we had tea on the porch at four. We continued to enjoy a great variety of flavors, courtesy of the creativity of Darren and Darius. It was a splendid spring day. Small waves from the river lapped against the shore. Birds were busy preparing their new homes. The twins were relieved not to have to patrol the grounds any more. Both spent no little time sprucing up the flower gardens. In fact, they did spend a great deal of time there, but the end result was worth it. Were I a more public person, I would have opened the gates to the hoi polloi and allowed them to enjoy this beauty.

We ate a light supper, and each of us retired for the night. I knew, though, that Abe would come back out to the porch and pace its length for another two hours or so. Such was his custom. Such was his need.

The next morning, we awakened refreshed. Our customary swim was followed by another breakfast on the *Mary Todd*. We had clotted cream on homemade blueberry muffins, slices of honeyed ham cooked on the grill, grapefruit juice, and chicory coffee—what a way to start the day! Abe inquired as to whether or not he could go out on his own now. I had no real reason to object, other than a bit of selfishness on my part. I could hardly deny his request, given his new public revelation.

"Anton," said Abe, "I've been readin' about a great work of art that includes me. It is at a place in South Dakota called Mt. Rushmore. Could you spare one of the twins to take me there? I'd like to see me!" He grinned.

"Yes, of course. If you leave early in the morning tomorrow, it will take about one hour to get there in a hovercar. You can choose which of the twins you want to accompany you, but I will need one here at the estate. By the way, I had a call from the Secret Service last night. It seems that we have sufficiently impressed the federal powers of your authenticity, and you have the right to protection as an ex-president. I think, at least for a while, it might be wise."

"Well, I want to cooperate. I also want to see that stone carving. Is tomorrow too soon?"

"No. I'll make all the arrangements. We can skip our swim and have an early breakfast. Is that satisfactory?"

"Yes. Thanks."

That afternoon, I invited the twins to join us for tea. They surprised us with yet another delicious brew and some Scottish shortbread—a great favorite of Abe's. We discussed the plans for the next day. Darius would accompany Abe, but he needed certainty that Darren would care for the garden—especially if there were no rain. Actually, the absence of the two would give me time to work in the lab without interruption. Because of recent events, it had been too long since I had lost myself in science. I had a project in mind: to simplify and amplify the genome accelerator. I wanted to make the gestation period shorter, with perhaps as much as one month of gestation accomplished in one day, not unlike the growth accelerator. I would speed that up as well.

The next day dawned a bit foggy and humid, but such is life in Sangamon County in late spring. I would be inside most of the day, so I didn't care. Abe and Darius would be off in the sky and then in South Dakota, in the dry, hot air of late spring typical of that place. When they returned that evening, Abe was as excited as a schoolboy after a picnic. He was astounded at the accomplishment of Gutzon Borglum and even purchased a small souvenir of the experience that he placed on the desk in his room. That evening, our conversation was solely about that human accomplishment. The sculpture was now almost 130 years old and was weathering well. Abe was particularly excited about the fact that after Gutzon's death, his son Lincoln completed the work. Abe was convinced that his son had been named for him, so he imagined a double self-dedication to the monument. I did find the enthusiasm a bit tedious, however. Gutzon had used all sorts of modern tools to accomplish his achievement, unlike the ancients who used brain and brawn.

My own day in the lab was quite successful. I accomplished all that I wanted to. My little invention was better than ever. Truthfully I had no plans to use it again, despite Abe's infrequent requests that I bring back one of his sons. I had proven to myself—and now to the world— that I had accomplished something new for science. I could live with that. Besides, I was eager to move on to new dimensions of research and accomplishment. It would be impossible, though, to do so in the public realm now. There would be too many prying eyes and overhearing ears. Whatever work I did, I would have to do it in my own laboratory. I refused to accept the dozens of invitations that arrived for publication rights, for honorary doctorates (like I needed another one!), and for tenured and adjunct professorships at prestigious universities. I also turned down scores of requests for profitable speaking engagements. Filthy lucre I had aplenty. Time, though, was beginning to run against me. I wanted to accomplish one more breakthrough.

Abe, too, was besieged by requests for public appearances. He received offers from all the major cyber-publishing houses for his memoirs. I encouraged him to accept. It would give him something to do and also give him some income of his own. I wanted to build up his self-esteem. On speaking tours, he would also acquire skills in the new communications tools. He was a proud man, recall, and having his own bank account was significant to him. With the twins providing some technical assistance, he worked on that endeavor, learning how to use the modern mental autoscriber. Abe received hundreds of invitations for public speaking. He demurred on anything that sought his opinion on current affairs, but he was amassing a small fortune by appearing in 1860s costume and simply repeating his Gettysburg Address at gatherings. He was crisscrossing the United States, getting to see more of the country than had existed in his first lifetime, always remaining eager to pose in front of a local statue of himself, meeting important civic leaders, and just enjoying himself. He took turns inviting the twins to join him, which was fine with me. His private wardrobe was contemporary, but for the speeches he still wore the 1860s frock coat and top hat. People expected it and loved it. He peppered his presentations with a few of his favorite stories. While he was gone, I worked in the lab and had my afternoon tea, always accompanied by some special baked treat.

Spring vanished, and summer was passing too quickly. The days were languid, especially when Abe was gone. The gardens were spectacular. The twins had planted just about every kind of herb, flower, shrub, and tree that could survive our climate.[210] It was a magnificent explosion of color. Flowers and vegetables included asparagus, asters, beans, beets, bell peppers, astilbe, apple trees, pear trees, peach trees, blackberries, blueberries, raspberries, strawberries, lettuce (several varieties), beans (several varieties), black-eyed Susans, onions, parsnips,

---

[210] It is still listed in all the horticultural references as Zone 5a.

turnips, yarrow, wisteria, lilies, broccoli, chives, celery, tomatoes, peonies, phlox, roses, hydrangeas, delphiniums, eggplant, cucumbers, pumpkins, and carrots—to name a few of the more familiar. They also planted other blooming things and food products that were a bit exotic for our area. They were beginning to make that monk Gregor Mendel look like an amateur. We enjoyed the fruits of their labors at our meals, and the house was always flush with the fragrance of fresh flowers.

Our conversations in late July and early August began to get political. I actually didn't much care about the topic, but it was paramount to Abe. That fall there would be an election for one of the three copresidents. The president for internal affairs, a Republican, an affable and competent enough fellow, Ebel W. Volker, was completing his term. He could not run again. The cast of characters coming forward to run for that office was not very impressive, and it seemed as though every legislator and other wannabe was seeking the position. I reviewed for Abe the new presidential system and how, with three presidents, one party always had an executive office majority. Most often the Congress was more evenly split, but in congressional sessions when the party representation was unbalanced, a general standstill took place. There was little forward motion. Decisions were postponed, especially if the executive branch had a different majority than the Congress. Our government limped, to put it mildly.

I have to admit that Abe did his homework. He studied the candidates and the history of the government since the 2032 initiation of the new system. He had strong opinions, but they were always backed up with good information and logic, and he always expressed them in unique language. In order to please him—and, I must admit, to keep him around a bit—I let myself indulge in the vulgar topic of political discourse. I was much more a "citizen of the world," but that was an area of experience that Abe knew little about. He was rather limited to understanding the major European powers of his previous time, their leadership (at that time mostly royal houses), and their roles in the still nascent United States. That man could talk! (Just look at his First Inaugural Address!)[211]

---

[211] See appendix G.

We always went our own ways after those discussions. Sometimes the boys joined us during afternoon tea. I was a bit surprised at how opinionated they were—less well informed than Abe, but still rather impressive.

On August 1, I received a very distressing cyber-message. My English friend Sir Percival Pettigrew had passed away.[212] He had stumbled while walking on the estate of Upton and hit his head against a rock. He never woke up. It was too late to make arrangements for us to go for his funeral. Fergus and Angus were able to attend. Later that evening, they contacted me. It seemed that Sir Percival had left his estate, Upton, his several other properties, his physical goods, and all his cash equity and investments to Fergus, Angus, and me! The only provision was that sufficient funds were to be available for one hundred years to run the several eye clinics that he had founded. I was stupefied. It was a most generous gesture from a boon companion. Even though the official cause of death was the blow to his head, I knew that he never really recovered from the series of events that took place during my last visit. I told Abe, and he was genuinely saddened by the news. He had liked Percival. Likewise, I informed the twins. They, too, were surprised and remembered well their time on his estate. (Oh, did they remember it!) The following morning, I phoned Angus and told him I would forward the necessary papers and signatures to have my third of the benefits divided equally between them. I had no need of the funds and did not want to have to bother with the running of another estate, especially from a distance. I had neither plans nor reason to return to England. The MacDougall brothers were overwhelmed at this added turn to their new prosperity. For my part, I simply sat on the porch that afternoon and drank my tea in silent reverie, recalling the good times—and the antics—that were my memories of Percy.

Abe and the boys knew to leave me to my own devices. I spent the next few days in the laboratory. When I finally felt sociable again (as much as I ever do, but Abe does have a way of bringing out the best in people), I returned to our afternoon tea. Abe was quite attentive to me, and I knew that the boys were always nearby, even when I didn't

---

[212] Why are you looking at me? I had nothing to do with it!

invite them to join us. We had another unusual tea, a bit bitter, but some delicious lemon bars accompanied the beverage. The two bitters equaled a sweet.

Abe continued to be busy traveling about the country and delivering the Gettysburg Address. I would have thought he would tire of that routine, but the opportunity to see familiar places as well as new ones was his delight. He insisted on wearing his 1860s clothing, and wherever it was possible, he stood in front of a statue of himself to deliver the speech. (Oh, I already mentioned that.) The pattern had become mind numbing in my opinion. A band would play one of the pieces from the Civil War era. Either a state or municipal authority would introduce Lincoln but would always first take the opportunity to somehow ingratiate himself to both Lincoln and the crowd. Then Abe would come on the dais and acknowledge the vociferous shouts of encouragement and respond to the applause. He would ask the people in the audience if they wanted to hear a story first, and the response, as you can guess, was always a resounding yes. Here is his response while in Los Angeles:

"Well, here's one that some of you old-timers might like. Tom Cruise, George Clooney, and Arnold Schwarzenegger all decide to go out trick-or-treating for Halloween. They decide to find costumes and dress as musical composers. They go into a costume store and look for masks and clothing. Cruise sees a costume that he likes and says, 'I'll be Beethoven.' George Clooney sees a costume that grabs his attention and says, 'I'll be Mozart.' Arnold had a tough time finding a costume that he liked and that fit him, but he eventually found one that appeased his interest and his size. He picks up the costume and says, 'I'll be Bach.'"

The crowd approved with laughter and applause.

"Do you want another one like that?" Abe asked.

"Yes!" cheered the crowd.

"All right, then. What do you call a lawyer that has gone bad?"

Abe paused a few seconds and then answered the question: "A senator!"

Again the crowd responded with enthusiastic approval. "More. More!"

"One more," said Abe, "then the Gettysburg Address. Once upon a time in Michigan, there was a fish-eating contest. You see, one day a fisherman caught a lot of fish. This type of fish was known locally as tench. The fisherman couldn't eat them all, so he gave them to the mayor of the town. The mayor wasn't sure what to do with them, but then he thought, 'Why not have a fish-eating contest?' Well, the town advertised the contest, and there were two finalists. One was a man from a small town in the Upper Peninsula. The town was named Fife. The contestant's name was Mr. Hicks. The other was a Swede, an import by way of Minnesota, and of course, his name was Sven. Oh, it was going to be an interesting final contest. The mayor rang the bell, and the competition began. Now, remember, they were eating that rare breed of Michigan fish known as tench. No sooner had the man named Mr. Hicks bitten into the first fish than one of his teeth fell out! He had to withdraw from the competition. The mayor, however, continued the competition. The Swede named Sven kept on eating and eating and ended up eating nine of those tench fish. The next day the headlines read, 'One Tooth Free for Fife Hicks, Sven Ate Nine Tench!'"

The crowd moaned at the joke, and Abe said that was enough. He invited the crowd to settle down and look into their souls for a moment, and then he played his part and pulled his notes out of his frockcoat pocket and read the Gettysburg Address. Naturally it was followed by applause, and then there was a display of fireworks. Abe's Secret Service detachment was always near. At each stop, it actually had to get larger because of the crowds. Either Darius or Darren also accompanied him—a little trust factor for Abe.

He had done dozens of these events when he got the request to participate in a special reenactment in Washington, DC. The National Association for the Advancement of Race and Gender Harmony, a successor to the old NAACP (National Association for the Advancement of Colored People), was going to hold its 2065 convention in Washington, DC. The date and place had been fixed long before Lincoln had made his first public appearance earlier that year in Springfield. Recall that he had been to Washington with me and was eager to return. The date for his presentation, the usual combination of a joke or two and then a recitation of the Address, was August 28. It marked the 102nd anniversary, to the day, of Dr. Martin Luther King Jr.'s famous address "I Have a Dream."

At the original speech in 1963, some 250,000 persons were gathered in the National Mall, spilling around the Lincoln Memorial, the Reflecting Pool, and the Washington Monument. Lincoln accepted, and when word of his acceptance was made public, the registration for the event, usually about five thousand people, multiplied exponentially. The crowd was expected to exceed 1.5 million people. The Washington Police, the FBI, the Secret Service, and hundreds of private security firms had to coordinate the effort to keep the crowd in order and safe. With contemporary communication it was not too difficult to arrange or to execute. (Bad choice of words there.)

August 28 came. The day was hot and sultry—a typical day for the former swamp known as Washington, DC. Registered attendees had special ID passes and were able to get the closest places. One thousand chairs had been set out for those in the audience who had special needs. The rest of the crowd had to stand, unless they brought their own cushions, blankets, or lawn chairs. In order to protect the crowd, aid stations were set up every one hundred feet. Water and fresh juices were available. Likewise, the air force flew military hovercars over the crowd, a mile and a half above them, and continuously sprayed out water. The air-cooled water turned to mist on its way down; it had the effect of cooling the gathering area down some twenty degrees.

Darius and Darren both went with Lincoln. He alone had a protective force of fifty Secret Service agents surrounding him. Other agents were secreted in the crowd. Everyone was prepared for the worst but hoping for the best.

The Marine Corps Band entertained the crowd from two until six. Then various leaders of the National Association for the Advancement of Race and Gender Harmony took to the rostrum. This year there was a Chinese speaker, a Hmong speaker, a Hispanic speaker, and an African American speaker. When they had finished, it was 7:30 p.m. The sun was still out. The sidewalks were sizzling, but the crowd was maintaining order. Being comfortable undoubtedly helped. Finally the president of NAARGH took to the podium and introduced the Reverend James Isaiah Goodspeed, the moral successor to Dr. King. His task was to read Dr. King's famous address from 1963. This he did, and he did it well. In the background, images of the original gathering were being projected onto the memorial. They were also simultaneously being broadcast into everyone's microchips.[213] When he finished, there was thunderous applause. When it finally calmed down, the Reverend James Isaiah Goodspeed spoke again. Without much flourish, but with enthusiasm, he said, "Ladies and gentlemen, members of the Association for the Advancement of Racial and Gender Harmony, honored guests all, it is my pleasure to introduce to you our next speaker, Abraham Lincoln, the sixteenth president of the United States."

To say the least, the crowd went wild. It was half an hour before Lincoln was able to speak, despite his sincere and continued efforts to begin his part in the day's rituals. As usual he asked if the crowd would like a joke, and the response, of course, was a vociferous "Yes!"

"Well, let's start here," said Abe. I was at a grade school in New York the other day, and one of the children asked me which state I was born in. I answered, 'The same as you, sonny. Nak'd and screamin'.'" Polite booing followed.

"Well, here's another. What do Christopher Columbus, George Washington and I have in common?"

The crowd looked puzzled, and a light rumbling went through the group.

"Give up?" asked Abe.

"Yes," shouted the crowd.

"We were all born on a holiday!"

More polite booing followed. Finally Lincoln stood straight and followed his customary routine. There he was, Abraham Lincoln, standing in front of the great statue that was a tribute to his wisdom, courage, and tenacity. To call the moment historic would be to state the obvious. He took his notes out of his frock pocket and, with great solemnity, proclaimed those famous 272 words in a little over two minutes. People in the crowd were crying. Banners were raised that read "Long Live Abraham Lincoln" and "Welcome Back, Abe!" The sustained applause matched that which had greeted his arrival.

While the applause and cheers thundered through the throng and echoed off the great buildings of the nation's capital, millions more were

---

[213] See appendix D.

viewing the experience through their microchips or through projections into their homes and offices. I was doing the same. I had the great event programmed to display on the laboratory wall. I skipped all the earlier histrionics, wanting solely to focus on Lincoln. I was worried that something might go wrong despite all the security measures that surrounded him. I saw Darren and Darius in the crowd; they were only two rows from Lincoln—farther from him than I would have preferred. While the great noise of the ovation continued, the Marine Corps Band played "Dixie" and then "The Battle Hymn of the Republic." Images of Old Glory were projected in virtual reality every two hundred feet, and then the Marine Corps Band began to play the national anthem—still "The Star-Spangled Banner." The chorus of over one million people singing that song moved even me.

The Reverend Goodspeed was trying to get Lincoln to leave the lectern, but Abe signaled him away. While the band played and the people sang, Lincoln stood there enjoying every moment of it. Finally things calmed down. Lincoln acknowledged the tribute and it picked up again for a few more minutes. Then he motioned for silence. This time everyone obeyed. The spectacle of that many people waiting for the next utterance was eerie. It was dusk now, moving into darkness. There was no breeze. All was still. The temperature had dropped a bit, and the air force was passing over at fewer intervals with the cooling spray. The usual ending to Abraham's presentation, a fireworks display, was still in the offing. The great man again signaled his appreciation, and then he began to speak once more. This was unscheduled and not part of the usual routine. I wondered what he was up to.

"Ladies and gentlemen, I appreciate your kindness. I appreciate your support for the mighty challenge of bringing full harmony to all the people of these United States. In my first life among you, people were divided by two colors: black and white. I wept when I read the text of the Thirteenth Amendment to the Constitution of the United States. You know the text as well as I do: 'Section One. Neither slavery nor involuntary servitude, except as a punishment for crime whereof the party shall have been duly convicted, shall exist within the United States, or any place subject to their jurisdiction. Section Two. Congress shall have power to enforce this article by appropriate legislation.' I consider my sacrifice upon the altar of freedom—a sacrifice made two hundred years ago—as fully worth the price of bringing these United States to the place where they stand upon the world stage today."

Again another ovation followed.

Where is he going with all this? I wondered.

"Your welcome to me in every place I have visited throughout this land has touched my heart. I want to publically acknowledge my gratitude to Dr. Anton Bauer for the science that has made this reincarnation possible." Applause rang out.

"The technological wonders that are part of this age, part of everything that is consistent with your everyday lives, are absolutely stunning, especially to a backwoodsman like myself. I have benefited from them every day of this new life. As you know, in my former life I enjoyed the sobriquet of 'Honest Abe.' Now, before you cheer me again, I beg your indulgence. You see, even in my primitive age in the 1800s, we were making incredible strides in technology. All of that was the birth pain of your current scientific world. Even then I observed, as I observe now, that the human spirit, that soul that binds us to one another under the Creator and under our marvelous Constitution, does not keep pace with the object world around us. In the reading and study that I was privileged to do before making my first public appearance, I cheered the Thirteenth Amendment. I applauded the great civil rights acts that became the law of the land five score years after my death. I also learned of the segregation that continued into the twenty-first century, including the sad year of 2015, when Ferguson, Baltimore, and Charleston became the battle cries of the continuing struggle in this nation for racial equality and understanding. I wept with relief and joy and wonder when I learned that the Confederate battle flag was lowered across the South. I learned of the horrible world wars and the powerful instruments of total annihilation that still exist on this earth, our common home.

"It has been with great personal interest that I have studied the development of your current federal leadership and the system of triumvirs that are the result of the Twenty-Ninth Amendment to that great Constitution. In fact, that study reminds me of a story. Would you like a story?" Abe knew well what the response would be.

"Well, there was a woman in a hot air balloon. And she got lost. She was floating over Lake Pontchartrain, and she trimmed her sail, so to speak, and hovered above a man in his boat who was fishing.[214] She shouted to the man, 'Pardon me. Can you assist me? I believe that I am lost. I told a friend of mine that I would meet her at the Royal Orleans Hotel an hour ago, but I don't know where I am.' The fisherman consulted the GPS function in his microchip and replied, 'You're in a hot air balloon, approximately twenty feet above the ground at an elevation of five feet above sea level. If you travel just five miles south, you will be in New Orleans, at twenty-nine degrees ninety-seven minutes north and ninety degrees six minutes west. And if you are not careful, you may end up below sea level, as is much of your destination!' She looked at the man and quipped, 'You must be a Republican.' 'I am,' replied the fellow. 'How did you know?' The woman answered from the balloon, 'Well, everything you told me is technically correct, but I have no idea of what to do with your detailed information, and I am still lost. In truth, you have not been much help to me.' The fisherman smirked and replied in turn, 'You must be a Democrat!' The lady in the hot air balloon responded, 'I am indeed, but how did you know?' The fisherman answered, 'Well, you don't know where you are or where you are going. You are where you are now because of a great quantity of hot air. You've made a promise to someone you have no idea how to keep, and now you expect me to solve your problem. You are in exactly the same position you were in before we met, but now, somehow, it is my fault!'"

The crowd, as they say, went wild. Once again Lincoln let the noise quiet down and then continued.

"Yes, I see that in many ways this nation is in the same situation it was two hundred years ago. And I see that the Democrats and the Republicans continue to struggle to outwit, outspend, and outmaneuver one another. I have looked carefully at your new system, and frankly, I find it wanting. I say that not to insult those who supported and framed the structures deemed necessary for a new world, but because, in my

---

[214] Lake Pontchartrain is the summer home of the St. Clare family in Harriet Beecher Stowe's novel *Uncle Tom's Cabin*.

own heart, experienced as it is in overseeing the destiny of a nation, I do not find it faithful to the Constitution. Therefore, I announce to you in this place and at this solemn event that I am going to start a new political party. Oh, it was around once until it ran out of enough steam to continue, but it is time to bring it back to life, just as I have been brought back to life. The current stalemates cannot continue if you wish, as a nation under God, to continue holding your place in this complicated new world. I invite anyone who is interested in joining me in this effort to return to this place next Sunday at three in the afternoon, and together we will launch a new political party. The party will be new, but it will be wrapped in an old name. I propose we call ourselves the Whigs. Great men such as Daniel Webster and Henry Clay shared that honor after the founding of the party in 1834. I do not purport to have their genius, but together we can bring this nation back to its origins: strength, courage, and incentive.

"Ladies and gentlemen, fellow citizens of these great United States: I have much enjoyed this new incarnation of mine. I have used this new lease on life to learn much, to ponder much, to strengthen myself, and to adjust to new times and new situations. But as you know, I have never been one to sit back and merely observe. I have always been a man of action—action that, I hope, makes me a man who does not just speak but who also puts his ideas into practice. Therefore, today, before this great throng, I announce my candidacy for the presidency of the United States."[215]

---

[215] Before his nomination in 1860, Lincoln had written a letter in which he stated the following about the presidency: "The taste is in my mouth a little."

CHAPTER 23

Redivivus

I was stunned as I watched and listened to Abe. This was completely unexpected. Then I saw Darren and Darius in the crowd, sporting those same small but significant knowing smirks I had seen before. My blood began to boil. Abe wanted to continue his surprising comments but was unable to do so.

Absolute pandemonium broke out. The twenty-one-gun salute took place, originally intended to sound immediately after the recitation of the Gettysburg Address. It deafened the ears of all those in Washington. Then the great fireworks display that always accompanied Abe's performances lit up the sky all over the federal area. Lincoln bowed deeply, put his great top hat on his head, and was ushered off the stage and into a hovercar manned by you know who—a certain set of twins.

Cybernews went into overtime. Every mode of communication carried the message instantly around the globe. The revivified Abraham Lincoln was once again entering the political arena. Wagers were placed quickly in Las Vegas regarding his odds of winning. And this was taking place long before anyone knew what Abe intended to do if elected to the presidency. The still ever-present talking heads were analyzing his every word. Yes, they were as annoying as ever.

The hovercar returned to Tadwil about two hours after the great announcement. I made sure to be in the laboratory—and no one ever disturbed me when I was in the laboratory. They would have to wait until morning to find out my reaction. I had to plan carefully now— more carefully than ever before. After a few hours of ruminating, I determined that Abe's chances of election were miniscule. The thrill of the moment would pass quickly. Such is the tenacity of the modern mind. In another day or two, some other flashy event would overshadow

Abe's proclamation. I rested better after I figured that out. I stayed in the lab, though, until teatime that afternoon. The boys put out a simple green tea and some peanut butter cookies. Abe came out the great front door of Tadwil and took his customary seat on the rocker. To be honest, he looked a bit sheepish. Perhaps he feared my reaction. He should have.

"Well, Abe," I said, "That was certainly a startling and historic announcement. I congratulate you and offer any assistance that the twins or I might be able to proffer.[216] How are you feeling today?"

"Well, Anton. I've had a lot of time to think things through. I truly am a man of action, not just words. Oh, I already knew in my first life that I could spin stories and craft words in clever ways, but there was also always a purpose to it. I was convinced that I could do something to better peoples' lives—especially those who were not able to do anything for themselves. This new life of mine, I determined, would be boring and without purpose if I continued to give the same speech over and over. Oh, I know I made a lot of money doing that, and I am ever grateful to you, Anton, but I need to stretch my whole self—not just these lanky legs."

Abe and I sat in silence for a bit. Then he continued.

"Anton, I would like to get my old Springfield house back. I would like to make that my campaign headquarters."

"Well, Abe, I can understand that, but there are two things you need to deal with. One is the fact that your son Robert gave the property to the State of Illinois as a perpetual monument to you.[217] The government will probably feel obligated to return it to you; however, think about the thousands and thousands of people who come to Springfield every year to see that house and that famous street, both of which have been so well preserved. If you reclaim the property, you will be denying the very people you say you want to help the chance to learn about history and to experience it in situ, as the archaeologists like to say. And it would deeply affect the economy of the place. Also, even if the state were to return it to you—or even if you were to purchase it—remember

---

[216] See, I can still lie. I bet you thought I was getting soft on Abe!

[217] Lincoln, although a lawyer, died without a will (intestate). His net worth at the time of his death was $85,000.

this: there is no running water in that house, no modern sanitary facilities, and no vector power to make light or run the machines that are part and parcel of our lives. Do you really want to do that?"

"As usual, you think things through better than I do. Maybe you ought to run for president!" He had the nerve to slap his thigh and laugh at this!

"I am a scientist, not a politician. But think it over, will you?"

We continued to talk about the house and the campaign. He had no idea that the kind of in-person, whistle-stop, baby-kissing, glad-handing that was part and parcel of political campaigns in the past was not part of the current modus operandi. The messages of the politicians were now cyberbeamed into our microchips. We could choose to turn the whole political announcement system off, keep it running, or pick and choose which messages we wished to receive. The endless, repetitive negative ads of the past were no longer legal. No one was allowed to state anything negative about one's opponent. A candidate could only review his or her own accomplishments and outline plans for the future of the nation and the world scene.[218] This reality took a lot of the wind out of Abe's sails. He rocked for a few moments, and then we agreed to continue our conversation after dinner.

Dinner that night was a smorgasbord of sausages, rolls, condiments, potato salads, Jell-O salads, and pastries. I particularly prefer *weißwurst* with mustard, even though eating it after the noon hour is a tad gauche.[219]

In the library, we continued where we had left off. Abe admitted he had not thought of the practical consequences of requesting his home. Instead he decided to open his campaign offices in Los Angeles, Saint Louis, Houston, Chicago, Atlanta, Boston, New York, and Washington, DC. With the contemporary methods of communication, each office would be instantly in contact with the others. I agreed with him that

---

[218] And you think that I lie!

[219] Weißwurst (vīce-vurst) is a white sausage made from pork back bacon and veal and flavored with a mixture of parsley, lemon, onions, mace, ginger, and cardamom. Each butcher determines his own mix. The mixture is stuffed into pork casings. It should be eaten in the morning, since the ingredients perish quickly. In fact, there is an old German saying that weißwurst should not hear the noon angelus chime of church bells.

this was a better plan. He still presumed I supported his candidacy, and I gave no contrary indication.

Abe asked the boys to get a hall rented for the hastily organized Whig convention in Washington, DC. Meanwhile, the number of cyber messages flooding the airwaves about Abe's announcement did not lessen. The boys took him to Washington, and I took myself to the lab. My newest project, I should mention, was about the only thing that could top my cloning of Abraham Lincoln. I was going after the God particle!

In DC

Thousands of people packed the hall. Many were the disenfranchised; others, the politically savvy. All were hoping that Lincoln would come forward as a viable candidate and win the election. Abe had some very definite plans for this party, its platform, and its future. He began with a brief review of the history of the old Whig party and the Whig presidents.[220] Then he spoke about how he became disenchanted with the internal problems of the party in the late 1850s, how the platform of the newly forming Republican Party caught his attention, and how he switched over to it primarily because of its clear abolitionist platform. Two startling announcements brought the assembly to its feet. The cheers were deafening.

"Your presence here," said Abe, "is sign and symbol of the desire of the people of these United States to change your government, to return to a system of government that was intended by the Constitution of this nation. I thank all of you for your enthusiasm, your support, and, of course, your finances!" Laughter and cheers ensued.

"As you know, I am here because of the brilliance of the scientist Dr. Anton Bauer. The work I had begun as the sixteenth president of the United States was cut short by an assassin's bullet. On one of my early forays into this modern world, I stood before the grave of my assassin, John Wilkes Booth, and announced my forgiveness for that act." At this there were more cheers, along with some tears.

---

[220] Harrison, Tyler, Taylor, and Fillmore.

"Firmness of purpose and honesty of character must be the hallmarks of this resurrected Whig Party. Without that, we deserve failure. The political correctness, the careful manipulation of symbols and persons, can have no place in our agenda. That era must end. If we win—no, *when* we win—we win honestly. If we lose, we lose honestly." Once again the typical cheers of a political convention filled the hall.

"As a candidate for the presidency, I intend to follow the campaign rules.[221] That is to say, the limitation on the number of cyberbroadcasts will be honored. However, there is nothing that says a candidate cannot travel the country to make his presence known, to make his positions clear, and to stand in front of people and engage them in discourse face-to-face. Well, folks, I know that my last train ride was not a cheerful one; however, I intend to visit every state on this continent by rail and to visit Hawaii and Alaska as well by this wonderful new mode of conveyance, the hovercar." To put it mildly, the crowd went wild again.

"Secondly, it will be the platform of this party that the system of three presidents be abolished and that the winner of this election be declared the sole president of these United States." An eerie and questioning silence ensued, only to be broken by sustained applause.

"My friends, in these last months while I have been catching up on the realities of my new time in life, I found in the print library of a dear friend, Sir Percival Pettigrew, a most interesting tome. I would like to quote a piece of it for you now:

> We are the centuries.
>
> We are the chin-choppers and the golly-whoppers, and soon we shall discuss the amputation of your head.
>
> We are your singing garbage men, Sir and Madam, and we march in cadence behind you, chanting rhymes that some think odd ...
>
> We have your eoliths and your mesoliths and your

---

[221] Ever honest, when running in 1846 for the Illinois State Legislature, friends collected $200 for him. After the election, he returned $199.25, stating he had used his own horse and stayed with friends, but had spent seventy-five cents on some cider. Later, as president, he would earn $25,000 a year.

neoliths. We have your Babylons and your Pompeiis, your Caesars and your chrome-plated (vital-ingredient-impregnated) artifacts.

We have your bloody hatchets and your Hiroshimas. We march in spite of Hell, we do---Atrophy, Entropy, and Proteus vulgaris,

Telling bawdy jokes about a farm girl name of Eve and a traveling salesman called Lucifer.

We bury your dead and their reputations. We bury you. We are the centuries.[222]

"My friends, I am the only one among you who has witnessed those centuries—although I admit I was more or less asleep during them." Nervous laughter ran through the crowd.

"I have the rare perspective of seeing how our great national institutions have fared—some for the better, some for the worse—over the course of these ten score years. I have seen the best of those times and the worst. For that reason, I have chosen the election campaign motto of 'Back to the past with the future.' This party will dedicate itself to reviving the best of the American past—a safe American past: a past filled with values and ethics and respect for all citizens, no matter their color, religion, race, orientation, or history. This party will also pledge itself to the ongoing pursuit of science and the humanities, which promise a future that will balance out the still-existent poverty of too many. It will staunchly defend the environmental concerns that weigh so heavily upon our younger citizens. This party will tolerate no dishonesty, no corruption, and no favoritism for the powerful. It is the party of the people of the United States, all of them, working together in this great endeavor to regenerate our place on the world stage.

"Ladies and gentlemen, let us get about the business of winning this election!"

The sound system played "The Star-Spangled Banner." Everyone stood, hands over hearts, and sang loudly and proudly. Then "Dixie"

---

[222] Walter M. Miller Jr., *A Canticle for Leibowitz*, (New York: Bantam-Dell, 1959), 245–6.

was played, and following that, "The Battle Hymn of the Republic." By nightfall, fifty-seven senators announced they were joining the Whig movement. They were joined by 351 members of the House of Representatives. The cybernews that evening ticked away in staccato beats as the government of the United States began to transform itself by popular approbation. I followed all of this carefully and warily. Perhaps I had created a monster equal to Frankenstein's. *How long would it be*, I wondered, *before the old lampoonists begin to characterize him once again as the "Great Ape"?* After all, nothing but beauty could be allowed in the White House! Even Stanton had referred to Abe as "that long-armed ape." That quote of Stanton's ought to go down in history along with his more famous "Now he belongs to the ages."

Well, Abe's chances of succeeding were minimal. The other parties had much more money, much more standing, and much more information about the current world—a world in which Lincoln was still a neophyte, a newborn, filled with naïveté. I turned my attention back to my God particle project.

Springfield, Early Autumn 2065

Abe returned home after his spectacular success in Washington. The defection of so many elected officials at the national level rattled the halls of Congress and especially flustered the staid and pompous stability of the other two presidents. Georgia Jefferson, president for external affairs, and Xander Zyxtos, president for space-time continuum affairs, were apoplectic. The mood of the nation, seemingly so fixed since the 2032 amendment, had been converted overnight. Those fleeing the Democratic and Republican parties were not so much convinced of the program put forward by Lincoln, but they certainly wanted to ride to their jobs on his proverbial frock tails.

Cabinet meetings, congressional caucuses, the Republican National Committee leadership, and the Democratic National Committee leadership all held countless sessions to determine a course of response. Nothing seemed satisfactory to stem the tide of defections to the new Whig Party. Adding insult to injury, the Greenpeace Party and the Independence Now Party, as well as Monroeist isolationist Libertarians, all joined the

Whigs in a united effort to unseat the current course of government. All this took place in just the few heady days after the Whig Convention.

I continued to dissemble about my support for Abe's efforts. He stayed at home for a few days. After my work in the lab each day, we did our customary afternoon tea. On Wednesday afternoon, after the convention, we sat watching the Sangamon River tumble past, enjoying autumn's annual Crayola exhibition, and sipping tea and munching on blueberry scones. I asked Abe, "How are things going? What's next? How can I help?"

His response was: "Well, Anton, I think it's all going faster than I expected. I do want to serve and to use my experience and ideas for the benefit of others, but all this attention—well, I guess I should have expected it. Frankly, I had forgotten how offensive some politicians could be, but the new laws forbidding negative ads will be a great help. Those rules would have driven the mudslingers of my former era right out of their minds. I will be starting the official campaigning with visits to Alaska and Hawaii. Is it all right with you if one of the twins drives and accompanies me?"

I was beginning to grow more and more suspicious of the relationship of those two butlers to Abraham, but I had promised him my help, and I would give it. Sort of. I did remember the fate of Humberto and Isabella as they went on their "vacation." Wouldn't it be a pity if Abe's craft went the way of Amelia Earhart and Buddy Holly?

Well, while they were gone, I could get some serious work done.

The Quest for the God Particle

I suppose some of you are offended at the term "God particle." For your information, most qualified physicists join in that offense. It was coined in a popular book in 1993.[223] Attempts to reinstate funds in the United States for the construction of a supercollider prompted the book. As usual, the hoi polloi grasped onto the term without bothering to deal with the science the book was so carefully trying to encourage and

---

[223] Leon Lederman and Dick Teresi, *The God Particle: If the Universe Is the Answer, What Is the Question?* (New York: Dell Publishing, 1993).

explain. All of this developed, of course, as a reaction to string theory and quantum chromodynamics. Those were the offspring of particle physics. My own work, you might recall, related to genomic physics. I was able to use that knowledge to create the genomic accelerator—the creative details of which I still refuse to reveal to fellow scientists, much less the masses. The theories of Max Planck had proven most useful.

You might be more familiar with the God particle as the Higgs boson or Higgs particle. The quest for a nonzero constant value drove the research, but the necessary particle excitations were very difficult to produce—hence the need for a supercollider. That Peck's Bad Boy of physics, Stephen Hawking, wrote earlier in this century that the kind of electron-positron collider needed to bring about the requisite actions and reactions (a true electron/positron accelerator) would require at least one hundred billion gigaelectronvolts, would be larger than our planet, and, if constructed, could initiate the end of the universe.[224] All the presumptions about the Standard Model needed to be rethought and deepened. While I was grateful to those physicists who accomplished this (Higgs won the Nobel Prize for Physics for his work), little had been done in the intervening decades. My work on the genomic accelerator was what piqued my interest in creating a supercollider that is not the size of the earth but a more manageable laboratory mainstay. What does all this mean, you ask? Well, in the simplest terms, it is the effort to discover (and then control—ha, ha, ha) the physical particle that was responsible for the big bang—the creation of the universe. That particle is particularly tiny and precariously unstable. In fact, it disintegrates at the breakpoint of ten sextillionths (10^{-22}) of a second. The Large Hadron Collider (LHC-H°) was built at the end of the twentieth century and the beginning of the twenty-first century near Geneva, Switzerland. Well, it was time for the United States (and for me) to replace it with a working unit that wasn't the size of a small country. And for that I ought to win

---

[224] The reference is to the famous serial articles of the 1880s and 1890s by George Wilbur Peck, and not to the 1921 Chaplin film *The Kid*, which starred Jackie Coogan. As long as clarifications are coming about, yes, this is the same Jackie Coogan who starred as Uncle Fester in the 1960s television series *The Addams Family*.

my own Nobel Prize! I knew that François Englert shared the prize with Higgs. I didn't intend to share mine with anyone.

My autumn was spent with endless hours in the lab, with experimentation, and with many challenging failures that kept leading me onward to accomplish my goal. The boys and Abe were curious about my work. When they asked about my newest project at an afternoon tea on one of Abe's breaks from campaigning, I simply reminded them that I was a physicist and that now I was working on the famous God particle. Little did I suspect that Abe could not have cared less, but that the twins were secretly scandalized at what they thought was an abominable effort to play God. If I had known they were such simpletons, I would have explained in clearer detail what this work was, but I presumed, since they worked for me, they would have some fundamental knowledge of the science of contemporary physics by now. They left our afternoon tea in a bit of awkward silence. Abe stayed behind and chatted endlessly about Hawaii and Alaska (he knew selecting Seward was a wise choice) and his time across the Southwest of the United States, in places that had only been Indian territory during his first life. In fact, after the Civil War, many soldiers, both Confederate and Union, took to the West to either continue their military lives, to seek their fortunes, or to go to ground.

That evening a visitor approached Tadwil. From the distant front gate, we viewed a young woman, rather attractive, standing at the checkpoint. She was requesting a meeting with Lincoln. Ever since Abe's "coming-out party," the Secret Service had insisted on patrolling the grounds and manning the gate. Little did they know about my own security system for the property. She gave her name as Jo-ēē Nicolay. The odds of her being related to Lincoln's well-liked personal secretary John Nicolay were small but possible. Abraham allowed her in. Two agents accompanied her. They sat on the porch, inviting me to join them. I asked the boys to bring some refreshments—not afternoon tea, but some appropriate evening digestifs. They appeared with some Chartreuse and Grand Marnier. A Waterford dish filled with Neuhaus chocolate was placed upon a beautiful Royal Doulton tray—a gift from Sir Percy.

Abe asked immediately whether she was related to John George

Nicolay. Her answer was affirmative. She stated that her name, Jo-ēē Georgia, was short for Johanna and that she had been named in honor of her great-great-great-great-great-great-great-uncle, John Nicolay, a German immigrant whose family moved from the Old Country (Bavaria) to Indiana and then Illinois when he was only five years old.[225] He had never lost his native accent, and Lincoln told us he enjoyed listening to John speak.

John had been a hard worker, working usually to the point of exhaustion.[226] Shortly before the assassination, Lincoln had promised Nicolay a position in Paris. That promise was kept by Lincoln's successor, Andrew Johnson. Nicolay had met Lincoln while he himself was a rising political star in Illinois. After that encounter with Lincoln, he resigned his work as a political editor and became Abe's devoted companion. Jo-ēē had followed in the family business of politics. She was the Republican senator from Tennessee and came to present herself for the role as Lincoln's vice-president.

"Well, Miss Nicolay," said Abe, "that is quite a presumption. Aren't you a Republican?"

"Yes, in fact I am. Our family has remained loyal to Uncle John's legacy. I am coming to you, though, because I have been disenchanted with my party for some time now. Also, I believe that I will be able to bring with me a great number of other Republicans, just as you brought Whigs into the Republican Party so long ago. It would also be an advantage to have a woman as your running mate. Another matter: I think my being a southerner might help as well. Imagine that! Andrew Johnson was from Tennessee also. We would enhance this little repetition of history."

"Well, I do like your pluck, Ms. Nicolay. Give me some time to study

---

[225] In other words, great[6].

[226] Nicolay died in 1901 and is buried in Oak Hill Cemetery in Georgetown (Washington, DC). He was so favored by Lincoln that he was treated as a son, as was John Hay, one of Lincoln's other three secretaries. Robert Lincoln often complained that Nicolay was treated better than he was. Nicolay, unlike Robert, never countermanded his father.

your positions and your posturin's and your pedigrees, and I will get back to you."[227]

"Thank you, Mr. Lincoln. That is all I ask."

During the next week, Lincoln did just that. He used his campaign team to vet the audacious woman from Tennessee, and he liked what he was told. Since he was the founder of the Whig Party of the twenty-first century, he was also its chairperson, and he communicated to Jo-ēē that the position was hers.

Once again the cyberpress went wild. "The perfect combination," they called it—"the past and the present, North and South, male and female." The old political systems were beginning to run scared as the election approached. Abe was gone a great deal, ever moving about the country, fulfilling his commitment to personal campaigning. I remained in the lab, ironing out the kinks in my supercollider as I came closer and closer to success.

Several times, while serving afternoon tea or dinner, the twins inquired about the God particle. I did my best to make it comprehensible to them, but the scientific details are infinitesimally boring to the nonspecialist. I tried to explain the nature of a particle detector and the problems with the swift decay of the Higgs boson. Comments about the Standard Model and the search for the inflationary epoch—that first millisecond in which the universe came about—were all beyond them. True, they had worked with Omar to create the sound drones that destroyed Stonehenge, but that was Physics 101 compared to this. They didn't even understand ferman-antiferman quarks. They did understand a bit when I gave them a little history lesson—how the work done in quantum physics in the twentieth century actually led to some of the developments that people enjoyed then and enjoyed well into the twenty-first century, resulting in items such as television, global positioning systems, the World Wide Web, and cloud storage capabilities. They seemed mollified to learn that there could be some

---

[227] As early as 1836, Lincoln wrote to the *Sangamo Journal* stating, "I go for admitting all whites to the right of suffrage who pay taxes or bear arms—by no means excluding females." He was quite ahead of his time.

practical applications for their lives. But like many others, the term "God particle" stuck in their craws.[228]

I nicknamed my project the Superconducting Supercollider. It was a project the US government cancelled in 1993. Shame! My big fear was the possibility of a magnet-quench event of the sort that delayed the usefulness of the great collider in Geneva (the Large Hadron Collider). Miniaturizing everything was painstaking, but it was the purpose of my efforts. Besides reducing the mechanism to something more manageable, I would also attempt to see if there was a particle beyond the Higgs boson. The Higgs boson was relatively fixed at a mass of 125GeV. I wondered whether something even smaller, even more "godly," might be lurking.

Meanwhile ... Abe

Abe continued traveling the country. I continued working in the lab. Abe continued racking up success after success on the campaign trail. My work was more demanding and more detailed. Success would be elusive, but oh, so worthwhile.

Abe was skilled at political manipulation. When he decried it in his Washington speech, he was lying. Well, imagine that! He controlled crowds easily. It was not only his natural forte, but the attraction of seeing Lincoln redivivus was more than most people could overlook.

He covered the western states and then the East Coast. The Middle West, his old stomping grounds, was his favorite. He had the cleverness to return to sites where he had campaigned before. He went to Milwaukee and stood at the site of an 1859 address to the Wisconsin Agricultural Society. At that time it was the grounds of the Wisconsin State Fair. It was now part of the campus of Marquette University, and the memorial plaque was at his feet as he addressed the energetic, youthful student crowd.

Just as in 1859, at the invitation of the Beloit City Republican Club, he went to Beloit, Wisconsin. He had been there during his Blackhawk War adventures in 1832, camping out on the site of today's Beloit College.

---

[228] A strange term, indeed, from Middle English.

Back in 1859, he spoke at Hanchett Hall, a building still standing in downtown Beloit. He had been scheduled to speak outdoors, but a rainstorm came and the crowd moved to the third floor of that building. A memorial plaque on the front of the old building marked the event. At that time, the controversy about abolition was the topic of the day. This time around Lincoln spoke on the need to return to "one nation, one leader."

A resident of nearby Janesville, William Tallman, then invited Lincoln to come and address the citizens of Janesville and to stay at his house. Lincoln obliged. The home was a spectacular Italianate design that boasted some of the first and finest features of the era: indoor gas lighting, central heating, walk-in closets, and an indoor toilet.[229]

Lincoln went with Tallman and stayed two nights. He would have stayed only one night, but he missed the train back to Springfield. At the original speech, he covered the usual Republican concerns of the day, focusing on abolition. He also recalled, to the joy of the crowd, an earlier visit to the area in 1832, when he was a soldier fighting in the Blackhawk War. His horse had been stolen at nearby Coldspring. This time around, he made the public announcement of his running mate, Johanna Georgia Nicolay, the senator from Tennessee. The campaign also initiated its motto: "Back to the past with the future."[230] The addition of Ms. Nicolay to the ticket thrilled the people of the country. Abe's campaign was steamrolling over its competition.

He basically sealed his election when he began to travel again to the Southwest, where he would deliver the Gettysburg Address in perfect Spanish and then address the crowd in that language.[231] During all those months of "ponderin'," he had been learning the language. He repeated

---

[229] Their wealth was ostentatious. Walk-in closets and indoor plumbing were novelties!

[230] It wasn't a great motto. In my humble opinion, it was a stupid motto, but it caught the media's attention and people loved it.

[231] In 2015 a former female vice presidential candidate who lost the 2008 election criticized another Republican for speaking Spanish at a campaign stop. She said that in the United States, everyone should speak "American."

that tour de force in Los Angeles, speaking in Hmong. There he added the short but powerful words of his Second Inaugural Address.[232]

Election Eve

It was November 2, 2065. Tomorrow was Election Day, that infamous first Tuesday of November. For thirty years now, schools had closed on the day. Business shut down. Everything paused. Beginning at noon on Election Day, every citizen would cast a ballot for the candidate of his or her choice. No one had to go out to a polling booth. The votes were cast by communicating one's choice through the microchip. No noncitizen, citizen not yet of age, or felon was programmed to use the chip for voting. All votes were cast between noon and 3:00 p.m. Votes from Hawaii and Alaska were transmitted at Eastern Time. (Astral Time, so useful for long-haul travel, was not used in domestic politics.) There was no longer a need for absentee ballots, since the government's super cybercomputer could receive its information on the same day from anywhere on the globe. By 6:00 p.m. eastern standard time, the election results would be known around the globe. Each citizen would receive the still-existing reverse 911 call to inform him or her of the results. Gone was the droning of the TV pundits.

Abe came back to Tadwil to await the results. He sat on the porch. He rocked. He paced. He learned well how to use cybercommunication and remained in contact with his campaign offices and, more significantly, with Ms. Nicolay.

At six that evening, while we were still sitting on the porch, but long after our afternoon tea, the news was flashed into our microchips: Abraham Lincoln had been elected as the fifty-third president of the United States.[233] The referendum to eliminate the triumvirate system passed. The Supreme Court met that evening and annulled the offending amendment and authorized the return to the original constitutional

---

[232] See appendix G.

[233] In 1860 Lincoln was the first president born from a place outside the original thirteen states. Therefore, he was, of course, the first president from Kentucky. Now he was the first clone to be elected president. Would he be the last?

plan. The legislative and the judicial branches of government acted with unusual swiftness and bipartisan cooperation. With the next inauguration, the triumvirate would vanish. The two presidents holding those offices would become portfolio vice presidents serving under Johanna Nicolay.

Millions of people sent congratulatory messages. The cybernetwork would have been overwhelmed in the past, but now an automated response acknowledged the greetings for all but the most important world and national leaders. Abe would speak with them in person.

Our dinner that evening had to be festive, although I was restive. The boys concocted a meal of barbecued ribs, new potatoes with rosemary butter, tenders of asparagus, and an orange-basil macerated cherry cloud for dessert. I shared the finest sherry with them after dinner, and then we retired to the porch. Abe did not sit down, however. He began his customary pacing. That great mind was already beginning to plan the future. So was I.

CHAPTER 24

Climax or Denouement (the Choice Is Yours)

The next morning, Johanna Georgia Nicolay, the newly elected vice president of the United States, once again presented herself at the gate to Tadwil. A perfunctory call to the main house was made by the Secret Service, and she arrived at the front door. I must say she looked spectacular. She wore a light tan Ralph Lauren dress, dark brown Gucci shoes, a Tiffany emerald necklace, and designer sunglasses. Her short bronze-colored hair, worn in the flapper style of the 1920s, accented the whole color scheme. The boys and the Secret Service certainly appreciated her presence. I could not have cared less. Abe came down the great stairway and stood in the hallway, gawking at her like a teenager. Then he quipped, "Well, I think from now on I will call you Penny—you know, like the color of your hair and the color of the old smallest denomination of coins once used in this land—the one they put my face on." Then they hustled off together, hand in hand, to the women's parlor to begin planning their transition to government.

Abe and Penny decided that they would also ask Congress and the Supreme Court to abrogate the Twentieth Amendment and thereby move the date of the inauguration to the more traditional March 4. It was pure nostalgia on Abe's part, but he was running high on that wave of popular emotion. Instead of the usual West Portico of the White House, the inauguration would take place in front of the Lincoln Memorial. Once again, Abe showed himself a master of the politically advantageous move. March 4 would be a Wednesday, and that whole inaugural week was declared a national holiday.

I had repaired to the laboratory. I paced. I fretted. I raged. I agonized. I worried. I strode around the laboratory seeking to settle the uncomfortable yet familiar feeling that was beginning to take control of me—that unstable, unhinged, emotional wobble known to me as the obtuse spirit. There was no denying it. It was there. And that meant something was going to happen: something evil, but something fun—for me.

Penny remained a guest at Tadwil for two weeks. She and Abe spent time riding, talking, consulting, deciding, planning, assessing, referring, and determining all that they hoped to accomplish together in their executive roles. I treated both with the respect due to them—that is, with the deference I so loathe (unless it is directed at me). Johanna was going to return to Washington to close her Senate office and whirl around Washington enjoying her newfound position, cajoling, entertaining, flattering, and probably bribing new Whig party members who won on the Lincoln frock coattails. We had a final high tea on the porch.

That night, the night before she was going to leave, I threw a wonderful dinner party in her honor. I invited the governors of Illinois and Tennessee, as well as the outgoing presidential triumvirate. By all visible accounts, I was honoring the new political reality and the new status of Abraham Lincoln redivivus.

The boys outdid themselves. Cocktails, wine, champagne, and a mixture of soft beverages were available in the library. Hors d'oeuvres consisted of oysters Bienville, Oysters Rockefeller, finger sandwiches of endless variation, and shrimp ceviche. Dinner was served at eight. To my surprise, the boys served wearing the footman uniforms they had mocked in England. The first course was lobster bisque with sherry. A small salad of mixed greens and grape tomatoes followed. There was a wonderful fish course: planked salmon served with garlic beurre and capers. Of course we used a proper fish fork for this course. The meat course was chateaubriand, with all the marvelous side dishes that always accompany that feast.

The reduction was made with shallots and tarragon grown from our own gardens. The lemons for the sauce were imported from southern California.[234] Dessert was that old New Orleans favorite, bananas Foster.

---

[234] The name of the dish comes from the personal chef of the Vicomte François-René de Chateaubriand. He had served under both Napoleon Bonaparte and King

Cognac and port followed in the library, along with some of the most interesting public conversation heard in Illinois since Lincoln's first victory so long ago.

The party broke up after midnight, well past my usual time of repose, but the publicity it gave to both Abe and me was well worth it. I congratulated the boys and told each of them that I had added $1000 NAD to their accounts in appreciation for their superb efforts.

In the intervening weeks, Abe was gone a great deal. He traveled the same route he had on the campaign, this time going to thank the people of the United States who had voted for him and trying to convince those who had voted otherwise that he would respect their opinions as well. Gone was the 1860s costume. Abe replaced it with the style of the day: a kind of modified Nehru jacket (so popular in the 1970s), a bright solid-colored shirt, and no hat. He had each of his suits tailor-made with extra zippered pockets. President or not, he loved those zippers. He did, promise though, as a nod to the electorate, to wear his historical clothing for the inauguration. He even went to Canada in an early effort to negotiate an end to the decades-long border conflict between the nations. In fact, he returned from there with a Newfoundland puppy. He wasn't sure what to name it—Honey, after his first dog, or Fido, after his Springfield dog. Finally he named the dog—you guessed it—Zipper.

Christmas came and went. So did New Year's Day 2066. Abe's inauguration committee met with him weekly. He had daily communication with the triumvirate and assured them of his admiration for them and his appreciation for their willingness to give up their exalted positions so graciously. The world was his oyster.[235] And I was beginning to fear all I would get out of this was the shell.

I continued the afternoon teas. When Abe was not there, I would often share the moment with the twins. They had managed to invent compost that allowed most of their perennial flowers and plants to

---

Louis XVIII.

[235] This strange phrase seems to have originated with William Shakespeare in the play *The Merry Wives of Windsor* (act 2, scene 2). The dialogue is this:
Falstaff: I will not lend thee a penny.
Pistol: Why then the world's mine oyster, Which I with sword will open.
Falstaff: Not a penny.

continue gracing the grounds throughout the seasons. Many hours were spent caring for that plot of beauty. Good thing they had no girlfriends, or jealousy would have entered in. (At least, as far as I knew, they had neither girlfriend nor boyfriend, but just each other. Neither ever mentioned Omar again, as far as that goes.)

It was getting closer to Inauguration Day. My obtuse spirit was in full gear. I wanted to hurt Abe. He was my creation. He was mine. I was not willing to share him with the world. I thought I was, but I wasn't. But what to do? The whole world knew about me and how Abe came back. I had basked in the accolades. There was nothing risible about any of it. There he was, this redivivus, the child of my brain.

The date of March 4 was long set. Abe was gone a great deal, coming home for the weekends. With the hovercars, it was easy to travel quickly wherever one wanted. He obtained one of the newer models that didn't require a human chauffeur. All one had to do was program a destination and select from a choice of routes. I abandoned, for the time being, my work on the God particle. I had more immediate concerns. I sat in front of the genome accelerator and let my head spin. Mathematical formulae and the known rules of the physical sciences whirred in my mind like items in a food blender. Slowly an idea was coming into focus. I took high tea with the twins that afternoon, and that is where my plan came together. Darren and Darius Didymus were impossible to distinguish physically. As long as they had been with me, the only way I could distinguish them was the slightest variation in the tones of their voices. Outsiders didn't stand a chance.

I went back to the laboratory and began my work. The scheming was finished. I had all the basic concepts mastered. I needed to adjust only a few things. I could vary the epigenetic constitution of the mitotic cell divisions. By accelerating that process, I could regenerate another human being in nine days. I would retain the maturation process at one year per day, lest the newly returned creature literally short-circuit. I would name this process "somatic acceleration." I had all the DNA of Abraham that I needed from the sad demise of Abe II. By accelerating the DNA acetylation and histone methylation, I could produce new beings in any amount of time I desired.

It was night, and I presumed the boys were out or asleep. They never entered the lab anyway. I went to the outer of the two great DNA storage vaults, dialed in the code (18-09-18-65) and scanned my retina.[236] (After that cataract surgery by Sir Percival so long ago, I'd had to recalibrate the retina scan to read my newly improved eyes.) The first lock whirred and clicked, and the door opened. The second vault, immediately behind the first, needed the retina scan and a fingerprint scan before entering the magic numbers. If any other sequence were initiated, the door would not open. Instead, a blast of acid would be sprayed from head to toe on the perpetrator. The mechanism signaled green with approval, and I entered the second code: 04-15-65 (the date of Abe's death) and 07-05-96 (the date of my birth). Each number had to be double-tapped or the aforementioned acid bath would issue forth and annihilate the intruder.

I took out two small vials of Lincoln blood/DNA. The old problem of finding a human uterus to carry the manipulated genetic material no longer existed. That which had led to the demise of the other mothers of the Abes was no longer a problem. I was able to directly manipulate the DNA into the now thawed nuclei of ninety-nine human eggs. Keeping them in a simple warming protocol would provide the right heat needed. Nourishment for the growing embryos could now be infused by an occasional nanosecond thermolaser blast.

I went to bed that night delighting in the knowledge that I had found a way to ruin Abe's big day. I just had to be patient. In the morning, I instructed the boys to convert the former Lincoln quarters in the barn and the hospital room birthing center into a great nursery, letting them know that within a week the nursery would have to become a dormitory. Plenty of sanitary stations were needed. I ordered crates of clothing in progressive sizes, knowing that the little clones would quickly outgrow their vesture by the day. We also ordered vast quantities of formula, solid baby food, a balanced diet for toddlers, then children's nourishment, then food for adolescents (and plenty of junk food—yes, it's still around), young adults, and finally full-grown adults. Imagine that! In no time, I would have another ninety-nine Abraham Lincolns strolling on this planet. The storage sheds were full. Darren

---

[236] The code was the years of Lincoln's first lifespan.

and Darius were delighted that so many vegetables, fruits, and herbs from their gardens had a practical use.

I did have to tell them what was going on. I didn't want to, but this was too big to manage without some conspiratorial assistance. I tried to couch it in friendly terms, with sufficient science to befuddle them and ample flattery to cajole them into cooperation. I announced to them that I was reproducing Lincoln on a large scale as a backup should anything similar to the events of April 1865 recur. They seemed to accept this explanation. ("Seemed" is the operative word.) I did order them not to tell Abraham, lying to them, that I didn't want Abe to live with any sense of day-to-day apprehension about his future.[237] This, too, they seemed to accept.

Lincoln came and went. Ms. Johanna Georgia Nicolay was our frequent guest. Little did Abe know that a mere five hundred yards away, each day, miniature Abraham Lincolns were maturing at a rapid pace. As with Abe III, I implanted microchips that would bring them up to the current year and month and day, ensuring that they reached their maturity on March 4. These boys ate and ate and ate. I let them out of the dormitory only when Abe III was gone. The microchips assured they could not escape from Tadwil. From the microphone and camera drones I had hidden in the dormitory, I was able to follow their conversations. Imagine ninety-nine lawyers in a room, all arguing the same thesis from the same premise in the same language. They knew that their lives were extraordinary, but they could not figure out where all this was going. Well, I knew!

Clothing them was easy. They were all the exact same size at any given time. At Tadwil, I let them wear comfortable modern clothing. They were rough on it as adolescents, with lots of torn shirts and pants. As with earlier Abes, I did not bother with shoes. That would have been a hopeless cause. I would wait until the culmination of my little scheme for that. This pod of Lincolns in the meantime ran, rode, swam, chopped, and ate and ate and ate. (Oh, I mentioned that already.)

Meanwhile, however, unknown to me, the twins were trying to figure out just what was really going on. My explanation was altogether

---

[237] I lied—imagine that!

reasonable, but by now they knew me better than to accept my word at face value. Their demeanor toward me was always exemplary. I would allow a few of the Abes to join us for afternoon tea. Caring for that many people under those special circumstances took a great deal of energy. The boys seemed to thrive on it, letting various Abes assist in cooking and cleaning—tasks that the boy Abes enjoyed as much as the fun activities of running and swimming. There was no way I was going to begin housing ninety-nine horses, so they had to take turns on the two that we had on the estate. I was able to return to the God particle project, but I was often tired. This was an unusual sensation for me, but I ascribed it to the constant companionship of ninety-nine Abraham Lincolns and to my own getting older. But my plan was congealing nicely. If I'd had a handlebar moustache like villains of old, I would have been twisting it.

What I did not know was anything about this little surreptitious conversation shared by the Didymus twins:

"Are you sure?" Darren asked.

"Yes," said Darius, "no doubt."

"Tell me again, just to be sure—what did you see?"

"It was the night before we were going to leave England. I was restless and couldn't sleep, so I decided to take a final tour through the back passages of Upton. I had just closed one of the linen closet doors on the second level to enter into the secret door behind it when Bauer came out of his room. He looked left and right and then quietly walked down the hallway to the grand staircase. I was able to follow him by paralleling his moves in the passages from priest hole to priest hole. He went into the servants' livery. I had to be very careful, as those old floorboards yield easily to any weight and squeak. Anyway, I stood behind the portrait of Giovanni Bertuccio—you recall, the butler in *The Count of Monte Cristo*.[238] I would have had a better advantage from the portrait of Anthony Hopkins in his role as the butler in *The Remains of the Day*,[239] but it was too new and didn't have spy holes cut into the locations of the eyes. I saw Bauer open the top drawer of the great oak

---

[238] Written by Alexandre Dumas in 1844.

[239] Released in 1993.

cabinet. He took out every pair of serving gloves and dusted the insides with some kind of powder. Every pair! He opened the wide end, held the glove in one hand, shook a small amount of some powder into each one, fluffed them a bit, and then returned them to the drawer in perfect position."

"That fiend!" Darren replied.[240]

"Yes. I am sure that had something to do with Omar's death. We can't go back to Upton. We can't prove it, but what else would that old kook be doing in the servants' livery in the middle of the night with some kind of powder?"

"Omar was our friend. He introduced us to Neo-Druidism.[241] This new Lincoln business—he's up to something, isn't he? He hurt Omar. In fact, I'm sure he is responsible for Omar's death. He is surely planning to do something similar to Abe."

"I have a plan," said Darius. "Trust me; he won't get away with whatever he is concocting now. Just play along, doing everything as usual. Eventually he will need us to assist in some way or another, and then we will act."

"Gladly."

The next morning, the twins were busy in the great garden. With all the Abes about, they had plenty of help to keep the weeds down and to prepare for the summer annuals. Their horticultural cleverness had left us with blooming flowers all winter, and now, as winter was slowly yielding to spring, new batches of blooms were bursting forth daily.

I needed that afternoon tea more than ever. I was slowing down; there was no question about it. That afternoon burst of caffeine gave me the boost I needed to get through the evening hours of my work on the God particle. The hum of everyday life at Tadwil was a balm. I liked routine—unless I chose to interrupt it.

The weekend before the inauguration, Abe and Johanna both came

---

[240] There is another term that could be inserted here, but that would make this tome X rated.

[241] The Neo-Druids are an actual semireligious cult whose members believe in many gods and goddesses and share a deep concern for the environment. They model their dress and worship after what they imagine the Druids of old would have done.

to Tadwil. Abe wanted to hand me the ticket for my place of honor in front of the Lincoln Memorial. I was touched at his thoughtfulness, but between my secret anger and my growing exhaustion, I didn't think a trip to Washington would be good for me. He understood and sympathized. He asked if the twins could come, and I denied him this request. I needed them to assist with the "multiplicated" Abes.[242] This Sunday evening would be our last dinner together at Tadwil. Should Abe return after that, there would be other dinners, but the chances were slim. He was out on his own now, and he was in the limelight. Once again, the boys outdid themselves. After preprandials, we went to the dining room. French onion soup was our starter. Roast squab stuffed with artichokes in a champagne demiglace was the entrée. Small fruit salads soaked in Grand Marnier sat in the Lismore Waterford dishes at each place. The starch for the meal was jasmine rice. Buttered peas and carrots, boiled in orange juice, complemented the artichokes in the squab. For dessert we had cherry compote with hand-cranked mango ice cream. As usual, we repaired to the great salon for some cognac and chocolate—this time Sprüngli, a special import from Zurich.

We rested well. In the morning, there was a mood of melancholy on the estate. We were all aware that this was the last time we would ever interact on this level. Abe, of course, had no idea that ninety-nine clones of him were breakfasting on a treat of the previous night's leftovers a few hundred yards away.

Shakespeare was right. "Parting is such sweet sorrow."[243] I promised Abe that I would visit him in the White House, but only if he let me sleep in the Lincoln Bedroom. He laughed, knowing that we were both aware of the truth about that fabled room. As a parting gift, I gave him the piece of cloth I had purloined from his coat at the Ford Theatre Museum. Again he chuckled. He gave me a Matthew Brady daguerreotype of him sitting on a chair, prebeard. It had to have cost him a fortune, but after all, I had made it possible for him to earn that fortune. I did assure him that I would watch the great events on the screen in my lab. The boys were nowhere to be seen, probably tending to the proverbial other

---

[242] Another neologism.

[243] *Romeo and Juliet*, act 2, scene 2.

ninety-nine sheep. Lincoln and Johanna got aboard the presidential hoverlimo and vanished from sight. Secret Service drones accompanied them. They were going to Washington to begin the new administration and a new era in America.

Monday of Inauguration Week passed. On Tuesday I ordered ninety-nine black hoverlimos. On Wednesday morning, the March 4, 2066, I had each of the Lincolns outfitted in the typical attire of classic Abe: Brooks Brothers frockcoats and tall black top hats. As a nod to his popularity in that outfit while campaigning, Abe had promised to wear it for the inauguration. Each of the hoverlimos arrived and took one Abe as its passenger. I had ordered the vehicles to arrive at Tadwil at 10:45 a.m. The trip to Washington, DC, would take about one hour. I plotted with the air traffic controllers in Washington. Like most of their ilk, they were ever grateful for a little baksheesh, and they allowed my vehicles to take a place in the great procession.[244] Usually it went from the White House to the Capitol Building, but Abe was going to be inaugurated in front of his own memorial. (Now that is hubris worthy of me!) The first cars in the procession were for the outgoing presidents, the Supreme Court judges, and family members. Since Abe had no living relatives, Vice President Nicolay's family and other Tennessee officials occupied those vehicles. To everyone's delight, Abe's new dog, Zipper, rode in an open hovercar by himself.

Finally Lincoln's hoverlimo came forward and stopped at the front of the platform erected for the great event. As he exited, he took one step toward the stand.

The sergeant at arms, as was his custom and duty, formally inquired, "Sir, who are you?"

Lincoln responded, "I am Abraham Lincoln, the fifty-third president of the United States."

At that same moment, the next hoverlimo arrived. Out stepped Abraham Lincoln. He, too, took a step toward the dais and was questioned by the sergeant at arms. "Who are you, sir?"[245]

---

[244] The Persian word "بخشش" ("*bakhshesh*") traces back to ancient Sanskrit. It has entered the parlance of the Middle East and means "tip." It also means "bribe."
[245] The sergeant at arms was Jason Summerfield Staples, a great-grandson, seven times removed, of John Summerfield Staples, the man who served as Lincoln's

He truthfully responded, "I am Abraham Lincoln, the fifty-third president of the United States." Confusion marked the countenance of the sergeant at arms. Then it happened again. And again. And again—for a total of ninety-nine perfect replicas of clone III of Abraham Lincoln. This foison of Lincolns was wreaking havoc in front of the great shrine. Each was insisting he was the true Lincoln. (Each was.) No one knew what to do. The great multitude that had gathered for the event was getting restless. The monitors that had been set up to publicize the event instead were broadcasting the melee. I was watching in my laboratory, laughing wildly at the pandemonium and confusion that was disrupting the event. But I was still feeling more and more tired.

The sergeant at arms looked at the Secret Service detail that surrounded the dais. Frantic calls were going out to Secret Service headquarters and to the CIA for more personnel to guard the growing clan of Lincolns. The Keystone Cops couldn't have responded any better![246] They simply shrugged. One of these gentlemen was the real Lincoln, but which one? Little did they know that each of them truly was the real Lincoln—100 percent. It was all due to my genius. I fixed Abe! I fixed them all. Well, how would the history books record this?

But I was tired. I shouldn't have been tired at noon, but I was. The planning and execution of this latest deviltry had worn me out. I wanted to work, but I couldn't concentrate. My vision began to blur, and I felt dizzy. There had been a little bit of that each day for about two weeks now, but today it was debilitating. I remembered the problem with Abe I—when I misread the multiplication level of acceleration—but this quite different. I reached for a chair, but I missed it, sitting down roughly with a hard fall to the floor. What was happening to me? I could hardly move.

Then I heard the voices. But they weren't some strange voices—not voices in my head. The voices were familiar. It was Darren and Darius. The sound was coming from a speaker somewhere in the lab ceiling.

---

substitute during the Civil War. If someone could afford a representative recruit, the going price was about $300. See The Enrollment Act of March 3, 1863.

[246] The Keystone Cops (aka Keystone Kops) was a series of early film comedies produced by Mack Sennett between 1912 and 1917.

"Professor," said Darren. "Dr. Bauer. Ohhhhh, Tony!" The mocking lilt of the call irritated me deeply, but still I couldn't move.

"Yes, Doctor, it's us, Darren and Darius," said Darius. "Aren't you feeling well? Should we come to your assistance?"

I could barely open my eyes, but I was able to gargle out a few syllables. They almost sounded like words. At least to me they did.

"What is going on? What's happening to me?"

"Oh, it's us, Your Royal Pompousness," said Darren. "We know what you did to Omar."

"What? Me? What are you talking about?"

"That drafty old castle is pockmarked with spy holes, you old goat. I followed you that last night in England to the servants' livery, and I saw what you did. And by the way, when we were making compost for our gardens, we came across some very unusual remains in the woods. We know what you have done, O Great One! By the way, how did you like our gardens?"

"Brrrrgghhh. Gaarrghhhh. Lllwyfhdk."

"What was that? It's hard to understand you. Is that one of your marvelous languages, Your Ostentatiousness? Not so glib now, are you?"

"Gkadebhf. Uakbelghe."

"Well, Your Pretentiousness," said Darius, "you liked our gardens. At least you said you did. In the middle of the all the purple flowers, amid the verbena, allium, catmint, bellflowers, and lavender, we planted and nourished and harvested a very healthy crop of aconite. Oh, Smart One, you might know it better as monkshood or wolfsbane. Beautiful flower, isn't it? But like many beautiful things, it is deadly—very deadly!"

"Oh Tony, Tony!" Darren called. "How did you like your tea this morning? Was it a little stronger than usual? A little more bitter than usual? Recall how every afternoon the past two weeks you commented on the unusual flavor and color of the tea? Yet you drank it eagerly, like the snob you are. Well, Tony, the tea was laced with aconite. Oh, yes, and a little touch of hemlock as well. That is why you are feeling so weak, so tired, so disabled, so dependent, and so needy. We've been dosing you a little bit every day at that preposterous afternoon tea you insist upon. Your body is becoming paralyzed even though that cauliflower mess of your brain is still active, listening to our every word and understanding completely what we have done to you.

"Oh, yes. Are you watching the screen? Are you enjoying the mayhem you have caused? Well, there's not much we can do about that, but we knew when all those hoverlimos began to appear this morning that you intended to hurt our friend Abe. That was when we decided today was the day to act."

"Getting drowsy?" Darius asked. "Need an aspirin, you old curmudgeon? Well, it won't do you any good. Do you feel your heartbeat beginning to slow? Oh, Arrogant One, your autopsy won't show any trace of either poison. It will show that you suffered an acute attack of arrhythmia. No sign of foul play—or, as that fat ass Dame Tallulah shouted, 'murder most foul.'"

"Oh yes," said Darren, "and the berries in your precious cream from your precious estate cows—there were a couple berries of belladonna included, just to make sure the dirty deed would be accomplished today."

"Arwohfflkh. Khafgeuh." (I thought I was making myself perfectly clear, but only gibberish escaped my constricting lips.)

"Oh, Anton—Tony—don't worry," said Darius. "No one will defile your body. There won't be any autopsy. There won't be anything left of your precious laboratory or of you to examine. Do you hear that noise? It sounds like a swarm of bees coming—a really, really big swarm of bees—doesn't it? Well, with all those double concrete walls around your precious laboratory, maybe you don't hear them. But they are coming—fast. You see, Your Haughtiness, I was watching when you distributed whatever it was you placed into the serving gloves back at Upton. I know that you were the cause of Omar's death. And now you plotted against Abe, who has done nothing but brought you fame and fortune."

"Yes, Your Pomposity," said Darren. "You thought you could become God by creating your precious little particle. Well, we Neo-Druids may believe in a multitude of deities, but we do not believe that you could possibly be one of them. We needed to stop you. And we wanted revenge for your murderous lechery. Not so good with words now, are you, Professor?"

"Fajhfkjga. Ncuadkjh. Dvbskjgf."

"Well," said Darius, "here we are chatting with the great Sir Dr. Bauer. Well, Your Portentousness, we are no dummies. We know you know that we know that you know we were the agents of the destruction of Stonehenge. And we learned well from our friend Omar how to create the little drones that brought about the fall of that ancient shrine. Well, Your Superciliousness, all that you hold so dear, so precious, is coming to an end. That wonderful sound you hear is the approach of one million drones programmed to blow up your precious lab—oh yes, and you along with it."

"Well, Your Egomaniacalness," said Darren, "what do you have to say now?"

"Pmsnkfjg. Sfksfffrrrrr."

Then there were no more words from me, Dr. Anton Bauer, and no more words from Darren or Darius. The sawmill buzzing of the approaching swarm of drones blackened the noon sky, and as the drones found their target sitting in the brilliance of the Sangamon County spring afternoon, the great laboratory and I vanished in a mushroom cloud of mist. *Pfffft*, and all was all gone.

No more laboratory.

No more clones.

No more genomic accelerator.

No more supercolliding God particle–producing machinery.

And yes, no more me, Dr. Anton Bauer.

Well, it may seem platitudinous, but platitudes, like stereotypes, have their origins in reality. And the reality is this, with a tad of a variation on a familiar theme: all that can be done at the end of this tale is to tell the truth—the simple, unvarnished truth. It is this: the butlers did it!

DISCLAIMERS AND AFTERMATH

1. No scholars, servants, or students were injured in the writing of this book.
2. All events narrated are fiction, unless they are true.
3. I used the phrase "of course" 111 times in this text, including the one in this sentence. In centuries to come, it will help source critics to identify the author.
4. All names of persons used in this work are fictitious, except those that are real. Any resemblance of fictitious names to real names is purely coincidental and not intentional. Real names are real names. What can be done about that? Nothing!
5. For lack of a will and any relatives on the part of Dr. Anton Bauer, the State of Illinois awarded the Didymus Twins the estate known as Tadwil. They turned it into a most profitable bed-and-breakfast.

This interview was conducted by Dr. Emile Râstille, book critic of the United Press International, on the veranda of the historic Mena House Hotel in Giza (Cairo), opposite the pyramids.

Râstille: "Well, Mr. Klein, your novel is making waves all over the world. Please tell me and your readers, do have plans for a sequel?"

Klein: "No."

Râstille: "Why not?"

Klein: "Have you read the book? The protagonist didn't survive." (to himself) "This man is an idiot."

Râstille: "What about plans for a screenplay?"

Klein: "That's up to others."

Râstille: "Rumor has it that Nikolaus Klein is a nom de plume. Is that correct?"

Klein: "Yes."

Râstille: "Would you mind telling us your real name?"

Klein: "Yes."

Râstille: "Will you be going on any of the talk shows to promote your book?"

Klein: "No."

Râstille: "Have you always had a special interest in Abraham Lincoln?"

Klein: "No."

Râstille: "Then what brought about your interest in Lincoln for this book?"

Klein: "I was driving through Illinois, returning from a brief holiday in New Orleans. The route took me through Springfield. I stopped to visit the regular tourist sites, and the rest, as they say, is history."

Râstille: "The work is an unusual combination of writing genres. How would you describe it?"

Klein: "Historical-future fiction."

Râstille: "I'm not sure I've ever heard of that before."

Klein: "Well, to quote a line from the book, 'Not my circus, not my monkey!'"[247]

Râstille: "Okay. I think I see where this is going. Is there anything you would like to share with your readers?"

Klein: "No."

Râstille walks off muttering to himself.
Klein sits back, smirks, and indulges in another mango frappé.

---

[247] See chapter 14.

APPENDIX A

The Real Text of "The Suicide's Soliloquy"[248]

Here, where the lonely hooting owl
Sends forth his midnight moans,
Fierce wolves shall o'er my carcass growl,
Or buzzards pick my bones.

No fellow-man shall learn my fate,
Or where my ashes lie;
Unless by beasts drawn round their bait,
Or by the ravens' cry.

Yes! I've resolved the deed to do
And this the place to do it:
This heart I'll rush a dagger through,
Though I in hell should rue it!

Hell!! What is hell to one like me
Who pleasures never knew;
By friends consigned to misery,
By hope deserted too?

To ease me of this power to think,
That through my bosom raves,

---

[248] The introduction of the poem in the *Sangamo Journal* read 'The following lines were said to have been found near the bones of a man supposed to have committed suicide in a deep forest on the flat branch of the Sangamon some time ago." It was originally published August 25, 1838.

I'll headlong leap from hell's high brink,
And wallow in its waves.

Though devils yell, and burning chains
May waken long regret;
Their frightful screams, and piercing pains,
Will help me to forget.

Yes! I'm prepared, through endless night,
To take that fiery berth!
Think not with tales of hell to fright
Me, who am damn'd on earth!

Sweet steel! Come forth from your sheath,
And glist'ning speak your powers;
Rip up the organs of my breath,
And draw my blood in showers!

I strike! It quivers in that heart
Which drives me to this end;
I draw and kiss the bloody dart,
My last-my only friend!

APPENDIX B

By William Knox[249]

Oh! why should the spirit of mortal be proud?
Like a swift-fleeting meteor, a fast-flying cloud
A flash of the lightning, a break of the wave
He passeth from life to his rest in the grave.

The leaves of the oak and the willow shall fade,
Be scattered around, and together be laid;
And the young and the old, and the low and the high,
shall moulder to dust, and together shall lie.

The infant a mother attended and loved;
The mother that infant's affection who proved;
The husband, that mother and infant who blest,--
Each, all, are away to their dwellings of rest.

The maid on whose cheek, on whose brow, in whose eye,
Shone beauty and pleasure, -- her triumphs are by;
And the memory of those who loved her and praised,
Are alike from the minds of the living erased.

The hand of the king that the sceptre hath borne,
The brow of the priest that the mitre hath worn,
The eye of the sage, and the heart of the brave,
Are hidden and lost in the depths of the grave.

---

[249] So familiar was Lincoln with this poem that some thought he wrote it. He is remembered to have said he wish he could have produced such fine words.

The peasant, whose lot was to sow and to reap,
The herdsman, who climbed with his goats up the steep,
The beggar, who wandered in search of his bread,
Have faded away like the grass that we tread.

The saint, who enjoyed the communion of Heaven,
The sinner, who dared to remain unforgiven,
The wise and the foolish, the guilty and just,
Have quietly mingled their bones in the dust.

So the multitude goes -- like the flower or the weed
That withers away to let others succeed;
So the multitude comes -- even those we behold,
To repeat every tale that has often been told.

For we are the same our fathers have been;
We see the same sights our fathers have seen;
We drink the same stream, we view the same sun,
And run the same course our fathers have run.

The thoughts we are thinking, our fathers would think;
From the death we are shrinking, our fathers would shrink;
To the life we are clinging, they also would cling; --
But it speeds from us all like a bird on the wing.

They loved -- but the story we cannot unfold;
They scorned -- but the heart of the haughty is cold;
They grieved -- but no wail from their slumber will come;
They joyed -- but the tongue of their gladness is dumb.

They died -- ay, they died; -- we things that are now,
That walk on the turf that lies over their brow,
And make in their dwellings a transient abode;
Meet the things that they met on their pilgrimage road.

Yea! hope and despondency, pleasure and pain,
Are mingled together in sunshine and rain;
And the smile and the tear, the song and the dirge,
Still follow each other, like surge upon surge.

'Tis the wink of an eye -- 'tis the draught of a breath--
From the blossom of health to the paleness of death,
From the gilded saloon to the bier and the shroud:--
Oh! why should the spirit of mortal be proud?

APPENDIX C

When Lilacs Last in the Dooryard Bloom'd (1865)
Walt Whitman (1819–1892)

1

When lilacs last in the dooryard bloom'd,
And the great star early droop'd in the western sky in the night,
I mourn'd, and yet shall mourn with ever-returning spring.

Ever-returning spring, trinity sure to me you bring,
Lilac blooming perennial and drooping star in the west,
And thought of him I love.

2

O powerful western fallen star!
O shades of night—O moody, tearful night!
O great star disappear'd—O the black murk that hides the star!
O cruel hands that hold me powerless—O helpless soul of me!
O harsh surrounding cloud that will not free my soul.

3

In the dooryard fronting an old farm-house near the white-wash'd palings,
Stands the lilac-bush tall-growing with heart-shaped leaves of rich green,
With many a pointed blossom rising delicate, with the perfume strong I love,
With every leaf a miracle—and from this bush in the dooryard,
With delicate-color'd blossoms and heart-shaped leaves of rich green,
A sprig with its flower I break.

4

In the swamp in secluded recesses,
A shy and hidden bird is warbling a song.

Solitary the thrush,
The hermit withdrawn to himself, avoiding the settlements,
Sings by himself a song.

Song of the bleeding throat,
Death's outlet song of life, (for well dear brother I know,
If thou wast not granted to sing thou would'st surely die.)

5

Over the breast of the spring, the land, amid cities,
Amid lanes and through old woods, where lately the violets peep'd from
the ground, spotting the gray debris,
Amid the grass in the fields each side of the lanes, passing the endless grass,
Passing the yellow-spear'd wheat, every grain from its shroud in the
dark-brown fields uprisen,
Passing the apple-tree blows of white and pink in the orchards,
Carrying a corpse to where it shall rest in the grave,
Night and day journeys a coffin.

6

Coffin that passes through lanes and streets,
Through day and night with the great cloud darkening the land,
With the pomp of the inloop'd flags with the cities draped in black,
With the show of the States themselves as of crape-veil'd women
standing,
With processions long and winding and the flambeaus of the night,
With the countless torches lit, with the silent sea of faces and the
unbared heads,
With the waiting depot, the arriving coffin, and the sombre faces,
With dirges through the night, with the thousand voices rising strong
and solemn,
With all the mournful voices of the dirges pour'd around the coffin,
The dim-lit churches and the shuddering organs—where amid these
you journey,

With the tolling tolling bells' perpetual clang,
Here, coffin that slowly passes,
I give you my sprig of lilac.
7
(Nor for you, for one alone,
Blossoms and branches green to coffins all I bring,
For fresh as the morning, thus would I chant a song for you O sane and
sacred death.

All over bouquets of roses,
O death, I cover you over with roses and early lilies,
But mostly and now the lilac that blooms the first,
Copious I break, I break the sprigs from the bushes,
With loaded arms I come, pouring for you,
For you and the coffins all of you O death.)
8
O western orb sailing the heaven,
Now I know what you must have meant as a month since I walk'd,
As I walk'd in silence the transparent shadowy night,
As I saw you had something to tell as you bent to me night after night,
As you droop'd from the sky low down as if to my side, (while the other
stars all look'd on,)
As we wander'd together the solemn night, (for something I know not
what kept me from sleep,)
As the night advanced, and I saw on the rim of the west how full you
were of woe,
As I stood on the rising ground in the breeze in the cool transparent
night,
As I watch'd where you pass'd and was lost in the netherward black
of the night,
As my soul in its trouble dissatisfied sank, as where you sad orb,
Concluded, dropt in the night, and was gone.
9
Sing on there in the swamp,
O singer bashful and tender, I hear your notes, I hear your call,
I hear, I come presently, I understand you,

But a moment I linger, for the lustrous star has detain'd me,
The star my departing comrade holds and detains me.

10

O how shall I warble myself for the dead one there I loved?
And how shall I deck my song for the large sweet soul that has gone?
And what shall my perfume be for the grave of him I love?

Sea-winds blown from east and west,
Blown from the Eastern sea and blown from the Western sea, till there
on the prairies meeting,
These and with these and the breath of my chant,
I'll perfume the grave of him I love.

11

O what shall I hang on the chamber walls?
And what shall the pictures be that I hang on the walls,
To adorn the burial-house of him I love?

Pictures of growing spring and farms and homes,
With the Fourth-month eve at sundown, and the gray smoke lucid and
bright,
With floods of the yellow gold of the gorgeous, indolent, sinking sun,
burning, expanding the air,
With the fresh sweet herbage under foot, and the pale green leaves of
the trees prolific,
In the distance the flowing glaze, the breast of the river, with a wind-
dapple here and there,
With ranging hills on the banks, with many a line against the sky, and
shadows,
And the city at hand with dwellings so dense, and stacks of chimneys,
And all the scenes of life and the workshops, and the workmen
homeward returning.

12

Lo, body and soul—this land,
My own Manhattan with spires, and the sparkling and hurrying tides,
and the ships,

The varied and ample land, the South and the North in the light, Ohio's
shores and flashing Missouri,
And ever the far-spreading prairies cover'd with grass and corn.
Lo, the most excellent sun so calm and haughty,
The violet and purple morn with just-felt breezes,
The gentle soft-born measureless light,
The miracle spreading bathing all, the fulfill'd noon,
The coming eve delicious, the welcome night and the stars,
Over my cities shining all, enveloping man and land.

13

Sing on, sing on you gray-brown bird,
Sing from the swamps, the recesses, pour your chant from the bushes,
Limitless out of the dusk, out of the cedars and pines.

Sing on dearest brother, warble your reedy song,
Loud human song, with voice of uttermost woe.

O liquid and free and tender!
O wild and loose to my soul—O wondrous singer!
You only I hear—yet the star holds me, (but will soon depart,)
Yet the lilac with mastering odor holds me.

14

Now while I sat in the day and look'd forth,
In the close of the day with its light and the fields of spring, and the
farmers preparing their crops,
In the large unconscious scenery of my land with its lakes and forests,
In the heavenly aerial beauty, (after the perturb'd winds and the storms,)
Under the arching heavens of the afternoon swift passing, and the voices
of children and women,
The many-moving sea-tides, and I saw the ships how they sail'd,
And the summer approaching with richness, and the fields all busy
with labor,
And the infinite separate houses, how they all went on, each with its
meals and minutia of daily usages,
And the streets how their throbbings throbb'd, and the cities pent—lo,
then and there,

Falling upon them all and among them all, enveloping me with the rest,
Appear'd the cloud, appear'd the long black trail,
And I knew death, its thought, and the sacred knowledge of death.

Then with the knowledge of death as walking one side of me,
And the thought of death close-walking the other side of me,
And I in the middle as with companions, and as holding the hands of companions,
I fled forth to the hiding receiving night that talks not,
Down to the shores of the water, the path by the swamp in the dimness,
To the solemn shadowy cedars and ghostly pines so still.

And the singer so shy to the rest receiv'd me,
The gray-brown bird I know receiv'd us comrades three,
And he sang the carol of death, and a verse for him I love.

From deep secluded recesses,
From the fragrant cedars and the ghostly pines so still,
Came the carol of the bird.

And the charm of the carol rapt me,
As I held as if by their hands my comrades in the night,
And the voice of my spirit tallied the song of the bird.

Come lovely and soothing death,
Undulate round the world, serenely arriving, arriving,
In the day, in the night, to all, to each,
Sooner or later delicate death.

Prais'd be the fathomless universe,
For life and joy, and for objects and knowledge curious,
And for love, sweet love—but praise! praise! praise!
For the sure-enwinding arms of cool-enfolding death.

Dark mother always gliding near with soft feet,
Have none chanted for thee a chant of fullest welcome?

Then I chant it for thee, I glorify thee above all,
I bring thee a song that when thou must indeed come, come unfalteringly.

Approach strong deliveress,
When it is so, when thou hast taken them I joyously sing the dead,
Lost in the loving floating ocean of thee,
Laved in the flood of thy bliss O death.

From me to thee glad serenades,
Dances for thee I propose saluting thee, adornments and feastings for thee,
And the sights of the open landscape and the high-spread sky are fitting,
And life and the fields, and the huge and thoughtful night.

The night in silence under many a star,
The ocean shore and the husky whispering wave whose voice I know,
And the soul turning to thee O vast and well-veil'd death,
And the body gratefully nestling close to thee.

Over the tree-tops I float thee a song,
Over the rising and sinking waves, over the myriad fields and the prairies wide,
Over the dense-pack'd cities all and the teeming wharves and ways,
I float this carol with joy, with joy to thee O death.
15
To the tally of my soul,
Loud and strong kept up the gray-brown bird,
With pure deliberate notes spreading filling the night.

Loud in the pines and cedars dim,
Clear in the freshness moist and the swamp-perfume,
And I with my comrades there in the night.

While my sight that was bound in my eyes unclosed,
As to long panoramas of visions.

And I saw askant the armies,
I saw as in noiseless dreams hundreds of battle-flags,
Borne through the smoke of the battles and pierc'd with missiles I saw them,
And carried hither and yon through the smoke, and torn and bloody,
And at last but a few shreds left on the staffs, (and all in silence,)
And the staffs all splinter'd and broken.

I saw battle-corpses, myriads of them,
And the white skeletons of young men, I saw them,
I saw the debris and debris of all the slain soldiers of the war,
But I saw they were not as was thought,
They themselves were fully at rest, they suffer'd not,
The living remain'd and suffer'd, the mother suffer'd,
And the wife and the child and the musing comrade suffer'd,
And the armies that remain'd suffer'd.

16

Passing the visions, passing the night,
Passing, unloosing the hold of my comrades' hands,
Passing the song of the hermit bird and the tallying song of my soul,
Victorious song, death's outlet song, yet varying ever-altering song,
As low and wailing, yet clear the notes, rising and falling, flooding the night,
Sadly sinking and fainting, as warning and warning, and yet again bursting with joy,
Covering the earth and filling the spread of the heaven,
As that powerful psalm in the night I heard from recesses,
Passing, I leave thee lilac with heart-shaped leaves,
I leave thee there in the door-yard, blooming, returning with spring.

I cease from my song for thee,
From my gaze on thee in the west, fronting the west, communing with thee,
O comrade lustrous with silver face in the night.

Yet each to keep and all, retrievements out of the night,

The song, the wondrous chant of the gray-brown bird,
And the tallying chant, the echo arous'd in my soul,
With the lustrous and drooping star with the countenance full of woe,
With the holders holding my hand nearing the call of the bird,
Comrades mine and I in the midst, and their memory ever to keep, for
the dead I loved so well,
For the sweetest, wisest soul of all my days and lands—and this for his
dear sake,
Lilac and star and bird twined with the chant of my soul,
There in the fragrant pines and the cedars dusk and dim.

The Lincoln Family Tree

Abraham Lincoln	Mary Todd
1809–1865	1818–1882
(56 years)	(63 years)

↓↓
↓↓
↓↓

Robert Todd	Edward Baker	William Wallace	Thomas
1843–1926	1846–1850	1850 – 1862	1853–1871
(82 years)	(3 years)	(11 years)	(18 years)

↓↓
　↓↓

Robert Todd married Mary Eunice Harlan

Mary Todd Lincoln (Isham)
married Charles Isham in 1891; nickname "Mamie"
1869–1938 (69 years) ↓

↓

Lincoln Isham
1892–1971
(79 years)
Married Leahalma Correa in 1919.
Helped raise a step-daughter, Frances Mantley.
Had no natural children.

Abraham Lincoln II
1873–1890 (16 years, no children)

↓↓
↓↓

Mary Lincoln Beckwith

1898–1975 (76 years)

Never married. Died an eccentric.

Robert Todd Lincoln Beckwith

1904–1985 (81 years)

Married a widow, Hazel Holland Wilson, who had a son ten years his junior. She died without further issue. Married a German immigrant, Annemaria Hoffmann, who bore a son, Timothy, in 1968. Beckwith was divorcing her when the child was born and proved he could not be his son since Robert had a vasectomy six years prior to this marriage. He finally married Margaret Hogan Fristoe, a divorcée with a daughter. She died in 2009.

He did own a rifle that had belonged to Lincoln and some pieces of the Lincoln White House Haviland china service. He also had a portrait of Mary Todd that was commissioned shortly before the assassination and was never given to Abe.

Robert Todd Lincoln Beckwith died without natural issue. He was the last of the Abraham Lincoln bloodline.

APPENDIX E

Letters between Grace Bedell and Abraham Lincoln

Hon A B Lincoln

Dear Sir

My father has just home from the fair and brought home your picture and Mr. Hamlin's. I am a little girl only 11 years old, but want you should be President of the United States very much so I hope you wont think me very bold to write to such a great man as you are. Have you any little girls about as large as I am if so give them my love and tell her to write to me if you cannot answer this letter. I have yet got four brothers and part of them will vote for you any way and if you let your whiskers grow I will try and get the rest of them to vote for you would look a great deal better for your face is so thin. All the ladies like whiskers and they would tease their husbands to vote for you and then you would be President. My father is going to vote for you and if I was a man I would vote for you to [sic] but I will try to get every one to vote for you that I can I think that rail fence around your picture makes it look very pretty I have got a little baby sister she is nine weeks old and is just as cunning as can be. When you direct your letter direct to Grace Bedell Westfield Chautauqua County New York.

I must not write any more answer this letter right off Good bye

Grace Bedell

Response of Abraham Lincoln to Grace Bedell, October 19, 1860

Springfield, Ill Oct 19, 1860
Miss Grace Bedell

My dear little Miss

Your very agreeable letter of the 15th is received. I regret the necessity of saying I have no daughters. I have three sons – one seventeen, one nine, and one seven, years of age. They, with their mother, constitute my whole family. As to the whiskers, having never worn any, do you not think people would call it a silly affection if I were to begin it now?

Your very sincere well wisher
Lincoln

Lincoln's First Inaugural Address

Fellow-Citizens of the United States:

In compliance with a custom as old as the Government itself, I appear before you to address you briefly and to take in your presence the oath prescribed by the Constitution of the United States to be taken by the President "before he enters on the execution of this office." I do not consider it necessary at present for me to discuss those matters of administration about which there is no special anxiety or excitement.

Apprehension seems to exist among the people of the Southern States that by the accession of a Republican Administration their property and their peace and personal security are to be endangered. There has never been any reasonable cause for such apprehension. Indeed, the most ample evidence to the contrary has all the while existed and been open to their inspection. It is found in nearly all the published speeches of him who now addresses you.

I do but quote from one of those speeches when I declare that— I have no purpose, directly or indirectly, to interfere with the institution of slavery in the States where it exists. I believe I have no lawful right to do so, and I have no inclination to do so. Those who nominated and elected me did so with full knowledge that I had made this and many similar declarations and had never recanted them; and more than this, they placed in the platform for my acceptance, and as a law to themselves and to me, the clear and emphatic resolution which I now read: *Resolved, That the maintenance inviolate of the rights of the States, and especially the right of each State to order and control its own domestic institutions according to its own judgment exclusively, is essential to that balance of power on which the perfection and endurance of our political fabric depend; and we denounce the lawless invasion by armed force of the* soil of any State or Territory, no matter what pretext, as among the gravest of crimes.

I now reiterate these sentiments, and in doing so I only press upon the public attention the most conclusive evidence of which the case is susceptible that the property, peace, and security of no section are to be in any wise endangered by the now incoming Administration. I add, too, that all the protection which, consistently with the Constitution and the laws, can be given will be cheerfully given to all the States when lawfully demanded, for whatever cause—as cheerfully to one section as to another.

There is much controversy about the delivering up of fugitives from service or labor. The clause I now read is as plainly written in the Constitution as any other of its provisions: No person held to service or labor in one State, under the laws thereof, escaping into another, shall in consequence of any law or regulation therein be discharged from such service or labor, but shall be delivered up on claim of the party to whom such service or labor may be due.

It is scarcely questioned that this provision was intended by those who made it for the reclaiming of what we call fugitive slaves; and the intention of the lawgiver is the law. All members of Congress swear their support to the whole Constitution— to this provision as much as to any other. To the proposition, then, that slaves whose cases come within the terms of this clause "shall be delivered up" their oaths are unanimous. Now, if they would make the effort in good temper, could they not with nearly equal unanimity frame and pass a law by means of which to keep good that unanimous oath?

There is some difference of opinion whether this clause should be enforced by national or by State authority, but surely that difference is not a very material one. If the slave is to be surrendered, it can be of but little consequence to him or to others by which authority it is done. And should anyone in any case be content that his oath shall go unkept on a merely unsubstantial controversy as to *how* it shall be kept?

Again: In any law upon this subject ought not all the safeguards of liberty known in civilized and humane jurisprudence to be introduced, so that a free man be not in any case surrendered as a slave? And might it not be well at the same time to provide by law for the enforcement of that clause in the Constitution which guarantees that "the citizens of each State shall be entitled to all privileges and immunities of citizens in the several States"?

I take the official oath to-day with no mental reservations and with no purpose to construe the Constitution or laws by any hypercritical rules; and while I do not choose now to specify particular acts of Congress as proper to be enforced, I do suggest that it will be much safer for all, both in official and private stations, to conform to and abide by all those acts which stand unrepealed than to violate any of them trusting to find impunity in having them held to be unconstitutional.

It is seventy-two years since the first inauguration of a President under our National Constitution. During that period fifteen different and greatly distinguished citizens have in succession administered the executive branch of the Government. They have conducted it through many perils, and generally with great success. Yet, with all this scope of precedent, I now enter upon the same task for the brief constitutional term of four years under great and peculiar difficulty. A disruption of the Federal Union, heretofore only menaced, is now formidably attempted.

I hold that in contemplation of universal law and of the Constitution the Union of these States is perpetual. Perpetuity is implied, if not expressed, in the fundamental law of all national governments.

It is safe to assert that no government proper ever had a provision in its organic law for its own termination. Continue to execute all the express provisions of our National Constitution, and the Union will endure forever, it being impossible to destroy it except by some action not provided for in the instrument itself.

Again: If the United States be not a government proper, but an association of States in the nature of contract merely, can it, as a contract, be peaceably unmade by less than all the parties who made it? One party to a contract may violate it— break it, so to speak—but does it not require all to lawfully rescind it? Descending from these general principles, we find the proposition that in legal contemplation the Union is perpetual confirmed by the history of the Union itself. The Union is much older than the Constitution. It was formed, in fact, by the Articles of Association in 1774. It was matured and continued by the Declaration of Independence in 1776. It was further matured, and the faith of all the then thirteen States expressly plighted and engaged that it should be perpetual, by the Articles of Confederation in 1778. And finally, in 1787, one of the declared objects for ordaining and establishing the Constitution was *"to form a more perfect Union."*

But if destruction of the Union by one or by a part only of the States be lawfully possible, the Union is *less* perfect than before the Constitution, having lost the vital element of perpetuity.

It follows from these views that no State upon its own mere motion can lawfully get out of the Union; that *resolves* and *ordinances* to that effect are legally void, and that acts of violence within any State or States against the authority of the United States are insurrectionary or revolutionary, according to circumstances.

I therefore consider that in view of the Constitution and the laws the Union is unbroken, and to the extent of my ability, I shall take care, as the Constitution itself expressly enjoins upon me, that the laws of the Union be faithfully executed in all the States. Doing this I deem to be only a simple duty on my part, and I shall perform it so far as practicable unless my rightful masters, the American people, shall withhold the requisite means or in some authoritative manner direct the contrary. I trust this will not be regarded as a menace, but only as the declared purpose of the Union that it *will* constitutionally defend and maintain itself.

In doing this there needs to be no bloodshed or violence, and there shall be none unless it be forced upon the national authority. The power confided to me will be used to hold, occupy, and possess the property and places belonging to the Government and to collect the duties and imposts; but beyond what may be necessary for these objects, there will be no invasion, no using of force against or among the people anywhere. Where hostility to the United States in any interior locality shall be so great and universal as to prevent competent resident citizens from holding the Federal offices, there will be no attempt to force obnoxious strangers among the people for that object. While the strict legal right may exist in the Government to enforce the exercise of these offices, the attempt to do so would be so irritating and so nearly impracticable withal that I deem it better to forego for the time the uses of such offices.

The mails, unless repelled, will continue to be furnished in all parts of the Union. So far as possible he people everywhere shall have that sense of perfect security which is most favorable to calm thought and reflection. The course here indicated will be followed unless current events and experience shall show a modification or change to be proper, and in every case and exigency my best discretion will be exercised, according to circumstances actually existing and with a view and a hope of a peaceful solution of the national troubles and the restoration of fraternal sympathies and affections.

That there are persons in one section or another who seek to destroy the Union at all events and are glad of any pretext to do it I will neither affirm nor deny; but if there be such, I need address no word to them. To those, however, who really love the Union may I not speak?

Before entering upon so grave a matter as the destruction of our national fabric, with all its benefits, its memories, and its hopes, would it not be wise to ascertain precisely why we do it? Will you hazard so desperate a step while there is any possibility that any portion of the ills you fly from have no real existence? Will you, while the certain ills you fly to are greater than all the real ones you fly from, will you risk the commission of so fearful a mistake?

All profess to be content in the Union if all constitutional rights can be maintained. Is it true, then, that any right plainly written in the Constitution has been denied? I think not. Happily, the human mind is so constituted that no party can reach to the audacity of doing this. Think, if you can, of a single instance in which a plainly written provision of the Constitution has ever been denied. If by the mere force of numbers a majority should deprive a minority of any clearly written constitutional right, it might in a moral point of view justify revolution; certainly would if such right were a vital one. But such is not our case. All the vital rights of minorities and of individuals are so plainly assured to them by affirmations and negations, guaranties and prohibitions, in the Constitution that controversies never arise concerning them. But no organic law can ever be framed with a provision specifically applicable to every question which may occur in practical administration. No foresight can anticipate nor any document of reasonable length contain express provisions for all possible questions. Shall fugitives from labor be surrendered by national or by State authority? The Constitution does not expressly say. *May* Congress prohibit slavery in the Territories? The Constitution does not expressly say. *Must* Congress protect slavery in the Territories? The Constitution does not expressly say.

From questions of this class spring all our constitutional controversies, and we divide upon them into majorities and minorities. If the minority will not acquiesce, the majority must, or the Government must cease. There is no other alternative, for continuing the Government is acquiescence on one side or the other. If a minority in such case will secede rather than acquiesce, they make a precedent which in turn will divide and ruin them, for a minority of their own will secede from them whenever a majority refuses to be controlled by such minority. For instance, why may not any portion of a new confederacy a year or two hence arbitrarily secede again, precisely as portions of the present Union now claim to secede from it? All who cherish disunion sentiments are now being educated to the exact temper of doing this.

Is there such perfect identity of interests among the States to compose a new union as to produce harmony only and prevent renewed secession?

Plainly the central idea of secession is the essence of anarchy. A majority held in restraint by constitutional checks and limitations, and always changing easily with deliberate changes of popular opinions and sentiments, is the only true sovereign of a free people. Whoever rejects it does of necessity fly to anarchy or to despotism. Unanimity is impossible. The rule of a minority, as a permanent arrangement, is wholly inadmissible; so that, rejecting the majority principle, anarchy or despotism in some form is all that is left.

I do not forget the position assumed by some that constitutional questions are to be decided by the Supreme Court, nor do I deny that such decisions must be binding in any case upon the parties to a suit as to the object of that suit, while they are also entitled to very high respect and consideration in all parallel cases by all other departments of the Government. And while it is obviously possible that such decision may be erroneous in any given case, still the evil effect following it, being limited to that particular case, with the chance that it may be overruled and never become a precedent for other cases, can better be borne than could the evils of a different practice. At the same time, the candid citizen must confess that if the policy of the Government upon vital questions affecting the whole people is to be irrevocably fixed by decisions of the Supreme Court, the instant they are made in ordinary litigation between parties in personal actions the people will have ceased to be their own rulers, having to that extent practically resigned their Government into the hands of that eminent tribunal. Nor is there in this view any assault upon the court or the judges. It is a duty from which they may not shrink to decide cases properly brought before them, and it is no fault of theirs if others seek to turn their decisions to political purposes.

One section of our country believes slavery is *right* and ought to be extended, while the other believes it is *wrong* and ought not to be extended. This is the only substantial dispute. The fugitive-slave clause of the Constitution and the law for the suppression of the foreign slave trade are each as well enforced, perhaps, as any law can ever be in a community where the moral sense of the people imperfectly supports the law itself. The great body of the people abide by the dry legal obligation in both cases, and a few break over in each. This, I think, can not be perfectly cured, and it would be worse in both cases *after* the separation of the sections than before. The foreign slave trade, now imperfectly suppressed, would be ultimately revived without restriction in one section, while fugitive slaves, now only partially surrendered, would not be surrendered at all by the other.

Physically speaking, we can not separate. We can not remove our respective sections from each other nor build an impassable wall between them. A husband and wife may be divorced and go out of the presence and beyond the reach of each other, but the different parts of our country can not do this. They can not but remain face to face, and intercourse, either amicable or hostile, must continue between them. Is it possible, then, to make that intercourse more advantageous or more satisfactory *after* separation than *before?* Can aliens make treaties easier than friends can make laws? Can treaties be more faithfully enforced between aliens than laws can among friends? Suppose you go to war, you can not fight always; and when, after much loss on both sides and no gain on either, you cease fighting, the identical old questions, as to terms of intercourse, are again upon you.

This country, with its institutions, belongs to the people who inhabit it. Whenever they shall grow weary of the existing Government, they can exercise their *constitutional* right of amending it or their *revolutionary* right to dismember or overthrow it. I can not be ignorant of the fact that many worthy and patriotic citizens are desirous of having the National Constitution amended. While I make no recommendation of amendments, I fully recognize the rightful authority of the people over the whole subject, to be exercised in either of the modes prescribed in the instrument itself; and I should, under existing circumstances, favor rather than oppose a fair opportunity being afforded the people to act upon it. I will venture to add that to me the convention mode seems preferable, in that it allows amendments to originate with the people themselves, instead of only permitting them to take or reject propositions originated by others, not especially chosen for the purpose, and which might not be precisely such as they would wish to either accept or refuse. I understand a proposed amendment to the Constitution—which amendment, however, I have not seen—has passed Congress, to the effect that the Federal Government shall never interfere with the domestic institutions of the States, including that of persons held to service. To avoid misconstruction of what I have said, I depart from my purpose not to speak of particular amendments so far as to say that, holding such a provision to now be implied constitutional law, I have no objection to its being made express and irrevocable.

The Chief Magistrate derives all his authority from the people, and they have referred none upon him to fix terms for the separation of the States. The people themselves can do this if also they choose, but the Executive as such has nothing to do with it. His duty is to administer the present Government as it came to his hands and to transmit it unimpaired by him to his successor. Why should there not be a patient confidence in the ultimate justice of the people? Is there any better or equal hope in the world? In our present differences, is either party without faith of being in the right? If the Almighty Ruler of Nations, with His eternal truth and justice, be on your side of the North, or on yours of the South, that truth and that justice will surely prevail by the judgment of this great tribunal of the American people.

By the frame of the Government under which we live this same people have wisely given their public servants but little power for mischief, and have with equal wisdom provided for the return of that little to their own hands at very short intervals. While the people retain their virtue and vigilance no Administration by any extreme of wickedness or folly can very seriously injure the Government in the short space of four years.

My countrymen, one and all, think calmly and *well* upon this whole subject. Nothing valuable can be lost by taking time. If there be an object to *hurry* any of you in hot haste to a step which you would never take *deliberately,* that object will be frustrated by taking time; but no good object can be frustrated by it. Such of you as are now dissatisfied still have the old Constitution unimpaired, and, on the sensitive point, the laws of your own framing under it; while the new Administration will have no immediate power, if it would, to change either. If it were admitted that you who are dissatisfied hold the right side in the dispute, there still is no single good reason for precipitate action. Intelligence, patriotism, Christianity, and a firm reliance on Him who has never yet forsaken this favored land are still competent to adjust in the best way all our present difficulty. In *your* hands, my dissatisfied fellow-countrymen, and not in *mine,* is the Momentous issue of civil war. The Government will not assail *you.* You can have no conflict without being yourselves the aggressors. *You* have no oath registered in heaven to destroy the Government, while I shall have the most solemn one to "preserve, protect, and defend it."

I am loath to close. We are not enemies, but friends. We must not be enemies. Though passion may have strained it must not break our bonds of affection. The mystic chords of memory, stretching from every battlefield and patriot grave to every living heart and hearthstone all over this broad land, will yet swell the chorus of the Union, when again touched, as surely they will be, by the better angels of our nature.

APPENDIX G

Lincoln's Second Inaugural Address

Fellow-Countrymen:

At this second appearing to take the oath of the Presidential office there is less occasion for an extended address than there was at the first. Then a statement somewhat in detail of a course to be pursued seemed fitting and proper. Now, at the expiration of four years, during which public declarations have been constantly called forth on every point and phase of the great contest which still absorbs the attention and engrosses the energies of the nation, little that is new could be presented. The progress of our arms, upon which all else chiefly depends, is as well known to the public as to myself, and it is, I trust, reasonably satisfactory and encouraging to all. With high hope for the future, no prediction in regard to it is ventured.

On the occasion corresponding to this four years ago all thoughts were anxiously directed to an impending civil war. All dreaded it, all sought to avert it. While the inaugural address was being delivered from this place, devoted altogether to *saving* the Union without war, insurgent agents were in the city seeking to *destroy* it without war— seeking to dissolve the Union and divide effects by negotiation. Both parties deprecated war, but one of them would *make* war rather than let the nation survive, and the other would *accept* war rather than let it perish, and the war came.

One-eighth of the whole population were colored slaves, not distributed generally over the Union, but localized in the southern part of it. These slaves constituted a peculiar and powerful interest. All knew that this interest was somehow the cause of the war. To strengthen, perpetuate, and extend this interest was the object for which the insurgents would rend the Union even by war, while the Government claimed no right to do more than to restrict the territorial enlargement of it. Neither party expected for the war the magnitude or the duration which it has already attained. Neither anticipated that the *cause* of the conflict might cease with or even before the conflict itself should cease. Each looked for an easier triumph, and a result less fundamental and astounding. Both read the same Bible and pray to the same God, and each invokes His aid against the other. It may seem strange that any men should dare to ask a just God's assistance in wringing their bread from the sweat of other men's faces, but let us judge not, that we be not judged. The prayers of both could not be answered.

That of neither has been answered fully. The Almighty has His own purposes. "Woe unto the world because of offenses; for it must needs be that offenses come, but woe to that man by whom the offense cometh." If we shall suppose that American slavery is one of those offenses which, in the providence of God, must needs come, but which, having continued through His appointed time, He now wills to remove, and that He gives to both North and South this terrible war as the woe due to those by whom the offense came, shall we discern therein any departure from those divine attributes which the believers in a living God always ascribe to Him? Fondly do we hope, fervently do we pray, that this mighty scourge of war may speedily pass away. Yet, if God wills that it continue until all the wealth piled by the bondsman's two hundred and fifty years of unrequited toil shall be sunk, and until every drop of blood drawn with the lash shall be paid by another drawn with the sword, as was said three thousand years ago, so still it must be said "the judgments of the Lord are true and righteous altogether."

With malice toward none, with charity for all, with firmness in the right as God gives us to see the right, let us strive on to finish the work we are in, to bind up the nation's wounds, to care for him who shall have borne the battle and for his widow and his orphan, to do all which may achieve and cherish a just and lasting peace among ourselves and with all nations.

Printed in the United States
By Bookmasters